Nebul

Nebula Awards ·31

SFWA's Choices
for the Best
Science Fiction
and Fantasy
of the Year

EDITED BY

PAMELA SARGENT

A HARVEST ORIGINAL

HARCOURT BRACE & COMPANY

San Diego   New York   London

In memory of:

Kingsley Amis

Claude Avice [Pierre Barbet]

Ian Ballantine

John Brunner

G. C. Edmondson

Jack Finney

Walter M. Miller, Jr.

Bob Shaw

Margaret St. Clair

Roger Zelazny

Contents

Introduction

PAMELA SARGENT

W e all have different temperaments, and I can tell you right now that the best temperament for a reader to have, or to develop, is a combination of the artistic and the scientific one." So wrote Vladimir Nabokov in his essay "Good Readers and Good Writers" in *Lectures on Literature,* and it strikes me as especially good advice for the reader of science fiction and fantasy. Nabokov has described the kind of temperament that should bring one to appreciate science fiction honed by both intelligence and an aesthetic sense, and fantasy that aspires to being one of the "great fairy tales," as Nabokov called all great novels.

That this kind of "good reader" is an increasingly endangered species can be inferred from the masses of mediocre science fiction and fantasy books that crowd bookstore shelves, threatening to overwhelm works of quality. The good reader has to look hard to find work that he can read, as Nabokov puts it, "not with his heart, not so much with his brain, but with his spine. It is there that occurs the telltale tingle even though we must keep a little aloof, a little detached when reading. Then with a pleasure that is both sensual and intellectual we shall watch the artist build his castle of cards and watch the castle of cards become a castle of beautiful steel and glass."

The Nebula Awards, given annually to authors of outstanding works of science fiction and fantasy, have been in existence for over thirty years. They are voted on by the members of the Science-fiction and Fantasy Writers of America, thus making this award unique in that it is the only award for science fiction given to writers by a popular vote of their peers. In an ideal world, this would be a guarantee that works honored with the award, or in contention for it, were inevitably ones that would reward the good reader. In this world, however, it is a fact that some of the finest writers in the genre have never won a Nebula and are rarely (if ever) in the running for one. It's also true that some winners and finalists in the past have owed their places on the ballot more to sentiment or to canny public relations efforts than to the merits of the work itself.

Any awards process has its flaws, and that of the Nebula is no exception. Perhaps the most one can ask is that the award call the good reader's attention to works that at least have a chance of repaying his careful reading. Fortunately, the Nebula Award accomplishes that; whatever the vagaries and injustices of the awards process, there are still Nebula winners and finalists every year that reward the conscientious reader; the list of past winners provides fine examples of science fiction at its best. The works on that list that repay the good reader's attention far outnumber those that may not.

Any anthologist should strive to be a good reader. This requires, as Nabokov asserts, being a rereader; it also necessitates the willingness to "get clear the specific world the author places at his disposal." One must enter the world invented by the writer without simply wallowing in it, identifying with the characters, or responding for purely personal reasons to the story or book.

What I did while reading for the three Nebula Awards volumes I have edited was to assume, from the outset, that any Nebula finalist was going to be well worth reading. I would read in the quietest and most pleasant spot I could find, and with as little distraction as possible, opening my mind to what the writer was presenting. Once all the finalists were read, I would reread each one, and that was an essential part of the process. Rereading allowed me to appreciate the best works more fully; it also made the flaws of the lesser ones more glaring. Occasionally, I found that I hadn't appreciated a particular story properly on the first reading; sometimes I discovered that the castle that had seemed to be made of beautiful steel and glass was only cards after all.

Selecting stories for an anthology is more complicated than it may appear. It isn't simply a matter of picking stories the editor personally likes, or those that have passed the test of rereading; limits on the length of a book impose their own restrictions. Anthologizing is also a kind of orchestration; the notes have to be arranged in a pleasing or appropriate order, and including too many pieces that sound similar notes can make for a monotonous book.

I would usually set down my ideal table of contents for each Nebula anthology before the winners were announced, listing everything that I would have included if the number of allotted pages were unlimited. From that list, I later winnowed and arranged the anthology, allowing for such additional features as essays about notable works of the year and tributes to fallen colleagues. Inevitably, works and writers I wanted to include had to be left out, but it was my good fortune to have enough fine work to choose from that such a dilemma was forced upon me. Better that than having mediocre novels and stories far outnumber good works on a final ballot, as they do on many publishers' lists. If that day ever comes, when an editor can't find enough good work on a ballot to fill the anthology, the Nebula Award will truly be no more than a marketing tool and a reward for clever networking and politicking. (Let me be blunt; it's drawn close to being that in some years.) Members of SFWA should aspire to honor only works that meet the highest standards, that offer examples of the many jewels still to be found in today's literary marketplace. Since we can't possibly honor every worthy work or writer, we should try at least to see that those who are honored are truly deserving.

The 1995 Nebula Awards Final Ballot

FOR NOVEL
Mother of Storms by John Barnes (Tor)
Beggars and Choosers by Nancy Kress (Tor)
Celestis by Paul Park (Tor)
°The Terminal Experiment by Robert J. Sawyer
    (HarperPrism; published as *Hobson's Choice* in *Analog*,
    December 1994–March 1995)
Metropolitan by Walter Jon Williams (Tor)
Calde of the Long Sun by Gene Wolfe (Tor)

FOR NOVELLA
"Soon Comes Night" by Gregory Benford
    (*Asimov's Science Fiction*, August 1994)
"Yaguara" by Nicola Griffith
    (*Asimov's Science Fiction*, March 1995)

°Indicates winner.

°"Last Summer at Mars Hill" by Elizabeth Hand
  (*The Magazine of Fantasy & Science Fiction*, August 1994)
"Bibi" by Mike Resnick and Susan Shwartz
  (*Asimov's Science Fiction*, Mid-December 1995)
"Mortimer Gray's History of Death" by Brian Stableford
  (*Asimov's Science Fiction*, April 1995)

FOR NOVELETTE
"The Resurrection Man's Legacy" by Dale Bailey
  (*The Magazine of Fantasy & Science Fiction*, July 1995)
"Tea and Hamsters" by Michael Coney
  (*The Magazine of Fantasy & Science Fiction*, January 1995)
"Jesus at the Bat" by Esther M. Friesner
  (*The Magazine of Fantasy & Science Fiction*, July 1994)
"Home for Christmas" by Nina Kiriki Hoffman
  (*The Magazine of Fantasy & Science Fiction*, January 1995)
"Think Like a Dinosaur" by James Patrick Kelly
  (*Asimov's Science Fiction*, June 1995)
°"Solitude" by Ursula K. Le Guin
  (*The Magazine of Fantasy & Science Fiction*, December 1994)
"When Old Gods Die" by Mike Resnick
  (*Asimov's Science Fiction*, April 1995)

FOR SHORT STORY
"Alien Jane" by Kelley Eskridge (*Century* #1)
°"Death and the Librarian" by Esther M. Friesner
  (*Asimov's Science Fiction*, December 1994)
"Grass Dancer" by Owl Goingback
  (*Excalibur*, Warner Aspect)
"The Narcissus Plague" by Lisa Goldstein
  (*Asimov's Science Fiction*, July 1994)
"The Kingdom of Cats and Birds" by Geoffrey A. Landis
  (*Science Fiction Age*, September 1994)
"The Lincoln Train" by Maureen F. McHugh
  (*The Magazine of Fantasy & Science Fiction*, April 1995;
  Alternate Tyrants, DAW)
"Short Timer" by Dave Smeds
  (*The Magazine of Fantasy & Science Fiction*, December 1994)

GRAND MASTER NEBULA AWARD
°A. E. van Vogt

Among the finalists in the novel category, "hard" science fiction predominated. (This made for an interesting contrast to the finalists in short fiction, where in many cases the story's resolution grew out of the hopes or fears of the central characters, almost as a kind of wish fulfillment, rather than from what we think we know, in our supposedly rationalist culture, about the "real" world. This particular tendency seems more pronounced in science fiction these days; we can speculate about what that may mean.) John Barnes, Nancy Kress, and Robert J. Sawyer are three of the most talented writers now writing rigorously realistic science fiction. Paul Park is an inventive and gifted writer who deserves a wider audience; Walter Jon Williams, with over a decade of fine work behind him, gets better all the time; and Gene Wolfe is quite simply one of the ornaments of the genre.

It's often said that much of any year's best science fiction and fantasy can be found in the novella form, and the 1995 finalists live up to that claim. Every one of this year's contenders in the novella category deserved a place here, and I strongly urge readers to seek out the works by Brian Stableford, Gregory Benford, Nicola Griffith, and Mike Resnick and Susan Shwartz that could not be included in this volume. In the shorter forms, in addition to the stories in this book, writers such as Geoffrey A. Landis, Dave Smeds, Mike Resnick, Michael Coney, and Nina Kiriki Hoffman put in welcome appearances.

I would also like to direct readers to works on this year's preliminary ballot, listed in an appendix in the back. Of the works listed there, several should amply reward the good reader.

One purpose of the Nebula Awards anthology is to display the Nebula Award winners in context, among other contenders equally deserving of the honor. I hope that this anthology, and its predecessors, have also served to give readers an idea of the many varieties of fine work, and the particular pleasures, to be found in science fiction and fantasy.

This is my last year as editor of the Nebula Awards anthology, and several people have earned my gratitude over the past three years.

George Zebrowski, Michael Bishop, and James Morrow, the previous editors in this series, gave me the fine examples of their meticulous editing and the benefit of their wise advice. John Radziewicz and Christa Malone, my editors at Harcourt Brace, were unfailingly patient and congenial while aiding me in managing the plethora of details and crises that come up during the editing of any anthology. Richard Curtis, SFWA's agent for the Nebula Awards anthology (and my own literary agent as well), negotiated the contracts, handled payments to the authors, and looked after the business of the book promptly and efficiently. Mark J. McGarry, editor of the *Bulletin of the Science-fiction and Fantasy Writers of America,* secured most of the comments by authors about their nominated works and got them to me when I needed them.

I would also like to thank all of the writers who have appeared in *Nebula Awards 29, 30,* and *31* for creating their fictional worlds, for allowing me to enter them, and for granting their permission to share those worlds with other readers.

Nebula Awards 31

The Year in Science Fiction and Fantasy: A Symposium

PAUL DI FILIPPO
NANCY SPRINGER
JUDITH MOFFETT
IAN WATSON
ROBERT SILVERBERG
MICHAELA ROESSNER

Science fiction and fantasy are genres that continue to attract a varied and diverse number of writers with very different literary goals. For any one commentator to have a coherent view of the field or to assess the relative importance of individual works is difficult at best. I have instead asked several knowledgeable and gifted writers to point out certain signposts, or to comment on the particular fictional territories they have recently explored.

Paul Di Filippo has been a Nebula Award finalist and is the author of *The Steampunk Trilogy* and *Ribofunk;* William Gibson has called his writing "spooky, haunting, hilarious." His short fiction has appeared in *The Magazine of Fantasy & Science Fiction (F&SF), Amazing Stories,* and several past Nebula Awards anthologies; his essays and reviews regularly appear in *Asimov's Science Fiction, Science Fiction Age,* and *F&SF.*

Nancy Springer has won two Edgar Allan Poe Awards, given by the Mystery Writers of America, for her novels *Toughing It* and *Looking for*

Jamie Bridger. She has also been honored with a James Tiptree Jr. Memorial Award for her novel *Larque on the Wing*. Among her other novels are *The Silver Sun, The Hex Witch of Seldom, The White Hart, Chains of Gold, Apⴰcalypse,* and *Metal Angel*. She lives in Pennsylvania.

Judith Moffett's many honors include a National Endowment for the Humanities Translation Fellowship in 1983, a National Endowment for the Arts Fellowship in 1984, two Fulbright grants, a Theodore Sturgeon Memorial Award for her 1986 story "Surviving," and a John W. Campbell Award for Best New Writer in 1988. Her books of poetry include *Keeping Time* and *Whinny Moor Crossing;* she is also the author of the novels *Pennterra, The Ragged World,* and *Time, Like an Ever-Rolling Stream.*

Ian Watson has won the Prix Apollo, given annually for the best science fiction novel published in France, and the British Science Fiction Association Award. Among his many novels are *The Embedding, The Martian Inca, Alien Embassy, Whores of Babylon, Lucky's Harvest, The Fallen Moon,* and *The Books of the Black Current* trilogy. His short fiction has appeared in *Omni, Asimov's Science Fiction, The Magazine of Fantasy & Science Fiction,* and several best-of-the-year anthologies. A graduate of Oxford, he lives in England.

Robert Silverberg, one of science fiction's most honored, prolific, and knowledgeable writers, has won five Nebula Awards and four Hugo Awards. He is the author of *Thorns, The Masks of Time, Downward to the Earth, Tower of Glass, The World Inside, The Book of Skulls, Dying Inside, Lord Valentine's Castle, Gilgamesh the King, Lord of Darkness, Kingdoms of the Wall, Hot Sky at Midnight,* and *Sorcerers of Majipoor,* to list only a few of his literate and elegantly written novels. His column of commentary appears monthly in *Asimov's Science Fiction.*

Michaela Roessner has won the John W. Campbell Award for Best New Writer and the Crawford Award for her first novel, *Walkabout Woman.* Her second novel, *Vanishing Point,* is set in and around the Winchester Mystery House, a noted landmark in San Jose, California, and she recently completed *The Stars Dispose,* a historical fantasy about Catherine de Medici. She is also an artist and teaches aikido, in which she holds a fourth-degree black belt.

Rummaging Through the Giant Purse

PAUL DI FILIPPO

Any reader who couldn't find a shiny, freshly minted example of her favorite kind of SF in 1995 wasn't looking very hard. From meticulously honed extrapolations straight from tomorrow's R&D labs to whimsical surreal head trips, the Magic Purse that is genre publishing continued to expand to cosmic interior dimensions seemingly inconsistent with its domestic exterior size. Although of course the Bottomless Poke contained the usual amount of fairy gold—books that turned to dead leaves or manure upon exposure to sunlight—there was more than enough quality reading material to occupy the most insatiable fan or irascible reviewer. Sometimes so much, in fact, that one occasionally felt like the Henry Kuttner protagonist who reached into a similar Miraculous Satchel and, greedily groping, squashed his own future head.

Out of the approximately one thousand new titles appearing in 1995 (a figure cited in the *Locus* year-end survey), here are my favorites from the ones I personally encountered, grouped by resemblances real or imagined.

The renaissance in Hard/Near Future SF continued to exfoliate lushly. John Barnes smeared our faces in the mud of a bloody, temporally twisted millennium with his *Kaleidoscope Century* (Tor), affirming his title of "new Heinlein"—if one can imagine a Heinlein whose sensibilities were honed amidst malls and edge cities on a diet of MTV. In *The Time Ships* (HarperCollins UK), a centennial sequel to Wells's *The Time Machine* (1895), Stephen Baxter proved that Victorian sensibilities would be no more or less adept at facing superscience realities than our own vaunted postmodern ones. Charles Pellegrino and George Zebrowski destroyed ninety-nine percent of humanity in the opening pages of their *The Killing Star* (AvoNova) and proceeded from there to unleash some *real* thrills. Newcomer Linda Nagata made an explosive entrance with *The Bohr Maker* and its prequel, *Tech-Heaven* (both Bantam). The former was reminiscent of Michael Swanwick's *Vacuum Flowers* (1987), while the latter was one of the most cogent explorations of cryonics and its societal effects I've ever seen. Simon Ings's *Hotwire* (HarperCollins UK) was headlong, ten-new-ideas-per-page Gen X cyberpunk that upped the wattage of its Boomer predecessors.

My favorite of the newer "hardies" (if I may be permitted the rather silly neologism), Greg Egan, can with some cheating be counted twice. His *Permutation City* (HarperPrism), an ontological-digital masterpiece of multiple layers of transcendence, saw its first U.S. publication in 1995, and his superb short-story collection *Axiomatic* (Millennium) appeared in the UK.

More on the space-opera tip was David Brin's *Brightness Reef* (Bantam). Set in his popular Uplift universe, the book literally jumped galaxies and explored tangential matters, postponing the answers to some big questions raised earlier in the series. And Gentry Lee, *sans* collaborator Clarke but still pursuing the mystery ship *Rama*, moved the series into near C. S. Lewis territory with *Bright Messengers* (Bantam).

If you were in the market for severely altered realities, the Copious Purse contained not only conventional coins but also psychotropic tablets placed there by various literary pushers. Jonathan Lethem fused Jack Kerouac's *On The Road* (1957) with Samuel Delany's *The Einstein Intersection* (1967) and came up with *Amnesia Moon* (Harcourt Brace), about the land where time was forgotten. Elisabeth Vonarburg's *Reluctant Voyagers* (Bantam) moved by subtle degrees from uchronia to Gnostic subcreation.

Richard Kadrey's *Kamikaze L'Amour* (St. Martin's Press) covered the U.S. West Coast with a mystical rain forest sprung more from Borges than from the greenhouse effect. In *An Exaltation of Larks* (Tor), Robert Reed postulated sequentially born and destroyed universes moving toward a strange attractor of either ultimate freedom or ultimate control. Whenever J. G. Ballard sets pen to page, our mundane world automatically assumes hyperreal tints, and in his *Rushing to Paradise* (Picador USA), eco-activists meet their destined soulmate in the form of a female Doctor Death. Ballard's protagonist would have felt right at home in the world of David Prill's *The Unnatural* (St. Martin's Press), which detailed with gleeful sardonicism mortuary science as a spectator sport. Perhaps the most daring and accomplished of these outré novels—in both literary and cultural terms—was Richard Calder's astounding *Dead Girls* (St. Martin's Press), the

Aubrey Beardsley–like tale of a fagged-out Peter Pan and a vampiric Wendy, updated for an audience—look in the mirror—sated with teenaged supermodels and juvenile ultraviolence.

Plain old high-quality SF of no particular camp was also abundant. Nicola Griffith made good on the promise of her first book, *Ammonite* (1993), with *Slow River* (Del Rey), a journey of feminist self-exploration amidst future urban squalor and the internecine playgrounds of the elite. In *Archangel* (Tor), Mike Conner managed to duplicate the desolation of George Stewart's *Earth Abides* (1949) while exploring racism and the nature of compassion in an alternative 1930s America. And he told a tale of detection at the same time! Catherine Asaro's *Primary Inversion* (Tor), fused romance with interstellar dynastic squabbling. *Child of the Light* (White Wolf), by Janet Berliner and George Guthridge, the opening salvo of a trilogy, was a sensitively told narrative that promised to invigorate the old sad story of our cataclysmic century through the medium of wild-talent protagonists.

Moving into the hazy interzone where SF bleeds into fantasy, we find several standout volumes. *Waking the Moon* (HarperPrism), by Elizabeth Hand, picked up a well-deserved Tiptree Award for its depiction of a secret contemporary war between paradigms, specifically that of the ancient matriarchal Moon Goddess culture versus its patriarchal successor. William Browning Spencer's *Zod Wallop* (St. Martin's Press) romped about like a Terry Gilliam film in the deadly headspace created by the author of a magical children's book. *Expiration Date* (HarperCollins UK) found Tim Powers in fine fettle, as his trademark humor—which went missing in *The Stress of Her Regard* (1989) but began to resurge in *Last Call* (1992)—speckled the tale of Thomas Edison's ghost on a rampage in modern California. And the Druidical Michael Moorcock used his *Blood: A Southern Fantasy* (AvoNova) to put the most optimistic and humanistic spin yet on his massive Multiverse.

Three reprint collections formed invaluable additions to the SF canon, rescuing important stories from the mulch of the ages. *The Ultimate Egoist* (North Atlantic Books) was volume one in the collected stories of past master Ted Sturgeon. *The Dragon Path* (Tor) brought the entire short-fiction output of neglected theosophical/ Dunsanyist fantasist Kenneth Morris to light. And *Ganglion and Other*

Stories (Tachyon Publications) made a strong case for boosting Wayne Wightman's reputation in the field. Virginal short fiction had two fine venues in Greg Bear's *New Legends* (Tor) and David Garnett's *New Worlds 4* (Gollancz).

It was a banner year for SF scholarship also, as critics poured forth their wisdom and scholarly gleanings. John Clute was a one-man tidal wave, collecting his most recent passionately acerbic essays in *Look at the Evidence* (Serconia Press); putting a public face on SF in *Science Fiction: The Illustrated Encyclopedia* (Dorling Kindersley); and porting an earlier work (shared with Peter Nicholls), *The Science Fiction Encyclopedia,* to CD-ROM (Grolier). Joanna Russ's *To Write Like a Woman* (Indiana University Press) marked the welcome return of an eminently sane and wry voice, matched by Brian Aldiss's witty salmagundi, *The Detached Retina* (Liverpool University Press). From St. James Press and the editorial guidance of Jay Pederson and Robert Reginald came *The St. James Guide to Science Fiction Writers,* a wrist-breaking, mesmerizing omnibus of essays and bibliographical material. And lucky readers were invited into Stanislaw Lem's formative childhood in his memoir, *Highcastle* (Harcourt Brace).

One final telling illustration of the newly enlarged capacity of SF's Wallet of Wonders was the publication of Harlan Ellison's determinedly Campbellian *I, Robot* (Warner Books), the Asimov-inspired screenplay of a never-produced film. Intriguing material that in past decades would have languished undeservedly in a writer's dusty trunk now gets its shot at a life in the Big Pouch, and we are, all of us, all the richer.

Touchstones for Gender-Benders
NANCY SPRINGER

Something I read years ago impressed me deeply, and I am embarrassed that I cannot remember who the author was, except that it's a good bet she or he was black. S/he said (obviously I'm paraphrasing) that a white writer can easily ignore the existence of blacks and usually does so, but that it is next to impossible for a black to write about blacks without dealing with the presence of whites in the world. I remember intuiting how true that statement was, and cringing because I myself, an archetypical WASP, had written whites-only novels without a second thought, and knowing that it was a shallow, easy sense of entitlement that let me do so.

That knowledge has been affecting my writing for ten or fifteen years, but it was only in 1995 that my reading in sf made me push the thought a bit further, thus: writers (usually male) can, and often do, write about men while barely acknowledging the existence of women (real women, not the literary equivalent of wet dreams) at all—but it is next to impossible for a writer (usually female) to write about women without dealing with the presence of men in the world.

It's true. I am sure it's true, because for the past year I've been reading for the Tiptree Award, the feminist sf award, an award conceived and nurtured by women, an award to which the publishers submit mostly material written by women. So what do we Tiptree judges end up talking about? The role of men in the stories, that's what.

Not that we shouldn't discuss male characters or works written by men. I know I just said "feminist award," but that's unfair to the Tiptree. In practice it is a feminist award, but that's because of the way the world is. Theoretically and philosophically, the James Tiptree Jr. Award encourages new ideas about either or any gender. It could go to a person of either gender writing a gender-bender about men—if somebody would just *do* that. The award is supposed to go to the work of sf that best utilizes the imaginative potential of the genre to explore/expand gender roles, period. I personally would love to see it go to a man for a fresh take on gender issues for men, but no such work was submitted this year, if ever. There were pregnant-man stories, of course, but written by women, and less in the spirit of gender exploration than in one of malicious glee.

I have nothing against malicious glee, but it gets boring and repetitious after a while. As a Tiptree judge, I saw too many male-bashing stories, most of them even more predictable than the chauvinist-pig-gets-preggers ones. So, sorting through feminist stories, I found myself using the roles of male characters as a touchstone on this basis: as long as women can't write stories about women without reflecting or deflecting them off men, then women haven't gotten very far.

I read some otherwise fine stories that failed the male-as-touchstone test. For instance, "The Birthday" by Esther Friesner (*The Magazine of Fantasy & Science Fiction)*, a strong, original, deeply felt story that slips over the edge into unbelievability because the male characters are uniformly loathsome. Or "De Secretis Mulierum" by L. Timmel Duchamp (also in *F&SF*), a story blessed with a wonderful, original premise but cursed with a male antagonist who is less a character than a caricature, a stereotypical chauvinist complete with the requisite tiny dick.

Or Kit Reed's *Little Sisters of the Apocalypse* (Black Ice Books), a slim volume which might better be named "Little Stick of Dynamite," a brilliantly written, incandescent firecracker of a book; I wish only that it gave off as much light as heat. In this book, the only good males are religious ecstatics; all the other men are necessary evils. Reed is such a good writer that, in her context of apocalyptic war, this sweeping characterization of an entire gender almost works—except that her female characters, painted with the same broad, fiery brush, fall far short of her descriptions of them. Her leader doesn't lead, her rebellious female rabble-rouser does not rebel. Despite the flaws, Reed writes such a scorcher, raising so many necessary questions about war and religion, that *Little Sisters of the Apocalypse* is a "keeper"; my copy has found a home on my bookshelf—even though, in the end, nothing happens except that the guys come home and everything returns to the status quo.

Which leads me to another touchstone, another issue that we (the few, the proud, the 1995 Tiptree judges) found ourselves addressing in almost every work we considered: the disappointing ending. For example, "De Secretis Mulierum," again, a story with a wonderful premise: a scientific advance has enabled historians to peek through the keyhole of time, discovering that both Thomas Aquinas and Leonardo da Vinci were women. What possibilities that idea opens up! But Duchamp contents herself with getting the female historian protagonist to break up with the oinker with the tiny dick. Her wonderful premise leads nowhere. Similarly, *Little Sisters of the Apocalypse* ultimately goes nowhere. Lisa Tuttle's "Food Man" (*Crank*), an insightful story about body image, slips into a standard horror ending. *The Raw Brunettes*, a chapbook by Lorraine Schein (Wordcraft of Oregon), goes nowhere except downhill from an exciting, psychedelic opening. These are only a few examples of the many, many works we considered for the Tiptree that ended not with a bang but with a whimper. Most frustrating, it was generally the strongest, most daring, most gender-bending stories that seemed to lack endings written with courage and authority. This problem was so prevalent, in both short and long narratives, that I became obsessed with it and began looking at my own work (or that of my work which is labeled "feminist"), wondering whether I, too, tend to wimp out in the final chapter—and, by damn, I think I do.

And I think I know why. Thanks to Joanna Russ, I have an idea why this problem occurs—and occurs, and occurs. In her recent collection, *To Write Like a Woman: Essays in Feminism and Science Fiction* (IUP Press), specifically in the essay entitled "What Can a Heroine Do? or Why Women Can't Write," Russ analyzes the plots that are traditionally available to women writers: Hello, dear, would you like to write a love story, a love story, or a love story? Or perhaps a story about a woman going crazy? That's it, darling; no other precedents exist. Therefore, women trying to write honestly about women are undertaking a great experiment. Women attempting gender-bending sf about women, even more so. It's no wonder the attempts get a bit gawky at times, no wonder that structures get leggy and sprawly and tend to crawl off in a downhill direction. The most difficult part, of course, is the ending. Give a woman writer a brilliant premise about women, and where does it lead? Nobody knows. There are no paths to follow.

Women's stories that predictably pillory male characters, women's stories with strong premises but endings that do not fulfill the promise of the beginnings—those two grumbles describe most of the material I read for the Tiptree this past year.

Show me a story by a woman or a man that comes up with a strong, original gender-bending premise and follows it through to a condign ending, and I'll show you a Tiptree winner.

Did we judges find a narrative like that to win this year's Tiptree Award?

In my opinion—no.

But we came close.

The two cowinners were, from Random House, *The Memoirs of Elizabeth Frankenstein* By Theodore Roszak and, from HarperPrism,

Waking the Moon by Elizabeth Hand. They're both brilliant books. They both develop high-concept gender-related premises. Read them and judge for yourself whether they treat both female characters and male characters as full human beings, and whether they flinch at the end.

These are exciting times. A touchstone of how far feminist sf has come: this year's jury did not consider that strong female characters in and of themselves made a story Tiptree material, because are not strong female protagonists the norm? Things may even get to the point where women writing stories about women will have endings available to them, and if there are men in the stories, it will be because the women want them there.

Planet Deseret

JUDITH MOFFETT

My husband and I moved to Salt Lake City from Philadelphia in August 1994, both looking forward to four or five years of postretirement Rocky Mountain High. I knew the special history of Utah, of course, but I'd lived all over the country and adapted time after time to local differences. Besides that, I'd grown up in a fundamentalist church, and, as a former religious fanatic myself, I felt I knew where the Mormons were coming from. Ted was worried about being plagued by missionaries; I wasn't, and we haven't been.

But I'd also lived abroad for extended periods; and after six months or so as a transplanted Utahn, I understood that Salt Lake wasn't just one more American town. The Church of Jesus Christ of Latter-day Saints, for all its many ultra-American qualities, imparts a color and flavor to Utah that make the place feel to me as truly foreign as England or Sweden ever did.

Alien-encounter sf is my favorite kind, so who's complaining? On the other hand, I do find Utah a peculiar place from which to view the whole field of the fantastic. The Beehive State's population is between two-thirds and three-fourths LDS; Salt Lake itself, it's said, is one-third Mormon, one-third non-Mormon, and one-third ex-Mormon. To insinuate that the main stomping ground of the LDS Church is *itself* a field of the fantastic is a cheap shot, and not a new one. But consider:

In 1827 a devout young man, Joseph Smith, is visited by an angel named Moroni (Mor-ohn-eye), who shows him where to find a stack of golden plates. Two magical devices, the Urim and Thummim, enable him to decode the encrypted writing etched upon them. Smith translates the plates—which contain *The Book of Mormon,* a fantastic retelling of history and a prophecy of events to come—and starts a religion. He makes many converts. The new church is persecuted ferociously.

The story of how Smith and/or his followers got from upstate New York to Utah—called Deseret by the early settlers, after a *Book of Mormon* word for honeybee—is blockbuster drama of the very highest caliber. The Alvin Maker series by Orson Scott Card, a native Utahn and the most famous of the LDS sf writers, is a fantastic transmogrification of an already fantastic story. For my money, the first two books in the series owe their excellence not only to Scott's mesmerizing tale-telling but also to two other factors: the wonderful material he was working with and the fact that Mormon culture is saturated with a sense of values.

Alas, it's a troublesome truth that, while many of these values seem to me very admirable, and the Mormon faithful admirable in the consistency with which they practice what they preach, other LDS values strike me as perfectly appalling. Since this is an essay about sf, not Mormon theocracy, I won't get into specifics here (but ask me at some con). What I had not at all anticipated is that, with one or two exceptions, the large and active group of sf and fantasy writers who live here either have LDS backgrounds or are practicing Mormons.

Why else, you ask, would a writer live in Utah, the state that gave us cold fusion, Orrin Hatch, Enid Greene Waldholtz (*our* representative, Ted's and mine!), and the school board that banned all clubs in order to stop gay and lesbian students from forming one? Right after we moved here, in fact, the *Salt Lake Tribune* ran a story about Brigham Young University English professor Brian Evans, a writer of mainstream fiction and horror, who was forced by Church authorities either to give up a National Endowment for the Arts fellowship or resign. (He resigned. As I recall, he was also excommunicated.) I mentioned this case at a dinner with some local sf writers I'd just met, expecting outrage. What I heard instead was that the NEA had *asked* for trouble, by funding Robert Mapplethorpe and other artists of dubious morals.

That conventional and docile response stopped me cold. How can serious writers submit to a religious institution that restricts what they say in print; and how are the rest of us supposed to take them seriously if they do?

I have pondered the question a good deal and have concluded that, from mid list to best-seller list, no LDS writer makes the grade who hasn't faced up to this conflict with integrity. But popular acclaim is important. I suspect things might have worked out differently for Brian Evans had his work been popular. Examples of *high-profile* Mormon writers who decline to toe the strict party line include the passionate environmentalist Terry Tempest Williams (the Church, like the West in general, favors multiple use) and, of course, our own immensely visible Orson Scott Card, who in *The Memory of Earth* (to cite one instance) turns Church practice on its head by making the priesthood available to women only (!).

There's also Dave Wolverton, an early grand-prize winner of the Writers of the Future Contest. Dave is a very smart guy. Church authorities found his first novel, *On My Way to Paradise*, disturbing; but he's also written a Star Wars novel, *The Courtship of Princess Leia*. Thanks to him I witnessed firsthand—at a bookstore signing in a Salt Lake mall—the media-driven creature our field has become, as copies of *Courtship* melted off the stacks on the table and awed children from Germany and England shyly asked to have their pictures taken with the author. Like Williams and Card, Wolverton appears to have found his own ways and means of acknowledging the Church's authority while still saying what he needs to say. Like them, he must know something I don't presume to know: how far he can be pushed without pushing back.

The Writers of the Future Contest has strong ties with Utah; Julia West recently became the state's second grand-prize winner, and a dozen or so quarterly winners and runners-up live here or used to. I have it on good authority that suspicions about a collusion between Dianetics and Mormonism are baseless. Dave Wolverton now does the preliminary judging for the contest and edits the anthologies of winners; he speculates that the numbers are so high because the judges have traditionally liked stories incorporating a sense of values, and the Utah writers' stories incorporate disproportionately more of them, for reasons likely having to do with their LDS background. It's a theory. Among the quarterly winners and placers with a national visage: Virginia Baker; M. Shayne Bell, whose story "Mrs. Lincoln's China" made the 1995 Hugo ballot; Diana Hoffman; Susan Kroupa; Brook West, the current Nebula Awards editor for the SFWA *Forum;* and Kathleen Woodbury, coordinator of the SFWA suite for the 1996 Worldcon. Elizabeth Boyer and Diann Thornley broke in without using the springboard of WOTF.

All the above, however, is but the tip of the iceberg. A few years back, Shayne Bell edited and Signature Books, a local small press, published the anthology *Washed by a Wave of Wind: Science Fiction from the Corridor.* In his editor's introduction, Shayne defines "the Corridor" as "the area of original Mormon settlement in the West stretching in a narrow band from Alberta to Sonora (but limited in this book to Utah and southeastern Idaho)." Twenty stories are included, all but three by writers who have published professionally elsewhere. The quality is uneven, and the *Locus* review wasn't very kind (though others were). For me, however, the extraordinary thing about the book is that it represents a phenomenon I've encountered nowhere else: the deep commitment of a core group of writers to each other, their region, and the genre.

Besides stories by Card, Wolverton, and Bell, and excellent pieces by Glenn L. Anderson, Carolyn Nicita, Michaelene Pendleton (a non-Mormon, by the way), and others, *WWW*'s table of contents includes a partial roster of the members of a group of writers who first met in a science fiction creative writing class at BYU in 1980. After the course ended, its members continued to meet and workshop stories. As of this writing, they've gone on meeting virtually *every single Saturday night* for sixteen years, either in Provo or in Salt Lake City. Sixteen years! (A recent shift to twice a month was offset by the instant formation of a reading group, which convenes on one of the vacated Saturdays, and the decision to devote a fifth Saturday, if any, to socializing.)

The group, called Xenobia, has endured marriages, divorces, children, a recent schism, the loss of old members and the addition of new ones (including me), and crises of every kind. (*Washed by a*

Wave of Wind is dedicated to the teacher of that landmark class, Marion K. Smith. Dr. Smith and his wife were among the guests at the last Xenobia Christmas party, in Shayne Bell's condo, for which occasion even the disaffected splinter group, Pilgrimage, turned out in force.)

There's more. In April 1996 Xenobia held a retreat, to which Pilgrimage and other groups were also invited. A house was rented at Homestead, a mountain resort, it being affordable in the off season. We arrived Friday evening for a potluck dinner and a presentation on Albert Zuckerman's *Writing the Blockbuster Novel.* All day Saturday, a dozen people sat around in a large living-dining room, laptops in laps, eyes glazed, writing writing writing. That evening after dinner we settled down to hear what everyone had produced. (At one extreme, I'd produced three pages and didn't read them; at the other, Shayne had written a whole story so good it was hard to believe he'd done it all that day.) The next morning we finished the readings and went home, many of us to church responsibilities.

Over the years, some Xenobians have achieved professional status; others still haven't; but the gritty persistence of the group over so long a time speaks volumes to me about the sf scene in Utah. Xenobia is still together for two reasons an outsider can observe: that Mormons like living in Utah, and that Church membership conditions people to group loyalty and commitment. But behind these lies a saga I've no space to go into here, involving an epic struggle on the part of dedicated young writers to get speculative fiction taken seriously at BYU, that is, by the LDS church. Xenobia emerged out of that struggle, and its veterans have turned down jobs and rejected graduate schools in order to stay where Xenobia is.

And, yes, the Xenobians—and their writing—do have values. I vividly recall the evening when a longtime member, LDS convert Dave Doering, burst out that the story under discussion (about a character's clever, cold-blooded efforts to manipulate an unsuspecting person to his own ends) was *immoral.* Morality used as a critical term, here in the sunset of Deconstruction? I don't mean to suggest that the Xenobians think morality the only important thing about a story, or even the most important thing. But they do think moral considerations are important in fiction, and, as a matter of fact, so do I. Even if I disagree, sometimes violently, with the way they define what is and isn't moral.

Maybe what I've been describing is less remarkable than I think it is, but I can assure you that, for better *and* for worse, it wasn't like this in Philadelphia.

So powerfully centrifugal is the local scene, indeed, that it's hard to see past it to what's going on in the field as a whole, though we do what we can. Everyone aspires to publish in the national markets and some succeed, several follow the on-line discussions, we attend the Worldcon. Our reading group devoted a session to the stories on the final Nebula ballot, some of which were much admired. Others, frankly, would have been smartly sent back to the drawing board; even members still struggling toward professional publication have become shrewd, insightful critics, after all those years of practice. (I'd been pretty satisfied with the first chapter of my novel-in-progress before the Xenobians sank their claws into it, but the postcritique revision is so much better it's embarrassing.)

At the supra-Xenobia level, Utah fans put on a con, called CONduit, every May. Also, for the past ten Februarys or so, former BYU students have sponsored an academic sf symposium: "Life, the Universe, and Everything." This is a big deal. The Provo writers kill themselves putting it together, pros fly in from distant places to participate, and guests of honor are drawn from the field's top names: Frederik Pohl, C. J. Cherryh, David Brin, Octavia Butler, Connie Willis, Lois McMaster Bujold. Last winter, when BYU threatened to withdraw its always tenuous support, the committee turned to Kristine Kathryn Rusch, last year's CONduit GOH (along with Dean Wesley Smith). Kris wrote a letter to the university committee testifying that LTUAE, as one of only three such academic symposia in the country, was of genuine value both to the field and to the university. It worked; the Y backed down and the symposium went forward. On the program: a presentation by Lee Allred, Xenobian, organizer, and Writers of the Future runner-up, discussing John Gardner's controversial 1978 book *On Moral Fiction.*

All of which is a partial answer to the question of why a writer like myself, a Gentile and a Democrat, would find it fascinating to live here. But I knew nothing about this gripping sf scene before I hit town. Things I did know: Mormons, at the personal level, are the nicest people imaginable and the best neighbors; Salt Lake City is blessed with one of the most spectacular natural settings of any city anywhere; the national parks of southern Utah—Canyonlands, Bryce Canyon, Capitol Reef, Arches, Zion—are names to conjure with around the world; and, finally, if you want to run the slopes where Olympic downhill skiers will set records in 2002, or raft the river wild, This Is The Place.

I got back just last weekend from a trip south, where for three days I stared at two-thousand-year-old petroglyphs and pictographs, scrambled over redrock and slickrock in the Needles district of Canyonlands, and huffed up the steep trail that bursts upon Delicate Arch. The mercury hit 98 and stuck. Unfiltered desert sunlight, bouncing off the white stone, sent camera light meters off the scale; but that country is beyond photography anyway, beyond description, almost beyond belief—as extreme and beautiful and strange as any otherworldly landscape I ever entered by means of a writer's imagination.

The leader of our little group was ex-Mormon Shayne Bell. For years, Shayne has spent as much time as he could in the parks, but the eleven-mile Needles hike stands out even in his experience. And all through those hours in the presence of ancient images and towering, violently colored, grotesquely eroded rock formations, story ideas kept leaping up and slapping us in the face.

Mormon history, Anasazi prehistory, landscape. I trust these make my point. No, it's not for everybody; yes, its policies, priorities, and social attitudes are often deplorable. But for now, while country still transcends the mess and greed of people, Utah is still a great place for writers in this field to be.

You even get to do a little missionary work on the side.

The British Scene
IAN WATSON

In Britain last year, hard-sf author Stephen Baxter celebrated the centenary of H. G. Wells's *The Time Machine* with an ambitious sequel, *The Time Ships*. This almost precipitated a cause célèbre (or, more likely—horrors—the pulping of the entire print run) when Wells's literary estate took umbrage at the use of "characters and plots" from HGW. The executors had never bothered about this, or maybe never noticed, when Christopher Priest's *The Space Machine* appeared in 1976 or Brian Aldiss's *Moreau's Other Island* in 1980. But on this occasion they scented . . . money.

In British copyright law there's no ownership of fictional characters or plots in general. Yet, like so much British law, this is a gray area. Obviously, outright plagiarism is illegal—but a spin-off from a book that was published when Queen Victoria was on the throne? Gadzooks!

Since defending such a ridiculous case could cost an author dearly, Baxter opted to hand over a slice of his earnings to Wells's estate. His publishers followed up swiftly with a paperback edition duly labeled "the authorized sequel to *The Time Machine*"—which is completely absurd.

And perhaps a dangerous precedent has been set, especially as science fiction is a genre that not infrequently remixes former themes and settings.

The Time Ships is a very clever pastiche incorporating our latter-day knowledge (or speculations) about Dyson spheres, physics, cosmology, et al. It's deliciously ironic in its moral education of the doughty Victorian time traveler, who is full of parochial chauvinist attitudes and impulses to trounce the natives with his fists, when actually the future Morlocks are much more advanced and subtle than he. One might cavil that there are really only two true characters in the book, one of whom is an enigmatic alien who remains enigmatic and the other the traveler equipped with his stereotyped attitudes; and that his quest to save the silly wimpish Weena is simply a waste of time. And one might regard the culminating cosmic panorama-trip as a hard-sf riff that would quite elude any ordinary reader led to expect an authentic Wellsian sequel. Helping to sustain a grand gonzo cavalcade are various alternate-history spear-carriers, such as Kurt Gödel, and assorted British buzznames of the Second World War.

Ian McDonald is an eloquent remix conjuror (and proud of it), who can write in anyone's style or milieu and make it his own, or even improve on it. In his distinctly Ballardian *Chaga*, part of East Africa (and elsewhere, too) is being remade by invasive enigmatic alien life, creating a dizzyingly beautiful mutagenic new landscape, which bids fair to sweep our civilization aside as it expands, but which also offers evolutionary transcendence. The majority of the book is awesome, poignant, thrilling, sublimely evocative; but then a version of Greg Bear's *Eon* puts in an appearance, swiftly mutating into Clarke's *Rama*, and there are just too many science-fictional homages.

As a tongue-in-cheek, or maybe a defiant, postscript, McDonald quotes Delany's comment that "in science fiction, everything should be mentioned twice, with the possible exception of science fiction." The moral here, I'd say, is that it would have been better not to mention science fiction at all; then the novel would have had fuller authenticity. Ultimately, too, everything has been arranged for us by a benevolent universe. After the pangs and anguish: the happy pill—as if Hollywood had insisted on an uplifting ending, courtesy of *Close Encounters*. "Message from Team Red. They say there are *figures*, moving down there in the mist."

A former remixer of Wells, Christopher Priest, who wouldn't dream of mentioning science fiction in an overtly literary novel that went on to win a mainstream literary award, has his tongue somewhat in his cheek in the splendid, though evasive, *The Prestige*. This tale of rival Victorian stage magicians is a tour de force of sleight of hand, both in subject matter and in style, with an "unreliable narrator" (or, rather, narrators, plural) teasingly affirming and withholding truth from the reader. Yes, no. Yes, no. Enter Nikola Tesla, who builds a fully functional matter transmitter for one of the magicians, a machine that subsequently gets relegated to the cellar to gather dust. Priest ingeniously centers his book around a science-fictional device while disguising from the public at large its family affinity, quite as thoroughly as other family affinities are cloaked in the narrative itself.

In *Seasons of Plenty* Colin Greenland continued in effervescent vein the trilogy begun with his much-admired *Take Back Plenty*. The British solar system is once again a domain of revitalized gonzo space opera, awash with aliens, mutants, and marvels. Not to mention interplanetary Victorian aether-ships, a different forte of Greenland's.

The wonders in *Seasons of Plenty* are perhaps a bit capricious compared with Christopher Evans's biotechnological solar system in *Mortal Remains*, with its highly original gossipy disgruntled organic spaceships (and organic everything else, lavishly visualized), though what is highly believable and serious eventually veers into a *Boy's Own* adventure yarn; and the extremely nifty narrative structure, using the dream visions of amnesiac resurrectees to dramatize events millions of miles apart, becomes almost too convenient as we bop from body to body, obedient to plot requirements.

Following up his *début d'estime* in *Vurt* (and proving that a small-press publication can come from outfield into swift bestsellerdom), Jeff Noon's *Pollen* is set in the same milieu of rainy magical-realist Manchester intersected with dreamland mediated by designer psychotropics. Seemingly influenced by Robert Holdstock's mythagos—incarnated myth figures—and by Ballard's *The Unlimited Dream Company* (in which suburban Shepperton, outside London, becomes a mutative orgiastic Garden of Eden), *Pollen* is an aboundingly lyrical, radiant, and moving account of humble heroisms when myths struggle to break into the real world, with apocalyptic consequences. Particularly poignant is the evolved-dog detective.

Another sequel, *Hotwire,* by cyber-meteor Simon Ings, is so much more lucid than its predecessor, *Hot Head,* which did read at times like fried brain. Partly set in Rio, *Hotwire* involves cities becoming sentient (a bit as in John Shirley's *City Come A Walkin',* written prior to the necessary info-technology), artificial intelligences called Massives which have gone their own (not very sane) way, as well as espionage and love and betrayal and obsession. Resolutely hip, an exuberant impresario display, *Hotwire* does strain unashamedly for effect, but most of the time Ings tosses the reader over his hip with a deft *o-goshi.*

The most innovative debut of the year was Scottish author Ken Macleod's appallingly titled *The Star Fraction.* Appallingly, because the cryptic puzzle of the title does no justice to this enthusiastic, invigorating, radical, hip-gritty story of a future wired Britain balkanized into competing semisovereign interest groups (all shades of reds, greens, wimmin, capitalist-anarchists, royalists, Islamic militants, what have you) and employing licensed mercenaries—whilst American-controlled United Nations zapper satellites peer down, ready to fry any signs of artificial intelligence emerging. For a while I suspected that this novel was an escapade of Trotskyist retro chic; but in fact it's genuinely revolutionary. Something completely different.

Paul McAuley (all these Macs!) is likewise gritty in *Fairyland*, his finest work yet. This very European novel starts in London, moves to Amsterdam and Prague and Paris (wondrously deconstructing Euro Disney), and climaxes in war-torn Albania. In fact there's constant civil war and turmoil in McAuley's near-future Europe, radically transformed by nanotechnology, meme bombs, and genetically engineered "doll" slaves, some of whom are uplifted by a wayward genius child to become the fairies of folklore. Memes (Richard Dawkins's "viral ideas") must be a genuine phenomenon, since the drummers of Neal Stephenson's *The Diamond Age* crop up in *Fairyland*, which was being written synchronously. It is for such prophetic insights into possible futures that one reads science fiction.

Gresham's Law and Science Fiction
ROBERT SILVERBERG

Gresham's law is at work in science fiction, and bad books are driving out good ones. The prospect is that the process will continue and grow even more harmful with time.

Sir Thomas Gresham was an English banker in the time of Queen Elizabeth I. Gresham's great contribution to economics was the idea of forming an equalization fund to support the exchange rate of his country's currency—an idea that the queen rejected, apparently because the royal treasury didn't have enough cash on hand to make the concept work, but which is common practice everywhere today.

One concept for which Gresham was *not* responsible was Gresham's law. The economist Henry D. Macleod, propounding it in 1857, attributed it erroneously to Gresham. It was, in fact, one of Gresham's contemporaries, Humphrey Holt, who in 1551 had observed that the debasement of English currency late in the reign of Henry VIII was causing coins of pure silver to disappear from circulation, leaving only base coins in use and bringing about severe inflation, "to the decay of all things." That is to say, bad money drives out good. People spend the debased coinage as fast as they can; coins of good metal vanish into hoards or are melted down for other uses, so that eventually there are none to be found in circulation at all.

What does this have to do with science fiction?

Simply this: since about 1975, when books based on popular s-f movies and television shows began to be published and to enjoy huge sales, a gradual debasement of the stuff we like to read has taken place. Once upon a time—when science fiction was exclusively the province of a few low-circulation magazines—s-f editors and readers put a premium on thoughtful, serious ideas and crisp, literate writing. That was the heyday of John W. Campbell's *Astounding Science Fiction* (now *Analog*) and, a little later, Horace Gold's *Galaxy* and the *Fantasy & Science Fiction* of Anthony Boucher and J. Francis McComas. It was the heyday, too, of the great writers who gave modern science fiction its character: Asimov, Heinlein, Sturgeon, De Camp, Simak, Kuttner, and the rest of Campbell's team in the 1940s, and Leiber, Kornbluth, Pohl, Clarke, Bradbury, Bester, Vance, Anderson, Blish, Dick, and many others a little later on.

Since the readers knew what they liked and magazine circulations varied very little from month to month, editors were motivated to publish the most challenging and vigorous stories they could find. They didn't have to worry about driving readers away by publishing excessively challenging and unusual fiction: the audience was steady, issue after issue, so long as the general quality level remained consistent. For young and unsophisticated readers, there were such action-oriented magazines as *Planet Stories* and *Amazing Stories;* when they were a little older, they would usually graduate to *Astounding* or one of its handful of adult-oriented competitors.

The coming of paperback publishing changed all that. Each book now was a unique item, with its own highly visible sales figures; but each of those unique books fell into a larger class of fiction according to type—the old Campbellian cerebral s-f, the wild-and-woolly *Planet Stories* type, the fantasy-tinged sword-and-sorcery type, and so on. Unsurprisingly, books of the more simpleminded sorts sold better— sometimes a great deal better. In a free-market economy there will always be more cash customers for Schwarzenegger-esque tales of violent conflict than for sober Campbellian examinations of the social consequences of technological developments.

Paperback publishers are not charitable institutions. They are in the business of what is accurately called "mass-market" publishing. The sales figures were unanswerable; and, gradually, over a period of ten or fifteen years, the older kind of science fiction, the kind that we who first discovered it thirty or forty years ago thought of as "good" science fiction, began to disappear.

You aren't likely to find many of the wonderful novels of Theodore Sturgeon, Fritz Leiber, or Alfred Bester in your neighborhood bookstore. Simak is a rarity; Blish is forgotten except (ironically) for his *Star Trek* novelizations; the work of Kornbluth and Kuttner is utterly unknown. Much great work of Vance, Dick, even Bradbury, Clarke, and Heinlein, has been shoved to the back rows in favor of the latest adventure of Princess Leia, the fourteenth volume in some popular robot-warrior series, and the ninth installment of a cops-and-robbers-in-the-asteroid-belt epic. I confess that I'm having trouble keeping some of my own best books in print these days. It isn't that these books of a generation ago are creaky and obsolete. They aren't. It's that they can't hold their own in the stores against the flashy new media-oriented kind of s-f and the interminable sequels to the mediocre books of a few years ago. Aside from the occasional brilliant Zeitgeist-shaping novel like *Neuromancer* or *Snow Crash,* just about the only s-f books that do well commercially nowadays are series books and Hollywood spin-offs.

This is sad on two accounts. One is that the books I'm talking about have a lot of great reading to offer. (Where are Sturgeon's *More than Human,* Ward Moore's *Bring the Jubilee,* Hal Clement's *Mission of Gravity* these days? In and out of print in the wink of an eye whenever some courageous publisher reissues them.)

Worse—far worse, I think—is the loss of these classics as exemplars of the type. Young science fiction writers traditionally take the work of their great predecessors as models for their own early books and stories. I grew up reading the classic s-f of what is still called the Golden Age, a period that began in 1939 and ran, by my estimate, to the early 1950s. When I began writing, my goal was to equal the attainments of those writers who, years before, had filled my head with their wondrous visions. I still keep that goal in mind with every word I write.

But what of the young writers of today, who have no access to those classics, and who may very well come to regard the crudely written and crudely conceived formula-ridden mass-market stuff of today's paperback racks as the proper ideal to follow? What they read is what they will write. Junk begets junk. So the newer writers will give us imitations of works that themselves would probably not have been able to see publication a generation ago.

When young writers no longer have access to a broad historical overview of science fiction—when they are unable to absorb and digest and transmute, as we did, such books as Heinlein's *Beyond This Horizon* and van Vogt's *The World of Null-A* and Sturgeon's *More Than Human* and Bester's *The Demolished Man,* then a whole world of creative possibilities is lost to them: either they merely strive to replicate the simple, badly written books that they think of as the best of s-f, or else they expend their creative energies reinventing wheels that were better designed by the writers of a generation ago.

Thus, as our classics go out of print, we lose touch with our ideals, our platonic forms of the finest s-f. Superb work is still being done by some writers, of course. Indeed, some of the best science fiction ever written has appeared in the last decade. But most of that high-quality work struggles in the marketplace and has a sadly short shelf life, driven out of sight by the vast tide of you-know-what, often causing its writers to wonder why they had bothered. And thus does Gresham's law operate in our bailiwick, "to the decay of all things." It's a problem I've been wrestling with for twenty years now, ever since the immense popularity of George Lucas's *Star Wars* brought hundreds of thousands of new s-f readers into the fold and forever changed the demographics of our field.

There has always been a place in our field for well-done action-adventure science fiction. I remember fondly the glorious space epics of Leigh Brackett and Poul Anderson and even Ted Sturgeon in the lively magazine *Planet Stories* of the 1940s; and I wrote plenty of stuff in the *Planet Stories* vein myself, later on. That kind of fast-moving, colorful, melodramatic fiction has a great deal to offer, especially to younger readers who might later go on to read the other sort of s-f.

What I *am* saying is that modern-day publishing's emphasis on the bottom line seems to be killing science fiction as an adult genre. I loved *Planet Stories,* sure, but I doubt that I would have stuck with s-f past the age of fifteen or so if I hadn't been able to move on to John Campbell's *Astounding Science Fiction* and Horace Gold's *Galaxy,* with their great array of stimulating stories by Asimov and Heinlein and Blish and Sturgeon and Kornbluth and Clement and so many other wonderful writers. We are heading to a point now, at least in book publishing, where the slam-bang kind of fiction is not only dominant but has driven our classics from print and is hurting the distribution and sales of new science fiction intended for an intelligent readership.

I see no remedy. In a free-market economy, the bottom line rules. (In the Soviet Union, state-controlled publishing houses served up a steady diet of classic Russian novels, poetry, and the collected works of Lenin to a huge audience starved for books of any sort, and scarcely any popular fiction was printed. In today's anything-goes Russia, Dostoyevsky and Chekhov are taking a backseat to pulp fiction of the tawdriest sort. The readers are voting with their rubles, and the publishers have to pay attention, or else.)

So I am playing the part, I guess, of that stuffiest of old bores, the *laudator temporis acti*—he who praises the glories of the past at the expense of the present. I can't help it. I've spent much of my life reading and writing science fiction. I love it for its visionary potential; I hate to see it turned into something hackneyed and cheap.

The torrent of bad s-f has the additional drawback of driving away mature readers who are just beginning to be curious about modern science fiction. Perhaps they read some Bradbury or Asimov long ago, and now they want to sample some of the current product; or it may be that they've never tried s-f at all, and somehow have decided to sample it now. So they wander into the bookstore, stare with glazing eyes at the garish covers in the science fiction section, finally pick up *Vengeance of the Galaxy Eaters* or the ninth volume of the *Glibabibion* saga or the novelization of *Vampires of the Void,* riffle through it in growing dismay, put it back, and cross the aisle to the mystery-novel section, where the interests of adult readers are currently being well attended to. And are lost to us forever.

It isn't the publishers' fault. They're simply delivering what the biggest segment of the audience wants, as they always do. If an audience for Grand Master X or Y or Z is no longer there, and if the work of modern writers of similar skill and ambition sells poorly also, they'll simply crank out the next *Glibabibion* volume, the one in which the

Wand of Total Power is recaptured by the Lord of Utter Evil. What choice do they have?

I don't begrudge the manufacturers of the interchangeable cotton-candy trilogies the readership and the concomitant fat royalty checks they have won. I just wish there were some way for the work of writers who ask more of themselves and of their readers to stay in print; and for that, I'm afraid, we need not only enlightened publishers—of whom we have a few already—but an intelligent and avid readership that demands not merely the same old stuff cubed but science fiction of the challenging, mind-expanding sort that brought us into the field in the first place.

Family Values
MICHAELA ROESSNER

Seems as if the science fiction aspect of speculative fiction is all that it ever was and more. The subject matter still covers the beloved ancient and not-so-ancient tropes: robots, time travel, empire-building space sagas, generation ships, alternate history, alternate universes, aliens, terraforming, bioengineering, etc., etc. Some of the old has become new again as current technology throws fresh light on venerable topics: Witness the recent rash of Martian-settlement novels. Then there are the more recent arrivals in town—virtual reality, nanotechnology, gene splicing, and so on—entrenched long enough that they're beginning to resemble once unruly gang-bangers who by surviving a self-selected brutal and uncertain youth now find themselves in the embarrassing position of becoming part of the establishment.

The end of every year finds writers in the field voting for those works they feel represent the best science fiction has to offer. With such a plethora to choose from, the winning works can sometimes provide interesting insights into the genre by virtue of their similarities or differences.

In last year's *Nebula Awards* volume symposium, James Gunn provided a salient analysis on what has driven the field over the years. He pointed out that it started as a "reader-driven category" in the days when editors enjoyed more freedom to buy books "that they themselves liked or respected." But once science fiction proved increasingly lucrative, it became a market-driven genre, with sales forces shaping choices on what is bought and how it is marketed. The end result is that in our increasingly television- and film-obsessed culture, the majority of commercial successes in the marketplace have proven to be the endless spin-offs of the *Star Wars* and *Star Trek* variety.

This has generated quite a debate in the field on the issues of literary values and compromises of writers' creativity. Although I think a good many writers feel threatened by this phenomenon, the point could be made that these sorts of series *do* serve a valid purpose beyond that of enabling authors an opportunity to actually earn a living. To wit, that there's a huge audience out there hungering for the good old pulp formula of a lot of action taking place on a vast intergalactic stage, peopled by ever more familiar characters and an ever more mapped-out infrastructure of culture, history, and technology.

It's a slightly different audience than that which consumed pulps in the past. These are readers introduced to their favorite universes via the initial visual and auditory input of television and film series. But they are still *readers*.

Bully for them, I say.

What about the writers? The colleagues involved in this sort of sharecropper writing that I've spoken to usually have a reaction to the work that falls at one end of the spectrum or the other. Either they enjoy the experience of submerging themselves in someone else's created reality, or they look at it simply as a way to pay the rent and put food on the table. On further conversation, both these camps tend to share one viewpoint: they don't view media tie-in labor to be their life's work. There is always that drive to create something that is uniquely one's own and into which one pours one's best efforts toward excellence.

But what is excellence? *Is* there a current unified-field theory of excellence evolving in speculative fiction? Keeping in mind that standards of "excellence" are subjective and constantly changing, there does seem to be such a standard at work in the selection of this year's Nebula winners.

In the early days, science fiction usually (but not always) tended to revolve around plot and nifty futuristic ideas. Not much else was necessary. The novelty and uniqueness of the genre were sufficient to charm, and the fact that the readers tended to be youthful didn't hurt, either.

As the readership and the writers grew up and became more sophisticated, so did their expectations for the field. Stories based solely on plot or nifty ideas began to seem flat. Authors dreamed of breaking away from the literary-ghetto aspects of the genre and gaining respect for their writing abilities.

One of the aspects of the craft, greater character development, allowed readers to care more for the stories' protagonists. Solar System Sidney was no longer out there repairing a leak in the space station's airlock while simultaneously fighting off antagonistic aliens in a (pardon the pun) vacuum as a historyless space-hero icon. Now you knew what events in his/her childhood had led him/her to this time and place, and whether he/she would survive the encounter to return to a meaningful significant other or a lonely yeoman's cabin. The craft of writing science fiction was growing up. Characters in stories had friends, enemies, families, and a personal history.

Then something else happened in science fiction. New writers were entering the field, but in a greater proportion than before they were "new" but not young. They brought with them an already well-developed maturity. Authors like Kate Wilhelm, Ursula K. Le Guin, Sheri Tepper, Lucius Shepard (the list could go on and on) started publishing speculative fiction long after they had been making their way in the world, raising families, and excelling in other venues.

Now we find writing in which fictional characters enjoy relationships and personal histories not simply to make them more engaging to the readership but because, just as in "real" life, it is exactly those relationships and personal histories that make things happen, that drive the plot.

Of course, this sort of writing was not revolutionary within the field. Nor was it confined to "thirty-somethings" and older. What was different was its prevalence.

And this is exactly what we find in all the Nebula winners and many of those works that made the final ballot this year: a maturity of writing that understands that it is the interactions of family and close relationships, or the failure of those interactions, that make things happen.

It would be unfair of me to spoil the reader's personal exploration into the works that follow by synopsizing them to make my point. But it is clearly there, and that depth in the authors' writing appears to be what other writers in the field have chosen to honor this year.

Solitude

URSULA K. LE GUIN

Ursula K. Le Guin was recently honored with one of the first retrospective James Tiptree Jr. Memorial Awards for her groundbreaking novel *The Left Hand of Darkness*. She accepted this award in May of 1996 at Wiscon 20, the only science fiction convention devoted to feminist issues, held every year in Madison, Wisconsin. (Le Guin was also the convention's guest of honor, and those fortunate enough to attend Wiscon were delighted and entertained by her speech about "Geriatrica," that land to which those of us who live long enough will inevitably be deported.) Among her many other honors are five Nebula Awards, five Hugo Awards, a National Book Award, The Pilgrim Award, the Pushcart Prize, and the Theodore Sturgeon Memorial Award. *The Encyclopedia of Science Fiction* describes her as "one of the most important writers within the field. . . . More attention has been paid to her by the academic community than to any other modern sf writer." Her books include *The Lathe of Heaven, Malafrena, The Dispossessed, Buffalo Gals and Other Animal Presences, Always Coming Home, A Fisherman of the Inland Sea, Four Ways to Forgiveness,* and her four Earthsea novels (*A Wizard of Earthsea, The Tombs of Atuan, The Farthest Shore,* and *Tehanu: The Last Book of Earthsea*).

About her novelette "Solitude," which won a 1995 Nebula Award, she writes:

"'Solitude' is one of a bunch of stories I have been writing which I call in my own mind *Swiving Through the Cosmos,* or *Galactic Nookie-Nookie,* because they all seem to have to do with love, sex, that sort of stuff. 'Solitude' comes at this interesting subject from a very odd angle, and there is very little nookie-nookie in the story, I'm sorry to say. What the story seems to be working on is how a society that had really fallen apart, keeping only the most minimal social and community bonds, would handle sex and male-female relationships and bringing up the kids. It was fun to write because I am an introvert, and this is a planet full of introverts."

An addition to "POVERTY: The Second Report on Eleven-Soro" by Mobile Entselenne'temharyonoterregwis Leaf, by her daughter, Serenity.

My mother, a field ethnologist, took the difficulty of learning anything about the people of Eleven-Soro as a personal challenge. The fact that she used her children to meet that challenge might be seen as selfishness or as selflessness. Now that I have read her report I know that she finally thought she had done wrong. Knowing what it cost her, I wish she knew my gratitude to her for allowing me to grow up as a person.

Shortly after a robot probe reported people of the Hainish Descent on the eleventh planet of the Soro system, she joined the orbital crew as back-up for the three First Observers down onplanet. She had spent four years in the tree-cities of nearby Huthu. My brother In Joy Born was eight years old and I was five; she wanted a year or two of ship duty so we could spend some time in a Hainish-style school. My brother had enjoyed the rainforests of Huthu very much, but though he could brachiate he could barely read, and we were all bright blue with skin-fungus. While Borny learned to read and I learned to wear clothes and we all had antifungus treatments, my mother became as intrigued by Eleven-Soro as the Observers were frustrated by it.

All this is in her report, but I will say it as I learned it from her, which helps me remember and understand. The language had been recorded by the probe and the Observers had spent a year learning it. The many dialectical variations excused their accents and errors, and they reported that language was not a problem. Yet there was a communication problem. The two men found themselves isolated, faced with suspicion or hostility, unable to form any connection with the native men, all of whom lived in solitary houses as hermits or in pairs. Finding communities of adolescent males, they tried to make contact with them, but when they entered the territory of such a group the boys either fled or rushed desperately at them trying to kill them. The women, who lived in what they called "dispersed villages," drove them away with volleys of stones as soon as they came anywhere near the houses. "I believe," one of them reported, "that the only community activity of the Sorovians is throwing rocks at men."

Neither of them succeeded in having a conversation of more than three exchanges with a man. One of them mated with a woman who came by his camp; he reported that though she made unmistakable and insistent advances, she seemed disturbed by his attempts to converse, refused to answer his questions, and left him, he said, "as soon as she got what she came for."

The woman Observer was allowed to settle in an unused house in a "village" (auntring) of seven houses. She made excellent observations of daily life, insofar as she could see any of it, and had several conversations with adult women and many with children; but she found that she was never asked into another woman's house, nor expected to help or ask for help in any work. Conversation concerning normal activities was unwelcome to the other women; the children, her only informants, called her Aunt Crazy-Jabber. Her aberrant behavior caused increasing distrust and dislike among the women, and they began to keep their children away from her. She left. "There's no way," she told my mother, "for an adult to learn anything. They don't ask questions, they don't answer questions. Whatever they learn, they learn when they're children."

Aha! said my mother to herself, looking at Borny and me. And she requested a family transfer to Eleven-Soro with Observer status. The Stabiles interviewed her extensively by ansible, and talked with Borny and even with me—I don't remember it, but she told me I told the Stabiles all about my new stockings—and agreed to her request. The ship was to stay in close orbit, with the previous Observers in the crew, and she was to keep radio contact with it, daily if possible.

I have a dim memory of the tree-city, and of playing with what must have been a kitten or a ghole-kit on the ship; but my first clear memories are of our house in the auntring. It is half underground, half aboveground, with wattle-and-daub walls. Mother and I are standing outside it in the warm sunshine. Between us is a big mudpuddle, into which Borny pours water from a basket; then he runs off to the creek to get more water. I muddle the mud with my hands, deliciously, till it is thick and smooth. I pick up a big double handful and slap it onto the walls where the sticks show through. Mother says, "That's good! That's right!" in our new language, and I realize that this is work, and I am doing it. I am repairing the house. I am making it right, doing it right. I am a competent person.

I have never doubted that, so long as I lived there.

We are inside the house at night, and Borny is talking to the ship on the radio, because he misses talking the old language, and anyway he is supposed to tell them stuff. Mother is making a basket and swearing at the split reeds. I am singing a song to drown out Borny so nobody in the auntring hears him talking funny, and anyway I like singing. I learned this song this afternoon in Hyuru's house. I play every day with Hyuru. "Be aware, listen, listen, be aware," I sing. When Mother stops swearing she listens, and then she turns on the recorder. There is a little fire still left from cooking dinner, which was lovely pigi root, I never get tired of pigi. It is dark and warm and smells of pigi and of burning duhur, which is a strong, sacred smell to drive out magic and bad feelings, and as I sing "Listen, be aware," I get sleepier and sleepier and lean against Mother, who is dark and warm and smells like Mother, strong and sacred, full of good feelings.

Our daily life in the auntring was repetitive. On the ship, later, I learned that people who live in artificially complicated situations call such a life "simple." I never knew anybody, anywhere I have been, who found life simple. I think a life or a time looks simple when you leave out the details, the way a planet looks smooth, from orbit.

Certainly our life in the auntring was easy, in the sense that our needs came easily to hand. There was plenty of food to be gathered or grown and prepared and cooked, plenty of temas to pick and rett and spin and weave for clothes and bedding, plenty of reeds to make baskets and thatch with; we children had other children to play with, mothers to look after us, and a great deal to learn. None of this is simple, though it's all easy enough, when you know how to do it, when you are aware of the details.

It was not easy for my mother. It was hard for her, and complicated. She had to pretend she knew the details while she was learning them, and had to think how to report and explain this way of living to people in another place who didn't understand it. For Borny it was ·easy until it got hard because he was a boy. For me it was all easy. I learned the work and played with the children and listened to the mothers sing.

The First Observer had been quite right: there was no way for a grown woman to learn how to make her soul. Mother couldn't go listen to another mother sing, it would have been too strange. The aunts all knew she hadn't been brought up well, and some of them taught her a good deal without her realizing it. They had decided her mother must have been irresponsible and had gone on scouting instead of settling in an auntring, so that her daughter didn't get educated properly. That's why even the most aloof of the aunts always let me listen with their children, so that I could become an educated person. But of course they couldn't ask another adult into their houses. Borny and I had to tell her all the songs and stories we learned, and then she would tell them to the radio, or we told them to the radio while she listened to us. But she never got it right, not really. How could she, trying to learn it after she'd grown up, and after she'd always lived with magicians?

"Be aware!" she would imitate my solemn and probably irritating imitation of the aunts and the big girls. "Be aware! How many times a day do they say that? Be aware of *what?* They aren't aware of what the ruins are, their own history,—they aren't aware of each other! They don't even talk to each other! Be aware, indeed!"

When I told her the stories of the Before Time that Aunt Sadne and Aunt Noyit told their daughters and me, she often heard the wrong things in them. I told her about the People, and she said, "Those are the ancestors of the people here now." When I said, "There aren't any people here now," she didn't understand. "There are persons here now," I said, but she still didn't understand.

Borny liked the story about the Man Who Lived with Women, how he kept some women in a pen, the way some persons keep rats in a pen for eating, and all of them got pregnant, and they each had a hundred babies, and the babies grew up as horrible monsters and ate the man and the mothers and each other. Mother explained to us that that was a parable of the human overpopulation of this planet thousands of years ago. "No, it's not," I said, "it's a moral story." — "Well, yes," Mother said. "The moral is, don't have too many babies." — "No, it's not," I said. "Who could have a hundred babies even if they wanted to? The man was a sorceror. He did magic. The women did it with him. So of course their children were monsters."

The key, of course, is the word "tekell," which translates so nicely into the Hainish word "magic," an art or power that violates natural law. It was hard for Mother to understand that some persons truly consider most human relationships unnatural; that marriage, for instance, or government, can be seen as an evil spell woven by sorcerors. It is hard for her people to believe in magic.

The ship kept asking if we were all right, and every now and then a Stabile would hook up the ansible to our radio and grill Mother and us. She always convinced them that she wanted to stay, for despite her frustrations, she was doing the work the First Observers had not been able to do, and Borny and I were happy as mudfish, all those first years. I think Mother was happy too, once she got used to the slow pace and the indirect way she had to learn things. She was lonely, missing other grown-ups to talk to, and told us that she would have gone crazy without us. If she missed sex she never showed it. I think, though, that her report is not very complete about sexual matters, perhaps because she was troubled by them. I know that when we first lived in the auntring, two of the aunts, Hedimi and Behyu, used to meet to make love, and Behyu courted my mother; but Mother didn't understand, because Behyu wouldn't talk the way Mother wanted to talk. She couldn't understand having sex with a person whose house you wouldn't enter.

Once when I was nine or so, and had been listening to some of the older girls, I asked her why didn't she go out scouting. "Aunt Sadne would look after us," I said, hopefully. I was tired of being the uneducated woman's daughter. I wanted to live in Aunt Sadne's house and be just like the other children.

"Mothers don't scout," she said, scornfully, like an aunt.

"Yes, they do, sometimes," I insisted. "They have to, or how could they have more than one baby?"

"They go to settled men near the auntring. Behyu went back to the Red Knob Hill Man when she wanted a second child. Sadne goes and sees Downriver Lame Man when she wants to have sex. They know the men around here. None of the mothers scout."

I realized that in this case she was right and I was wrong, but I stuck to my point. "Well, why don't you go see Downriver Lame Man? Don't you ever want sex? Migi says she wants it all the time."

"Migi is seventeen," Mother said drily. "Mind your own nose." She sounded exactly like all the other mothers.

Men, during my childhood, were a kind of uninteresting mystery to me. They turned up a lot in the Before Time stories, and the singing-circle girls talked about them; but I seldom saw any of them. Sometimes I'd glimpse one when I was foraging, but they never came near the auntring. In summer the Downriver Lame Man would get lonesome waiting for Aunt Sadne and would come lurking around, not very far from the auntring—not in the bush or down by the river, of course, where he might be mistaken for a rogue and stoned—but out in the open, on the hillsides, where we could all see who he was. Hyuru and Didsu, Aunt Sadne's daughters, said she had had sex with him when she went out scouting the first time, and always had sex with him and never tried any of the other men of the settlement.

She had told them, too, that the first child she bore was a boy, and she drowned it, because she didn't want to bring up a boy and send him away. They felt queer about that and so did I, but it wasn't an uncommon thing. One of the stories we learned was about a drowned boy who grew up underwater, and seized his mother when she came to bathe, and tried to hold her under till she too drowned; but she escaped.

At any rate, after the Downriver Lame Man had sat around for several days on the hillsides, singing long songs and braiding and unbraiding his hair, which was long too, and shone black in the sun, Aunt Sadne always went off for a night or two with him, and came back looking cross and self-conscious.

Aunt Noyit explained to me that Downriver Lame Man's songs were magic; not the usual bad magic, but what she called the great good spells. Aunt Sadne never could resist his spells. "But he hasn't half the charm of some men I've known," said Aunt Noyit, smiling reminiscently.

Our diet, though excellent, was very low in fat, which Mother thought might explain the rather late onset of puberty; girls seldom menstruated before they were fifteen, and boys often weren't mature till they were considerably older than that. But the women began looking askance at boys as soon as they showed any signs at all of adolescence. First Aunt Hedimi, who was always grim, then Aunt

Noyit, then even Aunt Sadne began to turn away from Borny, to leave him out, not answering when he spoke. "What are you doing playing with the children?" old Aunt Dnemi asked him so fiercely that he came home in tears. He was not quite fourteen.

Sadne's younger daughter Hyuru was my soulmate, my best friend, you would say. Her elder sister Didsu, who was in the singing circle now, came and talked to me one day, looking serious. "Borny is very handsome," she said. I agreed proudly.

"Very big, very strong," she said, "stronger than I am."

I agreed proudly again, and then I began to back away from her.

"I'm not doing magic, Ren," she said.

"Yes you are," I said. "I'll tell your mother!"

Didsu shook her head. "I'm trying to speak truly. If my fear causes your fear, I can't help it. It has to be so. We talked about it in the singing circle. I don't like it," she said, and I knew she meant it; she had a soft face, soft eyes, she had always been the gentlest of us children. "I wish he could be a child," she said. "I wish I could. But we can't."

"Go be a stupid old woman, then," I said, and ran away from her. I went to my secret place down by the river and cried. I took the holies out of my soulbag and arranged them. One holy—it doesn't matter if I tell you—was a crystal that Borny had given me, clear at the top, cloudy purple at the base. I held it a long time and then I gave it back. I dug a hole under a boulder, and wrapped the holy in duhur leaves inside a square of cloth I tore out of my kilt, beautiful, fine cloth Hyuru had woven and sewn for me. I tore the square right from the front, where it would show. I gave the crystal back, and then sat a long time there near it. When I went home I said nothing of what Didsu had said. But Borny was very silent, and my mother had a worried look. "What have you done to your kilt, Ren?" she asked. I raised my head a little and did not answer; she started to speak again, and then did not. She had finally learned not to talk to a person who chose to be silent.

Borny didn't have a soulmate, but he had been playing more and more often with the two boys nearest his age, Ednede who was a year or two older, a slight, quiet boy, and Bit who was only eleven, but boisterous and reckless. The three of them went off somewhere all the time. I hadn't paid much attention, partly because I was glad to be rid of Bit. Hyuru and I had been practicing being aware, and it was tiresome to always have to be aware of Bit yelling and jumping around. He never could leave anyone quiet, as if their quietness took something from him. His mother, Hedimi, had educated him, but she wasn't a good singer or story-teller like Sadne and Noyit, and Bit was too restless to listen even to them. Whenever he saw me and Hyuru trying to slow-walk or sitting being aware, he hung around making noise till we got mad and told him to go, and then he jeered, "Dumb girls!"

I asked Borny what he and Bit and Ednede did, and he said, "Boy stuff."

"Like what?"

"Practicing."

"Being aware?"

After a while he said, "No."

"Practicing what, then?"

"Wrestling. Getting strong. For the boygroup." He looked gloomy, but after a while he said, "Look," and showed me a knife he had hidden under his mattress. "Ednede says you have to have a knife, then nobody will challenge you. Isn't it a beauty?" It was metal, old metal from the People, shaped like a reed, pounded out and sharpened down both edges, with a sharp point. A piece of polished flintshrub wood had been bored and fitted on the handle to protect the hand. "I found it in an empty man's-house," he said. "I made the wooden part." He brooded over it lovingly. Yet he did not keep it in his soulbag.

"What do you *do* with it?" I asked, wondering why both edges were sharp, so you'd cut your hand if you used it.

"Keep off attackers," he said.

"Where was the empty man's-house?"

"Way over across Rocky Top."

"Can I go with you if you go back?"

"No," he said, not unkindly, but absolutely.

"What happened to the man? Did he die?"

"There was a skull in the creek. We think he slipped and drowned."

He didn't sound quite like Borny. There was something in his voice like a grown-up; melancholy; reserved. I had gone to him for reassurance, but came away more deeply anxious. I went to Mother and asked her, "What do they do in the boygroups?"

"Perform natural selection," she said, not in my language but in hers, in a strained tone. I didn't always understand Hainish any more and had no idea what she meant, but the tone of her voice upset me; and to my horror I saw she had begun to cry silently. "We have to move, Serenity," she said—she was still talking Hainish without realizing it. "There isn't any reason why a family can't move, is there? Women just move in and move out as they please. Nobody cares what anybody does. Nothing is anybody's business. Except hounding the boys out of town!"

I understood most of what she said, but got her to say it in my language; and then I said, "But anywhere we went, Borny would be the same age, and size, and everything."

"Then we'll leave," she said fiercely. "Go back to the ship."

I drew away from her. I had never been afraid of her before: she had never used magic on me. A mother has great power, but there is nothing unnatural in it, unless it is used against the child's soul.

Borny had no fear of her. He had his own magic. When she told him she intended leaving, he persuaded her out of it. He wanted to go join the boygroup, he said; he'd been wanting to for a year now. He didn't belong in the auntring any more, all women and girls and little kids. He wanted to go live with other boys. Bit's older brother Yit was a member of the boygroup in the Four Rivers Territory, and would look after a boy from his auntring. And Ednede was getting ready to go. And Borny and Ednede and Bit had been talking to some men, recently. Men weren't all ignorant and crazy, the way Mother thought. They didn't talk much, but they knew a lot.

"What do they know?" Mother asked grimly.

"They know how to be men," Borny said. "It's what I'm going to be."

"Not that kind of man—not if I can help it! In Joy Born, you must remember the men on the ship, real men—nothing like these poor, filthy hermits. I can't let you grow up thinking that that's what you have to be!"

"They're not like that," Borny said. "You ought to go talk to some of them, Mother."

"Don't be naive," she said with an edgy laugh. "You know perfectly well that women don't go to men to *talk*."

I knew she was wrong; all the women in the auntring knew all the settled men for three days' walk around. They did talk with them, when they were out foraging. They only kept away from the ones they didn't trust; and usually those men disappeared before long. Noyit had told me, "Their magic turns on them." She meant the other men drove them away or killed them. But I didn't say any of this, and Borny said only, "Well, Cave Cliff Man is really nice. And he took us to the place where I found those People things"—some ancient artifacts that Mother had been excited about. "The men know things the women don't," Borny went on. "At least I could go to the boygroup for a while, maybe. I ought to. I could learn a lot! We don't have any solid information on them at all. All we know anything about is this auntring. I'll go and stay long enough to get material for our report. I can't ever come back to either the auntring or the boygroup once I leave them. I'll have to go to the ship, or else try to be a man. So let me have a real go at it, please, Mother?"

"I don't know why you think you have to learn how to be a man," she said after a while. "You know how already."

He really smiled then, and she put her arm around him.

What about me? I thought. I don't even know what the ship is. I want to be here, where my soul is. I want to go on learning to be in the world.

But I was afraid of Mother and Borny, who were both working magic, and so I said nothing and was still, as I had been taught.

Ednede and Borny went off together. Noyit, Ednede's mother, was as glad as Mother was about their keeping company, though she said nothing. The evening before they left, the two boys went to every house in the auntring. It took a long time. The houses were each just within sight or hearing of one or two of the others, with bush and gardens and irrigation ditches and paths in between. In each house the mother and the children were waiting to say goodbye, only they didn't say it; my language has no word for hello or goodbye. They asked the boys in and gave them something to eat, something they could take with them on the way to the Territory. When the boys went to the door everybody in the household came and touched their hand or cheek. I remembered when Yit had gone around the auntring that way. I had cried then, because even though I didn't much like Yit, it seemed so strange for somebody to leave forever, like they were dying. This time I didn't cry; but I kept waking and waking again, until I heard Borny get up before the first light and pick up his things and leave quietly. I know Mother was awake too, but we did as we should do, and lay still while he left, and for a long time after.

I have read her description of what she calls "An adolescent male leaves the Auntring: a vestigial survival of ceremony."

She had wanted him to put a radio in his soulbag and get in touch with her at least occasionally. He had been unwilling. "I want to do it right, Mother. There's no use doing it if I don't do it right."

"I simply can't handle not hearing from you at all, Borny," she had said in Hainish.

"But if the radio got broken or taken or something, you'd worry a lot more, maybe with no reason at all."

She finally agreed to wait half a year, till the first rain; then she would go to a landmark, a huge ruin near the river that marked the southern end of the Territory, and he would try and come to her there. "But only wait ten days," he said. "If I can't come, I can't." She agreed. She was like a mother with a little baby, I thought, saying yes to everything. That seemed wrong to me; but I thought Borny was right. Nobody ever came back to their mother from boygroup.

But Borny did.

Summer was long, clear, beautiful. I was learning to starwatch; that is when you lie down outside on the open hills in the dry season at night, and find a certain star in the eastern sky, and watch it cross the sky till it sets. You can look away, of course, to rest your eyes, and doze, but you try to keep looking back at the star and the stars around it, until you feel the earth turning, until you become aware of how the stars and the world and the soul move together. After the certain star sets you sleep until dawn wakes you. Then as always you greet the sunrise with aware silence. I was very happy on the hills those warm great nights, those clear dawns. The first time or two Hyuru and I starwatched together, but after that we went alone, and it was better alone.

I was coming back from such a night, along the narrow valley between Rocky Top and Over Home Hill in the first sunlight, when a man came crashing through the bush down onto the path and stood in front of me. "Don't be afraid," he said. "Listen!" He was heavyset, half naked; he stank. I stood still as a stick. He had said "Listen!" just as the aunts did, and I listened. "Your brother and his friend are all right. Your mother shouldn't go there. Some of the boys are in a gang. They'd rape her. I and some others are killing the leaders. It takes a while. Your brother is with the other gang. He's all right. Tell her. Tell me what I said."

I repeated it word for word, as I had learned to do when I listened.

"Right. Good," he said, and took off up the steep slope on his short, powerful legs, and was gone.

Mother would have gone to the Territory right then, but I told the man's message to Noyit, too, and she came to the porch of our house to speak to Mother. I listened to her, because she was telling things I didn't know well and Mother didn't know at all. Noyit was a small, mild woman, very like her son Ednede; she liked teaching and singing, so the children were always around her place. She saw Mother was getting ready for a journey. She said, "House on the Skyline Man says the boys are all right." When she saw Mother wasn't listening, she went on; she pretended to be talking to me, because women don't teach women: "He says some of the men are breaking up the gang. They do that, when the boygroups get wicked. Sometimes there are magicians among them, leaders, older boys, even men who want to make a gang. The settled men will kill the magicians and make sure none of the boys gets hurt. When gangs come out of the Territories, nobody is safe. The settled men don't like that. They see to it that the auntring is safe. So your brother will be all right."

My mother went on packing pigi-roots into her net.

"A rape is a very, very bad thing for the settled men," said Noyit to me. "It means the women won't come to them. If the boys raped some woman, probably the men would kill *all* the boys."

My mother was finally listening.

She did not go to the rendezvous with Borny, but all through the rainy season she was utterly miserable. She got sick, and old Dnemi sent Didsu over to dose her with gagberry syrup. She made notes while she was sick, lying on her mattress, about illnesses and medicines and how the older girls had to look after sick women, since grown women did not enter one another's houses. She never stopped working and never stopped worrying about Borny.

Late in the rainy season, when the warm wind had come and the yellow honey-flowers were in bloom on all the hills, the Golden World time, Noyit came by while Mother was working in the garden. "House on the Skyline Man says things are all right in the boygroup," she said, and went on.

Mother began to realize then that although no adult ever entered another's house, and adults seldom spoke to one another, and men and women had only brief, often casual relationships, and men lived all their lives in real solitude, still there was a kind of community, a wide, thin, fine network of delicate and certain intention and restraint: a social order. Her reports to the ship were filled with this new understanding. But she still found Sorovian life impoverished, seeing these persons as mere survivors, poor fragments of the wreck of something great.

"My dear," she said—in Hainish; there is no way to say "my dear" in my language. She was speaking Hainish with me in the house so that I wouldn't forget it entirely. — "My dear, the explanation of an uncomprehended technology as magic *is* primitivism. It's not a criticism, merely a description."

"But technology isn't magic," I said.

"Yes, it is, in their minds; look at the story you just recorded. Before-Time sorcerors who could fly in the air and undersea and underground in magic boxes!"

"In *metal* boxes," I corrected.

"In other words, airplanes, tunnels, submarines; a lost technology explained as supernatural."

"The *boxes* weren't magic," I said. "The *people* were. They were sorcerors. They used their power to get power over other persons. To live rightly a person has to keep away from magic."

"That's a cultural imperative, because a few thousand years ago uncontrolled technological expansion led to disaster. Exactly. There's a perfectly rational reason for the irrational taboo."

I did not know what "rational" and "irrational" meant in my language; I could not find words for them. "Taboo" was the same as "poisonous." I listened to my mother because a daughter must learn from her mother, and my mother knew many, many things no other person knew; but my education was very difficult, sometimes. If only there were more stories and songs in her teaching, and not so many words, words that slipped away from me like water through a net!

The Golden Time passed, and the beautiful summer; the Silver Time returned, when the mists lie in the valleys between the hills, before the rains begin; and the rains began, and fell long and slow and warm, day after day after day. We had heard nothing of Borny and Ednede for over a year. Then in the night the soft thrum of rain on the reed roof turned into a scratching at the door and a whisper, "Shh—it's all right—it's all right."

We wakened the fire and crouched at it in the dark to talk. Borny had got tall and very thin, like a skeleton with the skin dried on it. A cut across his upper lip had drawn it up into a kind of snarl that bared his teeth, and he could not say p, b, or m. His voice was a man's voice. He huddled at the fire trying to get warmth into his bones. His clothes were wet rags. The knife hung on a cord around his neck. "It was all right," he kept saying. "I don't want to go on there, though."

He would not tell us much about the year and a half in the boy-group, insisting that he would record a full description when he got to the ship. He did tell us what he would have to do if he stayed on Soro. He would have to go back to the Territory and hold his own among the older boys, by fear and sorcery, always proving his strength, until he was old enough to walk away—that is, to leave the Territory and wander alone till he found a place where the men would let him settle. Ednede and another boy had paired, and were going to walk away together when the rains stopped. It was easier for a pair, he said, if their bond was sexual; so long as they offered no competition for women, settled men wouldn't challenge them. But a new man in the region anywhere within three days' walk of an auntring had to prove himself against the settled men there. "It would 'e three or four years of the same thing," he said, "challenging, fighting, always watching the others, on guard, showing how strong you are, staying alert all night, all day. To end up living alone your whole life. I can't do it." He looked at me. "I'ne not a 'erson," he said. "I want to go ho'e."

"I'll radio the ship now," Mother said quietly, with infinite relief.

"No," I said.

Borny was watching Mother, and raised his hand when she turned to speak to me.

"I'll go," he said. "She doesn't have to. Why should she?" Like me, he had learned not to use names without some reason to.

Mother looked from him to me and finally gave a kind of laugh. "I can't leave her here, Borny!"

"Why should you go?"

"Because I want to," she said. "I've had enough. More than enough. We've got a tremendous amount of material on the women, over seven years of it, and now you can fill the information gaps on the men's side. That's enough. It's time, past time, that we all got back to our own people. All of us."

"I have no people," I said. "I don't belong to people. I am trying to be a person. Why do you want to take me away from my soul? You want me to do magic! I won't. I won't do magic. I won't speak your language. I won't go with you!"

My mother was still not listening; she started to answer angrily. Borny put up his hand again, the way a woman does when she is going to sing, and she looked at him.

"We can talk later," he said. "We can decide. I need to sleep."

He hid in our house for two days while we decided what to do and how to do it. That was a miserable time. I stayed home as if I were sick so that I would not lie to the other persons, and Borny and Mother and I talked and talked. Borny asked Mother to stay with me; I asked her to leave me with Sadne or Noyit, either of whom would certainly take me into their household. She refused. She was the mother and I the child and her power was sacred. She radioed the ship and arranged for a lander to pick us up in a barren area two days' walk from the auntring. We left at night, sneaking away. I carried nothing but my soulbag. We walked all next day, slept a little when it stopped raining, walked on and came to the desert. The ground was all lumps and hollows and caves, Before-Time ruins; the soil was tiny bits of glass and hard grains and fragments, the way it is in the deserts. Nothing grew there. We waited there.

The sky broke open and a shining thing fell down and stood before us on the rocks, bigger than any house, though not as big as the ruins of the Before Time. My mother looked at me with a queer, vengeful smile. "Is it magic?" she said. And it was very hard for me not to think that it was. Yet I knew it was only a thing, and there is no magic in things, only in minds. I said nothing. I had not spoken since we left my home.

I had resolved never to speak to anybody until I got home again; but I was still a child, used to listen and obey. In the ship, that utterly strange new world, I held out only for a few hours, and then began to cry and ask to go home. Please, please, can I go home now.

Everyone on the ship was very kind to me.

Even then I thought about what Borny had been through and what I was going through, comparing our ordeals. The difference seemed total. He had been alone, without food, without shelter, a frightened boy trying to survive among equally frightened rivals against the brutality of older youths intent on having and keeping power, which they saw as manhood. I was cared for, clothed, fed so richly I got sick, kept so warm I felt feverish, guided, reasoned with, praised, befriended by citizens of a very great city, offered a share in their power, which they saw as humanity. He and I had both fallen among sorcerors. Both he and I could see the good in the people we were among, but neither he nor I could live with them.

Borny told me he had spent many desolate nights in the Territory crouched in a fireless shelter, telling over the stories he had learned from the aunts, singing the songs in his head. I did the same thing every night on the ship. But I refused to tell the stories or sing to the people there. I would not speak my language, there. It was the only way I had to be silent.

My mother was enraged, and for a long time unforgiving. "You owe your knowledge to our people," she said. I did not answer, because all I had to say was that they were not my people, that I had no people. I was a person. I had a language that I did not speak. I had my silence. I had nothing else.

I went to school; there were children of different ages on the ship, like an auntring, and many of the adults taught us. I learned Ekumenical history and geography, mostly, and Mother gave me a report to learn about the history of Eleven-Soro, what my language calls the Before Time. I read that the cities of my world had been the greatest cities ever built on any world, covering two of the continents entirely, with small areas set aside for farming; there had been 120 billion people living in the cities, while the animals and the sea and the air and the dirt died, until the people began dying too. It was a hideous story. I was ashamed of it and wished nobody else on the ship or in the Ekumen knew about it. And yet, I thought, if they knew the stories I knew about the Before Time, they would understand how magic turns on itself, and that it must be so.

After less than a year, Mother told us we were going to Hain. The ship's doctor and his clever machines had repaired Borny's lip; he and Mother had put all the information they had into the records; he was old enough to begin training for the Ekumenical Schools, as he wanted to do. I was not flourishing, and the doctor's machines were not able to repair me. I kept losing weight, I slept badly, I had terrible headaches. Almost as soon as we came aboard the ship, I had begun to menstruate; each time the cramps were agonizing. "This is no good, this ship life," she said. "You need to be outdoors. On a planet. On a civilized planet."

"If I went to Hain," I said, "when I came back, the persons I know would all be dead hundreds of years ago."

"Serenity," she said, "you must stop thinking in terms of Soro. We have left Soro. You must stop deluding and tormenting yourself, and look forward, not back. Your whole life is ahead of you. Hain is where you will learn to live it."

I summoned up my courage and spoke in my own language: "I am not a child now. You have no power over me. I will not go. Go without me. You have no power over me!"

Those are the words I had been taught to say to a magician, a sorceror. I don't know if my mother fully understood them, but she did understand that I was deathly afraid of her, and it struck her into silence.

After a long time she said in Hainish, "I agree. I have no power over you. But I have certain rights; the right of loyalty; of love."

"Nothing is right that puts me in your power," I said, still in my language.

She stared at me. "You are like one of them," she said. "You are one of them. You don't know what love is. You're closed into yourself like a rock. I should never have taken you there. People crouching in the ruins of a society—brutal, rigid, ignorant, superstitious— Each one in a terrible solitude— And I let them make you into one of them!"

"You educated me," I said, and my voice began to tremble and my mouth to shake around the words, "and so does the school here, but my aunts educated me, and I want to finish my education." I was weeping, but I kept standing with my hands clenched. "I'm not a woman yet. I want to be a woman."

"But Ren, you will be!—ten times the woman you could ever be on Soro—you must try to understand, to believe me—"

"You have no power over me," I said, shutting my eyes and putting my hands over my ears. She came to me then and held me, but I stood stiff, enduring her touch, until she let me go.

The ship's crew had changed entirely while we were onplanet. The First Observers had gone on to other worlds; our back-up was now a Gethenian archeologist named Arrem, a mild, watchful person, not young. Arrem had gone down onplanet only on the two desert continents, and welcomed the chance to talk with us, who had "lived with the living," as heshe said. I felt easy when I was with Arrem, who was so unlike anybody else. Arrem was not a man—I could not get used to having men around all the time—yet not a woman; and so not exactly an adult, yet not a child: a person, alone, like me. Heshe did not know my language well, but always tried to talk it with me. When this crisis came, Arrem came to my mother and took counsel with her, suggesting that she let me go back down onplanet. Borny was in on some of these talks, and told me about them.

"Arrem says if you go to Hain you'll probably die," he said. "Your soul will. Heshe says some of what we learned is like what they learn on Gethen, in their religion. That kind of stopped Mother from ranting about primitive superstition. . . . And Arrem says you could be useful to the Ekumen, if you stay and finish your education on Soro. You'll be an invaluable resource." Borny sniggered, and after a minute I did too. "They'll mine you like an asteroid," he said. Then he said, "You know, if you stay and I go, we'll be dead."

That was how the young people of the ships said it, when one was going to cross the lightyears and the other was going to stay. Goodbye, we're dead. It was the truth.

"I know," I said. I felt my throat get tight, and was afraid. I had never seen an adult at home cry, except when Sut's baby died. Sut howled all night. Howled like a dog, Mother said, but I had never seen or heard a dog; I heard a woman terribly crying. I was afraid of sounding like that. "If I can go home, when I finish making my soul, who knows, I might come to Hain for a while," I said, in Hainish.

"Scouting?" Borny said in my language, and laughed, and made me laugh again.

Nobody gets to keep a brother. I knew that. But Borny had come back from being dead to me, so I might come back from being dead to him; at least I could pretend I might.

My mother came to a decision. She and I would stay on the ship for another year while Borny went to Hain. I would keep going to school; if at the end of the year I was still determined to go back onplanet, I could do so. With me or without me, she would go on to Hain then and join Borny. If I ever wanted to see them again, I could follow them. It was a compromise that satisfied no one, but it was the best we could do, and we all consented.

When he left, Borny gave me his knife.

After he left, I tried not to be sick. I worked hard at learning everything they taught me in the ship school, and I tried to teach Arrem how to be aware and how to avoid witchcraft. We did slow-walking together in the ship's garden, and the first hour of the un-trance movements from the Handdara of Karhide on Gethen. We agreed that they were alike.

The ship was staying in the Soro system not only because of my family, but because the crew was now mostly zoologists who had come to study a sea animal on Eleven-Soro, a kind of cephalopod that had mutated toward high intelligence, or maybe it already was highly intelligent; but there was a communication problem. "Almost as bad as with the local humans," said Steadiness, the zoologist who taught and teased us mercilessly. She took us down twice by lander to the uninhabited islands in the Northern Hemisphere where her station was. It was very strange to go down to my world and yet be a world away from my aunts and sisters and my soulmate; but I said nothing.

I saw the great, pale, shy creature come slowly up out of the deep waters with a running ripple of colors along its long coiling tentacles and a ringing shimmer of sound, all so quick it was over before you could follow the colors or hear the tune. The zoologist's machine produced a pink glow and a mechanically speeded-up twitter, tinny and feeble in the immensity of the sea. The cephalopod patiently responded in its beautiful silvery shadowy language. "CP," Steadiness said to us, ironic—Communication Problem. "We don't know what we're talking about."

I said, "I learned something in my education here. In one of the songs, it says," and I hesitated, trying to translate it into Hainish, "it says, thinking is one way of doing, and words are one way of thinking."

Steadiness stared at me, in disapproval I thought, but probably only because I had never said anything to her before except "Yes." Finally she said, "Are you suggesting that it doesn't speak in words?"

"Maybe it's not speaking at all. Maybe it's thinking."

Steadiness stared at me some more and then said, "Thank you." She looked as if she too might be thinking. I wished I could sink into the water, the way the cephalopod was doing.

The other young people on the ship were friendly and mannerly. Those are words that have no translation in my language. I was unfriendly and unmannerly, and they let me be. I was grateful. But there was no place to be alone on the ship. Of course we each had a room; though small, the *Heyho* was a Hainish-built explorer, designed to give its people room and privacy and comfort and variety and beauty while they hung around in a solar system for years on end. But it was designed. It was all human-made—everything was human. I had much more privacy than I had ever had at home in our one-room house; yet there I had been free and here I was in a trap. I felt the pressure of people all around me, all the time. People around me, people with me, people pressing on me, pressing me to be one of them, to be one of them, one of the people. How could I make my soul? I could barely cling to it. I was in terror that I would lose it altogether.

One of the rocks in my soulbag, a little ugly gray rock that I had picked up on a certain day in a certain place in the hills above the river in the Silver Time, a little piece of my world, that became my world. Every night I took it out and held it in my hand while I lay in bed waiting to sleep, thinking of the sunlight on the hills above the river, listening to the soft hushing of the ship's systems, like a mechanical sea.

The doctor hopefully fed me various tonics. Mother and I ate breakfast together every morning. She kept at work, making our notes from all the years on Eleven-Soro into her report to the Ekumen, but I knew the work did not go well. Her soul was in as much danger as mine was.

"You will never give in, will you, Ren?" she said to me one morning out of the silence of our breakfast. I had not intended the silence as a message. I had only rested in it.

"Mother, I want to go home and you want to go home," I said. "Can't we?"

Her expression was strange for a moment, while she misunderstood me; then it cleared to grief, defeat, relief.

"Will we be dead?" she asked me, her mouth twisting.

"I don't know. I have to make my soul. Then I can know if I can come."

"You know I can't come back. It's up to you."

"I know. Go see Borny," I said. "Go home. Here we're both dying." Then noises began to come out of me, sobbing, howling. Mother was crying. She came to me and held me, and I could hold my mother, cling to her and cry with her, because her spell was broken.

From the lander approaching I saw the oceans of Eleven-Soro, and in the greatness of my joy I thought that when I was grown and went out alone I would go to the sea shore and watch the sea-beasts shimmering their colors and tunes till I knew what they were thinking. I would listen, I would learn, till my soul was as large as the shining world. The scarred barrens whirled beneath us, ruins as wide as the continent, endless desolations. We touched down. I had my soulbag, and Borny's knife around my neck on its string, a communicator implant behind my right earlobe, and a medicine kit Mother had made for me. "No use dying of an infected finger, after all," she had said. The people on the lander said goodbye, but I forgot to. I set off out of the desert, home.

It was summer; the night was short and warm; I walked most of it. I got to the auntring about the middle of the second day. I went to my house cautiously, in case somebody had moved in while I was gone; but it was just as we had left it. The mattresses were moldy, and I put them and the bedding out in the sun, and started going over the garden to see what had kept growing by itself. The pigi had got small and seedy, but there were some good roots. A little boy came by and stared; he had to be Migi's baby. After a while Hyuru came by. She squatted down near me in the garden in the sunshine. I smiled when I saw her, and she smiled, but it took us a while to find something to say.

"Your mother didn't come back," she said.

"She's dead," I said.

"I'm sorry," Hyuru said.

She watched me dig up another root.

"Will you come to the singing circle?" she asked.

I nodded.

She smiled again. With her rosebrown skin and wide-set eyes, Hyuru had become very beautiful, but her smile was exactly the same as when we were little girls. "Hi, ya!" she sighed in deep contentment, lying down on the dirt with her chin on her arms. "This is good!"

I went on blissfully digging.

That year and the next two, I was in the singing circle with Hyuru and two other girls. Didsu still came to it often, and Han, a woman who settled in our auntring to have her first baby, joined it too. In the singing circle the older girls pass around the stories, songs, knowledge they learned from their own mother, and young women who have lived in other auntrings teach what they learned there; so women make each other's souls, learning how to make their children's souls.

Han lived in the house where old Dnemi had died. Nobody in the auntring except Sut's baby had died while my family lived there. My mother had complained that she didn't have any data on death and burial. Sut had gone away with her dead baby and never came back, and nobody talked about it. I think that turned my mother against the others more than anything else. She was angry and ashamed that she could not go and try to comfort Sut and that nobody else did. "It is not human," she said. "It is pure animal behavior. Nothing could be clearer evidence that this is a broken culture—not a society, but the remains of one. A terrible, an appalling poverty."

I don't know if Dnemi's death would have changed her mind. Dnemi was dying for a long time, of kidney failure I think; she turned a kind of dark orange color, jaundice. While she could get around, nobody helped her. When she didn't come out of her house for a day or two, the women would send the children in with water and a little food and firewood. It went on so through the winter; then one morning little Rashi told his mother Aunt Dnemi was "staring." Several of the women went to Dnemi's house, and entered it for the first and last time. They sent for all the girls in the singing circle, so that we could learn what to do. We took turns sitting by the body or in the porch of the house, singing soft songs, child-songs, giving the soul a day and a night to leave the body and the house; then the older women wrapped the body in the bedding, strapped it on a kind of litter, and set off with it toward the barren lands. There it would be given back, under a rock cairn or inside one of the ruins of the ancient city. "Those are the lands of the dead," Sadne said. "What dies stays there."

Han settled down in that house a year later. When her baby began to be born she asked Didsu to help her, and Hyuru and I stayed in the porch and watched, so that we could learn. It was a wonderful thing to see, and quite altered the course of my thinking, and Hyuru's too. Hyuru said, "I'd like to do that!" I said nothing, but thought, So do I, but not for a long time, because once you have a child you're never alone.

And though it is of the others, of relationships, that I write, the heart of my life has been my being alone.

I think there is no way to write about being alone. To write is to tell something to somebody, to communicate to others. CP, as Steadiness would say. Solitude is non-communication, the absence of others, the presence of a self sufficient to itself.

A woman's solitude in the auntring is, of course, based firmly on the presence of others at a little distance. It is a contingent, and therefore human, solitude. The settled men are connected as stringently to the women, though not to one another; the settlement is an integral though distant element of the auntring. Even a scouting woman is part of the society—a moving part, connecting the settled parts. Only the isolation of a woman or man who chooses to live outside the settlements is absolute. They are outside the network altogether. There are worlds where such persons are called saints, holy people. Since isolation is a sure way to prevent magic, on my world the assumption is that they are sorcerors, outcast by others or by their own will, their conscience.

I knew I was strong with magic, how could I help it? and I began to long to get away. It would be so much easier and safer to be alone. But at the same time, and increasingly, I wanted to know something about the great harmless magic, the spells cast between men and women.

I preferred foraging to gardening, and was out on the hills a good deal; and these days, instead of keeping away from the men's-houses, I wandered by them, and looked at them, and looked at the men if they were outside. The men looked back. Downriver Lame Man's long, shining hair was getting a little white in it now, but when he sat singing his long, long songs I found myself sitting down and listening, as if my legs had lost their bones. He was very handsome. So was the man I remembered as a boy named Tret in the auntring, when I was little, Behyu's son. He had come back from the boygroup and from wandering, and had built a house and made a fine garden in the valley of Red Stone Creek. He had a big nose and big eyes, long arms and legs, long hands; he moved very quietly, almost like Arrem doing the untrance. I went often to pick lowberries in Red Stone Creek Valley.

He came along the path and spoke. "You were Borny's sister," he said. He had a low voice, quiet.

"He's dead," I said.

Red Stone Man nodded. "That's his knife."

In my world, I had never talked with a man. I felt extremely strange. I kept picking berries.

"You're picking green ones," Red Stone Man said.

His soft, smiling voice made my legs lose their bones again.

"I think nobody's touched you," he said. "I'd touch you gently. I think about it, about you, ever since you came by here early in the summer. Look, here's a bush full of ripe ones. Those are green. Come over here."

I came closer to him, to the bush of ripe berries.

When I was on the ship, Arrem told me that many languages have a single word for sexual desire and the bond between mother and child and the bond between soulmates and the feeling for one's home and worship of the sacred; they are all called love. There is no word that great in my language. Maybe my mother is right, and human greatness perished in my world with the people of the Before Time, leaving only small, poor, broken things and thoughts. In my language, love is many different words. I learned one of them with Red Stone Man. We sang it together to each other.

We made a brush house on a little cove of the creek, and neglected our gardens, but gathered many, many sweet berries.

Mother had put a lifetime's worth of nonconceptives in the little medicine kit. She had no faith in Sorovian herbals. I did, and they worked.

But when a year or so later, in the Golden Time, I decided to go out scouting, I thought I might go places where the right herbs were scarce; and so I stuck the little noncon jewel on the back of my left earlobe. Then I wished I hadn't, because it seemed like witchcraft. Then I told myself I was being superstitious; the noncon wasn't any more witchcraft than the herbs were, it just worked longer. I had promised my mother in my soul that I would never be superstitious. The skin grew over the noncon, and I took my soulbag and Borny's knife and the medicine kit, and set off across the world.

I had told Hyuru and Red Stone Man I would be leaving. Hyuru and I sang and talked together all one night down by the river. Red Stone Man said in his soft voice, "Why do you want to go?" and I said, "To get away from your magic, sorceror," which was true in part. If I kept going to him I might always go to him. I wanted to give my soul and body a larger world to be in.

Now to tell of my scouting years is more difficult than ever. CP! A woman scouting is entirely alone, unless she chooses to ask a settled man for sex, or camps in an auntring for a while to sing and listen with the singing circle. If she goes anywhere near the territory of a boy-group, she is in danger; and if she comes on a rogue she is in danger; and if she hurts herself or gets into polluted country, she is in danger. She has no responsibility except to herself, and so much freedom is very dangerous.

In my right earlobe was the tiny communicator; every forty days, as I had promised, I sent a signal to the ship that meant "all well." If I wanted to leave, I would send another signal. I could have called for the lander to rescue me from a bad situation, but though I was in bad situations a couple of times I never thought of using it. My signal was the mere fulfillment of a promise to my mother and her people, the network I was no longer part of, a meaningless communication.

Life in the auntring, or for a settled man, is repetitive, as I said; and so it can be dull. Nothing new happens. The mind always wants new happenings. So for the young soul there is wandering and scouting, travel, danger, change. But of course travel and danger and change have their own dullness. It is finally always the same otherness over again; another hill, another river, another man, another day. The feet begin to turn in a long, long circle. The body begins to think of what it learned back home, when it learned to be still. To be aware. To be aware of the grain of dust beneath the sole of the foot, and the skin of the sole of the foot, and the touch and scent of the air on the cheek, and the fall and motion of the light across the air, and the color of the grass on the high hill across the river, and the thoughts of the body, of the soul, the shimmer and ripple of colors and sounds in the clear darkness of the depths, endlessly moving, endlessly changing, endlessly new.

So at last I came back home. I had been gone about four years.

Hyuru had moved into my old house when she left her mother's house. She had not gone scouting, but had taken to going to Red Stone Creek Valley; and she was pregnant. I was glad to see her living there. The only house empty was an old half-ruined one too close to Hedimi's. I decided to make a new house. I dug out the circle as deep as my chest; the digging took most of the summer. I cut the sticks, braced and wove them, and then daubed the framework solidly with mud inside and out. I remembered when I had done that with my mother long, long ago, and how she had said, "That's right. That's good." I left the roof open, and the hot sun of late summer baked the mud into clay. Before the rains came, I thatched the house with reeds, a triple thatching, for I'd had enough of being wet all winter.

My auntring was more a string than a ring, stretching along the north bank of the river for about three kilos; my house lengthened the string a good bit, upstream from all the others. I could just see the smoke from Hyuru's fireplace. I dug it into a sunny slope with good drainage. It is still a good house.

I settled down. Some of my time went to gathering and gardening and mending and all the dull, repetitive actions of primitive life, and some went to singing and thinking the songs and stories I had learned here at home and while scouting, and the things I had learned on the ship, also. Soon enough I found why women are glad to have children come to listen to them, for songs and stories are meant to be heard, listened to. "Listen!" I would say to the children. The children of the auntring came and went, like the little fish in the river, one or two or five of them, little ones, big ones. When they came, I sang or told stories to them. When they left, I went on in silence. Sometimes I joined the singing circle to give what I had learned traveling to the older girls. And that was all I did; except that I worked, always, to be aware of all I did.

By solitude the soul escapes from doing or suffering magic; it escapes from dullness, from boredom, by being aware. Nothing is boring if you are aware of it. It may be irritating, but it is not boring. If it is pleasant the pleasure will not fail so long as you are aware of it. Being aware is the hardest work the soul can do, I think.

I helped Hyuru have her baby, a girl, and played with the baby. Then after a couple of years I took the noncon out of my left earlobe. Since it left a little hole, I made the hole go all the way through with a burnt needle, and when it healed I hung in it a tiny jewel I had found in a ruin when I was scouting. I had seen a man on the ship with a jewel hung in his ear that way. I wore it when I went out foraging. I kept clear of Red Stone Creek Valley. The man there behaved as if he had a claim on me, a right to me. I liked him still, but I did not like that smell of magic about him, his imagination of power over me. I went up into the hills, northward.

A pair of young men had settled in old North House about the time I came home. Often boys got through boygroup by pairing, and often they stayed paired when they left the Territory. It helped their chances of survival. Some of them were sexually paired, others weren't; some stayed paired, others didn't. One of this pair had gone off with another man last summer. The one that stayed wasn't a handsome man, but I had noticed him. He had a kind of solidness I liked. His body and hands were short and strong. I had courted him a little, but he was very shy. This day, a day in the Silver Time when the mist lay on the river, he saw the jewel swinging in my ear, and his eyes widened.

"It's pretty, isn't it?" I said.

He nodded.

"I wore it to make you look at me," I said.

He was so shy that I finally said, "If you only like sex with men, you know, just tell me." I really was not sure.

"Oh, no," he said, "no. No." He stammered and then bolted back down the path. But he looked back; and I followed him slowly, still not certain whether he wanted me or wanted to be rid of me.

He waited for me in front of a little house in a grove of redroot, a lovely little bower, all leaves outside, so that you would walk within arm's length of it and not see it. Inside he had laid sweet grass, deep and dry and soft, smelling of summer. I went in, crawling because the door was very low, and sat in the summer-smelling grass. He stood outside. "Come in," I said, and he came in very slowly.

"I made it for you," he said.

"Now make a child for me," I said.

And we did that; maybe that day, maybe another.

Now I will tell you why after all these years I called the ship, not knowing even if it was still there in the space between the planets, asking for the lander to meet me in the barren land.

When my daughter was born, that was my heart's desire and the fulfillment of my soul. When my son was born, last year, I knew there is no fulfillment. He will grow toward manhood, and go, and fight and endure, and live or die as a man must. My daughter, whose name is

Yedneke, Leaf, like my mother, will grow to womanhood and go or stay as she chooses. I will live alone. This is as it should be, and my desire. But I am of two worlds; I am a person of this world, and a woman of my mother's people. I owe my knowledge to the children of her people. So I asked the lander to come, and spoke to the people on it. They gave me my mother's report to read, and I have written my story in their machine, making a record for those who want to learn one of the ways to make a soul. To them, to the children I say: Listen! Avoid magic! Be aware!

Death and the Librarian

ESTHER M. FRIESNER

Esther M. Friesner holds a B.A. from Vassar College and a Ph.D. in Spanish from Yale, and is the prolific author of novels and short fiction. Her over seventy published stories have appeared in all of the major science fiction and fantasy magazines and in several anthologies; among her novels are *The Silver Mountain, Here Be Demons, Harlot's Ruse, Demon Blues, The Psalms of Herod, Majyk by Accident, Majyk by Design,* and *Majyk by Hook or Crook.*

Esther Friesner is justly renowned as one of the funniest and wittiest of fantasy writers, both in person and in print. Her Nebula Award–winning "Death and the Librarian" reveals that she can also write moving and delicately wrought fiction about love and loss. Of her inspiration for this story, she writes:

"During the recent Science Fiction World Convention in San Francisco, I had the pleasure of breakfasting with Terry Pratchett, who is not just a friend but one of my favorite authors. Creator of the Discworld fantasy series, he has proved again and again that humor can be funny and thought-provoking at the same time.

"The understandable popularity of his books has led to their adaptation into a host of other media, including games. At our breakfast, he gave me a pair of metal miniatures used in one of the Discworld games. These were the figures of Death (who is the typical robed and scythe-bearing skeleton, although that's about as far as the character's adherence to reader expectations goes) and the Librarian (of the wizardly Unseen University, who was transformed into an orangutan and elected to stay that way because it made it easier to do his job).

"I sat there playing with the miniatures in my hand and muttering, 'Death and the Librarian . . . Death and the Librarian . . . Death and the Librarian . . .' (Be it noted that Terry is a very long-suffering gentleman.) I just liked the sound of it. Okay, I admit that it was early and I needed more coffee, but I also contend that there are instances in a writer's life when a certain combination of words touches off a spark that won't blow out. All I know is that I thought that 'Death and the Librarian' sounded like a good title for *something*, and I was going to have to find out what that something was and write it or be haunted forever.

"Considering the source of my inspiration, I expected to write a funny story. Somewhere between there and here, the images of the robed skeleton and the bibliophilic orangutan went their own ways, and a whole new cast of characters showed up for work. I suppose I could say that a haunting title demanded a haunting story. I know where I *get* my ideas, but at times they're something else entirely by the time I finally set them down on paper."

In an October dusk that smelled of smoke and apples, a lady in a black duster coat and a broad-brimmed hat, heavily veiled, called at Rainey's Emporium in Foster's Glen, New York. She descended from the driver's seat of a black Packard, drawing the eye of every man who lounged on the wooden steps of the crossroads store and attracting a second murmuring throng of idlers from Alvin Vernier's barber shop across the way. The men of Foster's Glen had seen a Packard automobile only in the illustrated weeklies, but to see a woman driving such a dream-chariot—!

However, by the time the lady reached the steps of Rainey's and said, "I beg your pardon; I am seeking the home of Miss Louisa Foster," she had become a middle-aged man in a plain black broadcloth suit, a drummer with sample case in hand and a gleaming derby perched on his head, so that was all right.

"Miss Foster?" Jim Patton raised one eyebrow and tipped back his straw hat as he rubbed his right temple. "Say, you wouldn't be a Pinkerton, now would you?" And the other men on Rainey's steps all laughed, because Jim was reckoned a wit as wits went in Foster's Glen, New York.

The gentleman in black smiled politely, and a trim moustache sprouted across his upper lip to give him a more dapper, roguish air. (This at the expense of his drummer's case, which vanished.) "Yes, she's in trouble with the law again," he replied, turning the jape back to its source and stealing Jim's audience along with his thunder. "Lolling on the throne of an opium empire, I'm told, or was it a straightforward charge of breaking and entering?" He patted the pockets of his vest. "I'm useless without my notes." The idlers laughed louder, leaving poor Jim no hope but to drop the cap-and-bells and try the knight's helm on for size instead.

"That's a scandalous thing to say about a lady!" Jim snapped. "And about a lady like Miss Foster—! I can't begin to tell you all she's done hereabouts: church work, the Ladies' Aid, visiting the sick. . . . Why, she's even turned the east wing of the judge's house into a library for the town!"

"Is that so?" The stranger shot his crisp celluloid cuffs and adjusted a fat ring, pearl and silver, on his lefthand littlest finger. It twinkled into diamond and gold.

His remark was only a remark, but Jim Patton took it for a challenge to his honesty. "Yes, that's *so*," he blustered. "And she's even set aside the money to make the judge's house over to the town for use as a library entire after she's gone."

"What does the judge have to say to all this?"

"What does—?" Jim gaped. "Why, you scoundrel, old Judge Foster's been dead these twenty years! What's your business with his daughter but mischief if you don't even know that much about the family?"

"That would be business that concerns only Miss Foster and me," the stranger replied, and he grew a little in height and breadth of chest so that when Jim Patton stood up to face him they were an even match.

Still, Jim bellowed, "I'll make it my business to know!" and offered fists the size of small pumpkins for inspection. He was farm-bred and raised, born to a father fresh and legless returned from Gettysburg. Caleb Patton knew the value of begetting muscular sons to follow the plow he could no longer master, and Jim was his sire's pride.

The stranger only smiled and let his own muscles double in size until his right hand could cup Jim Patton's skull without too much strain on the fingers. But all he said was, "I am a friend of the family and I have been away." And then he was an old man, dressed in a rusty uniform of the Grand Old Army of the Republic, even though by rights the thick cloth should have been deep navy blue instead of black as the abyss.

The Packard snorted and became a plump, slightly frowsty-looking pony hitched to a dogcart. It took a few mincing steps forward, sending the Emporium idlers into a panic to seize its bridle and hold it steady until the gaffer could retake his seat and the reins. Most solicitous of all was Jim Patton, who helped the doddering veteran into the cart and even begged the privilege of leading him to Miss Foster's gate personally.

"That's mighty kind of you, sonny," the old man in black wheezed. "But I think I can find my way there right enough now."

"No trouble, sir; none at all," Jim pressed. "When your business with Miss Foster's done, I'd be honored if you'd ask the way to our farm after. My daddy'd be happy to meet up with a fellow soldier and talk over old times. Were you at Antietam?"

The old man's tears were lost in the twilight. "Son, I was there too." And he became a maiden wrapped in sables against the nipping air. She leaned over the edge of the dogcart to give Jim a kiss that was frost and lilacs. "Tell Davey to hug the earth of the Somme and he'll come home," she said. She drove off leaving Jim entranced and bewildered, for his Davey was a toddler sleeping in his trundle-bed at home and the Somme was as meaningless to his world of crops and livestock as the Milky Way.

The lady drove her pony hard, following the directions Jim and the rest had given. Her sable wraps whipped out behind her in the icy wind of her passage. The breath of a thousand stars sheared them to tattered wings that streamed from her shoulders like smoke. Her pony ran at a pace to burst the barrels of the finest English thoroughbreds, and his hooves carved the dirt road with prints like the smiling cut of a sword. They raced over distance and beyond, driving time before them with a buggywhip, hastening the moon toward the highpoint of the heavens and the appointed hour.

At length the road Jim Patton had shown her ended at the iron gates of a mansion at the westernmost edge of the town. By the standards of Boston or New York it was only a very fine house, but in this rural setting it was a palace to hold a princess. Within and without the grounds trees shielded it from any harm, even to the insinuating dagger of curious whispers. The judge himself had ordered the building of this fortification on the borders of his good name, and the strain of shoring up his innumerable proprieties had aged wood and stone and slate before their time.

The maiden stepped out of the dogcart and shook out her silvery hair. The black kitten mewed where the pony had stood and sniffed the small leather portmanteau that was the only tiding or trace of the dogcart.

The elderly woman gathered up portmanteau and kitten, pressing both to the soft fastness of her black alpaca-sheathed bosom with the karakul muff that warmed her hands. She glanced through the fence's tormented iron curlicues and her bright eyes met only darkened windows. She had ridden into town with the twilight, but now she stood on the hour before the clocks called up a new day.

"None awake? Well, I am not in the least surprised," she commented to the kitten. "At her age, quite a few of them grow tired at this hour. It's almost midnight. Let us try to conclude our business before then. I have a horror of cheap dramatics."

Then she caught sight of a glimmer of lamplight from a window on the eastern side of the house. "Ah!" she exclaimed, and her breath swung back the iron gates as she sailed through them and up the long white gravel drive.

The front doors with their glass lilies deferred to her without the hint of a squeak from latch or hinges. She took a moment in the entryway to arrange herself more presentably. Her black-plumed hat she left on a porcelain peg beside a far more modest confection of gray felt and ivory veils, then studied her reflection in the oak-framed glass the hat-pegs adorned.

"Mmmmmm." She laid soft pink fingers to her lips, evaluating the dimpled, dumpling face and all its studied benevolence. "Mmmmno," she concluded, and the black kitten mewed once more as the handsome young man in gallant's garb took final stock of every black-clad, splendid inch of his romantic immanence. He opened the portmanteau out upon itself, and it turned into an onyx orb. He felt that when a woman spent so much of her life circumscribed by domesticity and filial attentiveness, she at least deserved to depart in more dashing company than that of a fuddy-duddy refugee from a church bazaar. He sighed over the glowing orb before he knelt to touch the kitten's tail. Was that a purr he heard from the heart of the black sword he raised in the silent hall?

He passed through corridors where clutter reigned but dust was chastened out of existence. His gaze swept the house for life and saw the cook snoring in her room below the rooftree, the maids more decorously asleep in their narrow iron beds. A proper housecat patrolled the kitchen, the pantry, and the cellar, hunting heedless mice, dreaming oceans of cream. He noted each of them and sent his whispers into minds that slept or wakened:

"If you love him, tell him not to leave the farm for that factory job in New York City or the machines will have him."

"She must be born in the hospital, no matter how loudly your mother claims that hospitals are only for the dying, or she's as good as never born at all."

"Let the silly bird fly across the road; don't chase it there! The delivery man cannot rein back a motor-driven van in time and he does not know that you are a queen."

In certain times, in certain cases, he was allowed this much discretion: he might give them the means to forestall him, if they only had the wit to heed. Would he call it kindness? Ah, but in the end there were no whispered cautions that would avail. He could not change the fact he embodied, merely the time of its fruition. The grand black swan's wings he called into being as a final touch were neither grand nor black enough to hide him from the inevitability of himself.

Still, he thought she would appreciate the wings, and the way he made the black sword shine and sing. He came to the east wing, to the door past which the library lay. He knew the room beyond. Every wall of it was armored with bookshelves, except for the interruption of a massively manteled fireplace and where a pair of heavy French doors framed a view of the hill sloping down to the town. He had entered that room twenty years ago, wearing somber juridical robes and a bulldog's grim, resigned expression as he informed Judge Foster of the verdict *sans* appeal. Then his hands had been blunt as the words he had spoken. Now his fingers were long and pale as he touched the orb to the doorknob and let himself in.

She looked up from the book she was reading. "Hello," she said, closing the buff-colored volume and laying it aside on the great desk of rosewood and brass. A snowy wealth of hair crowned her finely featured face. Lamplight overlaid with a dappled pattern of roses shone on the fair hands she folded in the lap of her moiré dress, a gown so lapped in shades and meanings of black that it left his own dark livery looking shabby by comparison. Her expression held recognition without fear.

"Were you expecting me?" he asked, rather taken aback by the calm she wore draped so gracefully around her.

"Eventually," she replied. Her smile still had the power to devastate. "Isn't that the way it is supposed to be?" She rose from the high-backed chair and the bottle-green leather moaned softly to give her up from its embrace. "Father always told me I'd go to Hell, though he'd beat me black and blue if I so much as pronounced the word. Now that I've said it, I assume that's my destination." Her eyes twinkled, and in the air before them fluttered the ghost of a long-vanished fan. "Is it?"

The swan's wings slumped, then trickled away entirely. The gallant's costume diminished to the weedy suiting of a country parson. The sword lingered only long enough for him to realize it was still in his hands, an embarrassment. It shrank posthaste to become a raven that hopped onto the parson's shoulder and croaked its outrage at being transformed into so inappropriate an accessory. At least the orb had possessed the good taste to become a well-thumbed copy of Scripture.

"I—ah—do not discuss destinations."

"Not even to tell me whether it will be all that much of a change from Foster's Glen?" She owned the miraculous ability to be arch without descending to kittenishness.

"I am—er—I am not at liberty to say," he replied, polishing the lozenges of his pince-nez with a decidedly unclerical red kerchief he yanked from a trouser pocket.

"What are you at liberty to do, then?" she asked. "Collect the dead?"

"Er—ah—souls, yes. In specific, souls." He settled the lenses back on the bridge of his nose. "One does one's duty."

"One does it poorly, then," she said, and there was a great deal of bite to the lady's words.

Her vehemence startled him so that he did a little jump in place and bleated, "Eh?"

She was happy to explain. "If souls are what you gather, I said you do a shoddy job of work. You could have had mine twenty-five years ago. I had no further use for it. But to come now—! Hmph." Her small nose twitched with a disdainful sniff that had once broken aspiring hearts.

"Twenty-five years a—?" He made the pages of his Bible flutter as he searched them with a whirlwind's speed. His eyes remained blank as he looked up again and inquired, "I *am* addressing Miss Louisa Foster?"

The lady sighed and moved toward the nearest wall. From floor to ceiling it was a single, continuous tidal wave of books. The musty smell of aging ink and paper, the peculiarly enchanting blend of scents from cloth and leather bindings, sewn spines, and the telltale traces of all the human hands that had turned those pages enveloped her like a sacring cloud of incense as she took a single volume down.

"So it is true," she said, looking at the text in her hands instead of at him. "Death does mistake himself sometimes."

"But you are—?" he insisted.

"Yes, yes, of course I am!" She waved away his queries impatiently. "Louisa Jane Foster, Judge Theophilus Foster's only child, sure to make a brilliant marriage or Father would know the reason why. A brilliant marriage or none. Father gave me as few choices as you do."

She replaced the book and took down a second one, a cuckoo among the flock of fine leather-fledged falcons. It was only bound in yellowing pasteboards, but when she opened it a scattering of scentless flower petals sprinkled the library carpet. The laugh she managed as she paged through the crumbling leaves trembled almost as much as her smile.

"Have you ever heard of a man named Asher Weiss? More than just in the way of business, I mean. Did you know he was a poet?" She did not look disappointed when her caller admitted he did not. "I didn't think so." Her eyes blinked rapidly. "And the rest of the world is now as ignorant as you.

"There is a poem in here called 'For L.,'" she said. "I don't think seven people alive today ever read it. But I was one who did. He wrote it and I followed a trail of words into his heart, like Gretel seeking a way out of the darkling wood by following trails of pebbles and breadcrumbs." She stooped to gather up the petals in her palm and slip them back between the pages. "Not very brilliant, as matches go; nothing his faith or mine would willingly consecrate, so we made do without consecration. We two—we three soon learned how hard it is to live on pebbles and breadcrumbs." She slid the booklet back onto the shelf.

"May I?" He helped himself to the poet's pasteboard gravestone and read the dead man's name. "But this man died more than twenty-five years since!" he protested.

"And did I ever protest when you took him?" she countered. "At least you left me . . . the other." Her mouth hardened. She snatched the booklet from him and jammed it back between its more reputable kin. "A consolation, I imagined; living proof that God did not solely listen to Father's thundered threats. For a while I dreamed I saw the face of a god of love, not retribution, every time I looked down into his laughing eyes, so like his father's. Oh, what a fine joke!" She plucked a random volume from the shelf and flipped it open so that when she spoke, she seemed to take her words from the printed lines before her. "With all the best jokes, timing is everything."

She held the timorous parson's gaze without mercy. "Is sickness your purview too? Is hunger? Is fever? Or are you only there to settle their affairs in the end? That time—crouching by the bed, holding his hand—I wanted it to be me you took, not him. God knows how he would have gotten on without me—maybe Father's heart would have softened to an orphan's plight. . . . " Her smile was bitter as she shook her head. "No. I only read fairy tales. It is for the children to believe in them."

She looked up. "Do you like children, Death?"

Before he could answer, she folded the book shut. "I know," she said. "Ask no questions. Bow your head. Accept." She jabbed the book at the judge's portrait above the fireplace and her voice plunged to a baritone roar: *Your choices will be made for you, girl! When I want your opinion, I'll give it to you!* " She clapped the book between her hands and laughed. "You would think I would have learned my lessons better than that by now, living with the voice of God Almighty. Almighty . . . whose word remakes the world according to his desires. You know, I never had a Jewish lover, never had a bastard child. When I did not return with Father from New York City, all those years that I was gone from Foster's Glen, I was studying music abroad, living with a maiden aunt in Paris. So I was told. The townsfolk still think I am a lady."

"But you are!" he exclaimed, and the raven sprang from his shoulder to flit beneath the plaster sunbursts on the ceiling.

"You are as happily gulled as they, I see." She extended her hand and the bird came to rest upon it. "I am sorry," she told it. "We have no bust of Pallas for your comfort here, birdie. Father viewed all pagan art as disgraceful, because like my Asher, so few of its subjects seemed able to afford a decent suit of clothes."

"Well, ah—" The parson took a breath and let it out after he had comfortably become a gentleman in evening dress, offering her his arm and the tribute of a rose. "Shall we go?"

"No." The lady laughed and kissed the bird's gleaming plumage. "Not yet."

"Not—? But I thought—?" He cleared his throat and adjusted the starched bosom of his shirt. "From the warmth of your initial greeting, Miss Foster, I assumed you were quite willing to accept me as your escort tonight."

"How gallant," she said, her words dry as those ancient petals. "And at my age, how can I refuse so fine an offer? I cannot. I only wish to defer it."

"So do they all," he responded. "But this is the appointed time."

She ignored his summons, moving with a smooth, elegant carriage to the portrait above the mantel. She aped the judge's somber look to the last droop of jowl and beetling of brow as she thundered, *"Where is the blasted girl? Will these women never learn to be on time?"* She rested her free hand on the cool marble as she gazed up into the judge's painted scowl. "How long did you wait for me in the lobby of our hotel, Father, before you realized I had flown?" She looked back at her caller. "If I found the courage to keep him waiting, I have little to fear from baiting Death."

The stranger coughed discreetly into a black-gloved hand. "I am afraid that I really must insist you come with me now."

"Why should I come to you when you would not come to me?" Her eyes blazed blacker than the raven's feathers, blacker than the curl of downy hair encased in gold and crystal at the neck of her high-collared gown. "I called you and you would not come. Why? Couldn't you hear me? Was the rain falling too hard on the tiny box, or was the echo from the hole they'd dug for him too loud? I doubt it. They never dig the holes too deep in Potter's Field. Or was it the rumbling of the carriage wheels that drowned out my voice when *dear* Cousin Althea came to fetch me home again? Ah, no, I think perhaps it might have been impossible to hear my cries to you above the fuss she raised because she was so overjoyed to have 'found' me at last."

She slammed the book down on the mantel. "Of course it was impossible for her to have found me earlier, when all she had was my address on any of a dozen letters; letters I sent her pleading for money, for medicine, for the slightest hint of compassion. . . . " She sank down suddenly on the hearthstone, frightening the raven to flight.

He knelt beside her and took her in his arms. Her tears were strong reality against his form of smoke and whispers.

"You have waited so long," she murmured, her breath in his ear warm and alive. "Can't you wait a little longer?"

"How much longer?" He smelled the lavender water that she used after her bath and felt the weary softness of her old woman's skin, her old woman's hair.

"Only until I finish reading." She laid her hands on his shoulders and nodded toward the desk where the buff-covered book still lay.

"Is that all you ask? Not days, not months, only until—?"

"That is all." Her hands clasped his. "Please."

He consented, only half comprehending what he had granted her. All she had said was true: His was the discretion that had assumed there was no truth behind a woman's pleas. So many of them cried out, *Let me die!* who thought better of it later. Only when he was compelled to greet them below the railing of a bridge or with the apothecary bottle still in hand was he assured of their sincerity, and Miss Louisa Foster had not sought either of those paths after her cousin Althea fetched her home. *Hysterical* and *She'll get over it* tapped him on the shoulder, leering. He did have memories.

Still dressed for dancing, he helped her to her feet. She returned to her place in the green leather chair and took up the buff-covered book again. "To think I don't need spectacles at my age. Isn't it wonderful?" she said to him. And then: "You must promise not to frighten them."

He nodded obediently, although he had not the faintest idea of what she meant. He re-created himself as a lady of her own age and bearing, a tangle of dark tatting in her hands, a woolly black lapdog at her feet, the image of the poor relative whose bit of bread and hearthfire is earned with silence and invisibility.

The coach clock on the mantlepiece struck midnight.

The French doors creaked as a little hand shyly pushed them open. A dark head peered around the edge of the door. *Mother?* the wind sighed.

She did not look up from the open book as the child blew across the carpet and settled into her shadow. The small head rested itself against her knees, and thin, milky fingers that should have been pink and plump and scented with powder instead of mold reached up to close around her hand.

Read to me.

"Why, Danny, I am surprised at you," she said softly. "You know we can't begin without your friends."

The wind blew more phantoms through the open doors, gusts and wracks and tumbling clouds of children. They swept into the darkened library, whirling in eddies like the bright autumn leaves outside, catching in snug corners, in favorite chairs before the breath of their advent died away and left them all sitting in attentive order around Miss Louisa Foster's chair.

The stranger felt a tiny hand creep into hers, a hand whose damp clasp she had last disengaged as gently as she could from the breast of the young, despairing mother fated to survive the plunge the child did not. It was not the stranger's place to ask what became of her charges after she called for them. The child tugged insistently at her hand, then clambered up into her lap uninvited. She settled her head against the lady's shawled shoulder with a contented sigh, having found someone she knew. Her feet were bare and her golden hair smelled of factory smoke and river water.

"Now, shall we begin?" Miss Foster asked, beaming over the edge of the open book. Smiles answered her. "I think that if you are all very good, tonight we shall be finished with Tom Sawyer's adventures, and then—" Her voice caught, but she had been raised with what Judge Foster liked to call "breeding." She carried on. "—and then you shall rest."

She raised her eyes to the patient caller in the other chair. "You see how it is? Someone has to do this for them now. They were lost too young for anyone to share the stories with them—the old fairy tales, and Mother Goose, and *Kim,* and the legends of King Arthur, and *The Count of Monte Cristo,* and—and—oh! How can children be sent to sleep without stories? So I try."

"When—?" The lady with the lapdog wet her lips, so suddenly dry. "When did they first come to you?" The child leaning against her shoulder shifted, then pounced on the tangled tatting in her lap and sat happily creating a nest of Gordian knots as complex and as simple as the world.

"They came soon after I made over this room to be the town's library, after Father was dead. I scoured the shelves of his law books and filled them with all the tales of wonder and adventure and mischief and laughter they could hold. I was seated right here one midnight, reading aloud to myself from Asher's book of poetry, when the first one came." She leaned forward and fondly ruffled the hair of a little boy whose pinched face was still streaked with coal dust. "I never guessed until then that it was possible to hunger for something you have never known."

Then she bent and scooped up the child who held so tightly to her skirts. She set him on her lap and pressed his head to the high-necked, extremely proper sleekness of her dress front. The little ghost's black hair curled around the brooch that held his single strayed curl.

"One night, he was here with the rest. Come all the way from New York City, can you imagine that? And the roads so cold." Her lips brushed the white forehead. "So cold." She set him down again among the rest and gave the stranger a smile of forced brightness. "I've found that children sleep more peaceably after a story, haven't you?" Before her caller could reply, she added, "Please forgive me, but I don't like to keep them waiting."

Miss Foster began to read the last of Tom Sawyer's adventures. The oil lamp smoothed away the marks of fever and hunger and more violent death from the faces of the children who listened. As she read, the words slipped beneath the skin, brought a glow of delight to ravening eyes. In her own chair, Miss Foster's caller became conscious of a strange power filling the room. The ghosts were casting off their ghosts, old bleaknesses and sorrows, lingering memories of pain and dread. All that remained were the children, and the wonder.

At last, Miss Foster closed the book. "The End," she announced, still from behind the stiffness of her smile. The children looked at her expectantly. "That was the end, children," she said gently. "I'm afraid that's all." The small ghosts' eyes dimmed. By ones and twos they drifted reluctantly from the lamplight, back toward the moonlit cold.

"Wait."

The stranger stood, still holding the little girl to his chest. He was dressed as a road-worn peddler, with his goods on his back and a keen black hound at his heels. He dropped his dusty rucksack on the rosewood desk and plunged his arm inside. "Here's *Huckleberry Finn*," he said. "You'll have to read them that after they've heard *Tom Sawyer*." He dug more books from the depths of the bag, piling each on each. "Oh, and *The Three Musketeers. Uncle Tom's Cabin. Little Lord Fauntleroy* . . . well, it takes all kinds. And *David Copperfield, Treasure Island, Anne of Green Gables, 20,000 Leagues Under the Sea, Sarah Crewe*—" He stared at the tower of books he had erected and gave a long, low whistle. "I reckon you'll have the wit to find more."

She seized his wrist, her voice urgent as she asked, "Is this a trick? Another joke that Father's own personal god wants to play on me?"

"No trick," he said. "I shall come back, I promise you that, Miss Louisa. I'll come back because I must, and you know I must."

She touched the mourning brooch at her throat. "When?"

"When I promised." His eyes met hers. "When you've finished reading."

He placed the girl-child in her lap, then lifted up her own lost son; together they were no more burden than the empty air. Her arms instinctively crept around to embrace them both and he placed an open book in her hands to seal the circle. "Or when you will."

"I don't—" she began.

"Read."

He shouldered his rucksack and whistled up his hound. The ghostly throng of children gazed at him as he passed through their midst to the French doors. Outside there was still smoke and apples on the air, and a thousand tales yet to be told. He paused on the threshold and turned to see her still sitting there in the lamplight, staring at him.

"Give them their stories, Louisa," he said, his face now aged by winds and rains and summer days uncountable. "Give them back their dreams."

"Once—" She faltered. The children drew in nearer, faces lifted like flowers to the rain. "Once upon a time . . ."

He watched as the words took them all beyond his reach, and he willingly let them go. He bowed his head beneath the moon's silver scythe blade and took a new road, the black dog trotting beside him all the way.

Alien Jane

KELLEY ESKRIDGE

Kelley Eskridge's short fiction has appeared in *Century, Pulphouse, The Magazine of Fantasy & Science Fiction,* and *Little Deaths,* an anthology of erotic horror edited by Ellen Datlow. Her work has also appeared in *The Year's Best Fantasy and Horror.* She lives in Seattle, Washington, with her partner, writer Nicola Griffith.

"Alien Jane," a finalist for the Nebula Award, also won Kelley Eskridge the Astraea National Lesbian Action Foundation Writer's Award, an $11,000 prize. About this story, she writes:

"Congenital insensitivity to pain is a real condition. When I was young, I saw a feature on *60 Minutes* or one of its ilk about a family with three CIP kids. They had to be watched all the time because everything in the world—including themselves—was dangerous to them. They never knew that they needed to be healed.

"When I sat down to write 'Alien Jane,' I wanted to invert the idea of pain. I wanted to create a woman who needed to be healed because she did not hurt. And I wanted to think about what pain really means. We use physical pain as a barometer of so many things: self-worth (how well we resist pain and its debilitation); justification for attention (it's okay to ask for it as long as you really need it); how hard we've tried to achieve a physical goal (do you feel the burn?). But there are other kinds of pain, and they, too, have their function as a warning signal, a sign that we need to be healed: rage, loneliness, grief, helplessness, humiliation—all things that Jane has felt, that have led her to a place where the best option is to cut herself open to show that she is not, after all, so different from anyone else.

"The original story was full of horror and grue. I wrote from Jane's point of view and, as the writer, got caught up in the power of being able to hurt this character who couldn't feel it. I wrote enormous monologues, litanies of abuse. Wow, I thought, now I'm really exploring pain.

"Well, what a bunch of crap that was. What I was really doing was indulging myself in no-pay victimization—it was 'okay' because nobody got hurt. It upset me to realize it—and so, of course, back it went into the story, and emerged as all those people in the lab who turn the test dial all the way to the right just to see Jane burn without her knowing that she is being injured.

"It seemed such a strong image of alienation to me that I took from it the title of the story. Writing 'Alien Jane' gave me a more clear notion of my own definitions of science fiction and speculative fiction. For me, it's all about exploring the alien, exploring the difference until it's clear that there is no difference at all."

S he came in as a thinskin and we started off badly. Thinskins pissed me off. Everything about them was hopeless: their screams, their red faces, the smell of their blood, and there was always blood because it was night and they came from Emergency. They made me remember where I still was, and that was a terrible thing, a monster thing with nowhere to go but boiling out of me in a cloud of rage that fogged me for hours sometimes. The ward is where they put you when you have the rage.

"Don't you bring her in here."

"Calm down, Rita, go back to your own bed."

"Don't you bring her in here."

"Rita, I won't tell you again to behave yourself." Molasses voice and muscles and she meant it, Madge the Badge, chief white hat of the night shift. The thinskin lay silent as Madge and a no-name nurse made a sling of the sheet under her and moved her onto the empty bed, the one near the door because I liked the window view: it was just the sidewalk to the parking lot, but I could see people walking away. I thought about away for a while until the nurses finished with the sheets and the needles and left me alone with her. Then I got up and took the few steps across the linoleum floor.

"You shouldn't be in my room. I don't want you, and if you give me any hassle I'll hurt you, I swear."

She had her eyes closed until then but she opened them wide, bright blue. And she laughed, laughed. She howled. Two nurses came running into the room and one held her down while the other shot her up, and the whole time she made noises until her face turned purple.

They shot me, too. I hate that, but the worst was the thinskin and how she scared me.

She slept almost the whole next day. I got to where I could shake the sleepydrugs off pretty fast but she was an amateur, down for the long count. The nurses had her under Close Observation; they came in every fifteen minutes to check on her. "She's still gone, what did you people give her, can I have some?" I kept saying, until they finally made me leave the room. I thought maybe she didn't want to come back up, maybe wouldn't, but later I looked in from the hall and there she was cross-legged in the bed, looking fuzzbrained, the blankets and sheets twisted up around her waist.

"You're up. I've been up for ages. You missed breakfast, you missed lunch but it was crap, lunch I mean, so I guess you're better off and dinner'll be here soon. You wanna come down to the TV room and watch *Remington Steele*?"

She blinked for a while and then she said, "I have to go to the bathroom." She had a low voice, the kind that always makes me want to practice so I can sound like that. You can talk onto a tape to do it. I used to think about being an actress but that was all crap too, getting up in front of people and letting them see you cry.

I got my first good look at her while she was trying to get out of bed: older than me, maybe twenty-five, yellow dirty hair and those blue eyes. She was a mess, bandages everywhere, and where she wasn't all wrapped up she was the pastypale color that white people get when they eat meat all the time and don't work it off. She made my fingers itch to stuff an entire head of broccoli down her throat. She moved slow; and she looked at me. She pulled one leg out of the covers, and looked at me, then the other, and looked, until I finally said, "You see something you don't like?"

She shook her head. "Last night . . . you said . . ."

"Oh, *hijumadre*, forget it, I don't like nights and I don't like thinskins, but I won't hurt you. I was just being mean."

"Thinskins?"

"Yeah. New patients, you know, start by crying and yelling that they don't belong up here with all the rest of us really crazy people which of course *they* aren't, crazy I mean, and it's all a mistake. Then they get pitiful for a while and won't talk to anyone and shake all the time. They go off if you say boo to them. Thin skinned."

"Right." She was on her feet by this time, more bandage than body. "Well, I'll just have to try to remember that I belong here," and then she looked like she might cry, which I hate. I started to drift out and let her get herself back, but I don't know, something about her . . . I don't know. Anyway, I put out one arm and said, "Bathroom's over here," and walked her to the door.

A nurse came in then and took over, she gave me a look and said to the thinskin, "Everything okay here?"

"I didn't do anything," I said.

She was better when I came back, but I didn't want to talk and I guess neither did she, except she said what's your name and I said Rita and she said Jane.

She had Dr. Rousseau, who was my doctor and the best, not someone that I wanted to share with creepy Jane; Rousseau who half of us would have swallowed rocks for, and even the nurses liked. Rousseau spent a lot of time on Jane, but Jane wouldn't talk much more to her than she would to anybody else, which I respected in a way. She wouldn't even talk to Tommy Gee.

"Does she say much to you when you're together on your own, without any doctors around? Does she seem to communicate better with her peers?" Tommy Gee was always doing that, mixing up the stupid patients' talk with the doctor talk so you never knew if he meant it for you or some white coat standing behind you. His real name was Gian-something-Italian but we called him Tommy Gee-for-gee-whiz because that's how he was about everything, including being Rousseau's intern.

"If you mean does she relax when she's with the rest of us mentals then no, Dr. Gee, I guess she isn't comm-you-nee-cating well at all. Maybe they don't talk on whatever planet she's from."

"That doesn't sound very supportive, Rita."

"You're the doctor, you support her."

And he tried to, he was always coming around after her sessions with Rousseau, to talk to her, see if there was anything he could do to get her to open up. She was his special project.

I got used to having her in my room because she was so quiet I didn't notice her half the time. I talked to Rousseau about that during one morning session, and she just said *hmmm* and wrote it down.

"I think Tommy Gee likes her, too, but she probably hasn't even noticed how stupid he gets around her."

"Hmmm."

"I guess it'll be okay having her there. I mean, I probably won't even notice when she's gone until two days later."

Rousseau put the cap back on her pen and sat back in her chair. There was a little mended place near the pocket of her doctor coat. The first time I saw Rousseau was twenty hours after I came into Emergency, when they moved me up to the locked ward. She asked me if I wanted to talk and I said no like always, feeling like a rock in the gutter when the rainwater runs over it, pushing it little by little toward that big dark hole going down. I said no, and then I saw the mark on her coat, the careful clumsy darn, and I could never explain how it made me feel; but then it was okay to talk to this woman Rousseau.

She turned the pen over in her fingers, gave me a doctor look. "Haven't you ever thought that you might be the first to leave?" she asked.

I spent the rest of the morning like always, huddled up with Terry Louise on the bench down the hall from the nurses' station: her smoking cigarettes until she could hide behind the cloud they made; me trying to find some way to make my back comfortable against the wood slats, and making kissy noises at the boy orderlies when they went by, because I hated the way they always picked the little scared ones to rub up against when they thought no one was looking. They walked itchy around me after what happened that one time.

"I hate it when she does that," I said. "Why does she have to talk about me leaving?"

"Just say no, babe," Terry Louise said through a mouthful of smoke.

"Can't keep saying no forever."

Jane's bandages came off and she was all new pink skin on her arms and legs, like someone had decided she was a big fish that needed scaling. "She did it to herself," Terry Louise said one morning from behind her smoke.

"No way."

"Uh-huh. Why do you think she's in here? This isn't a plastic surgery ward."

"No one has the guts to do that to themselves. There's no way she could have got past the first leg."

"Madge the Badge was talking to one of the student nurses last night. So unless the meaning of 'self-inflicted' has changed while I've been away, No-Brain Jane is sicker than we are."

"We're not sick."

"Stop squirming around and sit still for half a minute, Rita. You look like something I'd like to bait a hook with," Terry Louise said. The old scars down the insides of her dark arms showed plainly when she raised the cigarette to her mouth. She smiled.

Susan came to see me over the weekend. She made me feel like she was holding my soul when she touched me: I wished Jane would disappear, but she was right there, watching.

"Suze, this is my new roommate Jane." I made a face, but not where Jane could see.

Susan leaned across the gap between our beds and held out her hand. "Hi."

Jane picked lint balls off her blanket.

Susan stood with her hand out. Jane wouldn't look at it.

"You shake her goddamned hand, you pink turd, or I'll hurt you worse than whoever did you the last time."

"Rita, shut up." Susan put her hand down. Jane was shaking and squeezing her fingers open and closed around great fistfuls of blanket. Her eyes were shut tight, so she didn't see me reach for her.

"*Back off, Rita.*"

Susan got me out of the room, down the hall. She left bruises on my arm.

"Don't hang on to it. I don't care, I don't even know her. Anyway, she must be hurt pretty bad."

"Fuck her. Everybody's hurt."

That was all it took to spoil my day with Susan, just ten seconds of goddamned Jane. When Suze finally left we were both strung tight, dancing around each other like beads on a wire. I glided back into my room like running on electric current.

It came out at Jane then, all my meanness in evil words, and Jane just closed her eyes and bit down on her lip to keep from crying; and when I finally stopped, she opened her mouth and said something that might have been, "I'm sorry, I'm sorry," but it was hard to tell around all the bright red where she had chewed her lip right through.

The lip needed stitches. "Frankenjane," Terry Louise chortled up and down the hall, "Frankenjane, feels no pain."

"Shut up, Terry Louise."

"Well, excuse me, honey, I meant to say *Princess* Jane. Princess Jane, so insane—"

"*Shut up.*"

"Humph," Terry Louise said, and lit another cigarette.

"She didn't even know she'd done it."

"I know. You told me seven times already—"

"She practically bit her lip *off,* I could see her teeth right through it, and her tongue was all dark red . . ."

"Rita—"

"Rousseau said it wasn't my fault but we all have to be careful, we have to be careful, she's always getting hurt and not knowing because she can't feel the pain and you were right, she did that other stuff to herself, to her own self, it's sick, how could anyone do that and not feel it, it's sick, she just chewed herself *up*—" and I couldn't stop talking, faster and faster, couldn't stop even when Terry Louise ran for Madge the Badge.

It took a long time to wake up from the needlesleep the next day. I was still in bed when Rousseau and Tommy Gee came in with Jane. I wanted to open my eyes, to say I'm sorry, but the drug was like a staircase that I had to climb, and every time I got to the top I would be back at the bottom again: like big wheels in my head turning all night, so I was more tired than if they had just let me cry for a while.

"Thank you for seeing Dr. Novak," Rousseau said to Jane. "Do you have any questions about the kind of testing he wants to do? I know he might not have explained things completely, he's so excited about your condition . . ."

Jane was quiet.

"Please understand how important this is," Rousseau went on. "No one here has had the opportunity to examine congenital insensitivity to pain. It's very rare, and there are so many things we want to know. . . ."

"I'm not a lab animal."

"No, you're not. No one will treat you that way. You're a person with an unusual condition, and with your help we can learn the best ways to deal with other people who have it. We may be able to help you find ways to live with it. I promise no one will hurt you . . . I mean . . ."

"I know what you mean, Doctor." Jane sounded a hundred years old, tired and thin-voiced.

"You don't have to do this if you don't want to. No one will make you," Tommy said gently.

"Will you excuse us for a moment, Jane?" Rousseau said. I felt her and Tommy move past me toward the window, their footsteps sending small shudders through the bed and the bones of my skull.

Rousseau kept her voice low. "Tommy, I expect you to back me up on this."

"I just don't think we should push her. She's only just started to connect with us. It's a little soon to ask her to include someone else in that trust."

"Dr. Novak is one of our best research neurologists. I think we should be supporting Jane's opportunity to work with him."

There was a silence that seemed long.

"I don't understand why you're doing this. I know you don't support his research funding, you even wrote a letter about it to the Chief of Neurology last year."

"How did you know about that?"

"Everybody knows."

Rousseau's voice suddenly sounded very close, sharp.

"Great. Then maybe everyone should know that I have since retracted that letter and encouraged several of my patients to participate
in Dr. Novak's studies. Including Jane, if she's willing."

"I still don't think—"

"Thank you, Doctor," and that didn't sound like any voice I'd ever
heard come out of Rousseau. *What's wrong?* I wanted to say but I
couldn't open my eyes. I heard Tommy Gee thump out of the room.

I heard Rousseau take in a deep breath and walk past me to
Jane's bed.

"Well, I just need you to sign this release."

I knew I should open my eyes but I couldn't stop climbing stairs
inside my head. No, I tried to say, no no but I could only make a little
noise. "Go to sleep, Rita," Rousseau said, and pulled the curtain across
between me and Jane.

She became silent Jane again, and I saw less and less of her because she had started the testing, and once the lab rats got hold of her
they didn't want to give her up. The nurses talked about it up and
down the halls, even Madge who was such a porcupine for rules, so we
all heard about Jane in the lab being electroshocked and pinpricked
and nerve pressed and never feeling a thing, and how it was something
you were born with and that nothing that happened to you ever hurt,
no matter how bad it was. Terry Louise said it was kind of neat and
Jane was like the star of one of those old flying saucer movies where
the alien takes over your body, so you look like a human but you're not.

One day in the room, I wanted to say I was sorry.

"Forget it."

"I didn't mean to hurt you."

"Stupid. Stupid, stupid. No one can hurt me. They've been trying
for a week now. Go ahead, do your best."

That wasn't what I meant, I thought, and I couldn't think of anything to say, so I just went on sitting on the edge of my bed rubbing
my fingers down the little nubby rows of the bedspread. Jane lay on
her back, arms straight by her sides, toes pointed at the ceiling. Her
pajamas were dirty around the seams. She looked very thin, greasy

with fatigue. She kept absolutely still. She moved only to breathe, and she wouldn't look at me.

I thought I would lie down like that too and look at the ceiling, and be very, very still. The ceiling was gray and restful. I wondered, if Jane and I lay in the same room long enough, would we start breathing together? When I closed my eyes I could hear everything. I heard orderlies wheeling medicine carts past our open door, the pills hissing in the tiny paper cups, little insects full of honey and poison; nurses in rubber soles; Terry Louise in paper slippers; Tommy Gee in his pointy leather shoes; Dr. Rousseau in heels: all stopping at our door, heads bent around the jamb looking in at Jane and me laid out like bodies on the back tables of funeral parlors, waiting to be made pretty enough to be seen by the living. Go away, I thought, go away and they all did, while Jane and I breathed together and the morning light turned gray under the weight of wet clouds and the light in the room dimmed into something soft and private.

After a long time the old pictures came back into my head and this time it was okay, okay to let the pictures move through me while the light was cool and the room was quiet with the sound of our breath like slow waves on a beach. The pictures turned into words, and I told myself to Jane.

"When I was little I wanted to wear jeans and climb up the big oak tree onto the garage roof and play pirates for the rest of my life. I could see everything from there. I thought I was queen of the world.

"Down the road from us was a big field where the grass grew as high as my waist, all green and reedy so it whispered when the wind went over it. I would run through it with my arms flung out wide, as fast as I could, so the wind would pick me up and fly me away. But I would always lose my breath too soon and fall down, into the green and the smell of warm wet dirt with just a strip of sky showing overhead, and I would have this whole world that was just for me, just mine."

I breathed gently and thought about my green place, and Jane was there; I could feel her in the grass wanting to run.

"When I was twelve, they took it away. They decided it was time for me to start being a girl like my sisters and my mother, and they took away my overalls and made me put on shoes that hurt my feet. I tried to climb anyway, and my dress got caught around my waist and under my arms so I couldn't move, and I knew I could never run in those shoes. I looked around and saw all the women I knew never running, never moving, weak and tired and bound up, and I couldn't believe my parents would do that to me, that they would tie me up like a box of groceries ready to be delivered. I said I wouldn't do it; I was standing in the dining room in these clothes that felt like ropes around me, and I said I won't, I won't. . . . My father took me by the arm and locked me in the hall closet with the winter coats. It was dark, and I couldn't move in those clothes, and the shoes were too narrow for my feet, they hurt. . . . I think it was those shoes did something funny to my mind. I think they were why I hung my Christmas doll up by one foot over my father's favorite chair in the living room and set fire to it—to the doll, I mean. I lit the match and put it right up against the hair and the whole thing melted and dripped onto the place in the chair that was rubbed shiny from my father. The house smelled for weeks.

"Then I was always in trouble. Always fighting. I burned more things, I tried to run away. I hurt my little sister bad one time with a rake. Everything just got worse. It's better now that I'm not with them anymore."

Jane said nothing.

"Maybe it's better you're here now."

Jane breathed.

"I stole things, I got caught. My parents gave me up to the court. My mother cried, said she couldn't do anything with me. She's Catholic, she'll carry it forever. I spit at the judge. That's what got me away from my folks, spitting at the judge. He didn't care about the broken windows and the badmouthing and the knife that time, he just didn't like me spitting at him. Spoiled his day."

Maybe Jane smiled, maybe not.

"But it all just hurt too much after a while. When you fall down out there in the world it isn't green and soft, it hurts. . . . I met Suze in that place for girls where they sent me . . . but it was too late and I felt so bad and I tried—"

I thought of Jane's legs and arms.

"They have to put you in here for that, and at first I hated it, it was like the closet again. But now there's Rousseau and Terry Louise.

"I don't do those things anymore, not really. I still . . . you know, I still say things sometimes, but even then it's like I only do it to make myself feel bad. I guess the meanness is going out of me. Rousseau says I'm better. She wanted me to leave a few months ago . . . but I screwed up, I did it again . . . one of the orderlies, that stupid Jackson, pissed me off. But I could have been out only I . . . I couldn't remember anymore how it felt, running in the grass."

Wax Jane, silent Jane. Ceiling-staring Jane.

"Suze is what I have left. If I mess that up I don't know what would happen. So I get funny sometimes. I guess you don't have to shake her hand if you don't want to."

I closed my eyes. It surprised me when she answered. Her voice sounded like she hadn't used it in a long time.

"I saw how she held you, how she touched you, you know? And I thought . . . how lucky you were that someone would touch you like that. And then she held out her hand to me. . . . I couldn't take it. It would kill me right now to have anyone be that nice to me. I'd rather spend all day with those doctors poking wires in me than one second with your girlfriend's hand in mine."

There was something in the way she said it; I saw again my father's face when he found the doll in a stinking puddle, and my mother saying *how could you, how could you* but never answering her own question. Jane reminded me of how the world can be so different sometimes from what we expect. I got up and poured her a cup of water and put it on the table by her bed. I knew she wouldn't want me to touch her, even though I would have liked maybe just to hold her hand, not like with Suze but only because she was scared and in a lonely place. I crawled back onto my bed and turned on my side away from her, blinking against the light. I thought that in my life I had been little Rita, and Rita full of rage, and crazy Rita, and now maybe I would be some other Rita: but I couldn't see her, I didn't know if she would be someone who could run through the world and not fall down.

———

Rousseau came into my room the next morning. She looked funny, and she said a strange thing: "Rita, please come with me down to the lab."

"Why?"

"Jane is asking for you. I'd like you to go be with her, if you don't mind."

We walked down the hall. Rousseau started for the elevator and I said, "I want the stairs, okay?"

She turned back so fast she almost caught Weird Bob's visiting sister with her elbow. "Sorry, I forgot about the claustrophobia." She didn't apologize to the sister. That and the forgetting and the asking in the first place made three strange things.

We walked down the stairs. I went first. "Three floors down," she said. She was close, only a step or two behind me. Her smell came down over me like green apples.

"Rita . . . you know that Jane agreed to work on these experiments with Doctor Novak. She's a volunteer. I just want you to remember when you see her . . . I don't want you to think . . . she isn't being hurt . . ." she said in a queer, rushed voice that didn't even sound like Rousseau. I stopped. Her hands were jammed into the pockets of her white coat and her face was turned to the wall, and she wouldn't look at me.

That was the strangest thing of all, and it scared me. It wasn't Rousseau standing over me, her red hair sparking under the stairwell light. My doctor wasn't scared; my doctor was an Amazon, a mother confessor, a carrier of fearlessness that she would breed into me like a new branch grafted onto a young tree. My doctor wasn't this person who was saying, "Just be calm and don't worry, everything will be fine."

"What's the matter with her?"

"Let's go."

My slippers rustled on the stair tread and on the linoleum of the hall when we went through the landing door. I followed the stripes painted on the wall, around and around the hallways like a maze. We came to a locked ward door and a nurses' station beyond it. The two men behind the desk wouldn't let me in until they checked with Novak on the telephone. The brown-haired one had a badge with a metal clip that he tried to put on me, and I wondered if I would have to hurt him, but Rousseau said, "Don't touch her."

"Doctor?"

"Let her put it on herself."

Brown-hair rolled his eyes and handed me the badge dangling between two fingertips, arm outstretched. Rousseau said nothing, but she was shaking just a little as we went down the hall. We could hear Brown-hair say something to the other one and they both laughed and I didn't like being there at all, in a place I didn't know, with strangers.

The hall was long and mostly bare, with only a few metal-backed chairs next to closed doors. The air smelled like ammonia and sweat and burned electrical wires. It was quiet except for our breathing, the *rsshhh rsshhh* sounds of our clothes, and Rousseau's hard-heeled, strong step. Then I began to hear another sound, a rise and fall of muffled noise like music, but something about it made me want to walk faster, and then it was Jane screaming and I began to run.

The place where they had her was at the end of the hall, a high-ceilinged room that made an echo out of Jane. The lab was full of white: white-coated doctors, orderlies in white pants and shirts, Jane in her cotton pajamas with her rolling eyes that showed white and blue, white and blue. She sat in a wooden chair with a high back and arms. Thin rainbows of color twisted out of her head, wires running out of her scalp into the machines around her. More wires with small disks on the end lay taped like lollipop strings against her neck; her left wrist; her pink-scarred calf; her ankle; under her pajamas at her heart. She sat very straight in the chair because her shins and forearms and ribs and head were belted against the wood with padded ties the color that white people call flesh, and I wondered if they thought that no one would see the ties because they were the flesh of Jane. Jane was screaming around a rubber mouthpiece that showed tan and wet from her saliva every time her lips pulled back—not terror screams but more like some giant grief, some last precious thing taken away. The room was full of her smell.

I couldn't go in. I stood at the door and I couldn't step into what I saw in that room. Everyone except Jane had stopped in mid-motion; they stared at us with the glazed otherplace look of people caught in the middle of some terrible thing like rape or butchery, the kind of act so horrible that while it is happening the doing of it removes you from all human space. I tried to turn around, but Rousseau was right behind me with her hands braced against the door frame, leaning into it like she would push the whole thing down. Then there was nowhere to go but ahead.

"Goddammit, goddammit," Rousseau was muttering as she moved in behind me.

"What are they doing, what are they doing to Jane?" I said, but she didn't hear me. Novak came over and stood in front of us like he was trying to keep us from coming in any farther.

"Jesus Christ, what is happening here? I told you to stop the goddamned test until I could get back." Rousseau's voice was low. I felt squeezed between her and Novak.

"Calm down, nothing happened, she's just upset—"

"She's still my patient. You had no right."

"Nobody has done anything to hurt her. Christ, Elaine, I'm a doctor, I don't—" Jane stopped screaming, suddenly, like a light turning off. Spit ran down her chin. The machines buzzed and the paper strips whispered onto the floor. A woman with a needle stepped over the coiled electrical cords toward Jane, and I could feel myself tense.

"It's okay, Rita," Rousseau said. "I'll get someone to take you back to the ward."

"No." I pulled out from between them, went toward Jane. Behind me I heard Rousseau start in on Novak. I felt proud of her again, fighting for Jane; then I was standing in front of the woman with the needle and she turned toward me. "Leave her alone," Rousseau said, and the needle went away. Jane saw me and tried to move. I didn't know if she was trying to get away or get closer, and for a moment I remembered the Jane who didn't want to be touched in love, the Jane who would rather stay different in her wires and straps, apart from people, alien Jane; and the Rita who always reached out with hurting hands. Then I unbuckled all the straps and put my arms around her, and she didn't pull away.

The other people in the lab began to move then, but they didn't seem to know what to do or where to go. I didn't want them to touch Jane but they did; they took the wires off her head and peeled them off her legs. They had to reach under me to get to her arms and chest.

There was a piece of metal under one white bandage on her arm. They took the metal and left the bandage. They took the mouthpiece, but no one wiped her wet chin so I dried her with the corner of my robe. There was a funny smell about her, something burning; fear sweat, I thought.

Rousseau came over, with Novak following. They squeezed around me. Jane closed her eyes.

"Let me see her, Rita." And so I had to let go. My hands still felt full of her even when they were empty.

Rousseau said something to Jane I couldn't hear. Jane shook her head, eyes still shut, face pale and moist under the hot lights.

"What's this?" Rousseau said.

She had found the bandage on Jane's arm. When she peeled it back, the arm was white around a stripe of red, and in the center of the stripe was a blister, raw and runny. The smell was worse with the bandage off.

Rousseau looked up at Novak. Being next to her made me feel cold.

"It was an accident," he said. "We were testing her for heat response, one of the techs pushed the dial up a little too high." He shifted, jammed his hands into his coat pockets, shrugged like he thought Rousseau was being ridiculous. She still hadn't spoken. She was so tense I thought she might break apart if she made a sound.

"Oh, come on, Elaine. Nobody got hurt."

"What do you call this?" Her voice was very soft.

"I call it an accident, for chrissakes. It's no big deal. She didn't feel a thing."

Jane began to cry.

Rousseau put the bandage back over the wound and smoothed down the tape. She stood up. "I'm reporting this," she said, still speaking softly. "I won't let you harm one of my patients, not that." It was like she was talking to herself.

"She's not really your patient anymore."

"You can't do that."

"I already have. She signed the consent form, she's a volunteer. I can do her a lot of good."

"You don't have enough clout for this. I don't care what kind of strings the Chief of Neuro pulls for you this time."

"Try me," Novak said. "But you'd better be ready, Elaine, because you'll have to go across country to find a job after I'm finished with you."

"Jesus," Rousseau said thickly.

"Jane is the professional opportunity of a lifetime," Novak went on, "and you don't have the slightest idea of what to do with her. But I do."

It felt like a punch in the stomach, the sick-making breathless kind. *It isn't true,* I wanted to say, and then I saw Rousseau's face like still water, and I turned away so I wouldn't have to watch while Novak put one arm around her and led her away, saying softly, persuasively, "Don't be upset. I didn't mean to upset you. Jane will be fine with me, I promise, she'll be fine and you can still manage her therapy, keep an eye on her. Why don't we just go have a cup of coffee and talk it over. . . ." And I moved closer to Jane and she grabbed me, pulled me in, and I realized she was whispering, her voice becoming clearer as Novak and Rousseau moved away.

". . . it keeps you safe, keeps you safe, the pain keeps you safe, because it hurts and you know something's wrong. People like me die if we're not careful; we pierce our lungs with a broken rib we didn't know we had; we smile and eat dinner while our appendix bursts inside us; we hold our hands out over the fire when we're children and laugh while the skin turns black. Pain keeps you safe. It's how you keep alive, how you stay whole, it's such a human thing and I don't have it. I don't have it. And you people . . . you think . . . no one ever asked if I could . . . but I can, I can, I can feel a touch or a kiss, I can feel your arms around me, I can feel my life, and I can feel hopeful, and scared, and I can see my days stretching out before me in this place while they forget and leave the heat on too long again and again and again, just to see, just to see me not knowing until I smell my own skin burning and realize. And when I look at them they aren't human anymore, they aren't the people that bring me ginger ale and smile at me. They're the people that turn up the dial . . . and they hate me because I didn't make them stop, and now they have to know this thing about themselves. They'll never let me go."

I held her tight. "Tell them," I said. "Tell them like you told me. You can make them stop, Jane, you don't have to—"

"I do have to, Rita, I do, I have to be . . . I keep thinking that they'll find a way to hurt me the way they want to, something that will work and then I'll be okay, I'll be safe, I'll be like everybody else, and I won't have to be alone anymore."

And then I understood that the smell in the room and the rawness under the bandage was her pain, her alien pain; and I suddenly knew how she might have taken a knife and stripped her own skin away, earnestly, fiercely, trying to see what made her different, find it and cut it out and take away the alien and just be Jane.

I held her. There was nothing I could say.

The next day Jane was transferred to the locked ward upstairs. Tommy Gee didn't want to let them take her. "There's a mistake," he said. "Wait for Dr. Rousseau. She'll be here in just a minute." But I knew she wasn't coming. "I'll find her," he said, and went running down the hall.

Jane stood just inside the room, one step from the hallway that would take her further inside her fear and her need, and she smiled. "I'll come see you when I'm better," she said. "You and Susan."

"Yes," I said.

"We'll go to the beach," she said. "We'll spend all day. We'll swim and lie on a blanket and eat sandwiches from a cooler. We'll get ice cream. We'll go for a walk and find crabs and sand dollars. We'll get sunburned and you'll press your finger against my shoulder, it will stand out white and oh, I'll say, oh, it hurts."

"Yes," I said. "It will hurt."

She looked at me like she was flying, and then she went out the door.

I found my jeans and a sweatshirt and sneakers and put them on, and packed my things into my duffel bag that had been stuffed into the back of the closet for so long. I went down to the nurses' station, passing Terry Louise on the way. "Where are you going?" she said.

"To the beach."

"What?"

"Bye," I said, and I could feel her watching me all the way down the hall, so surprised she forgot how much she liked to have the last word.

"You can't leave," the day nurse said uncertainly.

"This is the open ward, *amiga*, I can walk out of here anytime I want."

"You aren't a voluntary patient, you have to have your doctor's signature."

I don't have a doctor anymore, I wanted to say, and then Tommy Gee was there looking pale and tense. He saw my bag.

"I'll sign for this patient."

"Did you find Rousseau?" I said.

"I talked to her." He looked past me down the hall. "She's gone."

I wasn't sure who he meant, Rousseau or Jane, but I nodded.

I walked down five flights of stairs to the lobby entrance doors, and stopped. I looked back across the open space, full of people with flowers, new babies, people sleeping on couches, people crying, people going home. Two women went past me, one with a new white cast on her arm, the other one saying, "Are you okay? Does it hurt?"

The hurt one bit her lip and shrugged. "It doesn't matter."

"Oh yes it does," I said. I walked to the door and thought *I will be Rita running in the grass* and took the first step out.

Think Like a Dinosaur

JAMES PATRICK KELLY

James Patrick Kelly is a past Nebula Award finalist whose highly praised short fiction has appeared in many best-of-the-year volumes, including past volumes of *Nebula Awards* stories. He has published four novels: *Freedom Beach*, with John Kessel; *Look into the Sun; Planet of Whispers;* and *Wildlife;* he has also written plays, poems, essays, and a planetarium show. His first short story collection, *Think Like a Dinosaur and Other Stories*, will be published by Golden Gryphon Press. He lives in New Hampshire with his wife, Pam Kelly, and their three teenagers.

About his novelette "Think Like a Dinosaur," a Nebula finalist that was honored with the 1996 Hugo Award for novelette, he writes:

"The origins of 'Think Like a Dinosaur' are various. It actually began back in the Cretaceous period with some grouchy notes I wrote to myself about the unexamined philosophical implications of the transporter in, yes, *St°r Tr°k*. They did not, however, suggest a story until 1994, when my friend John Kessel sparked a controversy with a revisionist reading of a certain SF classic. Suffice it to say that for a time, the working title of this story was 'The Cold Equation'—but then that was when it was going to be a short-short shocker. As I wrote, I realized I wanted it to be more than just a commentary on Tom Godwin's story.

"The science is based in part on Kip Thorne's excellent *Black Holes and Time Warps: Einstein's Outrageous Legacy* (W. W. Norton, 1993). A tough-minded critique from the Cambridge Science Fiction Writers Workshop helped me add some new variables to the equation. The title came last of all."

Kamala Shastri came back to this world as she had left it—naked. She tottered out of the assembler, trying to balance in Tuulen Station's delicate gravity. I caught her and bundled her into a robe with one motion, then eased her onto the float. Three years on another planet had transformed Kamala. She was leaner, more muscular. Her fingernails were now a couple of centimeters long and there were four parallel scars incised on her left cheek, perhaps some Gendian's idea of beautification. But what struck me most was the darting strangeness in her eyes. This place, so familiar to me, seemed almost to shock her. It was as if she doubted the walls and was skeptical of air. She had learned to think like an alien.

"Welcome back." The float's whisper rose to a *whoosh* as I walked it down the hallway.

She swallowed hard and I thought she might cry. Three years ago, she would have. Lots of migrators are devastated when they come out of the assembler; it's because there is no transition. A few seconds ago Kamala was on Gend, fourth planet of the star we call epsilon Leo, and now she was here in lunar orbit. She was almost home; her life's great adventure was over.

"Matthew?" she said.

"Michael." I couldn't help but be pleased that she remembered me. After all, she had changed my life.

I've guided maybe three hundred migrations—comings *and* goings—since I first came to Tuulen to study the dinos. Kamala Shastri's is the only quantum scan I've ever pirated. I doubt that the dinos care; I suspect this is a trespass they occasionally allow themselves. I know more about her—at least, as she was three years ago—than I know about myself. When the dinos sent her to Gend, she massed 50,391.72 grams and her red cell count was 4.81 million per mm^3. She could play the *nagasvaram,* a kind of bamboo flute. Her father came from Thana, near Bombay, and her favorite flavor of chewyfrute was watermelon and she'd had five lovers and when she was eleven she had wanted to be a gymnast but instead she had become a biomaterials engineer who at age twenty-nine had volunteered to go to the stars to learn how to grow artificial eyes. It took her two years to go through migrator training; she knew she could have backed out at any time, right up until the moment Silloin translated her into a superluminal signal. She understood what it meant to balance the equation.

I first met her on June 22, 2069. She shuttled over from Lunex's

L1 port and came through our airlock at promptly 10:15, a small, roundish woman with black hair parted in the middle and drawn tight against her skull. They had darkened her skin against epsilon Leo's UV; it was the deep blue-black of twilight. She was wearing a striped clingy and Velcro slippers to help her get around for the short time she'd be navigating our .2 micrograv.

"Welcome to Tuulen Station." I smiled and offered my hand. "My name is Michael." We shook. "I'm supposed to be a sapientologist but I also moonlight as the local guide."

"Guide?" She nodded distractedly. "Okay." She peered past me, as if expecting someone else.

"Oh, don't worry," I said, "the dinos are in their cages."

Her eyes got wide as she let her hand slip from mine. "You call the Hanen dinos?"

"Why not?" I laughed. "They call us babies. The weeps, among other things."

She shook her head in amazement. People who've never met a dino tended to romanticize them: the wise and noble reptiles who had mastered superluminal physics and introduced Earth to the wonders of galactic civilization. I doubt Kamala had ever seen a dino play poker or gobble down a screaming rabbit. And she had never argued with Linna, who still wasn't convinced that humans were psychologically ready to go to the stars.

"Have you eaten?" I gestured down the corridor toward the reception rooms.

"Yes . . . I mean, no." She didn't move. "I am not hungry."

"Let me guess. You're too nervous to eat. You're too nervous to talk, even. You wish I'd just shut up, pop you into the marble, and beam you out. Let's just get this part the hell over with, eh?"

"I don't mind the conversation, actually."

"There you go. Well, Kamala, it is my solemn duty to advise you that there are no peanut butter and jelly sandwiches on Gend. And no chicken vindaloo. What's my name again?"

"Michael?"

"See, you're not *that* nervous. Not one taco, or a single slice of eggplant pizza. This is your last chance to eat like a human."

"Okay." She did not actually smile—she was too busy being

brave—but a corner of her mouth twitched. "Actually, I would not mind a cup of tea."

"Now, tea they've got." She let me guide her toward reception room D; her slippers *snicked* at the Velcro carpet. "Of course, they brew it from lawn clippings."

"The Gendians don't keep lawns. They live underground."

"Refresh my memory." I kept my hand on her shoulder; beneath the clingy, her muscles were rigid. "Are they the ferrets or the things with the orange bumps?"

"They look nothing like ferrets."

We popped through the door bubble into reception D, a compact rectangular space with a scatter of low, unthreatening furniture. There was a kitchen station at one end, a closet with a vacuum toilet at the other. The ceiling was blue sky; the long wall showed a live view of the Charles River and the Boston skyline, baking in the late June sun. Kamala had just finished her doctorate at MIT.

I opaqued the door. She perched on the edge of a couch like a wren, ready to flit away.

While I was making her tea, my fingernail screen flashed. I answered it and a tiny Silloin came up in discreet mode. She didn't look at me; she was too busy watching arrays in the control room. =A problem,= her voice buzzed in my earstone, =most negligible, really. But we will have to void the last two from today's schedule. Save them at Lunex until first shift tomorrow. Can this one be kept for an hour?=

"Sure," I said. "Kamala, would you like to meet a Hanen?" I transferred Silloin to a dino-sized window on the wall. "Silloin, this is Kamala Shastri. Silloin is the one who actually runs things. I'm just the doorman."

Silloin looked through the window with her near eye, then swung around and peered at Kamala with her other. She was short for a dino, just over a meter tall, but she had an enormous head that teetered on her neck like a watermelon balancing on a grapefruit. She must have just oiled herself because her silver scales shone. =Kamala, you will accept my happiest intentions for you?= She raised her left hand, spreading the skinny digits to expose dark crescents of vestigial webbing.

"Of course, I . . ."

=And you will permit us to render you this translation?=

She straightened. "Yes."

=Have you questions?=

I'm sure she had several hundred, but at this point was probably too scared to ask. While she hesitated, I broke in. "Which came first, the lizard or the egg?"

Silloin ignored me. =It will be excellent for you to begin when?=

"She's just having a little tea," I said, handing her the cup. "I'll bring her along when she's done. Say an hour?"

Kamala squirmed on the couch. "No, really, it will not take me . . ."

Silloin showed us her teeth, several of which were as long as piano keys. =That would be most appropriate, Michael.= She closed; a gull flew through the space where her window had been.

"Why did you do that?" Kamala's voice was sharp.

"Because it says here that you have to wait your turn. You're not the only migrator we're sending this morning." This was a lie, of course; we had had to cut the schedule because Jodi Latchaw, the other sapientologist assigned to Tuulen, was at the University of Hipparchus presenting our paper on the Hanen concept of identity. "Don't worry, I'll make the time fly."

For a moment, we looked at each other. I could have laid down an hour's worth of patter; I'd done that often enough. Or I could have drawn her out on why she was going: no doubt she had a blind grandma or second cousin just waiting for her to bring home those artificial eyes, not to mention potential spin-offs which could well end tuberculosis, famine, and premature ejaculation, *blah, blah, blah.* Or I could have just left her alone in the room to read the wall. The trick was guessing how spooked she really was.

"Tell me a secret," I said.

"What?"

"A secret, you know, something no one else knows."

She stared as if I'd just fallen off Mars.

"Look, in a little while you're going someplace that's what . . . three hundred and ten light years away? You're scheduled to stay for three years. By the time you come back, I could easily be rich, famous, and elsewhere; we'll probably never see each other again. So what have you got to lose? I promise not to tell."

She leaned back on the couch, and settled the cup in her lap. "This is another test, right? After everything they have put me through, they still have not decided whether to send me."

"Oh no, in a couple of hours you'll be cracking nuts with ferrets in some dark Gendian burrow. This is just me, talking."

"You are crazy."

"Actually, I believe the technical term is logomaniac. It's from the Greek: *logos* meaning word, *mania* meaning two bits short of a byte. I just love to chat is all. Tell you what, I'll go first. If my secret isn't juicy enough, you don't have to tell me anything."

Her eyes were slits as she sipped her tea. I was fairly sure that whatever she was worrying about at the moment, it wasn't being swallowed by the big blue marble.

"I was brought up Catholic," I said, settling onto a chair in front of her. "I'm not anymore, but that's not the secret. My parents sent me to Mary, Mother of God High School; we called it Moogoo. It was run by a couple of old priests, Father Thomas and his wife, Mother Jennifer. Father Tom taught physics, which I got a 'D' in, mostly because he talked like he had walnuts in his mouth. Mother Jennifer taught theology and had all the warmth of a marble pew; her nickname was Mama Moogoo.

"One night, just two weeks before my graduation, Father Tom and Mama Moogoo went out in their Chevy Minimus for ice cream. On the way home, Mama Moogoo pushed a yellow light and got broadsided by an ambulance. Like I said, she was old, a hundred and twenty something; they should've lifted her license back in the '50s. She was killed instantly. Father Tom died in the hospital.

"Of course, we were all supposed to feel sorry for them and I guess I did a little, but I never really liked either of them and I resented the way their deaths had screwed things up for my class. So I was more annoyed than sorry, but then I also had this edge of guilt for being so uncharitable. Maybe you'd have to grow up Catholic to understand that. Anyway, the day after it happened they called an assembly in the gym and we were all there squirming on the bleachers and the cardinal himself telepresented a sermon. He kept trying to comfort us, like it had been our *parents* that had died. When I made a joke about it to the kid next to me, I got caught and spent the last week of my senior year with an in-school suspension."

Kamala had finished her tea. She slid the empty cup into one of the holders built into the table.

"Want some more?" I said.

She stirred restlessly. "Why are you telling me this?"

"It's part of the secret." I leaned forward in my chair. "See, my family lived down the street from Holy Spirit Cemetery and in order to get to the carryvan line on McKinley Avenue, I had to cut through. Now this happened a couple of days after I got in trouble at the assembly. It was around midnight and I was coming home from a graduation party where I had taken a couple of pokes of insight, so I was feeling sly as a philosopher-king. As I walked through the cemetery, I stumbled across two dirt mounds right next to each other. At first I thought they were flower beds, then I saw the wooden crosses. Fresh graves: here lies Father Tom and Mama Moogoo. There wasn't much to the crosses: they were basically just stakes with crosspieces, painted white and hammered into the ground. The names were hand printed on them. The way I figure it, they were there to mark the graves until the stones got delivered. I didn't need any insight to recognize a once in a lifetime opportunity. If I switched them, what were the chances anyone was going to notice? It was no problem sliding them out of their holes. I smoothed the dirt with my hands and then ran like hell."

Until that moment, she'd seemed bemused by my story and slightly condescending toward me. Now there was a glint of alarm in her eyes. "That was a terrible thing to do," she said.

"Absolutely," I said, "although the dinos think that the whole idea of planting bodies in graveyards and marking them with carved rocks is weepy. They say there is no identity in dead· meat, so why get so sentimental about it? Linna keeps asking how come we don't put markers over our shit. But that's not the secret. See, it'd been a warmish night in the middle of June, only as I ran, the air turned cold. Freezing, I could see my breath. And my shoes got heavier and heavier, like they had turned to stone. As I got closer to the back gate, it felt like I was fighting a strong wind, except my clothes weren't flapping. I slowed to a walk. I know I could have pushed through, but my heart was thumping and then I heard this whispery seashell noise and I panicked. So the secret is I'm a coward. I switched the crosses back and I never went near that cemetery again. As a matter of fact," I nodded at the walls of reception room D on Tuulen Station, "when I grew up, I got about as far away from it as I could."

She stared as I settled back in my chair. "True story," I said and raised my right hand. She seemed so astonished that I started laughing. A smile bloomed on her dark face and suddenly she was giggling too. It was a soft, liquid sound, like a brook bubbling over smooth stones; it made me laugh even harder. Her lips were full and her teeth were very white.

"Your turn," I said, finally.

"Oh, no, I could not." She waved me off. "I don't have anything so good. . . ." She paused, then frowned. "You have told that before?"

"Once," I said. "To the Hanen, during the psych screening for this job. Only I didn't tell them the last part. I know how dinos think, so I ended it when I switched the crosses. The rest is baby stuff." I waggled a finger at her. "Don't forget, you promised to keep my secret."

"Did I?"

"Tell me about when you were young. Where did you grow up?"

"Toronto." She glanced at me, appraisingly. "There *was* something, but not funny. Sad."

I nodded encouragement and changed the wall to Toronto's skyline dominated by the CN Tower, Toronto-Dominion Centre, Commerce Court, and the King's Needle.

She twisted to take in the view and spoke over her shoulder. "When I was ten we moved to an apartment, right downtown on Bloor Street so my mother could be close to work." She pointed at the wall and turned back to face me. "She is an accountant, my father wrote wallpaper for Imagineering. It was a huge building; it seemed as if we were always getting into the elevator with ten neighbors we never knew we had. I was coming home from school one day when an old woman stopped me in the lobby. 'Little girl,' she said, 'how would you like to earn ten dollars?' My parents had warned me not to talk to strangers but she obviously was a resident. Besides, she had an ancient pair of exolegs strapped on, so I knew I could outrun her if I needed to. She asked me to go to the store for her, handed me a grocery list and a cash card, and said I should bring everything up to her apartment, 10W. I should have been more suspicious because all the downtown groceries deliver but, as I soon found out, all she really wanted was someone to talk to her. And she was willing to pay for it, usually five or ten dollars, depending on how long I stayed. Soon I was stopping by almost every day after school. I think my parents would have made me stop if they had known; they were very strict. They would not have liked me taking her money. But neither of them got home until after six, so it was my secret to keep."

"Who was she?" I said. "What did you talk about?"

"Her name was Margaret Ase. She was ninety-seven years old and I think she had been some kind of counselor. Her husband and her daughter had both died and she was alone. I didn't find out much about her; she made me do most of the talking. She asked me about my friends and what I was learning in school and my family. Things like that. . . ."

Her voice trailed off as my fingernail started to flash. I answered it. =Michael, I am pleased to call you to here.= Silloin buzzed in my ear. She was almost twenty minutes ahead of schedule.

"See, I told you we'd make the time fly." I stood; Kamala's eyes got very wide. "I'm ready if you are."

I offered her my hand. She took it and let me help her up. She wavered for a moment and I sensed just how fragile her resolve was. I put my hand around her waist and steered her into the corridor. In the micrograv of Tuulen Station, she already felt as insubstantial as a memory. "So tell me, what happened that was so sad?"

At first I thought she hadn't heard. She shuffled along, said nothing.

"Hey, don't keep me in suspense here, Kamala," I said. "You have to finish the story."

"No," she said. "I don't think I do."

I didn't take this personally. My only real interest in the conversation had been to distract her. If she refused to be distracted, that was her choice. Some migrators kept talking right up to the moment they slid into the big blue marble, but lots of them went quiet just before. They turned inward. Maybe in her mind she was already on Gend, blinking in the hard white light.

We arrived at the scan center, the largest space on Tuulen Station. Immediately in front of us was the marble, containment for the quantum nondemolition sensor array—QNSA for the acronymically inclined. It was the milky blue of glacial ice and big as two elephants. The upper hemisphere was raised and the scanning table protruded like a shiny gray tongue. Kamala approached the marble and touched her reflection, which writhed across its polished surface. To the right was a padded bench, the fogger, and a toilet. I looked left, through the control room window. Silloin stood watching us, her impossible head cocked to one side.

=She is docile?= She buzzed in my earstone.

I held up crossed fingers.

=Welcome, Kamala Shastri.= Silloin's voice came over the speakers with a soothing hush. =You are ready to open your translation?=

Kamala bowed to the window. "This is where I take my clothes off?"

=If you would be so convenient.=

She brushed past me to the bench. Apparently I had ceased to exist; this was between her and the dino now. She undressed quickly, folding her clingy into a neat bundle, tucking her slippers beneath the bench. Out of the corner of my eye, I could see tiny feet, heavy thighs, and the beautiful, dark smooth skin of her back. She stepped into the fogger and closed the door.

"Ready," she called.

From the control room, Silloin closed circuits which filled the fogger with a dense cloud of nanolenses. The nano stuck to Kamala and deployed, coating the surface of her body. As she breathed them, they passed from her lungs into her bloodstream. She only coughed twice; she had been well trained. When the eight minutes were up, Silloin cleared the air in the fogger and she emerged. Still ignoring me, she again faced the control room.

=Now you must arrange yourself on the scanning table,= said Silloin, =and enable Michael to fix you.=

She crossed to the marble without hesitation, climbed the gantry beside it, eased onto the table, and lay back.

I followed her up. "Sure you won't tell me the rest of the secret?"

She stared at the ceiling, unblinking.

"Okay then." I took the canister and a sparker out of my hip pouch. "This is going to happen just like you've practiced it." I used the canister to respray the bottoms of her feet with nano. I watched her belly rise and fall, rise and fall. She was deep into her breathing exercise. "Remember, no skipping rope or whistling while you're in the scanner."

She did not answer. "Deep breath now," I said and touched a sparker to her big toe. There was a brief crackle as the nano on her skin wove into a net and stiffened, locking her in place. "Bark at the ferrets for me." I picked up my equipment, climbed down the gantry, and wheeled it back to the wall.

With a low whine, the big blue marble retracted its tongue. I watched the upper hemisphere close, swallowing Kamala Shastri, then joined Silloin in the control room.

I'm not of the school who thinks the dinos stink, another reason I got assigned to study them up close. Parikkal, for example, has no smell at all that I can tell. Normally Silloin had the faint but not un-pleasant smell of stale wine. When she was under stress, however, her scent became vinegary and biting. It must have been a wild morning for her. Breathing through my mouth, I settled onto the stool at my station.

She was working quickly, now that the marble was sealed. Even with all their training, migrators tend to get claustrophobic fast. After all, they're lying in the dark, in nanobondage, waiting to be translated. Waiting. The simulator at the Singapore training center makes a noise while it's emulating a scan. Most compare it to a light rain pattering against the marble; for some, it's low-volume radio static. As long as they hear the patter, the migrators think they're safe. We reproduce it for them while they're in our marble, even though scanning takes about three seconds and is utterly silent. From my vantage I could see that the sagittal, axial, and coronal windows had stopped blinking, indicating full data capture. Silloin was skirring busily to herself; her comm didn't bother to interpret. Wasn't saying anything baby Michael needed to know, obviously. Her head bobbed as she monitored the enormous spread of readouts; her claws clicked against touch screens that glowed orange and yellow.

At my station, there was only a migration status screen—and a white button.

I wasn't lying when I said I was just the doorman. My field is sapientology, not quantum physics. Whatever went wrong with Kamala's migration that morning, there was nothing *I* could have done. The dinos tell me that the quantum nondemolition sensor array is able to circumvent Heisenberg's Uncertainty Principle by measuring space-time's most crogglingly small quantities without collapsing the wave/particle duality. How small? They say that no one can ever "see" anything that's only 1.62×10^{-33} centimeters long, because at that size, space and time come apart. Time ceases to exist and space becomes a random probabilistic foam, sort of like quantum spit. We humans call this the Planck-Wheeler length. There's a Planck-Wheeler time, too: 10^{-45} of a second. If something happens and something else happens and the two events are separated by an interval of a mere 10^{-45} of a second, it is impossible to say which came first. It was all dino to me—and that's just the scanning. The Hanen use different tech to create artificial wormholes, hold them open with electromagnetic vacuum fluctuations, pass the superluminal signal through, and then assemble the migrator from elementary particles at the destination.

On my status screen I could see that the signal which mapped Kamala Shastri had already been compressed and burst through the wormhole. All that we had to wait for was for Gend to confirm acquisition. Once they officially told us that they had her, it would be my job to balance the equation.

Pitter-patter, pitter-pat.

Some Hanen technologies are so powerful that they can alter reality itself. Wormholes could be used by some time-traveling fanatic to corrupt history; the scanner/assembler could be used to create a billion Silloins—or Michael Burrs. Pristine reality, unpolluted by such anomalies, has what the dinos call harmony. Before any sapients get to join the galactic club, they must prove total commitment to preserving harmony.

Since I had come to Tuulen to study the dinos, I had pressed the white button over two hundred times. It was what I had to do in order to keep my assignment. Pressing it sent a killing pulse of ionizing radiation through the cerebral cortex of the migrator's duplicated, and therefore unnecessary, body. No brain, no pain; death followed within seconds. Yes, the first few times I'd balanced the equation had been traumatic. It was still . . . unpleasant. But this was the price of a ticket to the stars. If certain unusual people like Kamala Shastri had decided that price was reasonable, it was their choice, not mine.

=This is not a happy result, Michael.= Silloin spoke to me for the first time since I'd entered the control room. =Discrepancies are unfolding.= On my status screen I watched as the error-checking routines started turning up hits.

"Is the problem here?" I felt a knot twist suddenly inside me. "Or there?" If our original scan checked out, then all Silloin would have to do is send it to Gend again.

There was a long, infuriating silence. Silloin concentrated on part of her board as if it showed her firstborn hatchling chipping out of its egg. The respirator between her shoulders had ballooned to twice its normal size. My screen showed that Kamala had been in the marble for four minutes plus.

=It may be fortunate to recalibrate the scanner and begin over.=

"*Shit.*" I slammed my hand against the wall, felt the pain tingle to my elbow. "I thought you had it fixed." When error-checking turned up problems, the solution was almost always to retransmit. "You're sure, Silloin? Because this one was right on the edge when I tucked her in."

Silloin gave me a dismissive sneeze and slapped at the error readouts with her bony little hand, as if to knock them back to normal. Like Linna and the other dinos, she had little patience with what she regarded as our weepy fears of migration. However, unlike Linna, she was convinced that someday, after we had used Hanen technologies long enough, we would learn to think like dinos. Maybe she's right. Maybe when we've been squirting through wormholes for hundreds of years, we'll cheerfully discard our redundant bodies. When the dinos and other sapients migrate, the redundants zap themselves—very harmonious. They tried it with humans but it didn't always work. That's why I'm here. =The need is most clear. It will prolong about thirty minutes,= she said.

Kamala had been alone in the dark for almost six minutes, longer than any migrator I'd ever guided. "Let me hear what's going on in the marble."

The control room filled with the sound of Kamala screaming. It didn't sound human to me—more like the shriek of tires skidding toward a crash.

"We've got to get her out of there," I said.

=That is baby thinking, Michael.=

"So she's a baby, damn it." I knew that bringing migrators out of the marble was big trouble. I could have asked Silloin to turn the speakers off and sat there while Kamala suffered. It was my decision.

"Don't open the marble until I get the gantry in place." I ran for the door. "And keep the sound effects going."

At the first crack of light, she howled. The upper hemisphere seemed to lift in slow motion; inside the marble she bucked against the nano. Just when I was sure it was impossible that she could scream any louder, she did. We had accomplished something extraordinary, Silloin and I; we had stripped the brave biomaterials engineer away completely, leaving in her place a terrified animal.

"Kamala, it's me. Michael."

Her frantic screams cohered into words. "Stop . . . *don't* . . . oh my god, someone *help!*" If I could have, I would've jumped into the marble to release her, but the sensor array is fragile and I wasn't going to risk causing any more problems with it. We both had to wait until the upper hemisphere swung fully open and the scanning table offered poor Kamala to me.

"It's okay. Nothing's going to happen, all right? We're bringing you out, that's all. Everything's all right."

When I released her with the sparker, she flew at me. We pitched back and almost toppled down the steps. Her grip was so tight I couldn't breathe.

"Don't *kill* me, don't, *please*, don't."

I rolled on top of her. "Kamala!" I wriggled one arm free and used it to pry myself from her. I scrabbled sideways to the top step. She lurched clumsily in the microgravity and swung at me; her fingernails raked across the back of my hand, leaving bloody welts. "Kamala, stop!" It was all I could do not to strike back at her. I retreated down the steps.

"You bastard. What are you assholes trying to do to me?" She drew several shuddering breaths and began to sob.

"The scan got corrupted somehow. Silloin is working on it."

=The difficulty is obscure,= said Silloin from the control room.

"But that's not your problem." I backed toward the bench.

"They lied," she mumbled and seemed to fold in upon herself as if she were just skin, no flesh or bones. "They said I wouldn't feel anything and . . . do you know what it's like . . . it's . . ."

I fumbled for her clingy. "Look, here are your clothes. Why don't you get dressed? We'll get you out of here."

"You bastard," she repeated, but her voice was empty.

She let me coax her down off the gantry. I counted nubs on the wall while she fumbled back into her clingy. They were the size of the old dimes my grandfather used to hoard and they glowed with a soft golden bioluminescence. I was up to forty-seven before she was dressed and ready to return to reception D.

Where before she had perched expectantly at the edge of the couch, now she slumped back against it. "So what now?" she said.

"I don't know." I went to the kitchen station and took the carafe from the distiller. "What now, Silloin?" I poured water over the back of my hand to wash the blood off. It stung. My earstone was silent. "I guess we wait," I said finally.

"For what?"

"For her to fix . . ."

"I'm not going back in there."

I decided to let that pass. It was probably too soon to argue with her about it, although once Silloin recalibrated the scanner, she'd have very little time to change her mind. "You want something from the kitchen? Another cup of tea, maybe?"

"How about a gin and tonic—hold the tonic?" She rubbed beneath her eyes. "Or a couple of hundred milliliters of serentol?"

I tried to pretend she'd made a joke. "You know the dinos won't let us open the bar for migrators. The scanner might misread your brain chemistry and your visit to Gend would be nothing but a three-year drunk."

"Don't you under*stand?*" She was right back at the edge of hysteria. "I am not *going!*" I didn't really blame her for the way she was acting but, at that moment, all I wanted was to get rid of Kamala Shastri. I didn't care if she went on to Gend or back to Lunex or over the rainbow to Oz, just as long as I didn't have to be in the same room with this miserable creature who was trying to make me feel guilty about an accident I had nothing to do with.

"I thought I could do it." She clamped hands to her ears as if to keep from hearing her own despair. "I wasted the last two years convincing myself that I could just lie there and not think and then suddenly I'd be far away. I was going someplace wonderful and strange." She made a strangled sound and let her hands drop into her lap. "I was going to help people see."

"You did it, Kamala. You did everything we asked."

She shook her head. "I couldn't *not* think. That was the problem. And then there she was, trying to touch me. In the dark. I had not thought of her since . . ." She shivered. "It's your fault for reminding me."

"Your secret friend," I said.

"Friend?" Kamala seemed puzzled by the word. "No, I wouldn't say she was a friend. I was always a little bit scared of her, because I was never quite sure of what she wanted from me." She paused. "One day I went up to 10W after school. She was in her chair, staring down at Bloor Street. Her back was to me. I said, 'Hi, Ms. Ase.' I was going to show her a genie I had written, only she didn't say anything. I came around. Her skin was the color of ashes. I took her hand. It was like picking up something plastic. She was stiff, hard—not a person anymore. She had become a thing, like a feather or a bone. I ran; I had to get out of there. I went up to our apartment and I hid from her."

She squinted, as if observing—judging—her younger self through the lens of time. "I think I understand now what she wanted. I think she knew she was dying; she probably wanted me there with her at the end, or at least to find her body afterward and report it. Only I could *not*. If I told anyone she was dead, my parents would find out about us. Maybe people would suspect me of doing something to her—I don't know. I could have called security but I was only ten; I was afraid somehow they might trace me. A couple of weeks went by and still nobody had found her. By then it was too late to say anything. Everyone would have blamed me for keeping quiet for so long. At night I imagined her turning black and rotting into her chair like a banana. It made me sick; I couldn't sleep or eat. They had to put me in the hospital, because I had touched her. Touched *death*."

=Michael,= Silloin whispered, without any warning flash. =An impossibility has formed.=

"As soon as I was out of that building, I started to get better. Then they found her. After I came home, I worked hard to forget Ms. Ase. And I did, almost." Kamala wrapped her arms around herself. "But just now she was with me again, inside the marble. . . . I couldn't see her but somehow I knew she was reaching for me."

=Michael, Parikkal is here with Linna.=

"Don't you see?" She gave a bitter laugh. "How can I go to Gend? I'm *hallucinating.*"

=It has broken the harmony. Join us alone.=

I was tempted to swat at the annoying buzz in my ear.

"You know, I've never told anyone about her before."

"Well, maybe some good has come of this after all." I patted her on the knee. "Excuse me for a minute?" She seemed surprised that I would leave. I slipped into the hall and hardened the door bubble, sealing her in.

"What impossibility?" I said, heading for the control room.

=She is pleased to reopen the scanner?=

"Not pleased at all. More like scared shitless."

=This is Parikkal.= My earstone translated his skirring with a sizzling edge, like bacon frying. =The confusion was made elsewhere. No mishap can be connected to our station.=

I pushed through the bubble into the scan center. I could see the three dinos through the control window. Their heads were bobbing furiously. "Tell me," I said.

=Our communications with Gend were marred by a transient falsehood,= said Silloin. =Kamala Shastri has been received there and reconstructed.=

"She migrated?" I felt the deck shifting beneath my feet. "What about the one we've got here?"

=The simplicity is to load the redundant into the scanner and finalize. . . . =

"I've got news for you. She's not going anywhere near that marble."

=Her equation is not in balance.= This was Linna, speaking for the first time. Linna was not exactly in charge of Tuulen Station; she was more like a senior partner. Parikkal and Silloin had overruled her before—at least I thought they had.

"What do you expect me to do? Wring her neck?"

There was a moment's silence—which was not as unnerving as watching them eye me through the window, their heads now perfectly still.

"No," I said.

The dinos were skirring at each other; their heads wove and dipped. At first they cut me cold and the comm was silent, but suddenly their debate crackled through my earstone.

=This is just as I have been telling,= said Linna. =These beings have no realization of harmony. It is wrongful to further unleash them on the many worlds.=

=You may have reason,= said Parikkal. =But that is a later discussion. The need is for the equation to be balanced.=

=There is no time. We will have to discard the redundant ourselves.= Silloin bared her long brown teeth. It would take her maybe five seconds to rip Kamala's throat out. And even though Silloin was the dino most sympathetic to us, I had no doubt she would enjoy the kill.

=I will argue that we adjourn human migration until this world has been rethought,= said Linna.

This was the typical dino condescension. Even though they appeared to be arguing with each other, they were actually speaking to me, laying the situation out so that even the baby sapient would understand. They were informing me that I was jeopardizing the future of humanity in space. That the Kamala in reception D was dead whether I quit or not. That the equation had to be balanced and it had to be now.

"Wait," I said. "Maybe I can coax her back into the scanner." I had to get away from them. I pulled my earstone out and slid it into my pocket. I was in such a hurry to escape that I stumbled as I left the scan center and had to catch myself in the hallway. I stood there for a second, staring at the hand pressed against the bulkhead. I seemed to see the splayed fingers through the wrong end of a telescope. I was far away from myself.

She had curled into herself on the couch, arms clutching knees to her chest, as if trying to shrink so that nobody would notice her.

"We're all set," I said briskly. "You'll be in the marble for less than a minute, guaranteed."

"*No*, Michael."

I could actually feel myself receding from Tuulen Station. "Kamala, you're throwing away a huge part of your life."

"It is my right." Her eyes were shiny.

No, it wasn't. She was redundant; she had no rights. What had she said about the dead old lady? She had become a thing, like a bone.

"Okay, then." I jabbed at her shoulder with a stiff forefinger. "Let's go."

She recoiled. "Go where?"

"Back to Lunex. I'm holding the shuttle for you. It just dropped off my afternoon list; I should be helping them settle in, instead of having to deal with you."

She unfolded herself slowly.

"Come on." I jerked her roughly to her feet. "The dinos want you off Tuulen as soon as possible and so do I." I was so distant, I couldn't see Kamala Shastri anymore.

She nodded and let me march her to the bubble door.

"And if we meet anyone in the hall, keep your mouth shut."

"You're being so mean." Her whisper was thick.

"You're being such a baby."

When the inner door glided open, she realized immediately that there was no umbilical to the shuttle. She tried to twist out of my grip but I put my shoulder into her, hard. She flew across the airlock, slammed against the outer door, and caromed onto her back. As I punched the switch to close the door, I came back to myself. *I* was doing this terrible thing—me, Michael Burr. I couldn't help myself: I giggled. When I last saw her, Kamala was scrabbling across the deck toward me but she was too late. I was surprised that she wasn't screaming again; all I heard was her ferocious breathing.

As soon as the inner door sealed, I opened the outer door. After all, how many ways are there to kill someone on a space station? There were no guns. Maybe someone else could have stabbed or strangled her, but not me. Poison how? Besides, I wasn't thinking, I had been trying desperately not to think of what I was doing. I was a sapiento-logist, not a doctor. I always thought that exposure to space meant instantaneous death. Explosive decompression or something like. I didn't want her to suffer. I was trying to make it quick. Painless.

I heard the whoosh of escaping air and thought that was it; the body had been ejected into space. I had actually turned away when thumping started, frantic, like the beat of a racing heart. She must have found something to hold onto. *Thump, thump, thump!* It was too much. I sagged against the inner door—*thump, thump*—slid down it, laughing. Turns out that if you empty the lungs, it is possible to survive exposure to space for at least a minute, maybe two. I thought it was funny. *Thump!* Hilarious, actually. I had tried my best for her—risked my career—and this was how she repaid me? As I laid my cheek against the door, the *thumps* started to weaken. There were just a few centimeters between us, the difference between life and death. Now she knew all about balancing the equation. I was laughing so hard I could scarcely breathe. Just like the meat behind the door. Die already, you weepy bitch!

I don't know how long it took. The *thumping* slowed. Stopped. And then I was a hero. I had preserved harmony, kept our link to the stars open. I chuckled with pride; I could think like a dinosaur.

I popped through the bubble door into reception D. "It's time to board the shuttle."

Kamala had changed into a clingy and Velcro slippers. There were at least ten windows open on the wall; the room filled with the murmur of talking heads. Friends and relatives had to be notified; their loved one had returned, safe and sound. "I have to go," she said to the wall. "I will call you when I land."

She gave me a smile that seemed stiff from disuse. "I want to thank you again, Michael." I wondered how long it took migrators to get used to being human. "You were such a help and I was such a . . . I was not myself." She glanced around the room one last time and then shivered. "I was really scared."

"You were."

She shook her head. "Was it that bad?"

I shrugged and led her out into the hall.

"I feel so silly now. I mean, I was in the marble for less than a minute and then—" she snapped her fingers—"there I was on Gend, just like you said." She brushed up against me as we walked; her body was hard under the clingy. "Anyway, I am glad we got this chance to talk. I really *was* going to look you up when I got back. I certainly did not expect to see you here."

"I decided to stay on." The inner door to the airlock glided open. "It's a job that grows on you." The umbilical shivered as the pressure between Tuulen Station and the shuttle equalized.

"You have got migrators waiting," she said.

"Two."

"I envy them." She turned to me. "Have *you* ever thought about going to the stars?"

"No," I said.

Kamala put her hand to my face. "It changes everything." I could feel the prick of her long nails—claws, really. For a moment I thought she meant to scar my cheek the way she had been scarred.

"I know," I said.

In Memoriam: John Brunner and Roger Zelazny

IAN WATSON

JACK DANN

JACK C. HALDEMAN II

In 1995, science fiction lost two of the most influential and important authors who ever graced the genre with their writing, intelligence, and wide learning. Any death in science fiction's closely knit community of writers is akin to a death in the family; the comparatively early passing of these two gifted and acclaimed authors makes their losses all the more painful.

John Brunner was one of the finest and most erudite writers of science fiction to come out of Britain. Among his honors were the British Fantasy Award, the Hugo Award, the British Science Fiction Association Award, the Prix Apollo, and the Cometa d'Argento (given for science fiction published in Italy). It is a measure of his talent to say that he deserved even more honors than that. He published his first novel, *Galactic Storm*, at the age of seventeen, and then went on to write a number of literate science fiction adventures, among them *Threshold of Eternity*, *Catch a Falling Star*, *Sanctuary in the Sky*, *Meeting at Infinity*, *Times Without Number*, *To Conquer Chaos*, and *The Rites of Ohe*. With the Hugo Award–winning *Stand on Zanzibar*, published in 1968, Brunner established himself as one of the most original and important writers of serious science fiction; this novel was followed by *The Jagged Orbit*, *The Sheep Look Up*, and *The Shockwave Rider*. Along with these dystopian works, the versatile Brunner continued to publish entertainments such as *Total Eclipse*, *The Dramaturges of Yan*, and *The Crucible of Time*, as well as several short-story collections, including *The Book of John Brunner* and *The Best of John Brunner* (edited by Joe Haldeman).

About his own writing, John Brunner once wrote:

"For me, the essence both of science fiction and of the necessity for it can be summed up by quoting the opening sentence of L. P. Hartley's *The Go-between:* 'The past is a foreign country; they do things differently there.' Given that we are all being deported willy-nilly towards that foreign country, the future, where we shall ultimately die, I'd rather make the journey as a tourist with no matter how fallible a Baedeker, than be deported as a refugee. . . .

"SF, like all printed fiction, belongs to the past. . . . But even metaphors drawn from an obsolete future can be invaluable in preparing us for eventual reality, whatever form—out of an infinite number—it may actually take."

John Brunner's life and work are recalled here by his colleague and friend Ian Watson, himself one of Britain's most inventive writers of science fiction.

Roger Zelazny published his first science fiction story in 1962; within only a few years, he had become one of the genre's most admired and praised writers. Along with the Americans Samuel R. Delany and Harlan Ellison and the British writers J. G. Ballard, Brian Aldiss, and Michael Moorcock, Zelazny was regarded as one of the pioneering figures of the New Wave, a group of writers who felt that science fiction should aspire to the highest literary standards. When the first Nebula Awards were given, for works published in 1965, Zelazny won two of them, one for his novella "He Who Shapes" and the other for his novelette "The Doors of His Face, the Lamps of His Mouth." In 1966, he won the Hugo Award for . . . *And Call Me Conrad,* the title under which his novel *This Immortal* was published in *The Magazine of Fantasy & Science Fiction.* His body of work contains some of the most poetic writing to be found in science fiction; among his most important novels are *This Immortal, The Dream Master, Lord of Light, Isle of the Dead,* and the nine volumes of his Amber series. He was also a master of the shorter form, winning awards for his stories "Home Is the Hangman," "Twenty-Four Views of Mount Fuji, by Hokusai," "Unicorn Variations," and "Permafrost." The year before his death, his novel *A Night in the Lonesome October* was a finalist for the 1994 Nebula. He was adept at serious work and lighter, humorous stories; he brought to both his science fiction and his fantasy a gift for creating memorable characters and his love of literature.

He could also, in his quiet way, be extremely funny. I was a witness to one example of his wit, when George Zebrowski was lamenting the disadvantages to a writer of having a last name beginning with z—being at the end of the last row on the bottom shelf of any bookstore's science fiction section, and thus presumably harder for readers to find. "But, George," Roger replied, "the readers must go down on their knees before us!"

As a person, Roger Zelazny endeared himself to everyone who knew him. His friend and fellow writer George R. R. Martin said about him: "Roger was as kind and generous as any man I have ever known. He was the best kind of company. Often quiet, but always interesting. Sometimes it seemed that he had read every book ever printed. He knew something about everything and everything about some things, but he never used his knowledge to impress or intimidate. In an age when everyone is a specialist, Roger was the last Renaissance man, fascinated by the world and all that's in it, capable of talking about Doc Savage and Proust with equal expertise and enthusiasm."

Roger Zelazny is remembered here by two colleagues and friends, Jack Dann and Jack C. Haldeman II. Jack Dann is the editor of over twenty anthologies and the author of *Starhiker, Timetipping, Junction,* and *The Man Who Melted;* his latest book is the critically acclaimed *The Memory Cathedral,* a novel about Leonardo da Vinci. Jack C. Haldeman II is the author of *Vector Analysis, There Is No Darkness* (with Joe Haldeman), *The Fall of Winter,* and *High Steel* (with Jack Dann). His short fiction has appeared in many magazines and anthologies.

At the Wrong End of Time: An Appreciation of John Brunner (1934–1995)
IAN WATSON

"And when he was come into his own country [they] said, Whence hath this man this wisdom, and these mighty works? . . . And they were offended in him. But [he] said unto them, A prophet is not without honour, save in his own country. . . ."

John Brunner died on August 25, 1995, as the result of a massive stroke that he had suffered the previous day, after arriving at the World Science Fiction Convention in Glasgow. He was sixty years old, and by this stage his books were almost entirely out of print in his native language, in Britain and in America, too.

A prophet? Well, if Arthur Clarke can quite rightly claim this status because of his prediction of the technology of communication satellites, it was John Brunner who predicted the Internet and computer viruses over twenty years ago in *The Shockwave Rider*. Nor was this all, by any means.

A prophet of doom? Certainly so, in his masterpiece about overpopulation, *Stand on Zanzibar*, and in his jeremiad about environmental pollution, *The Sheep Look Up*. But principally he was a prophet of sanity, of the belief that reason and goodwill can see us through; and he did his utmost to foster these qualities not only in his books but in his life, by furthering international dialogue, by campaigning against militarism and the evil of nuclear weapons, by funding out of his own scant money a literary prize to promote racial harmony in honor of Martin Luther King, Jr. He stamped his correspondence with the warning "Where books are burned, people will soon be burned too." Fluent in French, German, and Italian, John translated (beautifully) such novels as Gérard Klein's *The Overlords of War* so that European sf writers would have some voice in the Anglo-Saxon world that dominates sf internationally.

John wasn't Jesus, by any means; though he did feel in his later years that life was crucifying him, both professionally and personally.

He could be a bit pompous. Appearing at public events in an eyeboggling jacket or buzzing around Europe in his beloved Triumph Stag sports convertible, he somewhat resembled the comic royal elephant King Babar beloved of French children. Once when I was going through a rough patch, he grandly and generously offered to let me "tap him for a thousand" if I ever needed it. Later, when John himself was in stormy waters, I tried my best to get him a grant from the Royal Literary Fund, which was established in Britain way back in the eighteenth century to help out authors. A minor formality is to write a letter indicating that you are broke. John took the occasion to dispatch a detailed explanation which commenced (quoting from memory), "I have had unusual expenses recently. Because of the death of my beloved Marjorie I was obliged to fly to Bangkok to seek a new consort, unsuccessfully alas. . . ." The Royal Literary Fund did not give him anything.

John came to be perceived by publishers as difficult to deal with, and with some justification. Yet, equally, the publishing industry had not dealt very well by him. Singularly precocious, he collected his first rejection slip at the age of thirteen (because the British edition of *Astounding* didn't publish original material), sold his first paperback sf novel in Britain while still at school, and quickly left school, which he loathed, because—as he told his headmaster—it was interfering with his education. By the age of nineteen he had already broken into the American magazine market.

Compulsory military service wasted the next two years of his life, giving him a loathing of the military mind and the whole paraphernalia of war. Despite a flood of story sales to magazines, his subsequent effort to freelance in London on an average income of four pounds a week foundered, though he did "learn an awful lot of ways of cooking potatoes," prelude to a lifelong sideline in gastronomy. A stint at the Industrial Diamond Information Bureau and two years as an editor with the Books for Pleasure group culminated in his first novel sale to America, in 1958.

Thereafter he was up and running, and American publishers soaked up his output, largely of intelligent, well-paced space operas.

Upgrading himself to "mighty works" of the first rank was not so easy. His innovative atmospheric novel about a South American country under an ambiguously benevolent dictatorship, *The Squares of the City*—modeled on a classic chess game—was completed in 1960 but not published until five years later. *Stand on Zanzibar,* which was perhaps the longest sf novel anyone had so far written (and with a scope and vision to match its size), was the first novel by any Briton to win the Hugo Award, in 1968. But this was only after Penguin Books, which had contracted for the book, rejected it, and it was sold instead to Doubleday for a derisive minimal $1,500. A decade and a half later, when a feeding frenzy for big-scope sf was galvanizing publishers, *Stand on Zanzibar* would have been attracting bids of $1.5 million. To John, the deserved honor, a Hugo, and acclaim for "the most important science fiction novel of the last decade"; but not exactly the cash.

John wasn't exclusively a science fiction writer, by any means. He was a witty poet. He wrote the anthem of the British Campaign for Nuclear Disarmament, "Do You Hear the H-bomb's Thunder?," and one of his folk songs was recorded by Pete Seeger (though his novel about antinuclear protest, *The Days of March,* only appeared from a private press many years after it would have been urgently topical; such is the wisdom of commercial publishing). His fix-up fantasy novel of 1971, *The Traveller in Black*, expanded in 1987 as *The Compleat Traveller in Black*, was something entirely different from the Tolkien clones infesting the shelves. His mystery novels of the late sixties and early seventies featuring the socially conscious black detective Curfew would have been snapped up for a TV series nowadays, when, in Britain at least, producers fall over themselves to showcase the exploits of sleuths created by Colin Dexter, P. D. James, W. J. Burley, and socially conscious Ruth Rendell. However, Max Curfew was ahead of his time; and time moved on.

John devoted a sizable chunk of the late seventies and early eighties to a meticulously researched and ambitious historical saga set on the Mississippi in the last century, in a bid to make his fortune. Delayed by ill health, then overtaken by events (such as George Martin's best-selling *Fevre Dream*, intersecting steamboats with vampires), John's own *Steamboats on the River* fell flat on publication in 1983, with no American paperback edition and no British edition whatsoever. An sf thriller by John from 1971 is entitled *The Wrong End of Time,* and there seems to be a sad moral in this title. John was ahead of his time, to begin with, and he paid a price. Then, like elastic, time twanged—and he missed not only his steamboat but even, in his last years, much hope of being published at all. By then corporate accountants were calling the tune. Books as such weren't being bought, but career prospects were. John was perceived as having completed his career, and his out-of-print backlist was not located in any one place but was scattered all over; thus he was not an investment.

It's almost invidious to single out great titles when some of his nominally minor works are so fluent and moving and imaginative. I think at random of *The Stone That Never Came Down*, from 1973, a gritty, realistic tale about the imminent collapse of Europe in which a perception-enhancing virus unleashes a beneficial pandemic, converting a bombastic Mussolini type into an authentic political savior so that hardened newsmen weep to hear his proposals, and all men will be brothers. (I'll leave this in male-speak, since men usually do most of the fighting.)

Or, from the very same year, *The Dramaturges of Yan*, an alien-world adventure so very different, and colorful, and approaching the dimensions of sacred rite or medieval mystery play.

Or his theater-based sf novel from 1967, *The Productions of Time*, which a contemporary review hailed as *"ripe* for a Hollywood option . . . [as] a delicious horror movie"; no such luck, even though John subsequently spent several weeks in Hollywood being promised the moon, only to be dismissed from mind the moment he departed.

But yes, oh dear yes, the big four are *Stand on Zanzibar* (1968), its sibling *The Jagged Orbit* (1969), *The Sheep Look Up* (1972), and *The Shockwave Rider* (1975). Oh dear, because this supremely productive and magisterial period seemed to represent a summit of achievement from which thereafter the route was downhill. Writing an obituary in the British magazine *SFX*, John Grant phrases this in more upbeat vein: "I had the expectation that, any day soon, he was going to sit down and write the SF novel that would drive all the rest of us back to our caves to rethink where we could go from here." And it was possible. Yet really, health problems caused by stress got in the way; and the disruption of remarriage wound him up till he snapped; and ultimately, devoutly as his colleagues may have wished for Grant's outcome, the publishing industry couldn't have cared. A hand-to-mouth existence is conducive to grand conceptions only when one is younger.

Bizarrely, the value of John's estate, as reported by British newspapers, was just slightly over a quarter of a million pounds. This small fortune could only be the estimated imaginary future value of copyrights—for works that are all currently unavailable, and only trading as secondhand copies.

Stand on Zanzibar borrowed the kaleidoscopic multifaceted technique of John Dos Passos's radical *USA* trilogy (1930–36), but did so at a time when such a method had become culturally avant-garde because of the new critiques of capitalist imagery in the sixties, as life in the newly christened global village became increasingly like participation in a television advertisement. The ebullient split-up mixed-media style, with all its puns and consumerist satire, and its focus on medium as message, seems typically McLuhanite. John was writing *Stand on Zanzibar* during 1966, a couple of years after media guru

Marshall McLuhan's *Understanding Media: The Extensions of Man* first appeared, though a year before the quintessential hip McLuhan collage of imagery and epigrams, *The Medium Is the Massage: An Inventory of Effects.*

The British "New Wave," associated with *New Worlds* magazine under the editorship of Michael Moorcock, was beginning to plow this furrow with gusto, as Moorcock himself launched his parody "Swinging Sixties" hero Jerry Cornelius and as Ballard began exploiting the media landscape of car commercials and politics and war, Marilyn Monroe and napalm, cut with surrealism, which would lead on to the sexual iconography of car crashes.

Stand on Zanzibar is at once wildly experimental and basically conventional (though not at all in a derogatory sense). It is avowedly a consumer product "brought to you by John Brunner using Spicers Plus Fabric Bond and Commercial Bank papers interleaved with Serillo carbons," as the last page remarks brightly after the final acerbic roundup of the casualties. Public notices, obituaries, and reports punctuate the "tracking" of a multitude of characters in a stressed-out world of runaway overpopulation, as a black American executive tries to expedite economic penetration of the Third World while his New York flatmate, a white government agent, tries to get hold of a genetic discovery, and a supercomputer tries to hack a genetic fix to humanity's predicament, and a dropout pop sociological guru, Chad Mulligan, wryly observes before at last intervening.

The conventional element is that, via an adventure-story plot masquerading within all the virtuoso fireworks, protagonists will actually win some kind of heart-touching victory. Also, it isn't exactly "contemporary" in the way that Moorcock and Ballard were. It is futurological —if a concerned fascination with the future can be regarded as traditionalist. For Ballard, in a sense, the future had already happened; an artful autopsy should now be performed on our century. Moorcock would play a trickster, harlequin role, breakfasting in the ruins before exploring mythologized multiverses and slices of rejigged history, with a committed passion yet also with a certain dandyism.

Each of the four great books has a fascinating viewpoint-hero. Chad Mulligan of *Stand on Zanzibar* shares with Xavier Conroy of *The Jagged Orbit* an aggressively glib personality. The future America of the latter book is run by organized crime and the weapons industry, with the complicity of the media. Chad and Xavier have both dropped out of society almost as an act of petulance at human folly. Their sallies of savagely indignant wit and common sense—of the Ambrose Bierce variety—are quoted copiously from their own version of Devil's Dictionaries. When Chad capers back on stage, to pit his wits against the supercomputer, the challenge is principally to his self-esteem, and his intervention is an act of intellectual machismo. Likewise, rather, with Xavier. And this is possible because, give or take assorted horrors, the worlds of *Stand on Zanzibar* and *The Jagged Orbit* are ultimately habitable ones, curable ones.

Not so the world of *The Sheep Look Up;* and no bitter witty words are quoted from its resident doom watcher of the Rachel Carson death-of-the-planet school. No need; for Austin Train's message is written in the polluted sea and on the polluted wind.

Chad and Xavier might act the hobo and then spruce themselves up. No one in *Sheep* can clean the dirt up anymore. This book *crawls* with ringworm, sinusitis, lice, rats, festering sores. All in the midst of riches; and because of riches. Here is the ultimate doomsday book of the world shot to shit by the rape of our environment through greed. Heaved up for our appalled inspection is the whole iceberg of eco-catastrophe which is on a collision course with our ill-steered *Titanic*. Yet although all the characters in the book seem to be coughing their guts out, fouling their pants, losing their hair by the handful, being incinerated or driven mad, there isn't any sense of overkill. On the contrary, it's perfectly logical, necessary, and authentic (not a gratuitous bit of ghoulishness) when a woman's new microwave oven cooks her baby in her womb. The equation between death and injury and consumerism is tight. In the real world of the early seventies, the Automatic Sprinkler Corporation of America in Dallas was manufacturing cluster-bomb dispensers; what waters one fellow's lawn rips another's flesh. Cuttingly accurate is John's Dickensian humbug, Mr. Bamberley, who philanthropically provides free food (of a sort) to the Third World, funded from the sale of the best and stickiest napalm.

In sections introduced by skillful parodies of verses from Spenser's *The Shepheardes Calender* and such, *Sheep* is much less self-consciously stylistic than *Zanzibar* while still employing the same mixed-media multiview method. The exuberant hip-crime style of the earlier magnum opus has been honed into a tauter, fiercer instrument throughout, resulting in a complex tragic masterpiece.

Austin Train's followers, who believe in reordering the world along mutually helpful, ecologically sound, non-consumer-oriented lines, might call themselves "Trainites," but Train himself prefers the word "Commensalists," which naturally gets shortened to "commies"—a dipping of the lance to Pohl and Kornbluth's *The Space Merchants,* written back in McCarthyite days. When Train does speak out, in court, his appeal to humanity is almost embarrassingly sincere, a shock after the flip pontifications of Chad and Xavier. We only get his message of hope filtered through the viewpoint of a hard-boiled media lady who is converted on the spot. The outcome is the grimmest of cleansings, as America's citizens collectively set fire to what has at last become irredeemably obscene to them; and the smoke from the burning continent blows as far as Ireland. *Sheep* is a deeply moving work of art, but also a committed political and moral statement.

The Shockwave Rider's title is courtesy of Alvin Toffler's pop sociology best-seller, *Future Shock,* about the impact on people of the pace of change.

In a future America most citizens are plugged in to data nets. People are able to change their jobs and homes and lifestyles, and their partners, with total "plug-in" flexibility—apart from the inhabitants of the shantytowns west of the Rockies, the result of a massive Californian earthquake with which the government couldn't cope. In these shantytowns juveniles wage tribal warfare. But elsewhere children undergo behavior modification, often with harmful consequences that are kept secret. Despite a facade of public-opinion polling—by way of gambling on futures using Delphi oracle machines (a sideswipe at the Rand Corporation)—much is kept secret, including government attempts to force-feed the minds of promising young orphans and even to breed superhumans by genetic tampering, all part of a global "brain race."

Distrustful of a corrupt and manipulative government, most citizens glide through their ever-shifting, alienated lives, supposedly fulfilled by constant change but liable to paranoia and mental breakdown—until one of those bright orphans, Nick Haflinger, now an adult, escapes from government custody.

Much of the book consists of brilliantly handled flashbacks (or "fleshbacks") during Nick's interrogation by means of drugs and electronic stimulation of his brain to evoke memories. When, through the love of a good and wise woman, Nick writes a master program and unleashes this electronic tapeworm, all secrets are stripped bare and the people regain their sense of identity and free will. As two proposals are put to the nation as to how to improve the world, John finally addresses the reader directly: "How did you vote?" Again, a thrilling adventure story (and a work of art) is also a compassionate moral challenge.

The "big four" remain books of urgent relevance to the world today. Not only do they involve us emotionally because of their narrative skill and verve and breadth of reference, but they compel us to ask ourselves the Tolstoyan question, What Then Must We Do? The rest of John's considerable output contains many fluent, well-crafted works of minor classic status, and often rather more than that. He gave of himself liberally in his writing, for the sake of human togetherness, fulfillment, sanity, and, indeed, survival—as well as for entertainment, for this was his profession.

Now his voice is lost in the wilderness known as Out-Of-Print. But that voice changed lives, and will continue to do so for readers who are able to find John's many fine books.

Roger Zelazny
(1937–1995)
JACK DANN

I had just come home from an old-fashioned male-bonding bachelor party that Peter Nicholls had organized for me; and still feeling slightly tipsy, I checked my e-mail before retiring. It was there I found out that Roger Zelazny had died, and in that instant, as the screen seemed to dissolve before me, I flashed back to the early seventies when I first met Roger, in Baltimore. How could Roger be dead? It seems like only a few days ago that I was sitting around Jack Haldeman's old mansion in the Guilford section of Baltimore with Joe Haldeman,

Gardner Dozois, George Alec Effinger, Tom Monteleone, Bill Nabors, and Ted White. We would meet a few times a year to workshop our stories, drink, talk the talk . . . and see Roger Zelazny. We called ourselves the Guilford Gafia, a play on the Milford Mafia (which was what some SFWA members were calling the group of writers who wrote stories for Damon Knight's *Orbit* series and attended the Milford Writers Workshop at Damon and Kate Wilhelm's old mansion in Milford, Pennsylvania).

Roger described the "peculiar rites of the Guilford Gafia" in an introduction to my short-story collection, *Timetipping:* "Meeting in Haldeman Manor, a place reminiscent of a crowded Gormenghast with cats, the G. G. was a writing group that seemed to exist just at the periphery of Chaos or perhaps even a little nearer. Though I was not a member, I lived nearby and was occasionally bewildered by the strange lights and sounds, puzzled at the function served by the shark's brain in formaldehyde with a room all to itself, and enjoyably attracted by late-night invitations to artichoke cookouts."

Although Roger didn't attend the workshops, he was certainly a member. Although he was shy and quiet and unassuming—and would have chuckled over this description—he was the grand old man of the workshop. We would work like hell for a weekend, excoriate each other with the most constructive of constructive criticism, but there was always an incentive to survive: at the end of it all would be "the party," and at the party would be Roger. It was 1972. I was twenty-seven years old and had sold two or three stories. Gardner had brought me to Guilford, had introduced me to all these new writers, and there I was on a Sunday night sitting around with Roger Zelazny. What could be better? Here was the man who had written "The Doors of His Face, the Lamps of His Mouth," "A Rose for Ecclesiastes," "For a Breath I Tarry," *Isle of the Dead, The Dream Master, This Immortal.*

I would see Roger every year or two after those Baltimore days, which were my salad days, when everything was compressed and pure and full of the juice. Roger and I would bump into each other at conventions and sneak away for a drink, and I would insist that he pull out the string (which I *knew* he had hidden somewhere on his person) and make cat's cradles. Put a piece of string in Roger's hands, and he became a magician. He would sit there grinning at you like a Zen master while his hands would turn a circle of string into absolutely impossible shapes and forms.

And so we would meet at conventions, and somehow the years just piled up behind us. I became grayer and grayer, and friends started referring to me as "Andy Warhol," but Roger didn't seem to age. He was the same old Roger—tall, skinny, a bit stooped as if suddenly embarrassed, and quiet. For all of that, Roger was, of course, the trickster. There was something wonderfully childlike and impish about Roger, but he kept it well hidden. You would suddenly know that you were in the presence of a practical joker, of someone who was getting a huge kick out of life, who was dancing around on the ceiling at night, swinging on rafters, somersaulting across the lawn, someone who had fooled everyone into thinking that he was shy, quiet... Roger.

But something had slipped by March 1994.

My life had certainly changed. I was in the process of moving to Australia (and have been commuting back and forth ever since). I was meeting Janeen Webb at the Conference for the Fantastic in Florida, and then we were both flying back to Oz.

Roger was the guest of honor.

But Roger had finally aged. Seeing him was a shock. It was as if he had just decided to look old. He was, of course, ill; but he certainly didn't act it. In fact, he was all excited because he had just collaborated on a book with Alfred Bester. He had been commissioned to finish a book Alfie had started but had written only a few chapters. Roger told me that he had always wanted to be able to write like Alfie. He was worried that he couldn't do the flash and pyrotechnics the way Alfie could. Bester was a major influence on Roger, and Roger was nervous as a colt about having collaborated with the master. He told me that he had just finished the book and that he had a copy of the manuscript with him.

I spent the next day reading it. I gave Roger feedback on some minor quibbles and told him that I loved the book, that he had out-Bestered Bester. Roger seemed very pleased.

I didn't know that would be Roger's last book.

And so now I'm sitting here in Melbourne writing about Roger in the past tense. The book is closed, and, as Gardner Dozois once said,

"We're all stepping up to the line." There are others who can give you critical appraisals of Roger's work. But I felt I had to write something about Roger as I knew him. I guess this is my open letter to him, written, of course, too late.

I wish you peace, old friend, and I can't help but remember the thrill of reading those stories and novels of yours when I was starting out, how I would try to memorize passages to learn how you did it, how you turned prose into poetry; and when I think of you now, I once again remember the first lines of *Isle of the Dead,* and I can see you there, old trickster, walking along that eternal beach on Tokyo Bay.

In the freshening wind and sharp salt air.

Walking quietly away. . . .

Requiem for a Rare Bird
JACK C. HALDEMAN II

I imagine I've written a dozen or so pieces on Roger Zelazny for convention program books and such, but this is the one I never wanted to write.

Baltimore in the mid-sixties. It's a typical fannish party, complete with lots of beer, a mimeograph machine, much talk. Too much talk, so I climbed out a window to have a cigarette and a few minutes' peace. It was quiet on the roof. Baltimore was at my feet. The stars were out. I had a habit of sitting on roofs back then. It was something I did.

A young man, tall and lanky, came out through the window a few minutes later and joined me. He didn't say anything; he just sat down beside me and lit a pipe. We sat together a long time without words. It fit the moment. When we did start talking, it was about the stars. After a bit, I thought I should introduce myself. He said his name was Roger Zelazny. Our friendship had already begun.

It lasted thirty years. Not a bad run. Not nearly long enough.

I feel lucky to have had Roger for a friend for so many years. At times we lived around the corner from each other, at other times we lived far apart. During the distant times, we'd write each other. If he didn't hear from me for a while, he'd call, just to see how I was doing and to let me know what he'd been up to. So many memories.

We walked a lot of beaches, sat in a lot of bars and restaurants. We watched our kids play together and stood next to each other as men left this planet to walk the moon. There were some very good times. He sent me poetry for my fanzine *Tapeworm* during my fannish years and was very supportive of me when I started writing.

One time Roger and I were in a Baltimore bookstore. He'd just had a book come out, and the store had a display of them. We were wandering down separate aisles when I came across two kids standing in front of the display. "Oh, look," one of them said, "Roger Zelazny." At that point Roger poked his head around the corner and said, "Yes?" The grin he broke into at their shocked expressions is one of my most treasured memories.

Another memory I treasure is our Great Robert Heinlein Expedition. Roger had called me saying that Heinlein was going to speak at the U.S. Naval Academy and did I want to go with him. We went, and sat in the very top row of the balcony. Heinlein was a recluse of sorts in those years, and neither of us had met him. After he talked, and was being formally escorted out by the midshipmen, Roger asked me if I thought we could find him and meet him. I allowed as how it was another impossible thing we should try. Roger's announced strategy was to tell all the people we met that I was a big Heinlein fan and had a couple of books I'd like autographed. I told Roger that his strategy sucked, that we should say the famous science fiction writer Roger Zelazny would like to meet Robert Heinlein. Roger demurred, saying that Heinlein had probably never heard of him. So we played both strategies and an hour later found ourselves in the foyer of the admiral's quarters watching Heinlein, in formal attire, descend a monstrous curving staircase. Neither one of us could speak at first. It was an awesome moment. With my typical fannish blundering, I stammered something like "Mr. Heinlein, this is Roger Zelazny." Heinlein's face dropped its formal pose, and with a flash of genuine delight, he took Roger's hand. "Roger, you write a good stick," he said. Roger was so high, I don't think his feet touched the ground for a week.

Roger was a private person. In most situations he was shy and reserved. But if you knew him well enough, there was a veil he would drop, and doorways to other parts of Roger would open. He had a fantastic sense of humor and the quickest mind I've ever known. He had a fine sense of the absurd and used to send me clippings of the strange corners of human experience. I can see his pixie grin right now. Ah, yes, this hurts.

My fiancée, Barbara Delaplace, was the first to call me with the sad news that Roger had died. I slept badly that night. Then, just before I woke, I had a very strange dream. Roger was sitting in my room with me, my cat Oberon in his lap. The cat is named after *The Hand of Oberon*, the Amber book that Roger dedicated to me. We talked a lot in that dream, but mostly we laughed. At times he played string games with the cat. It was an easy, relaxed time; a time like we used to have years ago when there seemed to be so much time left. Then I woke up.

Understand that I am a working scientist. Understand that I am not much into mysticism. But in that moment of half awake, half asleep, I *knew* that Roger had been there. It was that real. It was comforting. Later that day, George R. R. Martin called me and said they were having a memorial service for Roger in New Mexico. I knew I had to go. After all, he had come to say good-bye to me.

For many reasons, I'm glad I went. I finally got to meet Jane Lindskold, whom I had previously only nodded to in passing, though Roger had mentioned her often in his telephone calls to me. I went to Santa Fe and talked to Judy Zelazny of old times, saw Roger's son Devin (my daughter Lori liked to put Devin in boxes and dresser drawers when they were very little) and daughter Shannon. But his son Trent was the key.

There were many young people at the memorial service. Beginning writers, musicians, game players. Most of them Roger had met through Trent and Jane. I could tell from what they said of him that they had seen the Roger behind the veil. His life had opened up again, even as it was closing. It brought joy to my heart in such a sad time. I'm so glad that Jane and Trent gave my friend so much in the last year. That last hard year.

Driving to the airport in Tampa to catch the plane to New Mexico, I was racked with anxiety. I was fussed about Roger. I was worried the old car I was driving would break down. Too many fusses. And then three sandhill cranes took flight across the highway in front of me, and I was oddly calmed.

Yes. For if I have an image of my friend Roger, it is of a crane. A whooping crane. Endangered and rare. Gawky and awkward at times, but with an innate grace and dignity beyond measure. I can see Roger as one of the trickster birds, grinning mischievously at us and winking, just before taking wing.

Good-bye, my friend. Fly well.

The Lincoln Train

MAUREEN F. McHUGH

Maureen F. McHugh won the James Tiptree Jr. Memorial Award, the Locus Award, and the Lambda Literary Award for her first novel, *China Mountain Zhang.* Her second novel, *Half the Day Is Night,* came out in 1994; her short fiction has been nominated for Nebula and Hugo Awards and has appeared in best-of-the-year anthologies. She has lived in Loveland, Ohio, New York City, and Shijiazhuang, China, and now lives in a suburb of Cleveland with her husband and son.

About her Nebula finalist "The Lincoln Train," which won the 1996 Hugo Award for short story, she has this to say:

"I have to thank Mike Resnick and the Cajun Sushi Hamsters from Hell for 'The Lincoln Train.' Mike commissioned the story for the last of his *Alternate* anthologies, *Alternate Tyrants.* I'd written two alternate history stories, but felt I hadn't really taken advantage of the form. I decided that I would pick a person whom everybody knew something about. My husband had recently read a *Scientific American* article about what kind of brain damage Lincoln would have suffered if he had survived, and with that as a springboard I decided to write about Lincoln. But the more of Lincoln's own writing I read, the less capable I felt of capturing the man on paper. So Lincoln is offstage in the story.

"In the first version of the story, I felt the ending was weak and rather sentimental, so I took the story to the Cajun Sushi Hamsters from Hell, my writers' group, which includes people like Geoff Landis, Mary Turzillo, Charlie Oberndorf, and S. Andrew Swann. Geoff and Charlie got into a discussion about how much insight the main character was capable of, and in the discussion they gave me the present ending, for which I am profoundly grateful."

Soldiers of the G.A.R. stand alongside the tracks. They are General Dodge's soldiers, keeping the tracks maintained for the Lincoln Train. If I stand right, the edges of my bonnet are like blinders and I can't see the soldiers at all. It is a spring evening. At the house the lilacs are blooming. My mother wears a sprig pinned to her dress under her cameo. I can smell it, even in the crush of these people all waiting for the train. I can smell the lilac, and the smell of too many people crowded together, and a faint taste of cinders on the air. I want to go home but that house is not ours anymore. I smooth my black dress. On the train platform we are all in mourning.

The train will take us to St. Louis, from whence we will leave for the Oklahoma territories. They say we will walk, but I don't know how my mother will do that. She has been poorly since the winter of '62. I check my bag with our water and provisions.

"Julia Adelaide," my mother says, "I think we should go home."

"We've come to catch the train," I say, very sharp.

I'm Clara, my sister Julia is eleven years older than me. Julia is married and living in Tennessee. My mother blinks and touches her sprig of lilac uncertainly. If I am not sharp with her, she will keep on it.

I wait. When I was younger I used to try to school my unruly self in Christian charity. God sends us nothing we cannot bear. Now I only try to keep it from my face, try to keep my outer self disciplined. There is a feeling inside me, an anger, that I can't even speak. Something is being bent, like a bow, bending and bending and bending—

"When are we going home?" my mother says.

"Soon," I say because it is easy.

But she won't remember and in a moment she'll ask again. And again and again, through this long long train ride to St. Louis. I am trying to be a Christian daughter, and I remind myself that it is not her fault that the war turned her into an old woman, or that her mind is full of holes and everything new drains out. But it's not my fault either. I don't even try to curb my feelings and I know that they rise up to my face. The only way to be true is to be true from the inside and I am not. I am full of unchristian feelings. My mother's infirmity is her trial, and it is also mine.

I wish I were someone else.

The train comes down the track, chuffing, coming slow. It is an old, badly used thing, but I can see that once it was a model of chaste and beautiful workmanship. Under the dust it is a dark claret in color. It is said that the engine was built to be used by President Lincoln, but since the assassination attempt he is too infirm to travel. People begin to push to the edge of the platform, hauling their bags and worldly goods. I don't know how I will get our valise on. If Zeke could have come I could have at least insured that it was loaded on, but the Negroes are free now and they are not to help. The notice said no family Negroes could come to the station, although I see their faces here and there through the crowd.

The train stops outside the station to take on water.

"Is it your father?" my mother says diffidently. "Do you see him on the train?"

"No, Mother," I say. "We are taking the train."

"Are we going to see your father?" she asks.

It doesn't matter what I say to her, she'll forget it in a few minutes, but I cannot say yes to her. I cannot say that we will see my father even to give her a few moments of joy.

"Are we going to see your father?" she asks again.

"No," I say.

"Where are we going?"

I have carefully explained it all to her and she cried, every time I did. People are pushing down the platform toward the train, and I am trying to decide if I should move my valise toward the front of the platform. Why are they in such a hurry to get on the train? It is taking us all away.

"Where are we going? Julia Adelaide, you will answer me this moment," my mother says, her voice too full of quaver to quite sound like her own.

"I'm Clara," I say. "We're going to St. Louis."

"St. Louis," she says. "We don't need to go to St. Louis. We can't get through the lines, Julia, and I . . . I am quite indisposed. Let's go back home now, this is foolish."

We cannot go back home. General Dodge has made it clear that if we did not show up at the train platform this morning and get our names checked off the list, he would arrest every man in town, and then he would shoot every tenth man. The town knows to believe him, General Dodge was put in charge of the trains into Washington, and he did the same thing then. He arrested men and held them and every time the train was fired upon he hanged a man.

There is a shout and I can only see the crowd moving like a wave, pouring off the edge of the platform. Everyone is afraid there will not be room. I grab the valise and I grab my mother's arm and pull them both. The valise is so heavy that my fingers hurt, and the weight of our water and food is heavy on my arm. My mother is small and when I put her in bed at night she is all tiny like a child, but now she refuses to move, pulling against me and opening her mouth wide, her mouth pink inside and wet and open in a wail I can just barely hear over the shouting crowd. I don't know if I should let go of the valise to pull her, or for a moment I think of letting go of her, letting someone else get her on the train, and finding her later.

A man in the crowd shoves her hard from behind. His face is twisted in wrath. What is he so angry at? My mother falls into me, and the crowd pushes us. I am trying to hold on to the valise, but my gloves are slippery, and I can only hold with my right hand, with my left I am trying to hold up my mother. The crowd is pushing all around us, trying to push us toward the edge of the platform.

The train toots as if it were moving. There is shouting all around us. My mother is fallen against me, her face pressed against my bosom, turned up toward me. She is so frightened. Her face is pressed against me in improper intimacy, as if she were my child. My mother as my child. I am filled with revulsion and horror. The pressure against us begins to lessen. I still have a hold of the valise. We'll be all right. Let the others push around, I'll wait and get the valise on somehow. They won't leave us travel without anything.

My mother's eyes close. Her wrinkled face looks up, the skin under her eyes making little pouches, as if it were a second blind eyelid. Everything is so grotesque. I am having a spell. I wish I could be somewhere where I could get away and close the windows. I have had these spells since they told us that my father was dead, where everything is full of horror and strangeness.

The person behind me is crowding into my back and I want to tell them to give way, but I cannot. People around us are crying out. I cannot see anything but the people pushed against me. People are still pushing, but now they are not pushing toward the side of the platform but toward the front, where the train will be when we are allowed to board.

Wait, I call out but there's no way for me to tell if I've really called out or not. I can't hear anything until the train whistles. The train has moved? They brought the train into the station? I can't tell, not without letting go of my mother and the valise. My mother is being pulled down into this mass. I feel her sliding against me. Her eyes are closed. She is a huge doll, limp in my arms. She is not even trying to hold herself up. She has given up to this moment.

I can't hold on to my mother and the valise. So I let go of the valise.

Oh merciful god.

I do not know how I will get through this moment.

The crowd around me is a thing that presses me and pushes me up, pulls me down. I cannot breathe for the pressure. I see specks in front of my eyes, white sparks, too bright, like metal and like light. My feet aren't under me. I am buoyed by the crowd and my feet are behind me. I am unable to stand, unable to fall. I think my mother is against me, but I can't tell, and in this mass I don't know how she can breathe.

I think I am going to die.

All the noise around me does not seem like noise anymore. It is something else, some element, like water or something, surrounding me and overpowering me.

It is like that for a long time, until finally I have my feet under me, and I'm leaning against people. I feel myself sink, but I can't stop myself. The platform is solid. My whole body feels bruised and roughly used.

My mother is not with me. My mother is a bundle of black on the ground, and I crawl to her. I wish I could say that as I crawl to her I feel concern for her condition, but at this moment I am no more than base animal nature and I crawl to her because she is mine and there is nothing else in the world I can identify as mine. Her skirt is rucked up so that her ankles and calves are showing. Her face is black. At first I think it is something about her clothes, but it is her face, so full of blood that it is black.

People are still getting on the train, but there are people on the platform around us, left behind. And other things. A surprising number of shoes, all badly used. Wraps, too. Bags. Bundles and people.

I try raising her arms above her head, to force breath into her lungs. Her arms are thin, but they don't go the way I want them to. I read in the newspaper that when President Lincoln was shot, he stopped breathing, and his personal physician started him breathing again. But maybe the newspaper was wrong, or maybe it is more complicated than I understand, or maybe it doesn't always work. She doesn't breathe.

I sit on the platform and try to think of what to do next. My head is empty of useful thoughts. Empty of prayers.

"Ma'am?"

It's a soldier of the G.A.R.

"Yes sir?" I say. It is difficult to look up at him, to look up into the sun.

He hunkers down but does not touch her. At least he doesn't touch her. "Do you have anyone staying behind?"

Like cousins or something? Someone who is not "recalcitrant" in their handling of their Negroes? "Not in town," I say.

"Did she worship?" he asks, in his northern way.

"Yes sir," I say, "she did. She was a Methodist, and you should contact the preacher. The Reverend Robert Ewald, sir."

"I'll see to it, ma'am. Now you'll have to get on the train."

"And leave her?" I say.

"Yes ma'am, the train will be leaving. I'm sorry ma'am."

"But I can't," I say.

He takes my elbow and helps me stand. And I let him.

"We are not really recalcitrant," I say. "Where were Zeke and Rachel supposed to go? Were we supposed to throw them out?"

He helps me climb onto the train. People stare at me as I get on, and I realize I must be all in disarray. I stand under all their gazes, trying to get my bonnet on straight and smoothing my dress. I do not know what to do with my eyes or hands.

There are no seats. Will I have to stand until St. Louis? I grab a seat back to hold myself up. It is suddenly warm and everything is distant and I think I am about to faint. My stomach turns. I breathe through my mouth, not even sure that I am holding on to the seat back.

But I don't fall, thank Jesus.

"It's not Lincoln," someone is saying, a man's voice, rich and baritone, and I fasten on the words as a lifeline, drawing myself back to the train car, to the world. "It's Seward. Lincoln no longer has the capacity to govern."

The train smells of bodies and warm sweaty wool. It is a smell that threatens to undo me, so I must concentrate on breathing through my mouth. I breathe in little pants, like a dog. The heat lies against my skin. It is airless.

"Of course Lincoln can no longer govern, but that damned actor made him a saint when he shot him," says a second voice. "And now no one dare oppose him. It doesn't matter if his policies make sense or not."

"You're wrong," says the first. "Seward is governing through him. Lincoln is an imbecile. He can't govern, look at the way he handled the war."

The second snorts. "He won."

"No," says the first, "we *lost,* there is a difference, sir. We lost even though the north never could find a competent general." I know the type of the first one. He's the one who thinks he is brilliant, who always knew what President Davis should have done. If they are looking for a recalcitrant southerner, they have found one.

"Grant was competent. Just not brilliant. Any military man who is not Alexander the Great is going to look inadequate in comparison with General Lee."

"Grant was a drinker," the first one says. "It was his subordinates. They'd been through years of war. They knew what to do."

It is so hot on the train. I wonder how long until the train leaves.

I wonder if the Reverend will write my sister in Tennessee and tell her about our mother. I wish the train were going east toward Tennessee instead of north and west toward St. Louis.

My valise. All I have. It is on the platform. I turn to go to the door. It is closed and I try the handle, but it is too stiff for me. I look around for help.

"It's locked," says a woman in gray. She doesn't look unkind.

"My things, I left them on the platform," I say.

"Oh, honey," she says, "they aren't going to let you back out there. They don't let anyone off the train."

I look out the window but I can't see the valise. I can see some of the soldiers, so I beat on the window. One of them glances up at me, frowning, but then ignores me.

The train blows that it is going to leave, and I beat harder on the glass. If I could shatter that glass. They don't understand, they would help me if they understood. The train lurches and I stagger. It is out there, somewhere, on that platform. Clothes for my mother and me, blankets, things we will need. Things I will need.

The train pulls out of the station and I feel so terrible I sit down on the floor in all the dirt from people's feet and sob.

The train creeps slowly at first, but then picks up speed. The clack-clack clack-clack rocks me. It is improper, but I allow it to rock me. I am in others' hands now and there is nothing to do but be patient. I am good at that. So it has been all my life. I have tried to be dutiful, but something in me has not bent right, and I have never been able to maintain a Christian frame of mind, but like a chicken in a yard, I have always kept my eyes on the small things. I have tended to what was in front of me, first the house, then my mother. When we could not get sugar, I learned to cook with molasses and honey. Now I sit and let my mind go empty and let the train rock me.

"Child," someone says. "Child."

The woman in gray has been trying to get my attention for a while, but I have been sitting and letting myself be rocked.

"Child," she says again, "would you like some water?"

Yes, I realize, I would. She has a jar and she gives it to me to sip out of. "Thank you," I say. "We brought water, but we lost it in the crush on the platform."

"You have someone with you?" she asks.

"My mother," I say, and start crying again. "She is old, and there was such a press on the platform, and she fell and was trampled."

"What's your name?" the woman says.

"Clara Corbett," I say.

"I'm Elizabeth Loudon," the woman says. "And you are welcome to travel with me." There is something about her, a simple pleasantness, that makes me trust her. She is a small woman, with a small nose and eyes as gray as her dress. She is younger than I first thought, maybe only in her thirties? "How old are you? Do you have a family?" she asks.

"I am seventeen. I have a sister, Julia. But she doesn't live in Mississippi anymore."

"Where does she live?" the woman asks.

"In Beech Bluff, near Jackson, Tennessee."

She shakes her head. "I don't know it. Is it good country?"

"I think so," I say. "In her letters it sounds like good country. But I haven't seen her for seven years." Of course no one could travel during the war. She has three children in Tennessee. My sister is twenty-eight, almost as old as this woman. It is hard to imagine.

"Were you close?" she asks.

I don't know that we were close. But she is my sister. She is all I have, now. I hope that the Reverend will write her about my mother, but I don't know that he knows where she is. I will have to write her. She will think I should have taken better care.

"Are you traveling alone?"

"My companion is a few seats farther in front. He and I could not find seats together."

Her companion is a man? Not her husband, maybe her brother? But she would say her brother if that's who she meant. A woman traveling with a man. An adventuress, I think. There are stories of women traveling, hoping to find unattached girls like myself. They befriend the young girls and then deliver them to the brothels of New Orleans.

For a moment Elizabeth takes on a sinister cast. But this is a train full of recalcitrant southerners, there is no opportunity to kidnap anyone. Elizabeth is like me, a woman who has lost her home.

It takes the rest of the day and a night to get to St. Louis, and Elizabeth and I talk. It's as if we talk in ciphers, instead of talking about home we talk about gardening, and I can see the garden at home, lazy with bees. She is a quilter. I don't quilt, but I used to do petit point, so we can talk sewing and about how hard it has been to get colors. And we talk about mending and making do, we have all been making do for so long.

When it gets dark, since I have no seat, I stay where I am sitting by the door of the train. I am so tired, but in the darkness all I can think of is my mother's face in the crowd and her hopeless open mouth. I don't want to think of my mother, but I am in a delirium of fatigue, surrounded by the dark and the rumble of the train and the distant murmur of voices. I sleep sitting by the door of the train, fitful and rocked. I have dreams like fever dreams. In my dream I am in a strange house, but it is supposed to be my own house, but nothing is where it should be, and I begin to believe that I have actually entered a stranger's house, and that they'll return and find me here. When I wake up and go back to sleep, I am back in this strange house, looking through things.

I wake before dawn, only a little rested. My shoulders and hips and back all ache from the way I am leaning, but I have no energy to get up. I have no energy to do anything but endure. Elizabeth nods, sometimes awake, sometimes asleep, but neither of us speak.

Finally the train slows. We come in through a town, but the town seems to go on and on. It must be St. Louis. We stop and sit. The sun comes up and heats the car like an oven. There is no movement of the air. There are so many buildings in St. Louis, and so many of them are tall, two stories, that I wonder if they cut off the wind and that is why it's so still. But finally the train lurches and we crawl into the station.

I am one of the first off the train by virtue of my position near the door. A soldier unlocks it and shouts for all of us to disembark, but he need not have bothered for there is a rush. I am borne ahead at its beginning but I can stop at the back of the platform. I am afraid that I have lost Elizabeth, but I see her in the crowd. She is on the arm of a younger man in a bowler. There is something about his air that marks him as different—he is sprightly and apparently fresh even after the long ride.

I almost let them pass, but the prospect of being alone makes me reach out and touch her shoulder.

"There you are," she says.

We join a queue of people waiting to use a trench. The smell is appalling, ammonia acrid and eye-watering. There is a wall to separate the men from the women, but the women are all together. I crouch, trying not to notice anyone and trying to keep my skirts out of the filth. It is so awful. It's worse than anything. I feel so awful.

What if my mother were here? What would I do? I think maybe it was better, maybe it was God's hand. But that is an awful thought, too.

"Child," Elizabeth says when I come out, "what's the matter?"

"It's so awful," I say. I shouldn't cry, but I just want to be home and clean. I want to go to bed and sleep.

She offers me a biscuit.

"You should save your food," I say.

"Don't worry," Elizabeth says. "We have enough."

I shouldn't accept it, but I am so hungry. And when I have a little to eat, I feel a little better.

I try to imagine what the fort will be like where we will be going. Will we have a place to sleep, or will it be barracks? Or worse yet, tents? Although after the night I spent on the train I can't imagine anything that could be worse. I imagine if I have to stay awhile in a tent then I'll make the best of it.

"I think this being in limbo is perhaps worse than anything we can expect at the end," I say to Elizabeth. She smiles.

She introduces her companion, Michael. He is enough like her to be her brother, but I don't think that they are. I am resolved not to ask, if they want to tell me they can.

We are standing together, not saying anything, when there is some commotion farther up the platform. It is a woman, her black dress is like smoke. She is running down the platform, coming toward us. There are all of these people and yet it is as if there is no obstacle for her. "NO NO NO NO, DON'T TOUCH ME! FILTHY HANDS! DON'T LET THEM TOUCH YOU! DON'T GET ON THE TRAINS!"

People are getting out of her way. Where are the soldiers? The fabric of her dress is so threadbare it is rotten and torn at the seams. Her skirt is greasy black and matted and stained. Her face is so thin. "ANIMALS! THERE IS NOTHING OUT THERE! PEOPLE DON'T HAVE FOOD! THERE IS NOTHING THERE BUT INDIANS! THEY SENT US OUT TO SETTLE BUT THERE WAS NOTHING THERE!"

I expect she will run past me but she grabs my arm and stops and looks into my face. She has light eyes, pale eyes in her dark face. She is mad.

"WE WERE ALL STARVING, SO WE WENT TO THE FORT BUT THE FORT HAD NOTHING. YOU WILL ALL STARVE, THE WAY THEY ARE STARVING THE INDIANS! THEY WILL LET US ALL DIE! THEY DON'T CARE!" She is screaming in my

face, and her spittle sprays me, warm as her breath. Her hand is all
tendons and twigs, but she's so strong I can't escape.

The soldiers grab her and yank her away from me. My arm aches
where she was holding it. I can't stand up.

Elizabeth pulls me upright. "Stay close to me," she says and starts
to walk the other way down the platform. People are looking up following the screaming woman.

She pulls me along with her. I keep thinking of the woman's
hand and wrist turned black with grime. I remember my mother's
face was black when she lay on the platform. Black like something
rotted.

"Here," Elizabeth says at an old door, painted green but now
weathered. The door opens and we pass inside.

"What?" I say. My eyes are accustomed to the morning brightness
and I can't see.

"Her name is Clara," Elizabeth says. "She has people in Tennessee."

"Come with me," says another woman. She sounds older. "Step
this way. Where are her things?"

I am being kidnapped. Oh merciful God, I'll die. I let out a moan.

"Her things were lost, her mother was killed in a crush on the
platform."

The woman in the dark clucks sympathetically. "Poor dear. Does
Michael have his passenger yet?"

"In a moment," Elizabeth says. "We were lucky for the commotion."

I am beginning to be able to see. It is a storage room, full of
abandoned things. The woman holding my arm is older. There are
some broken chairs and a stool. She sits me in the chair. Is Elizabeth
some kind of adventuress?

"Who are you?" I ask.

"We are friends," Elizabeth says. "We will help you get to your
sister."

I don't believe them. I will end up in New Orleans. Elizabeth is
some kind of adventuress.

After a moment the door opens and this time it is Michael with a
young man. "This is Andrew," he says.

A man? What do they want with a man? That is what stops me
from saying, "Run!" Andrew is blinded by the change in light, and I

can see the astonishment working on his face, the way it must be working on mine. "What is this?" he asks.

"You are with Friends," Michael says, and maybe he has said it differently than Elizabeth, or maybe it is just that this time I have had the wit to hear it.

"Quakers?" Andrew says. "Abolitionists?"

Michael smiles, I can see his teeth white in the darkness. "Just Friends," he says.

Abolitionists. Crazy people who steal slaves to set them free. Have they come to kidnap us? We are recalcitrant southerners, I have never heard of Quakers seeking revenge, but everyone knows the Abolitionists are crazy and they are liable to do anything.

"We'll have to wait here until they begin to move people out, it will be evening before we can leave," says the older woman.

I am so frightened, I just want to be home. Maybe I should try to break free and run out to the platform, there are northern soldiers out there. Would they protect me? And then what, go to a fort in Oklahoma?

The older woman asks Michael how they could get past the guards so early and he tells her about the madwoman. A "refugee" he calls her.

"They'll just take her back," Elizabeth says, sighing.

Take her back, do they mean that she really came from Oklahoma? They talk about how bad it will be this winter. Michael says there are Wisconsin Indians re-settled down there, but they've got no food, and they've been starving on government handouts for a couple of years. Now there will be more people. They're not prepared for winter.

There can't have been much handout during the war. It was hard enough to feed the armies.

They explain to Andrew and to me that we will sneak out of the train station this evening, after dark. We will spend a day with a Quaker family in St. Louis, and then they will send us on to the next family. And so we will be passed hand to hand, like a bucket in a brigade, until we get to our families.

They call it the underground railroad.

But we are slave owners.

"Wrong is wrong," says Elizabeth. "Some of us can't stand and watch people starve."

"But only two out of the whole train," Andrew says.

Michael sighs.

The old woman nods. "It isn't right."

Elizabeth picked me because my mother died. If my mother had not died, I would be out there, on my way to starve with the rest of them.

I can't help it but I start to cry. I should not profit from my mother's death. I should have kept her safe.

"Hush, now," says Elizabeth. "Hush, you'll be okay."

"It's not right," I whisper. I'm trying not to be loud, we mustn't be discovered.

"What, child?"

"You shouldn't have picked me," I say. But I am crying so hard I don't think they can understand me. Elizabeth strokes my hair and wipes my face. It may be the last time someone will do these things for me. My sister has three children of her own, and she won't need another child. I'll have to work hard to make up my keep.

There are blankets there and we lie down on the hard floor, all except Michael, who sits in a chair and sleeps. I sleep this time with fewer dreams. But when I wake up, although I can't remember what they were, I have the feeling that I have been dreaming restless dreams.

The stars are bright when we finally creep out of the station. A night full of stars. The stars will be the same in Tennessee. The platform is empty, the train and the people are gone. The Lincoln Train has gone back south while we slept, to take more people out of Mississippi.

"Will you come back and save more people?" I ask Elizabeth.

The stars are a banner behind her quiet head. "We will save what we can," she says.

It isn't fair that I was picked. "I want to help," I tell her.

She is silent for a moment. "We only work with our own," she says. There is something in her voice that has not been there before. A sharpness.

"What do you mean?" I ask.

"There are no slavers in our ranks," she says and her voice is cold.

I feel as if I have had a fever; tired, but clear of mind. I have never walked so far and not walked beyond a town. The streets of St. Louis are empty. There are few lights. Far off a woman is singing, and her voice is clear and carries easily into the night. A beautiful voice.

"Elizabeth," Michael says, "she is just a girl."

"She needs to know," Elizabeth says.

"Why did you save me then?" I ask.

"One does not fight evil with evil," Elizabeth says.

"I'm not evil!" I say.

But no one answers.

The Resurrection Man's Legacy

DALE BAILEY

Dale Bailey was born and grew up in Princeton, West Virginia; he now lives in Maryville, Tennessee, and is completing his Ph.D. in English. His stories have appeared in *The Magazine of Fantasy & Science Fiction*, *Amazing Stories*, and *Pulphouse*, and have been reprinted in *The Year's Best Fantasy and Horror* and *The Best From Fantasy & Science Fiction: A 45th Anniversary Anthology*. He recently completed his first novel.

His Nebula finalist, "The Resurrection Man's Legacy," is a moving and atmospheric look at one boy's childhood in an imagined past. About this novelette, Dale Bailey writes:

"'The Resurrection Man's Legacy' suggested itself to me as a title, and it took some time to find the story hidden inside it. The focus of the story—the grief a child feels at the loss of a parent—came later, and later still it became clear to me that the poignancy of the story would be enhanced if the loss were refracted through one of the central metaphors of the genre: the robot.

"In her introduction to the story in *F&SF*, Kris Rusch flattered me deeply by saying that the story combined the feel of Ray Bradbury and Isaac Asimov. While these writers were not consciously in my mind as I wrote, Kris's comment essentially reflects my intentions. The genius of Asimov's robot stories is that his robots always expose the weaknesses—and the strengths—of the human beings who made them. And Bradbury's greatest asset has always been his unparalleled skill at evoking emotion for a world that is irretrievably lost.

"I had both of these goals very much in mind as I began to put the story together. Because I hoped to arouse the sense of nostalgia central to grief, I deliberately set the story in a past that differs only slightly from the past we know. In doing so, I hoped to exploit our nostalgia for the simpler times of our own past; my reasons for using baseball, that mythic sport for which so many of us have nostalgic associations, were essentially the same. If the story has only a tenth of the emotional resonance of Bradbury at his best, then it succeeds better than I could have hoped.

"Another reason for setting this story in this slightly 'alternate' past is that it seems clear that essentially humanlike robots are unlikely to exist in any realistically extrapolated future. And yet I needed such a robot to effect the central irony of the piece. The end is (I hope) tragic, not because the boy has to destroy the robot, but because the robot doesn't have the capacity to understand the complex web of emotions the boy has woven around him. It is, after all, just a machine—and while the boy understands this fact, it cannot ameliorate his grief.

"Most of all, the story is about the influence of parents. I hope that 'The Resurrection Man's Legacy' gives readers a sense of the debt we owe our parents—both the literal parents who guide us from day to day and the whole community of role models who give us hopes and dreams we can aspire to. My mother and father first encouraged me to follow my dream of writing; but it was that community of science fiction and fantasy writers I read through an often lonely childhood who gave me the dream in the first place. In that sense, I want to dedicate the story to my mother and my father—and to the science fiction writers I read as a child, in some sense parents all."

I did not know the phrase "resurrection man" eighteen years ago. I was a boy then; such men were yet uncommon.

I know it now—we all know it—and yet the phrase retains for me a haunting quality, simultaneously wondrous and frightening. I met him only once, *my* resurrection man, on the cusp of a hazy August morning, but he haunts me still in subtle and unspoken ways: when I look in the mirror and see my face, like my father's face; or when I take the diamond, my uniform shining beneath the ranks of floodlights, and hear the infield chatter, like music if you love the game.

And I do. I do.

It was among the things he bequeathed to me, that love, though he could not have known it. We do not understand the consequences of the actions we take, the meaning of the legacies we leave. We cannot.

They are ghosts of sorts, actions in a vacuum where all action has passed, inheritances from the inscrutable dead. Legacies.

They can be gifts and they can be curses. Sometimes they can be both.

My father returned to the States in April of 1948, following the bloody, methodical invasion of Japan, and he married my mother the week he landed. She died in childbirth eleven months later, and I sometimes wonder if he ever forgave me. One other significant event occurred in '49: Casey Stengel, a ne'er-do-well journeyman manager, led the Yankees to the first of an unprecedented five straight victories in the World Series.

Twelve years later, in 1961, my father died too. That was the year Roger Maris came to bat in the fourth inning of the season's final game and drove his sixty-first home run into the right-field seats at Yankee Stadium, breaking Babe Ruth's record for single-season homers. In Baltimore, we still say that the new record is meaningless, that Maris played in a season six games longer than that of our home-grown hero; but even then, in our hearts, we knew it wasn't true.

Nothing would ever be the same again.

Two days after my father's death, the monorail whisked me from Baltimore to St. Louis. I had never been away from home. The journey was a nightmare journey. The landscape blurred beyond the shining curve of the window, whether through speed or tears, I could not tell.

My great aunt Rachel Powers met me at the station. Previously, I had known her only from a photograph pasted in the family album. A young woman then, she possessed a beauty that seemed to radiate color through the black and white print. She wore an androgynous flat-busted dress and her eyes blazed from above sharpened cheek bones with such unnerving intensity that, even in the photograph, I could not meet them for more than a moment.

The photograph had been taken forty years before my father's death, but I knew her instantly when I saw her on the platform.

"Jake Lamont?" she said.

I nodded, struck speechless. Tall and lean, she wore a billowing white frock and a white hat, like a young bride. The years had not touched her. She might have been sixteen, she might have been twenty. And then she lifted the veil that obscured her face, shattering the illusion of youth. I saw the same high, sharp cheek bones, the same intense eyes—blue; why had I never wondered?—but her flesh was seamed and spotted with age.

"Well, then," she said. "So you're a boy. I don't know much about boys." And then, when I still did not speak, "Are you mute, child?"

My fingers tightened around the handle of my traveling case. "No, ma'am."

"Well, good. Come along, then."

Without sparing me another glance, she disappeared into the throng. Half-fearful of being left in the noisy, crowded station, I lit out after her, dragging my suitcase behind me. Outside, in the clear midwestern heat, we loaded the suitcase into the trunk of a weary '53 Cadillac, one of those acre-long cars that Detroit began to produce in the fat years after the war.

We drove into farming country, on single-lane blacktop roads where you could cruise for hours and never see another car. We did not speak, though I watched her surreptitiously. Her intense eyes never deviated from the road, unswerving between the endless rows of corn. I cracked the window, and the car filled with the smell of August in Missouri—the smell of moist earth and cow manure, and green, growing things striving toward maturity, and the slow decline into September. That smell was lovely and alien, like nothing I had ever smelled in Baltimore.

At last, we came to the town, Stowes Corners, situated in a region of low, green hills. She took me through wide, tree-shadowed streets. I saw the courthouse, and the broad spacious lawn of the town square. On a quiet street lined with oak, my aunt pointed out the school, an unassuming antique brick, dwarfed by the monstrous edifice I had known in the city.

"That's where your father went to school when he was a boy," my aunt said, and a swift electric surge of anger—

—*how could he abandon me?*—

—jolted along my spine. I closed my eyes, and pressed my face against the cool window. The engine rumbled as the car pulled away from the curb, and when I opened my eyes again, we had turned into a long gravel drive. The Caddy mounted a short rise topped by a stand of maples, and emerged from the trees into sunlight and open air. My aunt paused there—in the days to come I would learn that she always paused there, she took a languorous, almost sensual delight in the land—and in the valley below I saw the house.

It had been a fine old farmhouse once, my aunt would later tell me, but that had been years ago; now, the surrounding fields lost to creditors, the house had begun the inevitable slide into genteel decay. Sun-bleached and worn, scabrous with peeling paint, it retained merely a glimmer of its former splendor. Even then, in my clumsy inarticulate fashion, I could see that it was like my aunt, a luminous fragment of a more refined era that had survived diminished into this whirling and cacophonous age.

"This is your home now," my aunt said, and without waiting for me to respond—what could I say?—she touched the gas and the car descended.

Inside, the house was silence and stillness and tattered elegance. The furnishings, though frayed, shone with a hard gloss, as if my aunt had determined, through sheer dint of effort, to hold back the ravages of years. A breeze stirred in the surrounding hills and chased itself through the open windows, bearing to me a faint lemony scent of furniture polish as I followed my aunt upstairs. She walked slowly, painfully, one hand bracing her back, the other clutching the rail. She led me to a small room and watched from the doorway as I placed my suitcase on the narrow bed. I did not look at her as she crossed the room and sat beside me. The springs complained rustily. I opened my suitcase, dug beneath my clothes, and withdrew the photograph I had brought from Baltimore. It was the only picture I had of my father and me together. Tears welled up inside me. I bit my lip and looked out the window, into the long treeless expanse of the backyard, desolate in a cruel fall of sunshine.

Aunt Rachel said, "Jake."

She said, "Jake, this isn't easy for either of us. I am an old woman and I am set in my ways. I have lived alone for thirty-five years, and I can be as ugly and unpleasant as a bear. I don't know the first thing about boys. You must remember this when things are hard between us."

"Yes, ma'am."

I felt her cool fingers touch my face. She took my chin firmly, and we stared into each other's faces for a time. She pressed her mouth into a thin indomitable line.

"You will look at me when I speak to you. Do you understand?"

"Yes, ma'am."

The fingers dropped from my face. "That's one of my rules. This isn't Baltimore, Jake. I'm not your father. He was a good boy, and I'm sure he was a fine man, but it strikes me that young people today are too lenient with their children. I will not tolerate disrespect."

"No, ma'am."

"Good," She smiled and smoothed her dress across her thighs. "I'm glad you've come to me, Jake," she said. "I hope we can be friends."

Before I could speak, she stood and left the room, closing the door behind her. I went around the bed and lifted the window. The breeze swept in, flooding the room with that alien smell of green things growing. I threw myself on the bed and drew my father's picture to my breast.

Among the photographs that are important to me number three relics of my youth. They are arranged across my desk like talismans as I write.

The first photograph, which I have already described to you, is that of my aunt as she must have looked in 1918 or '19, when she was a girl.

The second photograph is of my mother as she was in the days when my father knew her; aside from the photograph I have nothing of her. Perhaps my father felt that in hoarding whatever memories he had of her, he could possess her even in death. Or perhaps he simply could not bring himself to speak of her. I know he must have loved her, for every year on my birthday, the anniversary of her death, he drew into himself, became taciturn and insular in a way that in retrospect seems atypical, for he was a cheerful man, even buoyant. Beyond that I do not know; he was scrupulous in his destruction of every vestige of her. When he died, I found nothing. No photographs, but the one I still possess. No letters. Not even her rings; I suppose she wore them to the grave.

The third photograph I have mentioned also. It is of my father and me, when I was eleven, and it captures a great irony. Though it was taken in a ballpark—Baltimore's Memorial Stadium—my father did not love baseball. I don't remember why we went to that game—perhaps someone gave him the tickets—but we never attended another. That was when I felt it first, my passion for the sport; immediately, it appealed to me—its order and symmetry, its precision. Nothing else in sports rivals the moment when the batter steps into the box and faces the pitcher across sixty feet of shaven green. The entire game is concentrated into that instant, the skills of a lifetime distilled into every pitch; and no one, no one in the world but those two men, has any power to alter the course of the game.

In those days, of course, I did not think of it in such terms; my passion for the sport was nascent, rudimentary. All I knew was that I enjoyed the game, that someday I would like to see another. That much is my father's due.

The rest, indirectly anyway, was the resurrection man's gift, his legacy. But I have no photograph of him.

I slept uneasily that first night in Stowes Corners, unaccustomed to the rural quiet that cradled the house. The nightly symphony of traffic and voices to which I had been accustomed was absent, and the silence imparted a somehow ominous quality to the stealthy mouse-like chitterings of the automaids as they scurried about the sleeping house.

I woke unrested to the sound of voices drifting up from the parlor. Strange voices—my aunt's, only half-familiar yet, and a second voice, utterly unknown, mellifluous and slow and fawningly ingratiating.

This voice was saying, "You *do* realize, Miss Powers, there are limits to what we are permitted to do?"

I eased out of bed in my pajamas and crept along the spacious hall to the head of the stairs, the hardwood floor cool against my bare feet.

My aunt said, "Limits? The advertising gave me the impression you could do most anything."

I seated myself on the landing in the prickly silence that followed. A breeze soughed through the upstairs windows. Through the half-open door in the ornate foyer below, I could see a car parked in the circular drive. Beyond the car, the morning sun gleamed against the stand of maple and sent a drowsy haze of mist steaming away into the open sky.

My aunt was rattling papers below. "It doesn't say anything about limits here."

"No, ma'am, of course not. And I didn't mean to imply that our products were not convincing. Not by any means."

"Then what do you mean by limits?"

The stranger cleared his throat. "Not technological limits, ma'am. Those exist, of course, but they're not the issue here."

"Well, what in heaven's name *is* the issue?"

"It's a legal matter, ma'am—a constitutional matter, even. We're a young company, you know, and our product is new and unfamiliar and there's bound to be some controversy, as you might well imagine." He paused, and I could hear him fumbling about through his paraphernalia. A moment later I heard the sharp distinct *snick* of a lighter.

He smoked, of course. In those days, all men smoked, and the acrid gritty stink of tobacco smoke which now began to drift up the stairs reminded me of my father.

I do not smoke. I never have.

"Our company," he resumed, "we're cognizant of the objections folks might raise to our product. The Church—all the churches— are going to be a problem. And the doctors are going to have a field day with the need to come to terms with grief. We know that—our founder, Mr. Hiram Wallace, he *knows* that, he's an intelligent man, but he's committed. We're all committed. Do you know anything about Mr. Wallace, ma'am?"

"I'm afraid I don't."

"It's an inspiring story, a story I think you ought to hear. Anybody who's thinking of contracting with us ought to hear it. Do you mind?"

My aunt sighed. I heard her adjust herself in her chair, and I could imagine them in the quaint, spotless parlor I had seen the night before: my aunt in her white dress, her hands crossed like a girl's over the advertising packet in her lap; the resurrection man, leaning forward from the loveseat, a cigarette dangling between his fingers.

Aunt Rachel said, "Go ahead then."

"It's a tragedy, really," the resurrection man said, "but it ends in triumph. For you see, Mr. Wallace's first wife, she was hit by a bus on their honeymoon—"

"Oh, my!"

"Yes, ma'am, that's right, a bus." There was a hardy smack as the resurrection man slammed his hands together; I could hear it even at the top of the stairs. "Like that," he said, "so sudden. Mr. Wallace was heartbroken. He knows what you're feeling, ma'am, he knows what your boy upstairs is feeling, and he wants to help—"

With these words, an icy net of apprehension closed around my heart, and the tenor of my eavesdropping swerved abruptly from mild curiosity to a kind of breathless dread. The resurrection man's next words came sluggish and dim. I felt as if I had been wrapped in cotton. The landing had grown oppressively hot.

"The potential applications for this technology are mind-boggling," he was saying. "And I won't lie to you, ma'am, Mr. Wallace is exploring those avenues. But this, this service to the grief-stricken and the lonely, this is where his heart lies. That's why we're offering this service before any other, ma'am, and that's why there are limits to what we can do."

"But I'm afraid I still don't understand."

"Let me see if I can clarify, ma'am. Of all the forces arrayed against us—all the people like the churches and the doctors who'd like to see our enterprise go down the tubes—our single most dangerous adversary is the government itself. Our senators and representatives are frankly scared to death of this."

"But why?"

"It's the question of legal status, ma'am. What does it take to be a human being? That's the question. All the agreements we've worked out with congressional committees and sub-committees—it seems like a hundred of them—all the agreements boil down to one thing: these, these . . . beings . . . must be recognizably non-human, limited in intellect, artificial in appearance. No one wants to grapple with the big questions, ma'am. No one wants to take on the churches, especially our elected officials. They're all cowards."

Aunt Rachel said, "I see," in a quiet, thoughtful kind of voice, but she didn't say anything more.

In the silence that followed, something of the magnitude of my aunt's devotion came to me. I did not know much about Stowes Corners, but I suspected, with a twelve-year-old's inarticulate sense of such things, that the town was as rigidly provincial in perspective as in appearance. Whatever the stranger below was selling my aunt, he had clearly come a long way to sell it; there could be no need for such controversial ... beings, as he had called them ... here—here in a place where my aunt had told me that she was among the few folks in town who owned automaids.

I couldn't really afford them, Jake, she had said last night at supper, *but the work was getting to be too much for me. I'm glad you've come to help me.*

Now, with the sun rising over the maples and throwing sharp glints off the car in the drive, the resurrection man coughed. "I hope you're still interested, Miss Powers."

"Well, I don't know a thing about boys," she said. "And I don't want him growing up without a father. It isn't right that a boy grow up without a man in the house."

That icy net of apprehension drew still tighter about my heart. My stomach executed a slow perfect roll, and the sour tang of bile flooded my mouth. I leaned my head against the newel and shut my eyes.

"I agree entirely, ma'am," came the other voice. "A boy needs a father. You can rest assured we'll do our best."

From below, there came the rustle of people standing, the murmured pleasantries of leave-taking. My aunt asked how long it would take, and the resurrection man said not long, we'll simply modify a prefab model along the lines suggested by the photos and recordings— and through all this babble a single thought burst with unbearable clarity:

Nothing, nothing would ever be the same again.

I stood, and fled down the hall, down the back stairs. I slammed through the kitchen and into the gathering heat.

When the front door swung open, I was waiting. As the resurrection man—this stout, balding man dressed in a dark suit, and a wide bright tie; this unprepossessing man, unknowing and unknown, who would shape the course of my existence—as this man rounded the corner of his car, his case in hand, I hurled myself at him. Frenzied, I hurled myself at him, flailing at his chest. "What are you going to do?" I cried.

Strong hands pinned my arms to my sides and lifted me from the ground. The rancid odors of after-shave and tobacco enveloped me, and I saw that sweat stood in a dark ring around his collar. "Calm down!" he shouted. "Just calm down, son! Are you crazy?"

He thrust me from him. Half-blinded by tears, I stumbled away, swiping angrily at my eyes with my knuckles. Without speaking, the resurrection man dusted his suit and retrieved his case. He got in his car and drove away, and though I could not know it then, I would never see him again.

My father's body came by slowtrain several days later. He had returned to Stowes Corners only once in the years after the war, to see my mother into the earth where her family awaited her. Now, at last, he came to join her; we buried him in the sun-dappled obscurity of a Missouri noon.

As the minister quietly recited the ritual, a soft wind lilted through the swallow-thronged trees, bearing to me the sweet fragrances of freshly turned earth and new-mown grass. I watched an intricate pattern of light and leaf-shadow play across my aunt's face, but I saw no tears. Her still emotionless features mirrored my own. The service seemed appropriate—minimal and isolated, infinitely distant from the places and people my father had known. There was only the minister, my aunt, and myself. No one else attended.

When the minister had finished, I knelt before my mother's tombstone and reached out a single finger to trace her name. And then I clutched a handful of soil and let it trickle through my fingers into my father's grave. I shall never forget the sound it made as it spattered the casket's polished lid.

Several years ago, I chanced upon an archaeologist's account of his experience excavating a ruined city, abandoned beneath the sand for thousands of years. Such a project is an exercise in meticulous drudgery; the earth does not readily divulge her secrets. Stratum after stratum of sand must be sifted, countless fragments painstakingly extracted and catalogued and fitted together for interpretation. You are in truth excavating not one city, but many cities, each built on the rubble of the one which preceded it.

I am reminded of this now, for recollection, like archaeology, is a matter of sifting through ruins. Memory is frail and untrustworthy, tainted by desire; what evidence remains is fragmentary, shrouded in the mystery of the irretrievable past. You cannot recover history; you can only reconstruct it, build it anew from the shards that have survived, searching always for the seams between the strata, those places of demarcation between the city that was and the city that would be, between the self that you were and the self you have become.

How do you reconstruct a past, when only potsherds and photographs remain?

A moment, then.

An instant from the quiet, hot August day my father was interred— one of those timeless instants that stands like a seam between the geologic strata of a buried city, between the boy I was and the man I have become:

Afternoon.

In the room where I slept, the blinds rattled, but otherwise all was silent. Outside, somewhere, the world moved on. Tiny gusts leavened the heat and lifted the luminous scent of pollen into the afternoon, but through the open window there came only a cloying funerary pall. Far away, the sun shone; it announced its presence here only as an anemic gleam behind the lowered blinds, insufficient to dispel the gloom.

I stood before the closet, fumbling with my tie. My eyes stung and my stomach had drawn into an agonizing knot, but I refused to cry. I was repeating a kind of litany to myself—

—*I will not cry, I will not*—

—when a voice said:

"Hello, Jake."

My spine stiffened. The tiny hairs along my back stirred, as if a dark gust from some October landscape had swept into the room.

It was my father's voice.

I did not turn. Without a word, I shrugged off my jacket and swung open the closet door. In the dim reflection of the mirror hung inside, I could see a quiet figure, preternatural in its stillness, seated in the far shadowy corner by the bed.

I don't want him growing up without a father, my aunt had said. *It isn't right that a boy grow up without a man in the house.*

What in God's name had she done?

The figure said, "Don't be afraid, Jake."

"I'm not afraid," I said. But my hands shook as I fumbled at the buttons on my shirt. I groped for a hanger, draped the shirt around it, and thrust it into the depths of the closet, feeling exposed in my nakedness, vulnerable, but determined not to allow this . . . *being*, the resurrection man had called it . . . to sense that. Kicking away my slacks, I fished a pair of jeans out of the closet.

In the mirror, I saw the figure stand.

I said, "Don't come near me."

And that voice—*my God, that voice*—said, "Don't be afraid."

It smiled and lifted a hand to the window, each precise, economical gesture accompanied by a faint mechanical hum, as though somewhere far down in the depths of its being, flywheels whirred and gears meshed in intricate symphony. I watched as it gripped the cord and raised the blind.

The room seemed to ignite. Sunlight glanced out of the mirror and rippled in the glossy depths of the headboard and nightstand. A thousand spinning motes of dust flared, and I winced as my eyes adjusted. Then, my heart pounding, I closed the closet door, and at last, at last I turned around.

It was my father—from the dark hair touched gray at the temples to the slight smiling crinkles around the eyes to the slim athletic build, seeming to radiate poise and grace even in repose—in every detail, it was my father. It sat once again in the wooden chair by the nightstand, stiffly erect, its blunt fingers splayed on the thighs of its jeans, and returned my stare from my father's eyes. I felt a quick hot swell of anger and regret—

—*how could you abandon me?*—

—felt something tear away inside of me. I blinked back tears.

"My God, what are you?"

"Jake," it said. It said, "Jake, don't cry."

That swift tide of anger, burning, swept through me, obliterating all. "Don't you tell me what to do."

The thing seemed taken aback. It composed its features into an expression of startled dismay; its mouth moved, but it said nothing.

We stared across the room at one another until at last it looked away. It lifted the framed photograph that stood on the nightstand. A moment passed, and then another, while it gazed into the picture. I wondered what it saw there, in that tiny image of the man it was pretending to be.

One thick finger caressed the gilded frame. "Is that Memorial Stadium?"

It looked up, smiling tentatively, and I crossed the room in three angry strides. I tore the photograph out of the thing's hands, and then the tears boiled out of me, burning and shameful.

"You don't know anything about it!" I cried, flinging myself on the bed. The creature stood, its hands outstretched, saying, "Jake, Jake—" but I rushed on, I would not listen: "You're not my father! You don't know anything about it! Anything, you hear me? So just go away and leave me alone!" In the end, I was screaming.

The thing straightened. "Okay, Jake. If that's the way you want it." And it crossed the room, and went out into the hall, closing the door softly behind it.

I lay back on the bed. After a while, my aunt called me for supper, but I didn't answer. She didn't call again. Outside, it began to grow dark, and finally a heavy silence enclosed the house. Eventually, I heard tiny mutterings and whisperings as the automaids crept from their holes and crannies and began to whisk away the debris of another day, but through it all, I did not move. I lay wide awake, staring blindly at the dark ceiling.

During the days that followed my aunt and I moved about the house like wraiths, mute and insubstantial, imprisoned by the unacknowledged presence of this monstrous being, this creature that was my father and not my father. We did not mention it; I dared not ask, she proffered no explanation. Indeed, I might have imagined the entire episode, except I glimpsed it now and then—trimming the shrubs with garden shears or soaping down the Caddy in the heat, and once, in a tableau that haunts me still, standing dumb in the darkened parlor, gazing expressionlessly at the wall with a concentration no human being could muster.

Inexorably the afternoons grew shorter, the maple leaves began to turn, and somehow, somewhere in all the endless moments, August passed into September.

One morning before the sun had burned the fog off the hills, my aunt awoke me. I dressed quietly, and together we walked into the cool morning, the gravel crunching beneath our feet. She drove me to the school my father had attended all those long years ago, a mile away, and as I stepped from the car she pressed a quarter into my hand.

"Come here," she said, and when I came around the car to the open window, she leaned out and kissed me. Her lips were dry and hard, with the texture of withered leaves.

She looked away, through the glare of windshield, where morning was breaking across the town. A bell began to ring, and noisy clusters of children ran by us, shouting laughter, but I did not move. The two of us might have been enclosed in a thin impermeable bubble, isolated from the world around us. Her knuckles had whitened atop the steering wheel.

"You can walk home," she said, "you know the way," and when I did not answer, she cleared her throat. "Well, then, good luck," she said, and I felt a reply—what it might have been, I cannot know—catch in my throat. Before I could dislodge it, the car pulled from the curb.

I turned to the school. The bell continued to ring. Another clump of children swept by, and I drifted along like flotsam in their wake. I mounted the steps to the building slowly and carefully, as if the slightest jolt would destabilize the churning energies that had been compressed within me. I was a bomb, I could have ticked.

My aunt and I were in the kitchen, eating supper, that wall of impregnable silence between us. I ate with studied nonchalance, gazing steadfastly into my plate, or staring off into the dining room beyond the kitchen. The creature that looked like my father sat alone in there, shadowy and imperturbable, its hands folded neatly on the table.

Aunt Rachel said, "Jake, it's time to move on with your life. You must accept your father's death and go on. You cannot grieve forever."

I pushed my vegetables around my plate. Words swollen and poisonous formed in my gut; I could not force them into my throat.

She said, "Jake, I want to be your friend."

Again, I did not answer. I looked off into the dining room. The thing looked back, silent, inscrutable. And then, almost without thought, I began to speak, expelling the words in a deadly emotionless monotone: "You must be crazy. Do you think that thing can replace him?"

Aunt Rachel lowered her fork with shaking fingers. Her lips had gone white. "Of course not. Your father can never be replaced, Jake."

"That's not my father," I said. "It's nothing like him!"

"Jake, I know—"

But she could not finish. I found myself standing, my napkin clenched in one hand. Screaming: "It's not! It's not a thing like him! You must be crazy, you old witch—"

And then I was silent. A deadly calm descended in the kitchen. I felt light-headed, as though I were floating somewhere around the ceiling, tethered to my body by the most tenuous of threads. The things I had said made no sense, I knew, but they felt true.

My aunt said, "Look me in the eye, Jake."

I forced my stone-heavy eyes to meet hers.

"You must never speak to me like that again," she said. "Do you understand?"

Biting my lip, I nodded.

"Your father is dead," she told me. "I understand you are in pain, but it is time you face the facts and begin to consider the feelings of others again. You must never run away from the truth, Jake, however unpleasant. Because once you begin running, you can never stop."

She folded her napkin neatly beside her plate and pushed her chair away from the table. "Come here," she said. "Bend over and put your hands on your knees."

Reluctantly, I did as she asked. She struck me three quick painless blows across the backside, and I felt tears of humiliation well up in my eyes. I bit my lip—bit back the tears—and finished my meal in silence, but afterwards I crept upstairs to stretch on the narrow bed and stare at the familiar ceiling. A sharp woodsy odor of burning leaves drifted through the window, and shadows slowly inhabited the room. An orchestra of insects began to warm up in the long flat space behind the house.

I dozed, and woke later in the night to a room spun full of gossamer moonlight. The creature sat in the chair by the nightstand, cradling the photograph in its unlined hands. It looked up, something whirring in its neck, and placed the photograph on the nightstand where I could see it.

"I'll go if you like," it said.

I sat up, wincing. "Light, please," I told the lamp, and as the room brightened, I gazed into the picture. A boy curiously unlike myself gazed back at me, eyes shining, arm draped about the slim, dark-headed man next to him. My father's lean beard-shadowed face had already begun to grow unfamiliar. Looking at the photograph, I could see him—how could I not?—but at night, in the darkness, I could not picture him. His lips came to me, or his eyes, or the long curve of his jaw, but they came like pieces of a worn-out jigsaw puzzle—they would not fit together true. And now, of course, he is lost to me utterly; only sometimes, when I look into a mirror, I catch a glimpse of him there and it frightens me.

I reached out a finger to the photograph. Glass. Cold glass, walling me away forever.

I remembered the dirt as it trickled through my fingers; I remembered the sound it made as it spattered the lid of the casket.

"You're not my father," I said.

"No."

We were quiet for a while. Something small and toothy gnawed away inside me.

"What are you?" I asked.

"I'm a machine."

"That's all? Just a machine, like a car or a radio?"

"Something like that. More complicated. A simulated person, they call me—a sim. I'm a new thing. There aren't many machines in the world like me, though maybe there will be."

"I could cut you off," I said. "I could just cut you off."

"Yes."

"And if I do?"

The sim lifted its hands and shrugged. "Gone," it said. "Erased and irrecoverable. Everything that makes me me."

"Show me. I want to know."

The sim's expression did not change. It merely leaned forward and lifted the thick hair along its neck. And there it was: a tiny switch, like a jewel gleaming in the light. I reached out and touched it, ran my finger through the coarse hair, touched the skin, rubbery and cold, thinking of what he had said: *Erased and irrecoverable.*

"You're a machine," I said. "That's all." And everything—the fear and anger, the hope and despair—everything drained out of me, leaving a crystalline void. I was glass. If you had touched me, I would have shattered into a thousand shining fragments. "My aunt must be crazy."

"Perhaps she only wants to make you happy."

"You can't replace my father."

"I don't want to."

Insects had begun to hurl themselves at the window screen, and I told the light to shut itself off. The darkness seemed much thicker than before, and I could perceive the sim only as a silhouette against the bright moonlit square of the window. It reached out and picked up the photograph again and I thought: *It can see in the dark.*

Who knew what it could do?

The sim said, "Did you go to many games at Memorial Park?"

"You ought to know. You're supposed to be just like him."

"I hardly know a thing about him," the sim said. And then: "Jake, I'm not really a thing like him at all. I just look like him."

"That was the only game we ever went to."

"I see."

All at once that day came flooding back to me—its sights and sounds, its sensations. I wanted to describe the agony of suspense that built with every pitch, the hush of the crowd and the flat audible crack of the bat when a slugger launched the ball clear into the summer void, a pale blur against the vaulted blue. I remembered those things, and more: the oniony smell of the hot dogs and relish my father and I had shared, the bite of an icy Coke in the heat, and through it all the recurrent celebratory strain of the calliope. A thousand things I could not say.

So we sat there in silence, and finally the sim said, "Do you think we could be friends?"

I shrugged, thinking of my aunt. She too had wished to be my friend. Now, in the silent moonlit bedroom, the scene at the table came back to me. An oily rush of shame surged through me. "Is it really so bad, running away?"

"I don't know. I don't know things like that."

"What am I going to do?"

"Maybe you don't have to run away." The sim cocked its head with a mechanical hum. A soft crescent of moonlight illuminated one cheek, and I could see a single eye, flat and depthless as polished tin. But all the rest was shadow. It said, "I'm not your father, Jake. But I could be your friend."

Without speaking, I lay down, pulled the covers up to my chin, and listened for a while to the whispery chatter of the automaids as they scoured the bottom floor. A breeze murmured about the eaves, and somewhere far away in the hills, an owl hooted, comforting and friendly, and that was a sound I had never heard in Baltimore.

I had just begun to doze when the sim spoke again.

"Maybe sometime we can pitch the ball around," it said, and through the thickening web of sleep I thought, for just a moment, that it was my father. But, of course, it wasn't. An unutterable tide of grief washed over me, bearing me to an uneasy shore of dreams.

That October, I sat alone in the sun-drenched parlor and listened to the week-end games of the '61 World Series on my aunt's radio. The Yankee sluggers had gone cold. Mantle, recovering from late-season surgery, batted only six times in the whole series; Maris had spent himself in the chase for Babe Ruth's single-season home run record.

Yankee hurler Whitey Ford took up the slack. I read about his game-one shut-out in the newspaper. Four days later, when he took the mound again, I listened from hundreds of miles away. In the third inning, the sim came into the room and sat down across from me. It steepled its fingers and closed its eyes. We did not speak.

Ford pitched two more flawless innings before retiring with an injury in the sixth.

I stood up, suddenly angry, and glared at the sim. "You ought to have a name, I guess," I said.

The sim opened its eyes. It did not speak.

"I'll call you Ford," I said bitterly. "That's a machine's name."

Dreams plagued me that year. One night, I seemed to wake in the midst of a cheering crowd at Memorial Stadium. But gradually the park grew hushed. The game halted below, and the players, the bright-clad vendors, the vast silent throng—one by one, they turned upon me their voiceless gaze. I saw that I was surrounded by the dead: my father, the mother I had never known, a thousand others, all the twisted, shrunken dead. A tainted wind gusted among the seats, fanning my hair, and the silent corpses began to crumble. Desiccated flesh sloughed like ash from the bones, whirled in dark funnels through the stands. And then the air cleared, and I saw that the dead were lost to me forever. Silence reigned, and emptiness. Endless empty rows.

Day turned into dream-haunted night and into day again. My father receded in memory, as if I had known him a hundred years ago. My life in Baltimore might have been another boy's life, distant and unreal. I was agreeable, but distant with my aunt; I ignored Ford for the most part. I passed long stifling hours in school, staring dreamily, day after day, across the abandoned playground to the baseball diamond, dusty and vacant in the afternoon. I had no interest in studies. Even now, I remember my aunt's crestfallen expression as she inspected my report cards, the rows of D's and F's, or the section reserved for comments, where Mrs. O'Leary wrote, *Jake is well-behaved and has ability, but he is moody and lacks discipline.*

In March of '62, on my birthday, I came home from school to find a hand-stitched regulation baseball, a leather fielder's glove, and a Louisville Slugger, knotted with a shiny ribbon, arranged on my bed. I caressed the soft leather glove.

From the doorway, my aunt said, "Do you like them, Jake?"

I slipped on the glove, turned the ball pensively with my right hand, and flipped it toward the ceiling. It hung there for a moment, spinning like a jewel in the sunlight, and then it plunged toward the floor. My left hand leaped forward, the glove seemed to open of its own accord, and the ball dropped solidly into the pocket.

Nothing had ever felt so right.

I said, "I love them."

My aunt sat on the bed, wincing. Already, the arthritis had begun its bitter, surreptitious campaign. She smoothed her dress across her knees.

I brought the glove to my face. Closing my eyes, I drew in the deep, leathery aroma. "Gosh," I said, "they're fine . . . I mean, they're *really* fine. How did you ever know?"

My aunt smiled. "We're getting to know you, now. Besides I had some help."

"Help?"

She nodded, and touched the bat. "Only the best," she said. "Ford insisted on it."

"It's . . . well, it's just tremendous. I mean, thank you."

She leaned forward and pressed her lips to my cheek. "Happy birthday, Jake. I'm glad you like them." She lifted her hands to my shoulders and gently pushed me erect. "Now, look me in the eye," she said. "There's something we need to talk about."

"Yes, ma'am?"

"I've made some phone calls. I've talked to Mrs. O'Leary and some other folks at school."

I glanced away, let the baseball slip from my glove into my waiting hand. My aunt touched my chin, lifted my head so that I was looking in her eyes. "Listen, Jake, this is important."

"Okay."

"Mrs. O'Leary says you'll pass and go on to junior high, but it's a close thing. And starting next year your grades will count toward college. Did you know that?"

"No, ma'am."

"Every member of my family for two generations has gone to college. I do not intend for that to change."

I said nothing. Her eyes were a sharp intense blue. Penetrating. So we were family, I thought. She said, "Ford thinks you might like to try out for baseball next year. Is that true?"

I had never considered the possibility. Now, turning the ball in my hand, I said, "I guess."

"I talked to the junior high baseball coach, too. You have to bring your grades up or you won't be eligible for the team. Can you do that?"

"Yes, ma'am—it's not that I'm dumb or anything. It's just—" I paused, searching for words that would not come. How could I explain? "I don't know."

Aunt Rachel smiled. "But you'll do better, right?"

I nodded.

"Good." She smiled and reached out to squeeze my hand. I could feel the pressure of her fingers. I could feel the ball's seams dig into my palm. "Oh, that's fine, Jake. Have you ever played ball before?"

"No, ma'am," I said.

"Then you have some catching up to do. I think there's someone outside who'd like to help."

I stood and went to the window. Ford waited below, his shadow stretching across the grass. He wore a glove on his left hand, a baseball cap canted over his eyes. When he saw me, he lifted the glove and hollered, "Hey, Jake! Come on!"

I lifted my hand in a half-reluctant wave and just then Aunt Rachel stepped up behind me. She tugged a cap firmly over my head, and let her fingers fall to my shoulder. "Go ahead, have fun," she whispered. "But remember our deal."

"Yes, ma'am!" I shouted. Scooping up the bat, I ran out of the room. I bounded down the steps, through the kitchen, and into the sunlit backyard where Ford awaited me.

Ford pitched, and I batted.

The sun arced westward. Time and again, the Louisville Slugger whistled impotently in the air, until at last I threw it down in frustration.

"You're swinging wild," Ford said. "You're hacking at the ball."

He picked up the discarded bat, and swung it easily for a moment with his large and capable-looking hands.

"Like this," he told me. He planted his feet, and bounced a little on his knees. He held his elbows away from his body, tilted the bat over his shoulder, and swung smoothly and easily.

"Watch the ball," he said. "You've got to eye the ball in, and meet it smoothly. You want to try?"

I shrugged. Ford handed me the bat and took his position sixty feet away. I bobbed the bat, swung it once or twice the way I had seen the pros do, and relaxed into the stance Ford had shown me, the bat angled over my right shoulder. I tracked the ball as it left his hand, saw it hurtle towards me, but I held back, held back . . .

. . . and at the very last moment, just when it seemed the ball would whip by untouched, I swung.

I felt the concussion all along my shoulders and arms. My mouth fell open, and I tossed the bat into the grass, hooting in delight. Ford clapped his hands as the ball rocketed skyward, disappeared momentarily into the sun, and began to drop into the high grass beyond the yard.

Gone.

"Now we have to find it," Ford said.

I set off across the yard, jogging to keep up with Ford's long strides. My arms and shoulders ached pleasantly. I could taste a slight tang of perspiration on my upper lip. Half-curiously, I looked at the sim. Not a single droplet of sweat clung to his perfect, gleaming flesh. He walked smoothly, and easily, his knees humming with every step.

When we finally found the ball, far back in the field behind the house, I threw myself exhausted in the grass. Ford lowered himself beside me, propping his weight on his elbows, and we remained that way for a while, sucking thoughtfully on sweet blades of grass. An old game my father and I had played came back to me and I began to point out shapes in the clouds—a chariot, a skull, a moose—but the sim did not respond.

"Do you see anything?" I asked him, and when he did not answer I turned to eye him. "Well, do you?"

He chased the grass stalk to the far corner of his mouth and smiled. "Sure I do, when you point them out, Jake. You go ahead, I like to listen."

And so I did, until the charm of the game began to wear thin; after that we just lay quiet and restful for a while. At last, my aunt called me for supper. Inside, for the first time, the sim came into the kitchen and took a chair at the table while we ate. He shot me a glance as he sat down, as if I might have something to say about it, and I almost did. A quick flash of anger, like heat lightning, flickered through me. I looked away.

"Discipline," Ford told me that summer. "In baseball, discipline is everything."

That, too, was a legacy. And though I imagine Ford could not have known it—what could he really know, after all?—perhaps he sensed it somehow: this was a lesson with broader implications. Certainly Aunt Rachel knew it.

"For every hour you spend on baseball," she told me that night, "you must spend an hour reading or doing homework. Agreed?"

And so commenced my central obsessions, those legacies that have shaped my life. From that time onward, my youth was consumed by baseball and books. During that summer and the summers that followed—all through my high school career—Ford and I worked in the quiet isolation of the backyard. I took to baseball with a kind of innate facility, as if an understanding of the game had been encoded in my genes. I relished the sting of a line-drive into well-oiled leather, the inexorable trajectory of a flyball as it plummeted toward a waiting glove. I relish it still. There is an order and a symmetry to the game which counteracts the chaos that pervades our lives; even then, in some inchoate, inexpressible fashion, I understood this simple truth.

Every pitcher has to have a repertoire, Ford told me one day, a fastball and a curve. Leaning over me, he shaped my fingers along the seams of the ball. Hide it in your glove, he said. Don't tip off the batter.

Summer after summer, until the season broke and winter closed around the town, Ford coached me through the pitch—the grips, the wind-up and pivot, the follow-through on the release. I wanted to hurl with my arm. Save your arm, he told me; he showed me how to use my legs.

But it was more than merely physical discipline; Ford had a strategic grasp of the game, as well. He taught me that baseball was a cerebral sport, showed me that a well-coached team could prevail over talent and brawn. Some days we never touched a ball at all. We sat cross-legged in the grass, dissecting games we had heard on the radio or read about in the paper. He fabricated situations out of whole cloth and asked me to coach my way through them, probing my responses with emotionless logic.

Occasionally, in the frustration of the moment, I would stand and walk away from him, turning at last to gaze back to the far distant house, past the sim sitting patiently in the grass, to the back porch where my aunt waited, watching from the steps that first summer, and later, as the arthritis began to gnaw away inside her, from the hated prison of her powerchair.

In those later years, she preserved her dignity. On our infrequent excursions into town, she insisted on walking upright; she masked her pain and held her head rigidly erect, regal as a queen. She did not give up. Standing there in the open field, I would remember this, and her simple lesson, the litany she lived by, would come back to me: *You must never run away*. Chagrined, I would remember another thing that had been said to me—Ford's voice this time, saying, *Talent is never enough, Jake. Discipline is everything*—and I would walk back and take my place across from him.

Tell me again, I would say.

Tiny motors whirred beneath his flesh, drew a broad smile across his features; he would tell me again. Day after day, through the long summer months, he told me again. We hashed over countless situations, until the strategies came thoughtlessly to my lips, naturally, and I did not walk away in frustration anymore.

During these same years, I spent nights alone in my bedroom, studying during the school year, reading for pleasure in my stolen hours. At first, in a kind of half-conscious rebellion against my aunt's ultimatum, I read only about baseball—strategies and biographies, meditations on the game. But gradually my interests broadened. I read history and fiction and, one memorable summer, everything I could find about simulated people. I read about Hiram Wallace and his absurd tragedy. I read his encomiums for the specialized sims he called grief counselors—and opposing editorials from every perspective. The resurrection man had been right about one thing: Wallace had his critics.

But none of them convinced me.

At the school library one fall I researched the matter. I flipped anxiously through news magazines, half-hoping to run upon a picture of the stout, hearty salesman that had come to the house, half-fearing it as well. That night, I lay awake far into the morning, examining in a magazine graphic the wondrous intricacies of Ford's design. I remember being half-afraid the sim would walk in upon me, as if I were doing something vaguely shameful, though why I should have felt this way, I cannot say. After that, during sleepless nights, in the darkness when the image of my father would not cohere, I thought of Ford: I imagined the twisted involutions of his construction, the gears and cogs and whirring motors, the thousand electric impulses that sang along his nested wires, far down through his core, to the crystal-matrixed genius of his brain.

This is what I remember about high school:

Empty stands.

Not truly empty, you understand—the crowds came in droves by my senior year, when I won ten of eleven as a starter. By that time, a few local fellows, short on work, had even started looking in on practice. They lounged in the stands, trimming their nails or glancing through the want ads; every once in a while, if someone got a piece of the ball, they would holler and whistle.

And hundreds showed up for the last game of my high school career, when I gave up the winning run on a botched slider in the seventh. But the stands were empty all the same.

Afterward, I stood on the mound and watched the crowd disperse. A few teammates patted my shoulder as they headed in to see their families, but I just stood there in the middle of the diamond.

My aunt had never seen me play; she could barely leave the house by then. And Ford? Who would take him to the ballpark?

A jowly, red-faced man awaited me at school the following Monday. I had seen him in the stands during practice the last week or so, looking on with a kind of absent-minded regard, as if he had more important things on his mind. I assumed him an out-of-work gas jockey or a farmhand with time on his hands.

I was wrong.

He sat across from me in the cluttered office off the locker room, his beat-up oxfords propped carelessly on the corner of Coach Ryan's desk. He wore a shabby suit and a coffee-stained tie; his shirt gapped at the belly. Coach Ryan had introduced him as Gerald Haynes, a scout for the Reds.

"So what happened the other night?" Haynes asked.

I started to speak, but Coach Ryan interrupted. He fiddled with a pencil on his blotter. "Just an off game, Mr. Haynes—an off pitch, actually. The boy played a solid game." He looked at me as if he had just noticed I was there. "You played a solid game, Jake."

Haynes lifted an eyebrow. "What do *you* say, son?"

"I made a bad decision," I replied, when the silence had stretched a moment too long. "I went with the slider when the fastball had been working all day. It hung up on me." I shrugged.

"Jake's got a pretty good slider, actually—" Coach Ryan began, but Haynes held up his hand.

He picked up a paper cup that sat on the floor and dribbled a stream of tobacco juice into it. I could smell the tobacco juice, intermixed with the locker room's familiar stink of mold and sweat. "Why would you make a decision like that, son?"

"I knew there were some college scouts in the stands. I wanted to show them what I had."

Haynes chuckled.

"I didn't know *you* were there," I said.

Coach Ryan said, "I didn't tell him. I didn't want to make him nervous, you know?"

"So you pitched to impress the people watching, am I right?"

My bowels felt loose, like I might be sick, but I met his eyes. "Yes, sir."

Haynes put the cup down and leaned close to me. I could smell his polluted breath. "You pitch to win, Jake. That's the cardinal rule, okay?"

"Yes, sir."

"You aren't ready to throw sliders, and you certainly aren't ready to throw them on a three-two count in the last inning of a tied ballgame. You want to know about sliders, I'll tell you about sliders. A badly thrown slider can throw your arm out of whack for good, ruin your career. I've seen it once, I've seen it a thousand times."

"Yes, sir."

"You want to take care of yourself." Haynes leaned back and crossed his arms over his belly. He stared at me for a while.

I knew I shouldn't ask, but I couldn't help myself. "Why is that, sir?"

Haynes dug a clump of snuff from behind his lip and flipped it into the cup. He stood, wiped his hands on his pants, and extended his arm to me.

I reached out and took his grip. He squeezed hard and smiled. "I've seen better, son," he said. "But you ain't bad. You ain't bad."

Those were the days before ballplayers commanded the astronomical salaries they draw now, as Aunt Rachel quickly pointed out. "I'm entirely against it, Jake," she told me one evening early in July.

I sighed and shifted uncomfortably in one of the claw-footed chairs in the parlor. The Reds had, in fact, extended me an offer, but I had been chosen in the late rounds. My signing bonus was negligible, my proposed salary more so. *You've got talent, all right,* Haynes had told me, *but you ain't no ace, son.*

Not yet, I had thought.

Now, I glanced at Ford. He sat on the loveseat across the room, his back straight, his hands resting flat on his thighs. "Well, Ford," I said. "What do you think?"

The sim tilted his head with a faintly musical hum. He looked to my aunt and then back to me. "I don't know, Jake," he said at last. "I can't answer things like that."

"Well, wouldn't you like me to play pro ball?"

"Sure. I guess so."

"Don't you think he ought to go to college?" Aunt Rachel said drily.

"Yes, ma'am. I guess so."

I crossed my arms in exasperation and swung my legs over the arm of my chair. I managed to hold the pose for all of thirty seconds before my aunt's silent disapproval compelled me to lower my feet and sit up straight.

"Thank you," Aunt Rachel said. Then, after a brief silence, "Jake, you know that machine can't be a part of this."

I didn't answer.

"I only want what's best for you. You know that." She coughed weakly, grimacing, and straightened herself in the powerchair.

The doctor had told me she was in extraordinary pain, but it was easy to forget. She did not speak of her illness; she refused pain medication.

I felt awful. I wanted to apologize to her. But this was an opportunity that might never again present itself. I said, "College will wait. I can go to college anytime."

"Every member of my family for two generations has been to college."

"I didn't say I wouldn't go. I said it would wait."

My aunt guided her chair to the broad windows that overlooked the front. I could see the Caddy out there, more broken-down than ever, and on the knoll at the end of the long drive, the stand of maple overlooking the valley. I wondered what she could be thinking—if, like me, she was remembering the day she had brought me to this place, this home, and how she had paused up there to look out over the house and the land and to let me look out over them for the first time, too. I wondered what it had cost her to take me in, what it might cost her yet.

She said, "There are some things you should understand."

She did not turn around. I could see her gray hair, pulled into a loose bun, and the shawl she had taken to wearing across her shoulders even in July.

"Yes, ma'am?" I sought her eyes in the window, but her reflection shimmered, liquescent in the failing light.

She turned the chair and I cut my eyes to the sim, but he didn't say a word. He merely sat there, implacable and still, inhumanly so, watching.

My aunt cleared her throat. "Your father didn't leave much for you. He was a young man and hadn't much to leave. I don't have much either." She chuckled humorlessly. "I am an old woman, and I am sick. The doctors will have what remains to me. You understand?"

"But I can help. I can send you money. Some ballplayers make great money, more money than you can even imag—"

She held up her hand. "Not in the minors, Jake. What will you do if you injure yourself?"

"I can go to school if that happens."

"But how will you pay for it?"

I glanced at Ford, but the sim was quiet.

My aunt said, "Right now you have scholarship offers from three schools. If you injure yourself so you can't play ball that won't be true."

"And if I injure myself playing ball in school, I'll never play in the majors."

"In that case you'll have something to fall back on."

Again, there was silence. I stared at her resentfully for a moment, and then I looked away. I studied the faded floral pattern on the rug and nagged at my lower lip with my teeth.

Aunt Rachel said, "It's decided, then?"

Before I could think, the words were out: "Nothing's decided. I'm eighteen. I can do what I want."

My aunt drew her eyebrows together. "Of course, that's true. If that's the way you feel, you'll do whatever you wish." She touched a button on her powerchair, wheeled around, and zoomed out of the room.

"Christ."

I stood, walked through the dining room to the kitchen, and went outside. The sky had begun to grow dark, stippled with the first incandescent points of stars. Somewhere, I knew, players were taking the diamond, uniforms shining in the glare of banked floodlights. I could almost hear the good-natured give and take of the infield chatter, the mercurial chorus of the fans.

Dry grass crackled behind me, and turning, I saw Ford, one half of his face limned yellow in the light from the house. Up close, he smelled of machine oil and rubber, stretched taut over burnished steel.

"Are you okay?"

I stared away into the memory-haunted yard. Here, here was the place where it had begun, my passion for the game. Here, where we had so often thrown the ball around, honing my skills until I could send the ball sizzling over the plate in a single smooth motion, like a dancer.

"I shouldn't have said that about doing whatever I want."

The sim stood beside me. A breeze came up, leavening the night heat. "What are you going to do?" Ford asked.

"I don't know. Go to school, I guess."

"I see."

We were silent for a few moments, watching fireflies stencil glowing trails through the darkness. I said, "When I'm away, I'll miss you."

Ford cocked his head, something humming in his neck.

I said, "You'll take good care of her?"

"I will."

I raised a hand to the machine's shoulder and squeezed once, softly. I started back to the house. When I was halfway there, Ford said, "I'll miss you, too, Jake."

Smiling in the darkness, I said, "Thanks," and then I turned and went up the stairs and into the kitchen. I lay in my darkened bedroom for a long while before I heard the whine of the screen door and the sound of the sim coming into the house below.

The last time I saw the house in Stowes Corners, I was a senior in college. I have not been back since.

But the moment lingers in my mind, as timeless as the day my father was buried and Ford came to me in the humid stillness of a Missouri noon. Once again, I am reminded of the archaeologist, his search for the seams between the strata of the buried cities, built pell-mell one atop the rubble of another. This, too, is such a moment—a seam between the boy I had been, the man I would become:

I was twenty-three, informed by a grief pervasive in its devastation. My aunt had died two nights previous. A major stroke. Merciful, her doctor had called it. Painless. But how could he have known?

Three of us gathered that afternoon—the minister; a probate lawyer named Holdstock; myself. I had blown two weeks' work-study salary on the flowers which stood in ranks about the open grave, exuding a heady, cheerful perfume that seemed blasphemous. The sun printed the shadows of the tombstones across the grass, and the awning above us snapped in the breeze as the minister closed his book.

Once again, I crumbled dry earth between my fingers. I listened as it trickled against the coffin. Nothing changes.

I shook hands with the minister, walked the lawyer to his Lincoln.

"Everything's taken care of?" I asked.

Holdstock smiled at the question, asked twice in as many hours. "The auction's set for two weeks tomorrow. I'll be in touch."

We shook hands, and he opened his car door. He turned to look at me, and an odd expression—half embarrassment, half determination—passed over his face. He tugged nervously at the lapels of his dark jacket.

I knew what was coming.

"Listen," he said. "My boy's a big fan. He loves Tiger baseball. I was wondering, could I—" He held a pad in his hand.

"Sure." He fished a pen out of his coat, and I scrawled my name on the page.

"My boy has lots of autographs," he said. "We usually head down St. Louis for opening day and—" He shook his head. "Aw hell, I'm sorry."

He held out his hand again, said, "Best of luck, Jake," and shut the door. The Lincoln pulled away. A drop of perspiration slid between my shoulder blades. I shrugged off my jacket, slung it over my shoulder, and surveyed the cemetery. Everything was still. Yellow earthmoving machinery waited behind a screen of trees; I was delaying the inevitable.

I got in my car and drove away from the town, into a region of summer-painted hills. The house was to be sold, the furnishings auctioned. Medical expenses had taken everything, just as Aunt Rachel had predicted. I'd made a list for Holdstock; the few things I wished to keep had been delivered to the hotel. For reasons I had avoided analyzing, I couldn't bring myself to stay at the house.

Now, however, the funeral behind me, those reasons lingered like uneasy specters in my mind. *You must never run away from the truth,* Aunt Rachel had told me. *Once you begin running, you can never stop.*

Before I had gone twenty-five miles, I cursed and pulled to the side of the road. With a kind of nauseating dread, I swung the car back toward town. There was unfinished business.

A realtor's sign stood at the head of the long drive, but when I emerged from the maples and paused atop the hill, I saw that everything was the same. It seemed as if no time at all had passed. I might have been a boy again. Steeling myself, I touched the gas and started down.

The locks had been freshly oiled, and my key sent the tumblers silently home. As I stepped inside, something whirred at my feet; an automaid sped around the corner, treads blurring. Bulky and low, it looked curiously antiquated; the newer models were sleek, silent, somehow disquieting.

I closed the door. Afternoon sunlight slanted through half-closed blinds. The hardwood shone with a merciless gloss, but everything else seemed faded. The floral-patterned rugs had been drained of color, the pale sheets glimmered over furniture earmarked for auction. I could smell the musty odor of stale air and enclosed spaces, and the lemony ghost of my aunt's furniture polish, somehow disconcerting. It was a house where no one lived anymore.

I found Ford upstairs in my old bedroom. He sat rigidly in the chair by the window, his broad unlined hands flat against his thighs. He looked just the same.

"I wondered if you would come," he said.

I examined the dim room, lit only by an exterior glare cleft into radiant shards by the blinds. An old Orioles pennant dangled from one tack on the far wall, but the room was otherwise devoid of personality. The photo albums where I'd kept my baseball cards were gone, stored now in the shelf over my desk in Columbia. Gone too were the photographs—my aunt, my father, my mother. They stood now on the end tables in my apartment. Nothing remained.

"I've been reading about you in the papers," Ford said.

"I'm the big news, I guess," I said.

"Do you have a contract yet?"

"Soon. We're negotiating." I shrugged.

The sim didn't say anything, so I crossed the room and lifted the blind and gazed into the backyard for a moment. A bird chirped in the eaves.

"When do you graduate?"

"August." I laughed. "She couldn't hang on to see it, you know."

"I'm sure she would have liked to."

"Wouldn't have mattered anyway, I suppose. I'll be on the road in rookie league by August."

"And then?"

"Who knows? I saw Haynes recently. Remember him? He said, 'You ain't an ace yet, son, but you're getting better.' I plan to make it."

"So the old dream is coming true," Ford said.

"I guess. We'll see."

I sat on the denuded mattress. In here, in the room where I had been a boy, the years seemed to have fallen away. I felt as fractured and alone as when I had been twelve years old, as much a stranger to this room and house. I could not help but recall the day the resurrection man had come, could not help but remember his dark suit and garish tie, his unpleasant stink of after-shave and tobacco. *It isn't right that a boy grow up without a man in the house*, Aunt Rachel had said, and now, remembering this, I felt ice slide through my veins.

So this is what it all had come to.

I said, "I wanted to thank you. You've done everything for me."

"It's nothing," the sim said. "I understand."

We sat for a moment. Outside, a bird whistled merrily, as if it was the first bird, this the first day.

Ford turned to look at me, his neck swiveling with a hum so slight you could miss it if you weren't paying attention. He smiled, and I could hear tiny flywheels whir inside of him, and it all came back to me. Everything. The long days in the backyard, and Ford's strong hands gentle on my own, curving my fingers along the seams of the ball. The nights alone, here in this very room, when the darkness seemed to whirl and I could not remember my father's face. Ford— his vast intricacies, the thousand complicated mechanisms of his being—Ford had filled the void.

Ford said, "I didn't know about this part. I knew so much. They filled me up with so much knowledge about baseball and King Arthur and pirates and wars—all the things a boy might conceivably wish to know or learn. But they left this part out. I wonder if they knew?"

And then, for the first time, I thought of legacies. And though I did not say it, I thought: They didn't know. How could they?

But all I said was, "Nobody told me either."

I looked straight into his eyes, just as my aunt had taught me. "I'll be on the road a lot," I said, "there's nothing I can do. I'm sorry."

The sim smiled and bowed his head. The coarse hair at the base of his neck had neither grown nor been cut. It was the same color it had been always. And when he lifted a thick sheaf of it away, I saw what I knew I would see, what I had seen once before: a colored switch, like a tiny gem. The sunlight fell against it, and shattered into myriad colored fragments along the walls of the room.

Show me. I want to know, I had said all those years ago, and he had shown me, and I had seen that he was not my father, not even a man, but just a machine. A machine.

I reached out to the switch, touched it with trembling fingers, tensed to throw it home—

And if I do? I had asked him once.

Gone, he had told me. *Erased and irrecoverable. Everything that makes me me.*

Ford said, "We had some times, Jake."

"We had some times, Ford," I replied. "That's for sure."

And then I cut him off.

I remember it all. I remember the room as I saw it last, barren of everything that had made it mine. I remember Ford, slumped in the wooden chair, another lost possession—just furniture, awaiting auction. I turned away and walked down the stairs and through the foyer to the porch. I stood there for a long time, my eyes watering in the afternoon glare, and then I walked to the car and drove away.

I didn't look back.

But every day is a backwards glance. When I take the mound, I feel his fingers around my fingers, showing me the grips. And when I'm up by one in the ninth and the tying run is on third, it is his voice that I hear in my head.

I live in a fine house now, with my wife and son, and I play in Memorial Stadium more frequently than I might ever have hoped. My family attends every game.

But I have a recurrent dream.

In the dream, I stand on the mound, clutching a baseball and staring across the grass to the batter. The crowd is wild. If I look to the stands I can see them by the thousands, venting as one a full-throated roar. And with that enhanced acuity that comes to us in dreams, I see all the dead who are lost to me, scattered among the throng. The mother I could not know, the father I can barely remember. Aunt Rachel. Ford. The resurrection man, who unknowing shaped my destiny, and left for me this legacy, its blessing and its curse.

The game rides on a single pitch. The bases are loaded, one out remains in the final inning, the count stands at three and two. I have to throw a strike.

But even as the pitch leaves my outstretched fingers, I know that it is poorly thrown. A slider, it hangs up on me, seeming almost to float. The batter steps close, shoulders tensing with the pressure as he delays the swing, and then, in the final moment before the ball is over the bag, he whips the bat around in a single blurring motion.

You can hear the impact all over the park.

The ball leaps skyward. The crowd noise surges to a crescendo, and holds there momentarily, battering, contusive. And then, all at once, it is gone.

Silence fills the stadium.

I wheel around to track the progress of the ball, a diminishing speck as it climbs higher, still higher. I watch as it begins its long descent through the quiet air, plunging towards the second deck. And that is when I notice: my mother and father, Aunt Rachel and Ford, the resurrection man himself—gone, all of them, gone. As far as I can see, the empty stands, the endless empty rows.

Rhysling Award Winners

DAVID LUNDE

DAN RAPHAEL

The Rhysling Awards are named after the Blind Singer of the Spaceways featured in Robert A. Heinlein's "The Green Hills of Earth." They are given each year by members of the Science Fiction Poetry Association in two categories, best long poem and best short poem. Poets honored in the past with these awards include some of science fiction's finest writers; Michael Bishop, Gene Wolfe, Ursula K. Le Guin, Thomas M. Disch, Lucius Shepard, John M. Ford, Joe Haldeman, and Suzette Haden Elgin (who founded the Science Fiction Poetry Association in 1978) have all won the Rhysling Award.

The 1995 Rhysling Award for Best Long Poem went to David Lunde for his poem "Pilot, Pilot." David Lunde was born in California, grew up in Saudi Arabia, and is now Professor of English and Director of Creative Writing at the State University of New York College at Fredonia. He was honored with his first Rhysling Award in 1992 and won the Academy of American Poets Prize in 1967; his poems, short stories, and translations have been published in the *Iowa Review, Triquarterly, New Worlds, Aboriginal Science Fiction, Asimov's Science Fiction, Whispers,* and many other magazines and anthologies. His latest book is *Heart Transplants and Other Misappropriations* (Edwin Mellen Press, 1996).

"Pilot, Pilot" is one of a sequence of poems published in a chapbook, *Blues for Port City* (Mayapple Press, 1995), and it appears here with the preface to that book. David Lunde says about his poem:

"'Pilot, Pilot' was one of those infrequent and magical-seeming poems which come into one's head almost fully formed, or to be more exact, the scene described in the poem came to me as an extremely vivid mental image, but the words came very easily as well. Of course, it came about three in the morning—the same time my daughter was born!—and it took only about half an hour to complete the first full draft. I did a bit of polishing the next day, but the poem was essentially complete."

The 1995 Rhysling Award for Best Short Poem went to Dan Raphael for "Skin of Glass." His ninth book, *Molecular Jam,* was published in 1996 by Jazz Police Books (La Grande, Oregon). He lives in Portland, Oregon, and comments: "My chief poetic principle is that language knows more than I do. As my work is often nonlinear, people understand it better after witnessing one of my energetic performances."

About "Skin of Glass," he writes:

"I'm not sure how I came to write 'Skin of Glass.' Most of my poems come out spontaneously, often after some event like a movie or poetry reading. But trying to link some movie or book with this poem would be an educated guess (I did, around the time of writing the poem, read what I consider to be one of the best novels of the last ten or so years, *Steel Beach* by John Varley).

"More clearly influencing this poem is my interest in where religion and science, often seen as the opposite ends of a line, connect (following a relativistic model that turns a line into a sphere); for example, see Fritjof Capra's *Tao of Physics.* Thus the extended spaceship-body metaphor, and the ending linkage of the big bang with Buddha. High-energy physics shows us that matter is mostly space; Buddhism teaches us that matter is only our perception, that our bodies are energy trapped by our perceptions/limits."

Pilot, Pilot
DAVID LUNDE

Preface

These are the poems of Nulle, whose words captured better than those of any other writer the bitter longings and despair of the star-struck men and women who made the futile journey to Port City, the domed and tunneled asteroid that served as dock, refitting shop, warehouse, and launching-point for the Deepships—futile because only those who had been genetically and surgically altered and cyber-netically enhanced could become Pilots. Little is known of the shad-owy poet who wrote under the self-mocking pseudonym of 'Nulle' other than that she wrote in Port City during the latter half of the

22nd century and appears to have been of its *demi-monde*—occupying a position similar to that of the ancient French poet and thief François Villon in his city of Paris, though her sensibilities were more akin to those of the later French Symbolist poets whose voices she has borrowed in some of these poems. We note also borrowings from the great twentieth-century Welsh poet Dylan Thomas, particularly in her "Autoepitaph," while her device of speaking in the voices of typical citizens of Port City—including at times herself—echoes the *Spoon River Anthology* of the American poet Edgar Lee Masters. It is our hope that the publication of these long-forgotten verses will help readers of our own time to comprehend the emotional impact and attitudes of that turbulent transitional period in which humankind reconceived itself and realized at last the dream of stars—a thing which the study of mere historical fact can never accomplish.

—D. L., Regulated Spring, 2294

Your eyes were mirrors then,
silver as pressure domes, your
head raked back fifteen degrees.
The angle of your long neck
against the unwholesome horizontal
of that Port City street, the taut
cords of muscle straining
in my sweat-slick fingers,
are a senso I can't erase—
neither that image nor the shame,
knowing even then it wasn't you
I hated, brother, but myself, my life—
and at my back, suddenly, the laughter,
hurrying near, the great laughter,
and you beginning to, your lips
beginning to crimp at the edges
just a bit as if to smile—you!
smile!—and I stared hard
at your eyes—at, not into—
trying to scan His approach
and afraid, so afraid to turn,

as if by not seeing straight-on
I would not be seen. But I was.

That fearsome hand, irresistible
and deft as a waldo, slipped loose
my grip, set us apart by a meter,
you cursing weakly, rubbing your throat
where my thumbs had bruised it,
both of us weeping like children
caught in some infantile squabble,
pulled casually apart and forgotten,
while He cruised unruffled off,
murmuring, "Easy, grounders, easy there."
Oh, easy, always easy for Him!
cruising off to His future,
off to His ships and His stars.

"But we made you!" I screamed,
and the fury was in me then, so huge
I flicked out blade and flung it
hard at His enormous back—
and how He did what He did then
I can't tell you; I couldn't see
but whirling flash and blur and hear
the *shree-kaslam* of its return.
Then He was gone. My blade
was buried to its hilt in a wall
of solid ferrocrete. The empty street
still echoed with His laughter.

I am not Arthur Pendragon
and have no hope. I suppose
I could have left Port City,
walked off those bitter streets,
but where is there to go
that matters? I can't forget
the mirrors of your eyes,

how they could not frame
His fearful symmetry, how they
diminished and diminish me.

Skin of Glass

DAN RAPHAEL

surface that can be removed creates the problem of defining
what's underneath, having to go there to find out,
having to get the body involved, risk the senses, waste time
at least in cleaning up afterwards, in refuting the claims of others,
submitting to spectroscopic analysis, finding experts in
animal/vegetable/mineral icons/remains/signatures

no skin but a seed, not a seed but an entrance, an entrance i can't fit,
a new body i must— a probe, an extension,
                              projecting several feet from
my skin my spirit coheres as a lazy gelatinous rectangle,
            not what its made of but that it is, bigger but not more,
encasing more space not fed by molecular transmissions, lacking the
      antennae
to receive, through the membranes where something meets nothing,
                              where meat sums not,
                              things not,
      if so energized,
or shelled by that one way accretion of filtering all i'm capable of
like a song in one key in half an octave in four-four time,
a song that goes for fifteen minutes and can be repeated verbatim,
a song you can hear twenty years away, on your ship to who knows,
one technology racing another, hollow god-body-tree
filled with too many fish   with refugees   with poorly tanned furs,
an encyclopedia of non-seeding plants, spores in pores,
moisture interrupting everything,   thinning   defining
      making the colors run,   keeping my feet unsteady,
            water trying to get back into my eyes,
                  wanting to make my brain a chalice

the hull is our roof protecting me from the rain below,
                    the rain that mostly cant escape,
                is sad   amnesiac   content,
salt is its gravity,   fish are its wardens, its fantasies,
flying fish and diving birds,   walking catfish and aquatic mammals,
    huge subterranean pockets of symbiotic fungus
displaying the colonic intelligence of ants and bees,
        rocks that appreciate their own beauty, molten substance
that can neither be defined nor predicted, where heat and pressure
create the same relativistic curves as speed and gravity,

    the big bang is in each of us.
    the periodic table is in each part of us.
    the pantheon of buddhas, sattvas and boddhisattvas
            are waiting around curves of the brain,
        which is not in our heads but in our hearts,
        which are not in our chests but in each molecule
        unfurling to the sun which is not in the sky
                but everywhere
                at once

You See But You Do Not Observe

ROBERT J. SAWYER

The 1995 Nebula Award for Best Novel was given to Robert J. Sawyer's *The Terminal Experiment,* which was also published as a serial in *Analog* under the title *Hobson's Choice.* Sawyer, Canada's only native-born full-time science fiction writer, founded the Canadian region of the Science-fiction and Fantasy Writers of America and served on SFWA's board of directors from 1992 to 1995. He has won three Canadian Science Fiction and Fantasy Awards ("Auroras"), five HOMer Awards (voted on by the thirty thousand members of the Science Fiction and Fantasy Literature Forum on the on-line service CompuServe), and an Arthur Ellis Award from the Crime Writers of Canada. He is the author of the novels *Golden Fleece, Far-Seer, Fossil Hunter, Foreigner, End of an Era, Starplex,* and *Frameshift.* With his wife, Carolyn Clink, he edited *Tesseracts 6,* an anthology of Canadian science fiction and fantasy. He lives near Toronto.

About his Nebula Award–winning novel, he writes:

"Two of my favorite SF short stories are Arthur C. Clarke's 'The Nine Billion Names of God' and 'The Star.' Each asserts as real an aspect of religion normally taken on faith, and then examines the repercussions of that reality. Not many novels have done the same thing successfully, and so my goal in creating *The Terminal Experiment*—which begins with a man discovering scientific proof for the existence of the human soul—was to write such a book.

"I believe science fiction is at its best not when it's making predictions, and not even when it's sounding warning bells, but, rather, when it is giving us unique insights into what it means to be human, examining the human condition in ways that mainstream fiction simply *can't.* That's why Frederik Pohl's *Gateway* is my favorite SF novel: it looks at guilt under temporal circumstances that no one has yet experienced—and yet Fred's portrayal rings true. Well, *The Terminal Experiment* is my own attempt at uniquely science-fictional insights: an exercise in determining what a human mind might be like if it were aware either that it would live forever or that it was already dead. (The 'Hobson's choice' of the serial title is the choice between immortality or a scientifically verified life after death.)"

Readers are urged to seek out *The Terminal Experiment* and to read this inventive novel of "hard" science fiction. Instead of publishing an excerpt from Sawyer's novel, I have chosen, with his kind permission, to reprint his 1995 short story "You See But You Do Not Observe," which won both the Sixth Annual HOMer Award for Best Short Story and *Le Grand Prix de l'Imaginaire*, France's top SF award, for Best Foreign Short Story of the Year. About this tale, the author says:

"In some ways, no story could be further from being typical of my work: 'You See But You Do Not Observe' is a Sherlock Holmes tale, published with the permission of Dame Jean Conan Doyle and told, as closely as I could manage it, in Sir Arthur Conan Doyle's style. But it embodies, perhaps more clearly than anything else I've written, the central theme of all my work: namely, that clearheaded, unflinching, rational thinking is the only effective way to deal with reality. That was certainly the worldview from which I created *The Terminal Experiment*, which revolves around a *scientific* investigation into the nature of the human soul: no fuzzy New Age thinking for me, thanks—and, of course, none for Mr. Sherlock Holmes, either."

I had been pulled into the future first, ahead of my companion. There was no sensation associated with the chronotransference, except for a popping of my ears which I was later told had to do with a change in air pressure. Once in the twenty-first century, my brain was scanned in order to produce from my memories a perfect reconstruction of our rooms at 221B Baker Street. Details that I could not consciously remember or articulate were nonetheless reproduced exactly: the flock-papered walls, the bearskin hearth rug, the basket chair and the armchair, the coal scuttle, even the view through the window—all were correct to the smallest detail.

I was met in the future by a man who called himself Mycroft Holmes. He claimed, however, to be no relation to my companion, and protested that his name was mere coincidence, although he allowed that the fact of it was likely what had made a study of my partner's methods his chief avocation. I asked him if he had a brother called Sherlock, but his reply made little sense to me: "My parents weren't *that* cruel."

In any event, this Mycroft Holmes—who was a small man with reddish hair, quite unlike the stout and dark ale of a fellow with the same name I had known two hundred years before—wanted all details to be correct before he whisked Holmes here from the past. Genius, he said, was but a step from madness, and although I had taken to the future well, my companion might be quite rocked by the experience.

When Mycroft did bring Holmes forth, he did so with great stealth, transferring him precisely as he stepped through the front exterior door of the real 221B Baker Street and into the simulation that had been created here. I heard my good friend's voice down the stairs, giving his usual glad tidings to a simulation of Mrs. Hudson. His long legs, as they always did, brought him up to our humble quarters at a rapid pace.

I had expected a hearty greeting, consisting perhaps of an ebullient cry of "My dear Watson," and possibly even a firm clasping of hands or some other display of bonhomie. But there was none of that, of course. This was not like the time Holmes had returned after an absence of three years during which I had believed him to be dead. No, my companion, whose exploits it has been my honor to chronicle over the years, was unaware of just how long we had been separated, and so my reward for my vigil was nothing more than a distracted nodding of his drawn-out face. He took a seat and settled in with the evening paper, but after a few moments, he slapped the newsprint sheets down. "Confound it, Watson! I have already read this edition. Have we not *today's* paper?"

And, at that turn, there was nothing for it but for me to adopt the unfamiliar role that queer fate had dictated I must now take: our traditional positions were now reversed, and I would have to explain the truth to Holmes.

"Holmes, my good fellow, I am afraid they do not publish newspapers anymore."

He pinched his long face into a scowl, and his clear, gray eyes glimmered. "I would have thought that any man who had spent as much time in Afghanistan as you had, Watson, would be immune to the ravages of the sun. I grant that today was unbearably hot, but surely your brain should not have addled so easily."

"Not a bit of it, Holmes, I assure you," said I. "What I say is true, although I confess my reaction was the same as yours when I was first told. There have not been any newspapers for seventy-five years now."

"Seventy-five years? Watson, this copy of *The Times* is dated August the fourteenth, eighteen ninety-nine—yesterday."

"I am afraid that is not true, Holmes. Today is June the fifth, *anno Domini* two thousand and ninety-six."

"Two thou—"

"It sounds preposterous, I know—"

"It *is* preposterous, Watson. I call you 'old man' now and again out of affection, but you are in fact nowhere near two hundred and fifty years of age."

"Perhaps I am not the best man to explain all this," I said.

"No," said a voice from the doorway. "Allow me."

Holmes surged to his feet. "And who are you?"

"My name is Mycroft Holmes."

"Impostor!" declared my companion.

"I assure you that that is not the case," said Mycroft. "I grant I'm not your brother, nor a habitué of the Diogenes Club, but I do share his name. I am a scientist—and I have used certain scientific principles to pluck you from your past and bring you into my present."

For the first time in all the years I had known him, I saw befuddlement on my companion's face. "It is quite true," I said to him.

"But why?" said Holmes, spreading his long arms. "Assuming this mad fantasy is true—and I do not grant for an instant that it is—why would you thus kidnap myself and my good friend Dr. Watson?"

"Because, Holmes, the game, as you used to be so fond of saying, is afoot."

"Murder, is it?" asked I, grateful at last to get to the reason for which we had been brought forward.

"More than simple murder," said Mycroft. "Much more. Indeed, the biggest puzzle to have ever faced the human race. Not just one body is missing. Trillions are. *Trillions.*"

"Watson," said Holmes, "surely you recognize the signs of madness in the man? Have you nothing in your bag that can help him? The whole population of the Earth is less than two thousand millions."

"In your time, yes," said Mycroft. "Today, it's about eight thousand million. But I say again, there are trillions more who are missing."

"Ah, I perceive at last," said Holmes, a twinkle in his eye as he came to believe that reason was once again holding sway. "I have read in *The Illustrated London News* of these *dinosauria*, as Professor Owen called them—great creatures from the past, all now deceased. It is their demise you wish me to unravel."

Mycroft shook his head. "You should have read Professor Moriarty's monograph called *The Dynamics of an Asteroid*," he said.

"I keep my mind clear of useless knowledge," replied Holmes curtly.

Mycroft shrugged. "Well, in that paper Moriarty quite cleverly guessed the cause of the demise of the dinosaurs: an asteroid crashing into Earth kicked up enough dust to block the sun for months on end. Close to a century after he had reasoned out this hypothesis, solid evidence for its truth was found in a layer of clay. No, that mystery is long since solved. This one is much greater."

"And what, pray, is it?" said Holmes, irritation in his voice.

Mycroft motioned for Holmes to have a seat, and, after a moment's defiance, my friend did just that. "It is called the Fermi paradox," said Mycroft, "after Enrico Fermi, an Italian physicist who lived in the twentieth century. You see, we know now that this universe of ours should have given rise to countless planets, and that many of those planets should have produced intelligent civilizations. We can demonstrate the likelihood of this mathematically, using something called the Drake equation. For a century and a half now, we have been using radio—wireless, that is—to look for signs of these other intelligences. And we have found nothing—*nothing!* Hence the paradox Fermi posed: if the universe is supposed to be full of life, then where are the aliens?"

"Aliens?" said I. "Surely they are mostly still in their respective foreign countries."

Mycroft smiled. "The word has gathered additional uses since your day, good doctor. By aliens, I mean extraterrestrials—creatures who live on other worlds."

"As in the stories of Verne and Wells?" asked I, quite sure that my expression was agog.

"And even in worlds beyond the family of our sun," said Mycroft.

Holmes rose to his feet. "I know nothing of universes and other worlds," he said angrily. "Such knowledge could be of no practical use in my profession."

I nodded. "When I first met Holmes, he had no idea that the Earth revolved around the sun." I treated myself to a slight chuckle. "He thought the reverse to be true."

Mycroft smiled. "I know of your current limitations, Sherlock." My friend cringed slightly at the overly familiar address. "But these are mere gaps in knowledge; we can rectify that easily enough."

"I will not crowd my brain with useless irrelevancies," said Holmes. "I carry only information that can be of help in my work. For instance, I can identify one hundred and forty different varieties of tobacco ash—"

"Ah, well, you can let that information go, Holmes," said Mycroft. "No one smokes anymore. It's been proven ruinous to one's health." I shot a look at Holmes, whom I had always warned of being a self-poisoner. "Besides, we've also learned much about the structure of the brain in the intervening years. Your fear that memorizing information related to fields such as literature, astronomy, and philosophy would force out other, more relevant data is unfounded. The capacity for the human brain to store and retrieve information is almost infinite."

"It is?" said Holmes, clearly shocked.

"It is."

"And so you wish me to immerse myself in physics and astronomy and such all?"

"Yes," said Mycroft.

"To solve this paradox of Fermi?"

"Precisely!"

"But why me?"

"Because it is a *puzzle*, and you, my good fellow, are the greatest solver of puzzles this world has ever seen. It is now two hundred years after your time, and no one with a facility to rival yours has yet appeared."

Mycroft probably could not see it, but the tiny hint of pride on my longtime companion's face was plain to me. But then Holmes frowned. "It would take years to amass the knowledge I would need to address this problem."

"No, it will not." Mycroft waved his hand, and amidst the homely untidiness of Holmes's desk appeared a small sheet of glass standing vertically. Next to it lay a strange metal bowl. "We have made great strides in the technology of learning since your day. We can directly program new information into your brain." Mycroft walked over to the desk. "This glass panel is what we call a *monitor*. It is activated by the sound of your voice. Simply ask it questions, and it will display information on any topic you wish. If you find a topic that you think will be useful in your studies, simply place this helmet on your head"—he indicated the metal bowl—"say the words 'load topic,' and the information will be seamlessly integrated into the neural nets of your very own brain. It will at once seem as if you know, and have always known, all the details of that field of endeavor."

"Incredible!" said Holmes. "And from there?"

"From there, my dear Holmes, I hope that your powers of deduction will lead you to resolve the paradox—and reveal at last what has happened to the aliens!"

"Watson! Watson!"

I awoke with a start. Holmes had found this new ability to effortlessly absorb information irresistible, and he had pressed on long into the night, but I had evidently fallen asleep in a chair. I perceived that Holmes had at last found a substitute for the sleeping fiend of his cocaine mania: with all of creation at his fingertips, he would never again feel that emptiness that had so destroyed him between assignments.

"Eh?" I said. My throat was dry. I had evidently been sleeping with my mouth open. "What is it?"

"Watson, this physics is more fascinating than I had ever imagined. Listen to this, and see if you do not find it as compelling as any of the cases we have faced to date."

I rose from my chair and poured myself a little sherry—it was, after all, still night and not yet morning. "I am listening."

"Remember the locked and sealed room that figured so significantly in that terrible case of the Giant Rat of Sumatra?"

"How could I forget?" said I, a shiver traversing my spine. "If not for your keen shooting, my left leg would have ended up as gamy as my right."

"Quite," said Holmes. "Well, consider a different type of locked-room mystery, this one devised by an Austrian physicist named Erwin Schrödinger. Imagine a cat sealed in a box. The box is of such opaque material, and its walls are so well insulated, and the seal is so profound, that there is no way anyone can observe the cat once the box is closed."

"Hardly seems cricket," I said, "locking a poor cat in a box."

"Watson, your delicate sensibilities are laudable, but please, man, attend to my point. Imagine further that inside this box is a triggering device that has exactly a fifty-fifty chance of being set off, and that this aforementioned trigger is rigged up to a cylinder of poison gas. If the trigger is tripped, the gas is released, and the cat dies."

"Goodness!" said I. "How nefarious."

"Now, Watson, tell me this: without opening the box, can you say whether the cat is alive or dead?"

"Well, if I understand you correctly, it depends on whether the trigger was tripped."

"Precisely!"

"And so the cat is perhaps alive, and, yet again, perhaps it is dead."

"Ah, my friend, I knew you would not fail me: the blindingly obvious interpretation. But it is wrong, dear Watson, totally wrong."

"How do you mean?"

"I mean the cat is neither alive nor is it dead. It is a *potential* cat, an unresolved cat, a cat whose existence is nothing but a question of possibilities. It is neither alive nor dead, Watson—neither! Until some intelligent person opens the box and looks, the cat is unresolved. Only the act of looking forces a resolution of the possibilities. Once you crack the seal and peer within, the potential cat collapses into an actual cat. Its reality is *a result of* having been observed."

"That is worse gibberish than anything this namesake of your brother has spouted."

"No, it is not," said Holmes. "It is the way the world works. They have learned so much since our time, Watson—so very much! But as Alphonse Karr has observed, *Plus ça change, plus c'est la même chose.* Even in this esoteric field of advanced physics, it is the power of the qualified observer that is most important of all!"

I awoke again hearing Holmes crying out, "Mycroft! Mycroft!"

I had occasionally heard such shouts from him in the past, either when his iron constitution had failed him and he was feverish, or when under the influence of his accursed needle. But after a moment I realized he was not calling for his real brother but, rather, was shouting into the air to summon the Mycroft Holmes who was the twenty-first-century savant. Moments later, he was rewarded: the door to our rooms opened and in came the red-haired fellow.

"Hello, Sherlock," said Mycroft. "You wanted me?"

"Indeed I do," said Holmes. "I have absorbed much now on not just physics but also the technology by which you have re-created these rooms for me and the good Dr. Watson."

Mycroft nodded. "I've been keeping track of what you've been accessing. Surprising choices, I must say."

"So they might seem," said Holmes, "but my method is based on the pursuit of trifles. Tell me if I understand correctly that you reconstructed these rooms by scanning Watson's memories, then using, if I understand the terms, holography and micromanipulated force fields to simulate the appearance and form of what he had seen."

"That's right."

"So your ability to reconstruct is not just limited to rebuilding these rooms of ours, but, rather, you could simulate anything either of us had ever seen."

"That's correct. In fact, I could even put you into a simulation of someone else's memories. Indeed, I thought perhaps you might like to see the Very Large Array of radio telescopes, where most of our listening for alien messages—"

"Yes, yes, I'm sure that's fascinating," said Holmes dismissively. "But can you reconstruct the venue of what Watson so appropriately dubbed 'The Final Problem'?"

"You mean the Falls of Reichenbach?" Mycroft looked shocked. "My God, yes, but I should think that's the last thing you'd want to relive."

"Aptly said!" declared Holmes. "Can you do it?"

"Of course."

"Then do so!"

And so Holmes's and my brains were scanned, and in short order we found ourselves inside a superlative re-creation of the Switzerland of May 1891, to which we had originally fled to escape Professor Moriarty's assassins. Our reenactment of events began at the charming Englischer Hof in the village of Meiringen. Just as the original innkeeper had done all those years ago, the reconstruction of him exacted a promise from us that we would not miss the spectacle of the Falls of Reichenbach. Holmes and I set out for the falls, he walking with the aid of an alpenstock. Mycroft, I was given to understand, was somehow observing all this from afar.

"I do not like this," I said to my companion. "'Twas bad enough to live through this horrible day once, but I had hoped I would never have to relive it again except in nightmares."

"Watson, recall that I have fonder memories of all this. Vanquishing Moriarty was the high point of my career. I said to you then, and say again now, that putting an end to the very Napoleon of crime would easily be worth the price of my own life."

There was a little dirt path cut out of the vegetation running halfway round the falls so as to afford a complete view of the spectacle. The icy green water, fed by the melting snows, flowed with phenomenal rapidity and violence, then plunged into a great, bottomless chasm of rock black as the darkest night. Spray shot up in vast gouts, and the shriek made by the plunging water was almost like a human cry.

We stood for a moment looking down at the waterfall, Holmes's face in its most contemplative repose. He then pointed further ahead along the dirt path. "Note, dear Watson," he said, shouting to be heard above the torrent, "that the dirt path comes to an end against a rock wall there." I nodded. He turned in the other direction. "And see that backtracking out the way we came is the only way to leave alive: there is but one exit, and it is coincident with the single entrance."

Again I nodded. But, just as had happened the first time we had been at this fateful spot, a Swiss boy came running along the path, carrying in his hand a letter addressed to me which bore the mark of the Englischer Hof. I knew what the note said, of course: that an Englishwoman, staying at that inn, had been overtaken by a hemorrhage. She had but a few hours to live, but doubtless would take great comfort in being ministered to by an English doctor, and would I come at once?

"But the note is a pretext," said I, turning to Holmes. "Granted, I was fooled originally by it, but, as you later admitted in that letter you left for me, you had suspected all along that it was a sham on the part of Moriarty." Throughout this commentary, the Swiss boy stood frozen, immobile, as if somehow Mycroft, overseeing all this, had locked the boy in time so that Holmes and I might consult. "I will not leave you again, Holmes, to plunge to your death."

Holmes raised a hand. "Watson, as always, your sentiments are laudable, but recall that this is a mere simulation. You will be of material assistance to me if you do exactly as you did before. There is no need, though, for you to undertake the entire arduous hike to the Englischer Hof and back. Instead, simply head back to the point at which you pass the figure in black, wait an additional quarter of an hour, then return to here."

"Thank you for simplifying it," said I. "I am eight years older than I was then; a three-hour round trip would take a goodly bit out of me today."

"Indeed," said Holmes. "All of us may have outlived our most useful days. Now, please, do as I ask."

"I will, of course," said I, "but I freely confess that I do not understand what this is all about. You were engaged by this twenty-first-century Mycroft to explore a problem in natural philosophy—the missing aliens. Why are we even here?"

"We are here," said Holmes, "because I have solved that problem! Trust me, Watson. Trust me, and play out the scenario again of that portentous day of May the fourth, eighteen ninety-one."

And so I left my companion, not knowing what he had in mind. As I made my way back toward the Englischer Hof, I passed a man going hurriedly the other way. The first time I had lived through these terrible events I did not know him, but this time I recognized him for Professor Moriarty: tall, clad all in black, his forehead bulging out, his lean form outlined sharply against the green backdrop of the vegetation. I let the simulation pass, waited fifteen minutes as Holmes had asked, then returned to the falls.

Upon my arrival, I saw Holmes's alpenstock leaning against a rock. The black soil of the path to the torrent was constantly remoistened by the spray from the roiling falls. In the soil I could see two sets of footprints leading down the path to the cascade, and none returning. It was precisely the same terrible sight that had greeted me all those years ago.

"Welcome back, Watson!"

I wheeled around. Holmes stood leaning against a tree, grinning widely.

"Holmes!" I exclaimed. "How did you manage to get away from the falls without leaving footprints?"

"Recall, my dear Watson, that except for the flesh-and-blood you and me, all this is but a simulation. I simply asked Mycroft to prevent my feet from leaving tracks." He demonstrated this by walking back and forth. No impression was left by his shoes, and no vegetation was trampled down by his passage. "And, of course, I asked him to freeze Moriarty, as earlier he had frozen the Swiss lad, before he and I could become locked in mortal combat."

"Fascinating," said I.

"Indeed. Now, consider the spectacle before you. What do you see?"

"Just what I saw that horrid day on which I had thought you had died: two sets of tracks leading to the falls, and none returning."

Holmes's crow of "Precisely!" rivaled the roar of the falls. "One set of tracks you knew to be my own, and the other you took to be that of the black-clad Englishman—the very Napoleon of crime!"

"Yes."

"Having seen these two sets approaching the falls, and none returning, you then rushed to the very brink of the falls and found—what?"

"Signs of a struggle at the lip of the precipice leading to the great torrent itself."

"And what did you conclude from this?"

"That you and Moriarty had plunged to your deaths, locked in mortal combat."

"Exactly so, Watson! The very same conclusion I myself would have drawn based on those observations!"

"Thankfully, though, I turned out to be incorrect."

"Did you, now?"

"Why, yes. Your presence here attests to that."

"Perhaps," said Holmes. "But I think otherwise. Consider, Watson! You were on the scene, you saw what happened, and for three years—three years, man!—you believed me to be dead. We had been friends and colleagues for a decade at that point. Would the Holmes you knew have let you mourn him for so long without getting word to you? Surely you must know that I trust you at least as much as I do my brother Mycroft, who I later told you was the only one I had made privy to the secret that I still lived."

"Well," I said, "since you bring it up, I *was* slightly hurt by that. But you explained your reasons to me when you returned."

"It is a comfort to me, Watson, that your ill feelings were assuaged. But I wonder, perchance, if it was more you than I who assuaged them."

"Eh?"

"You had seen clear evidence of my death, and had faithfully if floridly recorded the same in the chronicle you so appropriately dubbed 'The Final Problem.'"

"Yes, indeed. Those were the hardest words I had ever written."

"And what was the reaction of your readers once this account was published in the *Strand*?"

I shook my head, recalling. "It was completely unexpected," said I. "I had anticipated a few polite notes from strangers mourning your passing, since the stories of your exploits had been so warmly received in the past. But what I got instead was mostly anger and outrage—people demanding to hear further adventures of yours."

"Which of course you believed to be impossible, seeing as how I was dead."

"Exactly. The whole thing left a rather bad taste, I must say. Seemed very peculiar behavior."

"But doubtless it died down quickly," said Holmes.

"You know full well it did not. I have told you before that the onslaught of letters, as well as personal exhortations wherever I would travel, continued unabated for years. In fact, I was virtually at the point of going back and writing up one of your lesser cases I had previously ignored as being of no general interest, simply to get the demands to cease, when, much to my surprise and delight—"

"Much to your surprise and delight, after an absence of three years less a month, I turned up in your consulting rooms, disguised, if I recall correctly, as a shabby book collector. And soon you had fresh adventures to chronicle, beginning with that case of the infamous Colonel Sebastian Moran and his victim, the Honorable Ronald Adair."

"Yes," said I. "Wondrous it was."

"But, Watson, let us consider the facts surrounding my apparent death at the Falls of Reichenbach on May the fourth, eighteen ninety-one. You, the observer on the scene, saw the evidence, and, as you wrote in 'The Final Problem,' many experts scoured the lip of the falls and came to precisely the same conclusion you had—that Moriarty and I had plunged to our deaths."

"But that conclusion turned out to be wrong."

Holmes beamed intently. "No, my good Watson, it turned out to be *unacceptable*—unacceptable to your faithful readers. And that is where all the problems stem from. Remember Schrödinger's cat in the sealed box? Moriarty and I at the falls present a very similar scenario: he and I went down the path into the cul-de-sac, our footprints leaving impressions in the soft earth. There were only two possible outcomes at that point: either I would exit alive, or I would not. There was no way out, except to take that same path back away from the falls. Until someone came and looked to see whether I had reemerged from the path, the outcome was unresolved. I was both alive and dead—a collection of possibilities. But when you arrived, those possibilities had to collapse into a single reality. You saw that there were no footprints returning from the falls—meaning that Moriarty and I had struggled until at last we had both plunged over the edge into the icy torrent. It was your act of seeing the results that forced the possibilities to be resolved. In a very real sense, my good, dear friend, you killed me."

My heart was pounding in my chest. "I tell you, Holmes, nothing would have made me more happy than to have seen you alive!"

"I do not doubt that, Watson—but you had to see one thing or the other. You could not see both. And, having seen what you saw, you reported your findings: first to the Swiss police, and then to the reporter for the *Journal de Genève,* and lastly in your full account in the pages of the *Strand.*"

I nodded.

"But here is the part that was not considered by Schrödinger when he devised the thought experiment of the cat in the box. Suppose you open the box and find the cat dead, and later you tell your neighbor about the dead cat—and your neighbor refuses to believe you when you say that the cat is dead. What happens if you go and look in the box a second time?"

"Well, the cat is surely still dead."

"Perhaps. But what if thousands—nay, millions!—refuse to believe the account of the original observer? What if they deny the evidence? What then, Watson?"

"I—I do not know."

"Through the sheer stubbornness of their will, they reshape reality, Watson! Truth is replaced with fiction! They will the cat back to life. More than that, they attempt to believe that the cat never died in the first place!"

"And so?"

"And so the world, which should have one concrete reality, is rendered unresolved, uncertain, adrift. As the first observer on the scene at Reichenbach, your interpretation should take precedence. But the stubbornness of the human race is legendary, Watson, and through that sheer cussedness, that refusal to believe what they have been plainly told, the world gets plunged back into being a wave front of unresolved possibilities. We exist in flux—to this day, the whole world exists in flux—because of the conflict between the observation you really made at Reichenbach and the observation the world *wishes* you had made."

"But this is all too fantastic, Holmes!"

"Eliminate the impossible, Watson, and whatever remains, however improbable, must be the truth. Which brings me now to the question we were engaged by this avatar of Mycroft to solve: this paradox of Fermi. Where are the alien beings?"

"And you say you have solved that?"

"Indeed I have. Consider the method by which mankind has been searching for these aliens."

"By wireless, I gather—trying to overhear their chatter on the ether."

"Precisely! And when did I return from the dead, Watson?"

"April of eighteen ninety-four."

"And when did that gifted Italian, Guglielmo Marconi, invent the wireless?"

"I have no idea."

"In eighteen hundred and ninety-*five*, my good Watson. The following year! In all the time that mankind has used radio, our entire world has been an unresolved quandary! An uncollapsed wave front of possibilities!"

"Meaning?"

"Meaning the aliens are there, Watson—it is not they who are missing, it is we! Our world is out of synch with the rest of the universe. Through our failure to accept the unpleasant truth, we have rendered ourselves *potential* rather than *actual.*"

I had always thought my companion a man with a generous regard for his own stature, but surely this was too much. "You are suggesting, Holmes, that the current unresolved state of the world hinges on the fate of you yourself?"

"Indeed! Your readers would not allow me to fall to my death, even if it meant attaining the very thing I desired most, namely the elimination of Moriarty. In this mad world, the observer has lost control of his observations! If there is one thing my life stood for—my life prior to that ridiculous resurrection of me you recounted in your chronicle of 'The Empty House'—it was reason! Logic! A devotion to observable fact! But humanity has abjured that. This whole world is out of whack, Watson—so out of whack that we are cut off from the civilizations that exist elsewhere. You tell me you were festooned with demands for my return, but if people had really understood me, understood what my life represented, they would have known that the only real tribute to me possible would have been to accept the facts! The only real answer would have been to leave me dead!"

———

Mycroft sent us back in time, but rather than returning us to 1899, whence he had plucked us, at Holmes's request he put us back eight years earlier, in May of 1891. Of course, there were younger versions of ourselves already living then, but Mycroft swapped us for them, bringing the young ones to the future, where they could live out the rest of their lives in simulated scenarios taken from Holmes's and my minds. Granted, we were each eight years older than we had been when we had fled Moriarty the first time, but no one in Switzerland knew us and so the aging of our faces went unnoticed.

I found myself for a third time living that fateful day at the falls of Reichenbach, but this time, like the first and unlike the second, it was real.

I saw the page boy coming, and my heart raced. I turned to Holmes, and said, "I can't possibly leave you."

"Yes, you can, Watson. And you will, for you have never failed to play the game. I am sure you will play it to the end." He paused for a moment, then said, perhaps just a wee bit sadly, "I can discover facts, Watson, but I cannot change them." And then, quite solemnly, he extended his hand. I clasped it firmly in both of mine. And then the boy, who was in Moriarty's employ, was upon us. I allowed myself to be duped, leaving Holmes alone at the falls, fighting with all my might to keep from looking back as I hiked onward to treat the nonexistent patient at the Englischer Hof. On my way, I passed Moriarty going in the other direction. It was all I could do to keep from drawing my pistol and putting an end to the blackguard, but I knew Holmes would consider robbing him of his own chance at Moriarty an unforgivable betrayal.

It was an hour's hike down to the Englischer Hof. There I played out the scene in which I inquired about the ailing Englishwoman, and Steiler the Elder, the innkeeper, reacted, as I knew he must, with surprise. My performance was probably halfhearted, having played the role once before, but soon I was on my way back. The uphill hike took over two hours, and I confess plainly to being exhausted upon my arrival, although I could barely hear my own panting over the roar of the torrent.

Once again, I found two sets of footprints leading to the precipice, and none returning. I also found Holmes's alpenstock, and, just as I had the first time, a note from him to me that he had left with it. The note read just as the original had, explaining that he and Moriarty were about to have their final confrontation, but that Moriarty had allowed him to leave a few last words behind. But it ended with a postscript that had not been in the original:

> My dear Watson [it said], you will honour my passing most of all if you stick fast to the powers of observation. No matter what the world wants, leave me dead.

I returned to London, and was able to briefly counterbalance my loss of Holmes by reliving the joy and sorrow of the last few months of my wife Mary's life, explaining my somewhat older face to her and others as the result of shock at the death of Holmes. The next year, right on schedule, Marconi did indeed invent the wireless. Exhortations for more Holmes adventures continued to pour in, but I ignored them all, although the lack of him in my life was so profound that I was sorely tempted to relent, recanting my observations made at Reichenbach. Nothing would have pleased me more than to hear again the voice of the best and wisest man I had ever known.

In late June of 1907, I read in *The Times* about the detection of intelligent wireless signals coming from the direction of the star Altair. On that day, the rest of the world celebrated, but I do confess I shed a tear and drank a special toast to my good friend, the late Mr. Sherlock Holmes.

Old Legends

GREGORY BENFORD

"Of all current science fiction writers," scholar and critic Gary K. Wolfe writes about Gregory Benford, "he may stand the best chance to finally dissolve the arbitrary barrier between the 'two cultures' of science and literature." Benford won the 1980 Nebula Award for his novel *Timescape,* highly praised for its realistic and detailed depiction of scientists at work, and was a Nebula finalist this year for his novella "Soon Comes Night." He is both one of the most prominent writers of "hard" science fiction and a working physicist, who holds the position of Professor of Physics at the University of California at Irvine. His novels include *The Stars in Shroud, Jupiter Project, In the Ocean of Night, Against Infinity, Artifact, Great Sky River, Tides of Light, Furious Gulf,* and *Sailing Bright Eternity;* much of his short fiction has been collected in *Matter's End* and *In Alien Flesh.*

Benford has said about his fiction that "my major concerns are the vast landscape of science, and the philosophical implications of that landscape on mortal, sensual human beings." In the following essay, he explores a fascinating corner of twentieth-century history: the relationship of science fiction to science itself.

L ong before I became interested in science itself, I was a science fiction reader. The Space Age changed that in 1957. At the time it seemed that the central metaphor of science fiction had become real, foggy legend condensing into fact.

I read about Sputnik on the deck of the *S.S. America,* sailing back from Germany, where I had lived for three years while my father served in the occupying forces. The one-page mimeographed ship's newsletter of October 4 gave that astonishing leap an infuriatingly terse two sentences.

By the time I re-entered high school in the U.S., just emerging from years when the Cold War seemed to fill every crevice of the world, the previously skimpy curriculum was already veering toward science, a golden, high-minded province. Suddenly I found that I could take a full year of calculus and physics in my senior year. This was quite a change. I put aside my devoted reading of the sf magazines and launched myself into science, the real thing.

I began to think seriously that a career of simply studying the physical world, which I had often read about in fiction, could be open to such as me. I had done reasonably in high school up until Sputnik, getting Bs and As, but not thinking of myself as one of the really bright members of the class. I imagined that I would probably end up as an engineer, but I really wanted to be a writer. When I scored high in the national scholastic exams of 1958 nobody was more surprised than I. But those scores opened the advanced classes to me in my senior year, and a whole new landscape.

This fresh path led directly to an early afternoon in 1967, when two physicists and a clerk from the personnel office at the Lawrence Radiation Laboratory ushered me into a large office without preamble, and there sat a distracted Edward Teller behind a messy desk piled high with physics journals.

To my surprise, the other physicists quickly excused themselves and left. Teller was scientific director of the Laboratory then, fabled for his work developing the A-bomb and H-bomb, and his epic split with Robert Oppenheimer.

They sprang Teller on me without warning. I had gone up to Livermore to discuss working there as a research physicist, following my doctoral thesis at the University of California at San Diego. Nobody told me that Teller insisted on taking the measure of every candidate in the program. "We didn't want you to be nervous," one said later. It worked; I was merely terrified.

He was the most daunting job interviewer imaginable. Not merely a great physicist, he loomed large in one of the central mythologies of modern science fiction, the A-bomb. In the next hour no one disturbed us as Teller quizzed me about my thesis in detail.

Attentively he turned every facet over and over, finding undiscovered nuances, some overlooked difficulty, a calculation perhaps a bit askew.

He was brilliant, leaping ahead of my nervous explanations to see implications I had only vaguely sensed. His mind darted as swiftly as any I had ever encountered, including some Nobel Laureates. To my vast surprise, I apparently passed inspection. At the end, he paused a long moment and then announced that he had "the most important kvestion of all." Leaning closer, he said, "Vill you be villing to vork on veapons?"

Unbidden, images from Stanley Kubrick's film *Dr. Strangelove* leaped to mind. But Teller had impressed me as a deep, reflective man. I said I would—occasionally, at least. I had grown up deep in the shadow of the Cold War. My father was a career army officer, and I had spent six years living with my family in occupied post-war Japan and Germany. It seemed to me that the sheer impossibility of using nuclear weapons was the best, indeed the only, way to avoid strategic conventional war, whose aftermath I had seen in shattered Tokyo and Berlin. Paralleling this direct experience was my reading in science fiction, which had always looked ahead at such issues, working out the future implied by current science.

That afternoon began my long, winding involvement with modern science and fiction, the inevitable clash of the noble and imaginary elements in both science and fiction with the gritty and practical. I have never settled emotionally the tensions between these modes of thinking. Growing up amid the shattered ruins of Germany and Japan, with a father who had fought through World War II and then spent long years occupying the fallen enemy lands, impressed me with the instability of even advanced nations. The greatest could blunder the most.

I quit Livermore in 1971 to become a professor at the University of California at Irvine. In novels such as *In the Ocean of Night,* written after my "Rad Lab" days, I see in retrospect that I was thrashing out my mixed feelings. I often turned to other scientists to fathom how my own experience fit with the history of both science and fiction in our time. I did not see then how intertwined they were and are, and how much we face the future using the legends of the past.

SIXA VS. SEILLA

"Veapons" called immediately to mind the central fable of sf in those days—the event which seemed to put the stamp on John Campbell's

Astounding magazine. In the spring of 1944 Cleve Cartmill published a clear description of how an atomic bomb worked in *Astounding,* titled "Deadline." Actually, Cartmill's bomb would not have worked, but he did stress that the key problem was separating non-fissionable isotopes from the crucial Uranium 235.

This story became legend, proudly touted by fans after the war as proof of sf's predictive powers. It was a tale of an evil alliance called the Axis—oops, no, the Sixa—who are prevented from dropping the A-bomb, while their opponents, the Allies—no, oops, that's the Seilla—refrain from using the weapon, fearing its implications.

In March 1944 a captain in the Intelligence and Security Division and the Manhattan Project called for an investigation of Cartmill. He suspected a breach in security, and wanted to trace it backward. U.S. security descended on Campbell's office, but Campbell truthfully told them that Cartmill had researched his story using only materials in public libraries.

A Special Agent nosed around Cartmill himself, going so far as to enlist his postman to casually quiz him about how the story came to be written. The postman remembered that John Campbell had sent Cartmill a letter several days before the Special Agent clamped a mail cover on Cartmill's correspondence. This fit the day when agents had already visited Campbell's office. Campbell was alerting his writer, post-haste. Soon enough, Security came calling.

Sf writers are often asked where they get their ideas. This was one time when the answer mattered. Cartmill had worked for a radium products company in the 1920s, he told the agent, which had in turn interested him in uranium research. He also fished forth two letters from Campbell, one written ten days short of two years before the Hiroshima bombing, in which Campbell urged him to explore these ideas: "U 235 has—I'm stating fact, not theory—been separated in quantity easily sufficient for preliminary atomic power research, and the like. They got it out of regular uranium ores by new atomic isotope separation methods; they have quantities measured in pounds . . ." Since a minimum critical mass is less than a hundred pounds, this was sniffing close to Top Secret data.

"Now it might be that you found the story worked better in allegory," Campbell advised, neatly leading Cartmill to distance the yet unwritten tale from current events. Plainly Campbell was trying to skirt close to secrets he must have guessed. Literary historian Albert Berger obtained the formerly secret files on the Cartmill case, and as he points out in *Analog* (September, 1984), Campbell never told Cartmill that wartime censorship directives forbade *any* mention of atomic energy. Campbell was urging his writer out into risky territory.

Cartmill was edgy, responding that he didn't want to be so close to home as to be "ridiculous. And there is the possible danger of actually suggesting a means of action which might be employed." Still, he had used the leaden device of simply investing the Axis and Allies names, thin cover indeed. Campbell did not ask him to change this, suggesting that both men were tantalized by the lure of reality behind their dreams.

The Office of Censorship came into play. Some suggested withholding *Astounding*'s mailing privileges, which would have ended the magazine. In the end, not attracting attention to the Cartmill story and the magazine seemed a smarter strategy. Security feared that ". . . such articles coming to the attention of personnel connected with the Project are apt to lead to an undue amount of speculation." Only those sitting atop the Manhattan Project knew what was going on. "Deadline" might make workers in the far-flung separation plants and machining shops figure out what all this uranium was for, and talk about it. The Project was afraid of imagination, particularly disciplined dreaming with numbers and facts well marshaled. They feared science fiction itself.

All this lore I already accepted, but I was curious about those at the top of the Project, such as Teller. Self-cautious, a mere, fresh postdoctoral physicist, I did not at first ask him about any of these legendary events. I was busy, too, learning how science works in such lofty realms.

I discussed both physics and politics with Teller while at the Lab, finding him delightfully eccentric and original. One hammering-hot summer day in Livermore, we continued well into the lunch hour. Teller wanted to go swimming, but refused to break off discussions. "Ve must not be all in our minds, all the time." I went with him. He cut an odd figure as he threaded among the muscular sunbathers, mind fixed on arcane points of theoretical physics, his skin pale as the underbelly of a fish. He sat at the pool edge and shed his suit, tie, shirt, the works right down to—instead of underwear—a swim suit. This man plans ahead, I thought.

As a boy in Budapest he had come in second in a contest with a streetcar, losing a foot. Beside the pool he unfastened his artificial foot, unembarrassed. (In *Dr. Strangelove*, I couldn't help recalling, it was an artificial hand.) He kept talking physics even as he wriggled over to the edge. He earnestly concluded his point, nodded earnestly, satisfied, and then seemed to realize where he was. I could almost hear him think, *Ah, yes, next problem. Svimming. Vere iss . . . ?* "Edward," I began—and Teller instantly flung himself like an awkward frog into the water, obliviously comic.

Moments like these led me to finally see through the cultural aura that obscures figures like Teller. They are more vast and various than we think, funnier and odder and warmer. Dr. Strangelove doesn't exist. Teller had made a name for himself at Los Alamos by thinking ahead. He proposed the hydrogen fusion bomb, the Super, while the A-bomb was under development—and lobbied to skip the A-bomb altogether, leapfrogging to the grander weapon.

With his penchant for problem-solving, Teller was a symbol of the "techno-fix" school of warfare, and by the 1960s the times were running against him. At one Livermore lunch, an arms control negotiator furiously said to me, "He's the Satan of weapons! We've got to stop him." Many scientists felt just as strongly.

H. Bruce Franklin's *War Stars: The Superweapon and the American Imagination* made the case that sf, particularly in the pulp magazines, strongly influenced U.S. foreign policy. In the 1930s Harry Truman had read lurid pulp magazine sf yarns of super weapons settling the hash of evil powers. Often they were held in readiness after, insuring the country against an uncertain future.

Truman wasn't alone. Popular culture's roots run deep. Time and again at Livermore I heard physicists quote sf works as arguments for or against the utility of hypothetical weapons. As I came to know the physics community more widely, this complex weave deepened.

BEEPS

At Livermore I got involved with the theory of tachyons, the theoretically possible particles which can travel faster than light. Not the sort of thing one imagines a "weapons lab" allowing, but Teller allowed the theorists a wide range. When the tachyon idea popped up in the physics journals, I discussed it with Teller. He thought they were highly unlikely, and I agreed, but worked on them anyway out of sheer speculative interest. With Bill Newcomb and David Book, I published in *Physical Review* a paper titled "The Tachyonic Antitelephone." We destroyed the existing arguments, which had avoided time-travel paradoxes by re-interpreted tachyonic trajectories moving backward in time as their anti-particles moving forward in time. It was simple to show that imposing a signal on the tachyons (sending a message) defeated the re-interpretation, so the causality problem remained. If sending a tip-off about a horse race to your grandfather made him so rich he jilted your grandmother and ran off to Paris, that was just as bad a violation of cause and effect.

Teller invoked a different argument against tachyons, which recalled the casual lunchtime discussions at Los Alamos, which were legendarily fruitful. At one, Enrico Fermi asked his famous question, "Where are they?"—and raised the still fiercely contentious issue of why aliens, if they are plentiful in the galaxy, haven't visited us by now. (That question undoubtedly inspired the proposal that radio listening might turn up alien broadcasts, made by Giuseppe Cocconi and Philip Morrison in 1959—the same Morrison who had worked in the Manhattan Project.) Using similar logic, Teller noted that tachyons could be used to send messages backward in time. "Vhy haven't they been sent? Vere are our messages from the future?"

Our answer was that nobody had built a tachyon receiver yet. Neat, perhaps, but a bit too neat. Surely somehow nature would not disguise such a profound trick. There had to be a way of seeing from theory why such disturbing things could not occur.

I was so intrigued by these hypothetical particles that I wrote papers investigating their consequences. That drew me into a distant friendship with Gerald Feinberg of Columbia University, who had introduced some of the ideas of tachyonic field theory. He was an amiable, concentrated man, always thinking through the broad implications of the present. He was also a first-class physicist who had edited a science fiction fanzine in high school with two other upstart Bronx Science High School students, Sheldon Glashow and Steven Weinberg—who later won the Nobel Prize for their theory which united the weak and electromagnetic forces. Titled ETAOIN SHRDLU for the frequency of letter use in English, the only fanzine ever edited by Nobel Prize winners stressed science with earnest teenage energy. (A generation later Stephen Hawking spent most of his free time reading sf paperbacks. Enthusiastically discussing them decades later with me, he was like most readers, able to recall plots and ideas easily, but not titles or authors.)

Tachyons were the sort of audacious idea that comes to young minds used to roving over the horizon of conventional thought. Because of Feinberg I later set part of my tachyon novel at Columbia. By the late 1970s I thought tachyons quite unlikely, since several experiments had failed to find them (after an exciting but erroneous detection in 1972). Still, the issue of how physics could *prove* that time communication is impossible remained—the primary issue for all of us, including Teller. Tachyons seemed a better way to address this than the more exotic beasts of the theorists' imaginations, such as spacetime wormholes.

So I framed the issue using tachyons, exploring how people in the future might get around the problem of having no receiver: by using energetic tachyons to disturb a finely tuned experiment in a physics lab in the past. Gerry chuckled when he heard this notion, pleased that his theoretical physics had spawned a novel about how scientists actually worked. He was rather bemused by the continuing cottage industry of tachyon papers, now numbering in the several hundreds. When an Australian experiment seemed to find cosmic rays moving over twice the speed of light, the field had a quick flurry of interest. Gerry was intrigued, then crestfallen when the results weren't confirmed.

He told me years later that he had begun thinking about tachyons because he was inspired by James Blish's short story, "Beep." In it, a faster-than-light communicator plays a crucial role in a future society, but has an annoying final *beep* at the end of every message. The communicator necessarily allows sending of signals backward in time, even when that's not your intention. Eventually the characters discover that all future messages are compressed into that *beep*, so the future is known, more or less by accident. Feinberg had set out to see if such a gadget was theoretically possible.

This pattern, speculation leading to detailed theory, I encountered more and more in my career. The litany of science is quite prissy, speaking of how anomalies in data lead theorists to explore new models, which are then checked by dutiful experimenters, and so on. Reality is wilder than that.

No one impressed me more with the power of speculation in science than Freeman Dyson. Without knowing who he was, I found him a like-minded soul at the daily physics department coffee breaks, when I was still a graduate student at the University of California at San Diego. I was very impressed that he had the audacity to give actual department colloquia on his odd ideas. These included notions about space exploration by using nuclear weapons as explosive pushers, and speculations on odd variants of life in the universe. He had just published a short note on what came to be called Dyson spheres—vast civilizations which swarm around their star, soaking up all available sunlight and emitting infrared, which we might study to detect them. (This was a direct answer to both Fermi's question and the Cocconi-Morrison proposal—more links in a long chain.) Dyson had read Jules Verne while a child, and at age eight and nine wrote an sf novel, *Sir Phillip Roberts's Erolunar Collision*, about scientists directing the orbits of asteroids. He was unafraid to publish conjectural, even rather outrageous ideas in the solemn pages of physics journals. When I remarked on this, he answered with a smile, "You'll find I'm not the first." Indeed, he descended from a line of futurist British thinkers, from J. D. Bernal of *The World, the Flesh and the Devil*, to Olaf Stapledon to Arthur C. Clarke. In *Infinite in All Directions*, Dyson remarked that "Science fiction is, after all, nothing more than the exploration of the future using the tools of science."

This was a fairly common view in those burgeoning times. In my first year of graduate school in La Jolla I noticed Leo Szilard at department colloquia, avidly holding forth on his myriad ideas. Szilard had persuaded Einstein to write the famous letter to Roosevelt explaining that an A-bomb was possible, and advocating the Manhattan Project. He had a genius for seizing the moment. Szilard had seen the potential in nuclear physics early, even urging his fellow physicists in the mid-1930s to keep their research secret. I had read Szilard's satirical sf novel *The Voice of the Dolphins* in 1961, and his sf short stories, and decided to wait until I had time from a weathering round of classes to speak to him. I was just taking some difficult examinations in late May 1964 when Dyson told me that Szilard had died of a heart attack that morning. It was a shock, though I had scarcely exchanged a dozen words with him. (Of his rather cerebral fiction he had said, "I am emotionally moved by extraordinary reasoning.") I had not seized the moment.

Szilard was obsessed with nuclear dangers, and Dyson carried some of Szilard's thinking forward. A student of Dyson's made head-lines in 1976 by designing a workable nuclear weapon using only published sources. I recalled the Cartmill episode. When I remarked on this, Dyson said, "The link goes back that far, yes." At the time I didn't know what he meant.

ROCKETS AND WAR STARS

Scientists often read sf at an early age and then drift away, but many maintain a soft spot in their hearts for it. Some, like me, bridge the two communities.

So it was no surprise to me when Teller enlisted sf allies in his policy battles. Especially effective in the 1980s was Jerry Pournelle, a rangy, technophilic, talented figure. With a .38 automatic he could hit a beer can at fifty yards in a cross wind. As needed, he could also run a political campaign, debug a computer program, or write a best-selling science fiction novel—simultaneously. When he asked me to serve on the Citizens' Advisory Council on National Space Policy in 1982, at first I didn't realize that Jerry wasn't proposing just another pressure group. This was a body which had direct lines to the White House, through the National Security Advisor. Teller, too, was "in the loop."

Pournelle dominated the Council meetings with his Tennessee charm, techno-conservative ideas, and sheer momentum. An oddly varied crew assembled: writers, industrial researchers, military and civilian experts on subjects ranging from artificial intelligence to rock-etry. The Council, a raucous bunch with feisty opinions, met at the spacious home of science fiction author Larry Niven. The men mostly talked hard-edge tech, the women policy. Pournelle stirred the pot and turned up the heat. Throughout all this, politics was not an issue. I was a registered Democrat, others were Republican, but our positions did not evolve from our politics. Amid the buffet meals, saunas and hot tubs, well-stocked open bar, and myriad word processors, fancies simmered and ideas cooked, some emerging better than half-baked.

Blocking nuclear weapons had always appealed to me. My misgivings about military involvement in the space program and other areas, which had surfaced in my novels repeatedly, vanished in matters which clearly were the military's province. Never, in all the policy and technical consulting I did while a professor at UCI, did I doubt that solving the immense problem of nuclear war lay somehow outside the province of the physicists who had started it all. But physicists could contribute—indeed, they had to try.

I favored as a first goal defending missiles and military command centers, using ground-based systems of swift, non-nuclear-tipped rockets. Technically this was small potatoes, really, not much beyond the capacity already available under existing treaties, which after all had allowed the Soviets to ring Moscow with a hundred fast defensive rockets, nuclear-tipped and still in place today.

The more ambitious specialists talked of war stars—great bunkers in the sky, able to knock down fleets of missiles. I doubted they could deal with the tens of thousands of warheads that could be launched in a full exchange. Still, to me that fact was a better argument against the existence of those thousands of warheads, rather than an argument against defense.

Finally, we settled on recommending a position claiming at least the moral high ground, if not high orbits. Defense was inevitably more stabilizing than relying on hair-trigger offense, we argued. It was also more principled. And eventually, the Soviet Union might not even be the enemy, we said—though we had no idea it would fade so fast. When that happened, defenses would still be useful against any attacker, especially rogue nations bent on a few terrorist attacks. There were plenty of science fiction stories, some many decades old, dealing with that possibility.

The Advisory Council met in August of 1984 in a mood of high celebration. Their pioneering work had yielded fruits unimaginable in 1982—Reagan himself had proposed the Strategic Defense Initiative, suggesting that nuclear weapons be made "impotent and obsolete." The Soviets were clearly staggered by the prospect. (Years later I heard straight from a senior Soviet advisor that the U.S. SDI had been the straw that broke the back of the military's hold on foreign policy. That seems to be the consensus now among the diplomatic community, though politically SDI is a common whipping boy, its funding cut.)

None of this was really unusual in the history of politics, policy, and science fiction. H. G. Wells had visited with both presidents Roosevelt, Stalin, Churchill, and other major figures. In 1906 Theodore Roosevelt was so dismayed by the Wellsian portrait of a dark future that he asked him to the White House for a long talk about how to avoid drifting that way. Wells's attention to war as the principal problem of the modern era found a ready audience among world leaders. Jules Verne had not commanded such respect in the corridors of power, and no writer since Wells has, but in the late twentieth century it seemed that science fiction's grasp of possibilities was once more called forth, this time by the same government which had fretted over Cleve Cartmill.

In the summer of 1984 all things seemed possible. I was not surprised that Robert Heinlein attended the Advisory Council meetings, dapper and sharp-witted. And out of the summer heat came a surprise visitor—Arthur C. Clarke, in town to promote the opening of the film made from his novel, *2010*. Clarke had testified before Congress against the Strategic Defense Initiative, and regarded the pollution of space by weapons, even defensive ones, as a violation of his life's vision.

Heinlein attacked as soon as Clarke settled into Larry Niven's living room. The conversation swirled around technical issues. Could SDI satellites be destroyed by putting into orbit a waiting flock of "smart rocks" (conventional explosives with small rockets attached)? Would SDI lead to further offensive weapons in space?

Behind all this lay a clear clash of personalities. Clarke was taken aback. His old friend Heinlein regarded Clarke's statements as both wrong-headed and rude. Foreigners on our soil should step softly in discussions of our self-defense policies, he said.

It was, at best, bad manners. Perhaps Clarke was guilty of "British arrogance."

Clarke had not expected this level of feeling from an old comrade. They had all believed in the High Church of Space, as one writer present put it. Surely getting away from the planet would diminish our rivalries? Now each side regarded the other as betraying that vision, of imposing unwarranted assumptions on the future of mankind. It was a sad moment for many when Clarke said a quiet good-bye, slipped out, and disappeared into his limousine, stunned.

In that moment I saw the dangers of mingling the visionary elements of sf with the hard-nosed. The field welcomed both, of course, but the world chewed up those of such ample spirit.

Behind much of this was Teller, close advisor to Reagan. He got involved with exotica such as X-ray lasers, which I thought beside the point. The answer lay not in vastly different, new technology, but using tried-and-true methods with a different strategic vision.

I was naive about what would follow, while the Soviets got the message quite clearly—because they watched what we did, and didn't merely listen to the public debate—and began thinking about throwing in the towel altogether. Meanwhile, over the Strategic Defense Initiative issue Nobel Laureates ground their axes, techno-patter rained down, politicians played to the gallery—ships passing in the night, their fog horns bellowing.

Our present had become, for that sf fan reading a newspaper report of Sputnik, completely science fictional. Even in the 1980s, though, I did not know how deep the science and science fiction connection went.

OLD LEGENDS

I had always wondered about Teller's effectiveness at influencing policy. In the 1940s, as James Gleick remarks in *Genius*, a biography of Richard Feynman, Teller was as imaginative and respected as Feynman. He was the great idea man of the Manhattan Project. So it was natural for me to ask him finally about science fiction's connection with both scientific discovery (tachyons) and science policy (the Manhattan Project).

"For long range thinking I trust in the real visionaries—the ones I prefer to read, at least. The science fiction writers. I haf always liked

Mr. Heinlein, Mr. Asimov, of course Mr. Clarke—they are much more important in the long run than any Secretary of Defense."

So we talked on about how he had read magazines in the 1940s in Los Alamos, bought similar hardbacks as they began to appear in the 1950s, and eventually from the press of events kept up with only a few favorites—the hard sf types, mostly but not exclusively.

He pointed out to me an interesting paragraph in an old paperback.

> We were searching . . . for a way to use U 235 in a controlled explosion. We had a vision of a one-ton bomb that would be a whole air raid in itself, a single explosion that would flatten out an entire industrial center. . . . If we could devise a really practical rocket fuel at the same time, one capable of driving a war rocket at a thousand miles an hour, or more, then we would be in a position to make almost anybody say "uncle" to Uncle Sam.
>
> We fiddled around with it all the rest of 1943 and well into 1944. The war in Europe and the troubles in Asia dragged on. After Italy folded up . . .

That was Robert A. Heinlein as "Anson MacDonald" in "Solution Unsatisfactory," in the May 1941 *Astounding*. It even gets the principal events in the war in the right order.

"I found that remarkable," Teller said, describing how Manhattan Project physicists would sometimes talk at lunch about sf stories they had read. Someone had thought that Heinlein's ideas were uncannily accurate. Not in its details, of course, because he described not a bomb, but rather using radioactive dust as an ultimate weapon. Spread over a country, it could be decisive.

I recalled thinking in the 1950s that in a way Heinlein had been proved right. The fallout from nuclear bursts can kill many more than the blast. Luckily, Hiroshima and Nagasaki were air bursts, which scooped up little topsoil and so yielded very low fallout. For hydrogen bombs, fallout is usually much more deadly.

In Heinlein's description of the strategic situation, Teller said, the physicists found a sobering warning. Ultimate weapons lead to a strategic standoff with no way back—a solution unsatisfactory. How to avoid this, and the whole general problem of nuclear weapons in the hands of brutal states, preoccupied the physicists laboring to make them. Nowhere in literature had anyone else confronted such a Faustian dilemma as directly, concretely.

Coming three years later in the same magazine, Cleve Cartmill's "Deadline" provoked astonishment in the lunch table discussions at Los Alamos. It really did describe isotope separation and the bomb itself in detail, and raised as its principal plot pivot the issue the physicists were then debating among themselves: should the Allies use it? To the physicists from many countries clustered in the high mountain strangeness of New Mexico, cut off from their familiar sources of humanist learning, it must have seemed particularly striking that Cartmill described an allied effort, a joint responsibility laid upon many nations.

Discussion of Cartmill's "Deadline" was significant. The story's detail was remarkable, its sentiments even more so. Did this rather obscure story hint at what the American public really thought about such a superweapon, or would think if they only knew?

Talk attracts attention. Teller recalled a security officer who took a decided interest, making notes, saying little. In retrospect, it was easy to see what a wartime intelligence monitor would make of the physicists' conversations. Who was this guy Cartmill, anyway? Where did he get these details? Who tipped him to the isotope separation problem? "And that is vhy Mr. Campbell received his visitors."

So the great, resonant legend of early hard sf was, in fact, triggered by the quiet, distant "fan" community among the scientists themselves. For me, closing the connection in this fundamental fable of the field completed my own quizzical thinking about the link between the science I practice, and the fiction I deploy in order to think about the larger implications of my work, and of others'. Events tinged with fable have an odd quality, looping back on themselves to bring us messages more tangled and subtle than we sometimes guess.

I am sure that the writers of that era, and perhaps of this one as well, would be pleased to hear this footnote to history. Somebody really was listening out there. I suspect today is no different. Perhaps the sf writers are indeed the unacknowledged legislators of tomorrow.

Grand Master
A. E. van Vogt

HARLAN ELLISON
CHARLES L. HARNESS

The Grand Master Nebula Award is given to a living writer for a lifetime of achievement. At the height of his career, in the forties, A. E. van Vogt was justly regarded as one of the most important writers of science fiction. Born in Canada in 1912, he came to Los Angeles during the forties. By then, he was already a prolific writer for John W. Campbell's legendary *Astounding* (later *Analog*) magazine and was considered one of the foremost writers, along with Isaac Asimov and Robert A. Heinlein, during what would later be called science fiction's Golden Age. By the fifties, he had won a permanent place for himself in the science fiction pantheon with his work, and was among the first science fiction writers to be eagerly snapped up by major hardcover publishers. Yet for various reasons —a long period during which he did not write, critical attacks from those who misunderstood his specific and idiosyncratic literary goals, changing tastes among readers, and an ever more prevalent cultural amnesia in his adopted land of the United States—A. E. van Vogt was increasingly overlooked and neglected even in science fiction circles.

In an essay published by *Science Fiction Age*, "Ten Neglected SF Writers: A Reader's Guide," George Zebrowski wrote:

"A. E. van Vogt's works exude a steel blue strangeness, at once in love with the stylized surfaces of technology but reminding us that barbarians are in control of the toys. His best works were the magazine stories of the 1940s, collected into book form in the '50s and '60s: *The Weapon Shops of Isher* (1951) and its sequel, *The Weapon Makers* (1952); *Empire of the Atom* (1957) and its sequel, *The Wizard of Linn* (1962). The well-known *Slan* (1951) and the first two World of Null-A novels—*The World of Null-A* (1948) and *The Players of Null-A* (1956)— hold some of the most dreamlike enjoyments to be found in SF, beauties to be found nowhere else. *The Mixed Men* (1952) is vividly beautiful; *The*

Voyage of the Space Beagle (1950) is better than any *Star Trek* story. The novella 'Recruiting Station' (1942) will twist your mind with hallucinatory imagery.

"Yet today this author who helped make hardcover SF publishing in the 1950s a success is all but forgotten. . . . Van Vogt's influence can clearly be seen in Alfred Bester's first two novels, especially in *The Stars My Destination* (1957); in the early work of Philip K. Dick, most obviously in *Solar Lottery* (1955) and *The World Jones Made* (1956); in the work of Charles L. Harness (probably his greatest disciple); in Kurt Vonnegut's *The Sirens of Titan* (1959); and, now that I can look back across two decades as a writer, in my own *The Omega Point Trilogy* (1983). Here is one of the last living masters of SF's Golden Age of the 1940s, yet he has no Hugo, no Nebula . . . and his work is nearly unavailable."

Happily, with this Grand Master Nebula, this cycle of neglect is finally broken: publishers, take note!

The award was presented to A. E. van Vogt on April 27, 1996, in the ballroom of the *Queen Mary* in Long Beach, California, where the 1995 Nebula Awards banquet was held. The author was accompanied by his wife, Lydia Brayman van Vogt, who was at his side during the presentation. SFWA president Barbara Hambly presented the trophy, and van Vogt received a standing ovation from the audience. SFWA's newest Grand Master was also given a birthday cake decorated with the words "Happy Birthday, Van" in honor of his eighty-fourth birthday. After accepting his award, van Vogt gave the following speech:

"Thank you very much.

"Among all of the awards and honors I have received, this Grand Master Award is indeed a special one. Coming from my fellow writers and professionals, it means a great deal to me.

"I have rubbed elbows with quite a few writers of science fiction, some you might have heard of. Most are gone now, but I am still here. I turned eighty-four years old yesterday.

"The thing is, longevity will get you something good. Sometimes another birthday cake, sometimes a wonderful honor such as this one.

"To the board of directors of SFWA and to the president, Barbara Hambly, I offer sincere admiration and thanks—not only from myself, but also from my wife, Lydia, who is by my side always.

"Thank you and good night."

In this volume, writer Harlan Ellison offers an eloquent and moving tribute to A. E. van Vogt. Ellison's many honors include multiples of

Nebula Awards, Hugo Awards, Lifetime Achievement Awards from both the World Fantasy Convention and the Horror Writers Association, the PEN Silver Pen Award for Journalism, and the Mystery Writers of America Edgar Allan Poe Award.

Charles L. Harness, a writer deeply influenced by van Vogt, also contributes an essay about the man's work. Harness, called "the great poet-philosopher of science fiction" by Brian Aldiss, is the author of *The Rose, The Paradox Men,* and *The Ring of Ritornel;* his recent novels *Krono* and *Lurid Dreams* won praise from the *New York Times Book Review.*

In addition, I have the pleasure of presenting here one of A. E. van Vogt's classic short stories, "Enchanted Village," first published in 1950.

A. E. van Vogt: Prefatory Remarks

HARLAN ELLISON

Even the brightest star shines dimly when observed from too far away. And human memory is notoriously unreliable. And we live in ugly times, when all respect for that which has gone before suffers crib death beneath the weight of youthful arrogance and ignorance. But a great nobility has, at last, been recognized and lauded. Someone less charitable than I might suggest the honor could have been better appreciated had it not been so tardy, running its race with a foe that blots joy and destroys short-term memory. But I sing the Talent Electric and, like all the dark smudges of history, nothing but the honor and the achievement remain for the myth-makers.

Alfred E. van Vogt has been awarded the Grand Master trophy of the Science-fiction and Fantasy Writers of America. He is not the first person to receive this accolade . . . given only to those whose right to possess it is beyond argument or mitigation. But . . .

Were we in 1946, or even 1956, van Vogt would have already been able to hold the award aloft. Had SFWA existed then, and had the greatest living sf authors been polled as to who was the most fecund, the most intriguing, the most innovative, the most influential of their number, Isaac and Arthur and Cyril and Hank Kuttner and Ron Hubbard would all have pointed to the same man, and Bob Heinlein would've given him a thumbs-up. Van Vogt was the pinnacle, the source of power and ideas; the writer to beat. Because he embodied in his astonishing novels and assorted stories what we always say is of prime importance to us in this genre—the much vaunted *Sense of Wonder*.

Van Vogt *was* the wellspring of wonder.

Youthful memory is filled with gaps and insolent of history, but for those who were there, and for those who care, it was van Vogt's books that were among the very first published in the mainstream from the despised realm of science fiction. When the first specialty houses were formed, they went after *The Weapon Shops of Isher* and *Slan* and *Masters of Time*. But when Simon & Schuster got into the game, most prestigious of the mainstream houses taking a chance on sf, it was van Vogt they sought, and *The World of Ā* and *Voyage of the Space Beagle* were the high-water marks.

That's how important he was.

And then came dark years during which the man was shamefully agented and overlooked; and even the brightest star loses its piercing light if observed through the thickening mists of time and flawed memory.

Now it is lifetimes later, and the great award has, at last, been presented. To some, less charitable than I, something could be said about a day late and a dollar short; but not I. I am here to sing the Talent Electric, and it is better now than never. He is the Grand Master. A. E. van Vogt, weaver of a thousand ideas per plot-line, creator of alien thoughts and impossible dreams that rival the best ever built by our kind.

This dear, gentlemanly writer whose stories can still kill you with a concept or warm you with a character, now joins the special pantheon.

Isaac and Alfie B. and Arthur and those rare, few others have been waiting for him to step up onto the dais. As one who read Van's "The Shadow Men" in the very first sf magazine he ever bought, I bless those who have presented him with the physical token of the greatness we knew all along. Written in enormous spray-painted letters on the Great Wall of China are the unarguable words VAN RULES! And don't you forget it.

A. E. van Vogt: An Appreciation
CHARLES L. HARNESS

John Thomas Cross, a nine-year-old telepath, IQ 300-plus, two hearts, abnormal strength, has just watched the police shoot his mother. As she dies she orders him, when he reaches fifteen, to go to a secret place where he will find a fantastic invention left by his murdered father. "Use it to kill our great enemy, Kier Gray."

They are *slans* (from S. Lann, who originated them centuries ago), and the human public believes they are conspiring to overthrow the government. Kier Gray's police have standing orders to shoot the "snakes" on sight. (They read minds via sensitive golden tendrils in their hair.)

A. E. van Vogt presents the whole theme of his story on page one, naming the major players and the conflicts to come. This was an extraordinary innovation in the genre at the time and must be considered the act of a supreme artist: rather like Beethoven setting out the whole scheme of the Ninth Symphony with the introductory bars, or Wagner stating the theme of Lohengrin in the prelude.

So begins *Slan*, probably van Vogt's most popular SF novel. And like the Ancient Mariner clutching the Wedding Guest, it never lets us go. We're carried along by a wild momentum.

So let's rejoin Jommy Cross as he weaves through the crowd, looking for a way out. He does indeed escape—by grabbing the rear bumper of a car moving through traffic. And not just any car. As he discovers by reading the minds of the occupants, it's the car of Kier Gray's Chief of Security, who is at that very moment looking for him! He escapes again, hides in a hole under a condemned building, is finally caught by Granny, a bleary-eyed alcoholic crone.

Granny is one of van Vogt's most memorable characters. Incidentally, he has few cardboard characters. Even some of his buildings qualify as characters. "[Kier Gray's Palace] . . . glowed with a soft, living, wonderful flame that was never the same color for more than an instant." Another is "polyphonic." Almost everybody is at least three-dimensional. Granny is four-plus: "[Jommy] had never seen a face that more nearly expressed the malignant character behind the mask of old flesh. . . . Every twisted line in that wrecked face had its counterpart in the twisted brain. A whole world of lechery dwelt within the confines of that shrewd mind." (Beautiful!)

They cut a deal. She'll hide him, he'll steal for her. (Fagin and Oliver!)

He stays with her six years. He flourishes in mind and body. By dint of telepathically auditing numerous university classes, he acquires the equivalent of several Ph.D.'s in sundry arts and sciences. And on his fifteenth birthday he recovers the device left by his father, Peter Cross: a handheld atomic weapon. He does wonders with it, including fastening it to the nose of a captured craft and blasting an underground escape tunnel eight miles long under the city. Thus he eludes another class of enemies, the *tendrilless* slans, deadlier even than the humans.

The charm and the suspense generated by this book do indeed depend in large part on Jommy's escapes from forces that would love to kill him. The individual chapters are just separate components of one big escape, leading finally to his confrontation with Kier Gray. Rather like looking closely at a fractal and finding that it is composed of smaller fractals, each of which is itself made up of elements of the identical design, and so on down the line. Van Vogt uses great artistry in this.

The book necessitates a great deal of explanation of the historical events and science of the day. Van Vogt presents it in small doses during rapid action sequences. We are rushed along and never notice that we have been instructed (sometimes at length) as to some factual element critical for the story line.

He has a profound grasp of the elements of suspense. We suspect that he could take the opening chapter of the U.S. census report for 1990 and turn it into a thriller that would have us sitting pop-eyed on the edge of our recliners.

He seems to bring in a brand-new mystery every couple of chapters. The new ones build pyramidally on the ones already there. Suspense builds.

Another famous van Vogtian suspense device is the conference of powerful men to decide somebody's fate, generally that of one of the conferees. Thus—Kier Gray: "John Petty is making this bid to depose me and no matter who wins between us, some of you are going to be dead before morning." (He was quite right.) Jommy Cross is involved in several similar life-threatening jams and is always able to talk himself out of trouble. It's fascinating to follow the conflicting lines of argument in these deadly dialogues.

We bear in mind that *Slan* was serialized in *Astounding* in late 1940, five years before Hiroshima. When the time came to bring the book out in hardcover (1946), the author had to acknowledge that nuclear power would be commonplace in the future world of *Slan*. On the other hand, the great superiority of Jommy's atomic weapon had to be retained. Van Vogt handled the problem with great skill and aplomb.

The world in which van Vogt wrote *Slan* proved the scope of his imagination. In the mid 1940s we had no computers (and certainly no Internet), no orbiting satellites, little or no TV. We hadn't been to the moon. Nearly all cars still had the old stick shift. There were no test-tube babies or heart transplants, no carbon dating. No transistors or microchips or genetic engineering or lasers or pulsars or quasars. DNA was still a mystery. These little deficiencies didn't bother him. He provided sophisticated substitutes.

He develops escape themes further in *The World of Ā*. (Yes, he hands us a mystery in the very title! How do we pronounce "Ā"? Eventually, we are told "Null A," meaning non-Aristotelian—meaning what? Read the book!)

It's 2650, the country is run by leaders selected by the Machine. Gilbert Gosseyn, a hotel guest, is in town to participate in the Machine's "games"—actually tests to determine fitness for advancement in the hierarchy of leaders. Since it is the custom to withdraw police protection in the city during the games, the guests must provide their own. As the group closes ranks, suspicion falls on Gosseyn. Is he who he claims to be, a law-abiding citizen from Cress Village, Florida? To his horror and amazement, he flunks a lie-detector test. Somebody has been messing with his mind. He doesn't know who he is. They toss him out into the night. And there his adventures really begin. He is murdered. Yet he awakens, alive and well, in a Venusian forest. The Machine-controlled roboplane sent for him gives him a status report: "Your existence and the mystery of your mind potential has caused a great war machine to mark time, while its leaders frantically try to find out who is behind you. . . . Don't underestimate the potentialities of a man who has been killed but is still alive."

One of the most fascinating of van Vogt's many scientific inventions is Gosseyn's ability to memorize the superficial molecular structure of a given scene, store it away in memory, then, from any place or time, materialize his body there. With the aid of his strange powers and a non-Aristotelian population, he thwarts an invasion of Venus by a Galactic Empire. But is all this under the control of a Cosmic Chessplayer? The book races to its destined end and we discover the truth. The last sentence of the novel (stunning last sentences are his trademark) leaves our ears ringing.

We move on. In *Empire of the Atom* Lord Clane of the ruling House of Linn is a mutant. Born frail, and never expected to amount to much, he rises in the dynastic ranks to control Earth. He alone has the power to resist the barbaric invader. They meet in classic van Vogtian mode: "[Czinczar] fingered the rod of force suggestively. 'So far as I can see, we can kill you in less than a second whenever we desire.' Clane shook his head. 'You are in error. It is quite impossible for you to kill me.'" (And he was right. Great stuff!)

So now to two books about the weapon shops: *The Weapon Shops of Isher* and its sequel, *The Weapon Makers*. ("The Right to Bear Arms Is the Right to Be Free.") We are once more in the far future (4784), where the weapon shops are a thorn in the side of the Isher Empire, ruled presently by the Empress Innelda. The doors of the shops are psychically tuned to permit entry to anyone who needs a weapon for defensive purposes or is otherwise peaceably inclined, but will deny entry to agents of the Empress.

Robert Hedrock, who accidentally became immortal several millennia ago, has created the weapon shops to counterbalance (not overthrow) the Isher Empire. Only toward the end of the narratives do his associates discover his immortality.

Innelda, in the eyes of Robert Hedrock: "The tigress had shown her claws, and they were made of steel and quiescent violence. The soul of this woman must be pure fire." He respects her and has plans for her.

Innelda brings to bear a new and enormously destructive weapon against one of the shops. The resulting blast hurls the shop back in time, to the twentieth century. MacAllister, a reporter, walks in to investigate. The shop manages to return to its own time and place in the future, but MacAllister is caught between past and future and begins to seesaw back and forth in time every couple of hours, with the weapon shop as the fulcrum. "In all the universe there had never been anything like the power that was accumulating, swing by swing, in his body. Released, the explosion would rock the fabric of space. All time would sigh to its echoes and the energy tensions that created the illusion of matter might collapse before the strain."

Hedrock plays only a background role in the first of the two books, *The Weapon Shops of Isher*. The main story here deals with Fara, who operates a repair shop and initially is a faithful subject of the Empress. After Fara is cheated, bankrupted, and evicted from his shop by scoundrels, he turns to the weapon shops. From there on in, it's a heart warming tale of how he gets his own back.

The weapon shops saga showed (perhaps for the first time) that science fiction could build around, indeed be *based* on, the highest levels of human altruism, decency, and love. Van Vogt's development of these themes has never been surpassed.

Hedrock returns in force in *The Weapon Makers*. The author wastes no time. Page 1: Innelda orders, "General Grall, you will, as a purely precautionary measure, arrest Captain Hedrock an hour after lunch and hang him."

How Hedrock gets out of this makes tight reading. In fact, the chief Councilors of the Weapon Shops agree that he shows an unacceptably high level of courage in dealing with Innelda's death sentence and that, therefore, he is a very suspicious character and should be shot.

He escapes from the Councilors via secret-matter transport into his private laboratory—where he is immediately attacked by a giant rodent, which he kills.

The major conflict in *The Weapon Makers* turns on Innelda's big secret: a starship, and the attempts of the weapon shops to acquire the design, if not the ship. Hedrock is able to get inside the ship, but is discovered, and he escapes in the star-powered lifeboat. We accept without a murmur that Hedrock's body can handle several million gravities and velocities of four hundred million miles per second.

He wakes up in a faraway system, where he finds he has been captured by greatly superior spiderlike creatures. They recognize only logical processes, and are puzzled that Hedrock additionally has feelings and emotions. They want to study him before they kill him. Spacetime is no problem to them, and they return him to Earth to continue their analyses in his home environment. What they find both amazes and enlightens them. The volume closes with their Delphic pronouncement: "Here is the race that shall rule the sevagram."

Sevagram?

What *is* the sevagram? Van Vogt had never before mentioned the word. Never mind. The very fact of the omission tells us what it is. He leaves it up to each of us to define it, within the unlimited realms of our own van Vogtiana. We know how to do this. He has given us the power. Just as in his stories, anything we say will be right and true.

Enchanted Village

A. E. VAN VOGT

E xplorers of a new frontier" they had been called before they left for Mars.

For a while after the ship crashed into a Martian desert, killing all on board except—miraculously—this one man, Bill Jenner spat the words occasionally into the constant, sand-laden wind. He despised himself for the pride he had felt when he first heard them.

His fury faded with each mile that he walked, and his black grief for his friends became a gray ache. Slowly he realized that he had made a ruinous misjudgment.

He had underestimated the speed at which the rocketship had been traveling. He'd guessed that he would have to walk three hundred miles to reach the shallow, polar sea he and the others had observed as they glided in from outer space. Actually, the ship must have flashed an immensely greater distance before it hurtled down out of control.

The days stretched behind him, seemingly as numberless as the hot, red, alien sand that scorched through his tattered clothes. This huge scarecrow of a man kept moving across the endless, arid waste— he would not give up.

By the time he came to the mountain, his food had long been gone. Of his four water bags, only one remained, and that was so close to being empty that he merely wet his cracked lips and swollen tongue whenever his thirst became unbearable.

Jenner climbed high before he realized that it was not just another dune that had barred his way. He paused, and as he gazed up at the mountain that towered above him, he cringed a little. For an instant he felt the hopelessness of this mad race he was making to nowhere— but he reached the top. He saw that below him was a depression surrounded by hills as high as or higher than the one on which he stood. Nestled in the valley they made was a village.

He could see trees and the marble floor of a courtyard. A score of buildings were clustered around what seemed to be a central square. They were mostly low-constructed, but there were four towers pointing gracefully into the sky. They shone in the sunlight with a marble luster.

Faintly, there came to Jenner's ears a thin, high-pitched whistling sound. It rose, fell, faded completely, then came up again clearly and unpleasantly. Even as Jenner ran toward it, the noise grated on his ears, eerie and unnatural.

He kept slipping on smooth rock, and bruised himself when he fell. He rolled halfway down into the valley. The buildings remained new and bright when seen from nearby. Their walls flashed with reflections. On every side was vegetation—reddish-green shrubbery, yellow-green trees laden with purple and red fruit.

With ravenous intent, Jenner headed for the nearest fruit tree. Close up, the tree looked dry and brittle. The large red fruit he tore from the lowest branch, however, was plump and juicy.

As he lifted it to his mouth, he remembered that he had been warned during his training period to taste nothing on Mars until it had been chemically examined. But that was meaningless advice to a man whose only chemical equipment was in his own body.

Nevertheless, the possibility of danger made him cautious. He took his first bite gingerly. It was bitter to his tongue, and he spat it out hastily. Some of the juice which remained in his mouth seared his gums. He felt the fire of it, and he reeled from nausea. His muscles began to jerk, and he lay down on the marble to keep himself from falling. After what seemed like hours to Jenner, the awful trembling finally went out of his body and he could see again. He looked up despisingly at the tree.

The pain finally left him, and slowly he relaxed. A soft breeze rustled the dry leaves. Nearby trees took up that gentle clamor, and it struck Jenner that the wind here in the valley was only a whisper of what it had been on the flat desert beyond the mountain.

There was no other sound now. Jenner abruptly remembered the high-pitched, ever-changing whistle he had heard. He lay very still, listening intently, but there was only the rustling of the leaves. The noisy shrilling had stopped. He wondered if it had been an alarm, to warn the villagers of his approach.

Anxiously he climbed to his feet and fumbled for his gun. A sense of disaster shocked through him. It wasn't there. His mind was a blank, and then he vaguely recalled that he had first missed the weapon more than a week before. He looked around him uneasily, but there was not a sign of creature life. He braced himself. He couldn't leave, as there was nowhere to go. If necessary, he would fight to the death to remain in the village.

Carefully Jenner took a sip from his water bag, moistening his cracked lips and his swollen tongue. Then he replaced the cap and started through a double line of trees toward the nearest building. He made a wide circle to observe it from several vantage points. On one side a low, broad archway opened into the interior. Through it, he could dimly make out the polished gleam of a marble floor.

Jenner explored the buildings from the outside, always keeping a respectful distance between him and any of the entrances. He saw no sign of animal life. He reached the far side of the marble platform on which the village was built, and turned back decisively. It was time to explore interiors.

He chose one of the four tower buildings. As he came within a dozen feet of it, he saw that he would have to stoop low to get inside.

Momentarily, the implications of that stopped him. These buildings had been constructed for a life form that must be very different from human beings.

He went forward again, bent down, and entered reluctantly, every muscle tensed.

He found himself in a room without furniture. However, there were several low marble fences projecting from one marble wall. They formed what looked like a group of four wide, low stalls. Each stall had an open trough carved out of the floor.

The second chamber was fitted with four inclined planes of marble, each of which slanted up to a dais. Altogether there were four rooms on the lower floor. From one of them a circular ramp mounted up, apparently to a tower room.

Jenner didn't investigate the upstairs. The earlier fear that he would find alien life was yielding to the deadly conviction that he wouldn't. No life meant no food or chance of getting any. In frantic haste he hurried from building to building, peering into the silent rooms, pausing now and then to shout hoarsely.

Finally there was no doubt. He was alone in a deserted village on a lifeless planet, without food, without water—except for the pitiful supply in his bag—and without hope.

He was in the fourth and smallest room of one of the tower buildings when he realized that he had come to the end of his search. The room had a single stall jutting out from one wall. Jenner lay down wearily in it. He must have fallen asleep instantly.

When he awoke he became aware of two things, one right after the other. The first realization occurred before he opened his eyes— the whistling sound was back; high and shrill, it wavered at the threshold of audibility.

The other was that a fine spray of liquid was being directed down at him from the ceiling. It had an odor, of which technician Jenner took a single whiff. Quickly he scrambled out of the room, coughing, tears in his eyes, his face already burning from chemical reaction.

He snatched his handkerchief and hastily wiped the exposed parts of his body and face.

He reached the outside and there paused, striving to understand what had happened.

The village seemed unchanged.

Leaves trembled in a gentle breeze. The sun was poised on a mountain peak. Jenner guessed from its position that it was morning again and that he had slept at least a dozen hours. The glazing white light suffused the valley. Half hidden by trees and shrubbery, the buildings flashed and shimmered.

He seemed to be in an oasis in a vast desert. It was an oasis, all right, Jenner reflected grimly, but not for a human being. For him, with its poisonous fruit, it was more like a tantalizing mirage.

He went back inside the building and cautiously peered into the room where he had slept. The spray of gas had stopped, not a bit of odor lingered, and the air was fresh and clean.

He edged over the threshold, half-inclined to make a test. He had a picture in his mind of a long-dead Martian creature lazing on the floor in the stall while a soothing chemical sprayed down on its body. The fact that the chemical was deadly to human beings merely emphasized how alien to man was the life that had spawned on Mars. But there seemed little doubt of the reason for the gas. The creature was accustomed to taking a morning shower.

Inside the "bathroom," Jenner eased himself feet first into the stall. As his hips came level with the stall entrance, the solid ceiling sprayed a jet of yellowish gas straight down upon his legs. Hastily Jenner pulled himself clear of the stall. The gas stopped as suddenly as it had started.

He tried it again, to make sure it was merely an automatic process. It turned on, then shut off.

Jenner's thirst-puffed lips parted with excitement. He thought, "If there can be one automatic process, there may be others."

Breathing heavily, he raced into the outer room. Carefully he shoved his legs into one of the two stalls. The moment his hips were in, a steaming gruel filled the trough beside the wall.

He stared at the greasy-looking stuff with a horrified fascination—food—and drink. He remembered the poison fruit and felt repelled, but he forced himself to bend down and put his finger into the hot, wet substance. He brought it up, dripping, to his mouth.

It tasted flat and pulpy, like boiled wood fiber. It trickled viscously into his throat. His eyes began to water and his lips drew back convulsively. He realized he was going to be sick, and ran for the outer door—but didn't quite make it.

When he finally got outside, he felt limp and unutterably listless. In that depressed state of mind, he grew aware again of the shrill sound.

He felt amazed that he could have ignored its rasping even for a few minutes. Sharply he glanced about, trying to determine its source, but it seemed to have none. Whenever he approached a point where it appeared to be loudest, then it would fade or shift, perhaps to the far side of the village.

He tried to imagine what an alien culture would want with a mind-shattering noise—although, of course, it would not necessarily have been unpleasant to them.

He stopped and snapped his fingers as a wild but nevertheless plausible notion entered his mind. Could this be music?

He toyed with the idea, trying to visualize the village as it had been long ago. Here a music-loving people had possibly gone about their daily tasks to the accompaniment of what was to them beautiful strains of melody.

The hideous whistling went on and on, waxing and waning. Jenner tried to put buildings between himself and the sound. He sought refuge in various rooms, hoping that at least one would be soundproof. None were. The whistle followed him wherever he went.

He retreated into the desert, and had to climb halfway up one of the slopes before the noise was low enough not to disturb him. Finally, breathless, but immeasurably relieved, he sank down on the sand and thought blankly:

What now?

The scene that spread before him had in it qualities of both heaven and hell. It was all too familiar now—the red sands, the stony dunes, the small, alien village promising so much and fulfilling so little.

Jenner looked down at it with his feverish eyes and ran his parched tongue over his cracked, dry lips. He knew that he was a dead man unless he could alter the automatic food-making machines that must be hidden somewhere in the walls and under the floors of the buildings.

In ancient days, a remnant of Martian civilization had survived here in this village. The inhabitants had died off, but the village lived on, keeping itself clean of sand, able to provide refuge for any Martian who might come along. But there were no Martians. There was only Bill Jenner, pilot of the first rocketship ever to land on Mars.

He had to make the village turn out food and drink that he could take. Without tools, except his hands, with scarcely any knowledge of chemistry, he must force it to change its habits.

Tensely he hefted his water bag. He took another sip and fought the same grim fight to prevent himself from guzzling it down to the last drop. And, when he had won the battle once more, he stood up and started down the slope.

He could last, he estimated, not more than three days. In that time he must conquer the village.

He was already among the trees when it suddenly struck him that the "music" had stopped. Relieved, he bent over a small shrub, took a good firm hold of it—and pulled.

It came up easily, and there was a slab of marble attached to it. Jenner stared at it, noting with surprise that he had been mistaken in thinking the stalk came up through a hole in the marble. It was merely stuck to the surface. Then he noticed something else—the shrub had no roots. Almost instinctively, Jenner looked down at the spot from which he had torn the slab of marble along with the plant. There was sand there.

He dropped the shrub, slipped to his knees, and plunged his fingers into the sand. Loose sand trickled through them. He reached deep, using all his strength to force his arm and hand down; sand— nothing but sand.

He stood up and frantically tore up another shrub. It also came easily, bringing with it a slab of marble. It had no roots, and where it had been was sand.

With a kind of mindless disbelief, Jenner rushed over to a fruit tree and shoved at it. There was a momentary resistance, and then the marble on which it stood split and lifted slowly into the air. The tree fell over with a swish and a crackle as its dry branches and leaves broke and crumbled into a thousand pieces. Underneath where it had been was sand.

Sand everywhere. A city built on sand. Mars, planet of sand. That was not completely true, of course. Seasonal vegetation had been observed near the polar icecaps. All but the hardiest of it died with the coming of summer. It had been intended that the rocketship land near one of those shallow, tideless seas.

By coming down out of control, the ship had wrecked more than itself. It had wrecked the chances for life of the only survivor of the voyage.

Jenner came slowly out of his daze. He had a thought then. He picked up one of the shrubs he had already torn loose, braced his foot against the marble to which it was attached, and tugged, gently at first, then with increasing strength.

It came loose finally, but there was no doubt that the two were part of a whole. The shrub was growing out of the marble.

Marble? Jenner knelt beside one of the holes from which he had torn a slab, and bent over an adjoining section. It was quite porous—calciferous rock, most likely, but not true marble at all. As he reached toward it, intending to break off a piece, it changed color. Astounded, Jenner drew back. Around the break, the stone was turning a bright orange-yellow. He studied it uncertainly, then tentatively he touched it.

It was as if he had dipped his fingers into searing acid. There was a sharp, biting, burning pain. With a gasp, Jenner jerked his hand clear.

The continuing anguish made him feel faint. He swayed and moaned, clutching the bruised members of his body. When the agony finally faded and he could look at the injury, he saw that the skin had peeled and that blood blisters had formed already. Grimly Jenner looked down at the break in the stone. The edges remained bright orange-yellow.

The village was alert, ready to defend itself from further attacks.

Suddenly weary, he crawled into the shade of a tree. There was only one possible conclusion to draw from what had happened, and it almost defied common sense. This lonely village was alive.

As he lay there, Jenner tried to imagine a great mass of living substance growing into the shape of buildings, adjusting itself to suit another life form, accepting the role of servant in the widest meaning of the term.

If it would serve one race, why not another? If it could adjust to Martians, why not to human beings?

There would be difficulties, of course. He guessed wearily that essential elements would not be available. The oxygen for water could come from the air . . . thousands of compounds could be made from sand. . . . Though it meant death if he failed to find a solution, he fell asleep even as he started to think about what they might be.

When he awoke it was quite dark.

Jenner climbed heavily to his feet. There was a drag to his muscles that alarmed him. He wet his mouth from his water bag and staggered toward the entrance of the nearest building. Except for the scraping of his shoes on the "marble," the silence was intense.

He stopped short, listened, and looked. The wind had died away. He couldn't see the mountains that rimmed the valley, but the buildings were still dimly visible, black shadows in a shadow world.

For the first time, it seemed to him that, in spite of his new hope, it might be better if he died. Even if he survived, what had he to look forward to? Only too well he recalled how hard it had been to rouse interest in the trip and to raise the large amount of money required. He remembered the colossal problems that had had to be solved in building the ship, and some of the men who had solved them were buried somewhere in the Martian desert.

It might be twenty years before another ship from Earth would try to reach the only other planet in the Solar System that had shown signs of being able to support life.

During those uncountable days and nights, those years, he would be here alone. That was the most he could hope for—if he lived. As he fumbled his way to a dais in one of the rooms, Jenner considered another problem: How did one let a living village know that it must alter its processes? In a way, it must already have grasped that it had a new tenant. How could he make it realize he needed food in a different chemical combination than that which it had served in the past; that he liked music, but on a different scale system; and that he could use a shower each morning—of water, not of poison gas?

He dozed fitfully, like a man who is sick rather than sleepy. Twice he wakened, his lips on fire, his eyes burning, his body bathed in perspiration. Several times he was startled into consciousness by the sound of his own harsh voice crying out in anger and fear at the night.

He guessed, then, that he was dying.

He spent the long hours of darkness tossing, turning, twisting, befuddled by waves of heat. As the light of morning came, he was vaguely surprised to realize that he was still alive. Restlessly he climbed off the dais and went to the door.

A bitingly cold wind blew, but it felt good to his hot face. He wondered if there were enough pneumococci in his blood for him to catch pneumonia. He decided not.

In a few moments he was shivering. He retreated back into the house, and for the first time noticed that, despite the doorless doorway, the wind did not come into the building at all. The rooms were cold but not draughty.

That started an association: Where had his terrible body heat come from? He teetered over to the dais where had spent the night. Within seconds he was sweltering in a temperature of about one hundred and thirty.

He climbed off the dais, shaken by his own stupidity. He estimated that he had sweated at least two quarts of moisture out of his dried-up body on that furnace of a bed.

This village was not for human beings. Here even the beds were heated for creatures who needed temperatures far beyond the heat comfortable for men.

Jenner spent most of the day in the shade of a large tree. He felt exhausted, and only occasionally did he even remember that he had a problem. When the whistling started, it bothered him at first, but he was too tired to move away from it. There were long periods when he hardly heard it, so dulled were his senses.

Late in the afternoon he remembered the shrubs and the tree he had torn up the day before and wondered what had happened to them. He wet his swollen tongue with the last few drops of water in his bag, climbed lackadaisically to his feet, and went to look for the dried-up remains.

There weren't any. He couldn't even find the holes where he had torn them out. The living village had absorbed the dead tissue into itself and had repaired the breaks in its "body."

That galvanized Jenner. He began to think again . . . about mutations, genetic readjustment, life forms adapting to new environments. There'd been lectures on that before the ship left Earth, rather generalized talks designed to acquaint the explorers with the problems men might face on an alien planet. The important principle was quite simple: adjust or die.

The village had to adjust to him. He doubted if he could seriously damage it, but he could try. His own need to survive must be placed on as sharp and hostile a basis as that.

Frantically Jenner began to search his pockets. Before leaving the rocket he had loaded himself with odds and ends of small equipment.

A jackknife, a folding metal cup, a printed radio, a tiny super-battery that could be charged by spinning an attached wheel—and for which he had brought along, among other things, a powerful electric fire lighter.

Jenner plugged the lighter into the battery and deliberately scraped the red-hot end along the surface of the "marble." The reaction was swift. The substance turned an angry purple this time. When an entire section of the floor had changed color, Jenner headed for the nearest stall trough, entering far enough to activate it.

There was a noticeable delay. When the food finally flowed into the trough, it was clear that the living village had realized the reason for what he had done. The food was a pale, creamy color, where earlier it had been a murky gray.

Jenner put his finger into it but withdrew it with a yell and wiped his finger. It continued to sting for several moments. The vital question was: Had it deliberately offered him food that would damage him, or was it trying to appease him without knowing what he could eat?

He decided to give it another chance, and entered the adjoining stall. The gritty stuff that flooded up this time was yellower. It didn't burn his finger, but Jenner took one taste and spat it out. He had the feeling that he had been offered a soup made of a greasy mixture of clay and gasoline.

He was thirsty now with a need heightened by the unpleasant taste in his mouth. Desperately he rushed outside and tore open the water bag, seeking the wetness inside. In his fumbling eagerness, he spilled a few precious drops onto the courtyard. Down he went on his face and licked them up.

Half a minute later, he was still licking, and there was still water.

The fact penetrated suddenly. He raised himself and gazed wonderingly at the droplets of water that sparkled on the smooth stone. As he watched, another one squeezed up from the apparently solid surface and shimmered in the light of the sinking sun.

He bent, and with the tip of his tongue sponged up each visible drop. For a long time he lay with his mouth pressed to the "marble," sucking up the tiny bits of water that the village doled out to him.

The glowing white sun disappeared behind a hill. Night fell, like the dropping of a black screen. The air turned cold, then icy. He shivered as the wind keened through his ragged clothes. But what finally stopped him was the collapse of the surface from which he had been drinking.

Jenner lifted himself in surprise, and in the darkness gingerly felt over the stone. It had genuinely crumbled. Evidently the substance had yielded up its available water and had disintegrated in the process. Jenner estimated that he had drunk altogether an ounce of water.

It was a convincing demonstration of the willingness of the village to please him, but there was another, less satisfying, implication. If the village had to destroy a part of itself every time it gave him a drink, then clearly the supply was not unlimited.

Jenner hurried inside the nearest building, climbed onto a dais—and climbed off again hastily, as the heat blazed up at him. He waited, to give the Intelligence a chance to realize he wanted a change, then lay down once more. The heat was as great as ever.

He gave that up because he was too tired to persist and too sleepy to think of a method that might let the village know he needed a different bedroom temperature. He slept on the floor with an uneasy conviction that it could *not* sustain him for long. He woke up many times during the night and thought, "Not enough water. No matter how hard it tries—" Then he would sleep again, only to wake once more, tense and unhappy.

Nevertheless, morning found him briefly alert; and all his steely determination was back—that iron will power that had brought him at least five hundred miles across an unknown desert.

He headed for the nearest trough. This time, after he had activated it, there was a pause of more than a minute; and then about a thimbleful of water made a wet splotch at the bottom.

Jenner licked it dry, then waited hopefully for more. When none came he reflected gloomily that somewhere in the village an entire group of cells had broken down and released their water for him.

Then and there he decided that it was up to the human being, who could move around, to find a new source of water for the village, which could not move.

In the interim, of course, the village would have to keep him alive, until he had investigated the possibilities. That meant, above everything else, he must have some food to sustain him while he looked around.

He began to search his pockets. Toward the end of his food supply, he had carried scraps and pieces wrapped in small bits of cloth. Crumbs had broken off into the pocket, and he had searched for them often during those long days in the desert. Now, by actually ripping the seams, he discovered tiny particles of meat and bread, little bits of grease, and other unidentifiable substances.

Carefully he leaned over the adjoining stall and placed the scrappings in the trough there. The village would not be able to offer him more than a reasonable facsimile. If the spilling of a few drops on the courtyard could make it aware of his need for water, then a similar offering might give it the clue it needed as to the chemical nature of the food he could eat.

Jenner waited, then entered the second stall and activated it. About a pint of thick, creamy substance trickled into the bottom of the trough. The smallness of the quantity seemed evidence that perhaps it contained water.

He tasted it. It had a sharp, musty flavor and a stale odor. It was almost as dry as flour—but his stomach did not reject it.

Jenner ate slowly, acutely aware that at such moments as this the village had him at its mercy. He could never be sure that one of the food ingredients was not a slow-acting poison.

When he had finished the meal he went to a food trough in another building. He refused to eat the food that came up, but activated still another trough. This time he received a few drops of water.

He had come purposefully to one of the tower buildings. Now he started up the ramp that led to the upper floor. He paused only briefly in the room he came to, as he had already discovered that they seemed to be additional bedrooms. The familiar dais was there in a group of three.

What interested him was that the circular ramp continued to wind on upward. First to another, smaller room that seemed to have no particular reason for being. Then it wound on up to the top of the tower, some seventy feet above the ground. It was high enough for him to see beyond the rim of all the surrounding hilltops. He had thought it might be, but he had been too weak to make the climb before. Now he looked out to every horizon. Almost immediately the hope that had brought him up faded.

The view was immeasurably desolate. As far as he could see was an arid waste, and every horizon was hidden in a midst of wind-blown sand.

Jenner gazed with a sense of despair. If there was a Martian sea out there somewhere, it was beyond his reach.

Abruptly he clenched his hands in anger against his fate, which seemed inevitable now. At the very worst, he had hoped he would find himself in a mountainous region. Seas and mountains were generally the two main sources of water. He should have known, of course, that there were very few mountains on Mars. It would have been a wild coincidence if he had actually run into a mountain range.

His fury faded because he lacked the strength to sustain any emotion. Numbly he went down the ramp.

His vague plan to help the village ended as swiftly and finally as that.

The days drifted by, but as to how many he had no idea. Each time he went to eat, a smaller amount of water was doled out to him. Jenner kept telling himself that each meal would have to be his last. It was unreasonable for him to expect the village to destroy itself when his fate was certain now.

What was worse, it became increasingly clear that the food was not good for him. He had misled the village as to his needs by giving it stale, perhaps even tainted, samples, and prolonged the agony for himself. At times after he had eaten, Jenner felt dizzy for hours. All too frequently his head ached and his body shivered with fever.

The village was doing what it could. The rest was up to him, and he couldn't even adjust to an approximation of Earth food.

For two days he was too sick to drag himself to one of the troughs. Hour after hour he lay on the floor. Some time during the second night the pain in his body grew so terrible that he finally made up his mind.

"If I can get to a dais," he told himself, "the heat alone will kill me; and in absorbing my body, the village will get back some of its lost water."

He spent at least an hour crawling laboriously up the ramp of the nearest dais, and when he finally made it, he lay as one already dead. His last waking thought was: "Beloved friends, I'm coming."

The hallucination was so complete that momentarily he seemed to be back in the control room of the rocketship, and all around him were his former companions.

With a sigh of relief Jenner sank into a dreamless sleep.

He woke to the sound of a violin. It was a sad-sweet music that told of the rise and fall of a race long dead.

Jenner listened for a while and then with abrupt excitement realized the truth. This was a substitute for the whistling—the village had adjusted its music to him!

Other sensory phenomena stole in upon him. The dais felt comfortably warm, not hot at all. He had a feeling of wonderful physical well-being.

Eagerly he scrambled down the ramp to the nearest food stall. As he crawled forward, his nose close to the floor, the trough filled with a steamy mixture. The odor was so rich and pleasant that he plunged his face into it and slopped it up greedily. It had the flavor of thick, meaty soup and was warm and soothing to his lips and mouth. When he had eaten it all, for the first time he did not need a drink of water.

"I've won!" thought Jenner. "The village has found a way!"

After a while he remembered something and crawled to the bathroom. Cautiously, watching the ceiling, he eased himself backward into the shower stall. The yellowish spray came down, cool and delightful.

Ecstatically Jenner wriggled his four-foot tail and lifted his long snout to let the thin streams of liquid wash away the food impurities that clung to his sharp teeth.

Then he waddled out to bask in the sun and listen to the timeless music.

It'll Float, but Can It Fly?: Science Fiction and Fantasy Films of 1995

KATHI MAIO

No Nebula Award is given for science fiction on film or television, but it is customary to include an essay in the *Nebula Awards* anthology about the year's notable science fiction and fantasy in visual form. Kathi Maio, author of *Feminist in the Dark* and *Popcorn and Sexual Politics,* also writes on movies for *The Magazine of Fantasy & Science Fiction* and *Sojourner;* this is her third appearance in these volumes.

She begins her commentary on the films of 1995 with a comment on the "blockbuster fever" that seemed to dominate the movie industry that year. "In fact," she writes, "that particular sickness—of throwing big stars, bigger explosions, and the biggest possible, nonstop FX at a stupidly written script—reached epidemic proportions during the year."

Since then, in the view of many, that particular epidemic has become a plague.

Blockbuster fever continued to grip conglomeratic Hollywood in 1995. In fact, that particular sickness—of throwing big stars, bigger explosions, and the biggest possible nonstop FX at a stupidly written script—reached epidemic proportions during the year. And one particularly soggy SF epic, about a webfooted Mariner and the *Waterworld* he navigates, came to represent all that had gone wrong with the studio film.

Envisioned as a low-budget, aquatic *Mad Max* rip-off when Peter Rader first pitched and scripted it in the eighties, *Waterworld* was still a highly derivative postapocalyptic adventure movie by the time of its release nearly a decade (and countless rewrites) later. But its budget had grown to *at least* $150 million. (Most estimates, including domestic marketing costs, put the film's price tag at well over $200 million.)

Much of the film's budget is right on the screen to see: in the surly countenance of the film's decidedly unmacho star, Kevin Costner, and in the elaborate water-tossed sets he visits. (The artificial scrap-metal atoll, a quarter mile in circumference, alone cost $5 million.) Director Kevin Reynolds (*Robin Hood: Prince of Thieves*) couldn't control costs, Hawaii weather, or the overweening ego of his star. So he ended up with his name attached to a film that is almost, but not quite, as bad as the negative buzz that preceded its release had predicted it would be.

We American viewers tried to entertain ourselves with the film's many absurdities (for example, where *did* the "smokers" get all those cigarettes from, hundreds of years after the world went underwater?). And we tried to revel in all the wave-tossed action, as well as Dennis Hopper's scene-stealing (but seen before) madman antics. But *Waterworld's* uninvolving characters and plot got in the way of these simple pleasures. And so we turned our backs on the film when it had grossed a mere $88 million.

I'd like to say that the rest of Hollywood looked upon Universal's embarrassment with *Waterworld* and learned its lesson. But the corporate belief in overkill cinema just isn't that easily shaken. Especially since, in the long run, extravagant, laughable *Waterworld* was, shockingly, a profitable film. The lucrative (and very action-oriented) international box office added another $260 million to *Waterworld's* war chest, thus putting the film over the top and reinforcing the very excesses the film represented.

In the long run, the lesson of *Waterworld* was much different from the one many of us had hoped for. 1995 was the year it became unmistakably clear that the tastes of the global marketplace would dictate the decisions made by the "American" movie industry. That being the case, the trend toward overblown action and cartoonish stories would undoubtedly persist. Likewise, the major studios' overreliance on established movie franchises seemed a certainty.

Forget all that's challenging and new. Studios wanted to put their money on a Sure Thing.

But some sure things are also very bad movies. Take *Congo,* for instance. This jungle adventure (with sf touches related to satellites, laser weaponry, and a high-tech "talking" gorilla) is just about as inept as a major motion picture can be. It's too straight for high camp and too utterly stupid to be taken seriously. It couldn't even claim any name stars. But Paramount was nonetheless able to successfully market the film (written for the screen by John Patrick Shanley) as coming from "the best-selling author of *Jurassic Park.*" Michael Crichton gave the film its modest, and completely undeserved, success. His name proved golden once more.

Less successful, but equally bad—not even the international market could make this one a hit—was *Judge Dredd.* Sylvester Stallone is supposed to be a box-office guarantee. Or, at least, that's *supposed* to be the reason he gets the big bucks. But even he of the slurred speech and the bulging neck veins could put no pizzazz in this dull, self-serious adaptation of the British comic book *2000AD.* Without the social satire of the original, this fable about a judge/jury/executioner lawman in the anarchic days of the Mega Cities to come was just no fun.

And speaking of British cult comics that tanked with American audiences, *Tank Girl* was an even bigger flop. Yet this tale of an arid future in which a hedonistic punker (Lori Petty) with her own armored vehicle does battle with the evil bureaucrats of the Department of Water and Power is actually a much better sf romp than its abysmal receipts would indicate. But with no sex-kitten allure, and no super-powers (and no star power, either), this Tank Girl just couldn't attract an audience.

Such failures had some of us, briefly, dreaming (foolishly, again) of a day in which Hollywood would finally abandon the notion that if it's science fiction, it must come from a comic book. But the movie industry won't be turning its back on zap-powee source material for its fantasy films any time soon. And the reason's simple: *Batman.* The most successful cinematic comic-book franchise struck gold for a third time in 1995. Change helmets, switch leading men—nobody seemed to care. (The Dark Knight is the kind of sure thing those suits dream about.)

Batman Forever came in as the official domestic box-office champ for the year, with receipts of $184 million. Joel Schumacher knew enough not to copy the dark vision of the first two films, directed by Tim Burton. So he went for glitz and energy. He made his *Batman* an all-out camped-up cartoon. Val Kilmer and Chris O'Donnell were beefcake poster boys in their fetishist rubber suits. And Jim Carrey's Riddler, a zany dervish in bright green spandex, was an even bigger audience lure.

Since safe bets rule the industry today, the success of another blockbuster, *Toy Story*, was doubly sweet. Oh, there's little real risk in a venture that combines animation with the name (and marketing know-how) of Disney. Still, this particular project was something new, and relatively daring for the House of Mouse. It was the first full-length computer-animated feature. Produced by Disney partner Pixar, in northern California, this eye-popping feast of CGI (computer-generated imagery) was directed by John Lasseter, following up on his Oscar win for a computer-animated short called *Tin Toy* (1989).

Using a cast of toy heroes was a brilliant stroke. Three-dimensional but frankly artificial—they're made of plastic, metal, wood, and cloth—the cowpoke doll, Woody; the space ranger action figure, Buzz Lightyear; and all of their toy-box cohorts look real. Wondrously so. (By comparison, the rarely glimpsed humans of the film are woefully inadequate imitations.)

But the CGI breakthroughs of *Toy Story* aren't the only reason for its phenomenal success. (It actually made more money than *Batman Forever*, but a good chunk of its earnings came in 1996.) I like to think that *Toy Story* was a monster hit because it is actually a well-written and involving buddy picture. Buzz and Woody are three-dimensional both in the way they look *and* in the way they act. And, as voiced by Tim Allen and Tom Hanks, they were two of the most attractive leading men of the year.

Toy Story wasn't the only movie triumph Tom Hanks was attached to in 1995. He also led the cast of Ron Howard's smash hit, *Apollo 13*. As heightened as the story and its visual effects were, the film (based on Jim Lovell's memoir, *Lost Moon*) is science fact and not science fiction. But since it provided the most inspirational example of believable, smart (nonviolent and cooperative) space valor in recent memory, it's definitely worth noting here.

Audiences are drawn to realistic heroism. Perhaps that helps to explain why the history-based sword-fight epics *Braveheart* and *Rob Roy* did significantly better than the Arthurian fable (and undeniable flop) *First Knight*. Of course, besides a ponderous pace, casting was the biggest problem with *First Knight*. Sean Connery and the utterly American Richard Gere were both too old for their respective Arthur and Lancelot roles. And Julia Ormond was just a little too chilly as Guinevere.

Unusual casting choices were made for another film, the medical thriller *Outbreak*. Happily, the resulting movie was much more entertaining. Dustin Hoffman wouldn't have been my choice as leading man in a movie about brave virologists fighting a new plague, but he gives his character an intense everyman quality that works. He and Rene Russo (as his ex-wife and co-bug-hunter) may seem like a real odd couple, too. But then, implausibilities abound in this particular story of a Motaba virus decimating a sleepy California town and threatening the nation. By the time the story gets too absurd, though, director Wolfgang Petersen already has the audience hooked. Playing on our AIDS-induced fears of coming plagues, *Outbreak* provided a cure for the spring movie doldrums.

Another tale of the plague years provided a much less comforting, and much more atmospheric, movie experience. It was *12 Monkeys*, a film directed by Terry Gilliam from a screenplay by David and Janet Peoples ("inspired" by Chris Marker's short masterpiece, *Le Jetee*). Only nominally a 1995 release, the film opened in New York and L.A. in the final days of the year to qualify for Oscar consideration. (It was a strategy that worked, too, notably in Brad Pitt's nomination for best supporting actor.)

In the year 2035, only a fraction of the earth's human population remains, in a desolate, heavily controlled underground environment. A "volunteer," Cole (Bruce Willis), is sent back to the year 1996 to try to discover the origins of the virus that has nearly wiped out humanity. But time travel is an inexact science, and Cole doesn't always end up at the right time or place. Worse, the citizens of the American past view doomsayer Cole as a delusional wacko.

And perhaps he is. Or, at the very least, he'd like to be.

12 Monkeys isn't a perfect film. Bruce Willis's truculent performance is far too problematic, for a start. But there is an intelligence at work in this movie that is sorely absent from most of those comic-book-based science fiction flicks of this year, or any other. This is a movie that people saw a second time for the story instead of for the special effects. And then they actually discussed it with one another. (Incredible.)

With *12 Monkeys*, Terry Gilliam has once again shown himself to be one of our foremost contemporary fantasy filmmakers.

But not all plagues are the literal variety explored in films like *Outbreak* and *12 Monkeys*. To many, the growth of automation and virtual reality is a pestilence of equal peril. True, there's nothing new about this fear and loathing of new technologies. But you'd think there was, the way movieland exploited computer paranoia in 1995. You could even call this the year of the rise—and immediate fall—of the computer/VR thriller.

Appropriately enough, the bad guy in a film called *Hackers* even goes by the nom de computing The Plague. And real-life hackers viewed this particular teen thriller as a contagion of the first order. They defaced the film's posters. They slammed the movie on-line. But they needn't have gotten so hot and bothered about it. It bombed. And it's not hard to see why.

The plot, involving corporate extortionists (who skateboard) and the sweet-faced Rollerblading punk hackers whom the baddies have set up to take the fall, is a tad ludicrous. And, in an attempt to make a task like locating and downloading a file look exciting, Iain Softley and his crews have transformed nuts-and-bolts computing into a 3-D video game. A mistake, but an understandable one—computers are boring; it's what they can do that is sometimes exciting.

Sacrilegious as it is for me to say this, I nonetheless rather enjoyed this film. If you could set aside the realities of hacking and were willing to view the film as an odd little teen adventure yarn with a romantic subplot, it really wasn't half bad.

I'll also confess to a grudging enjoyment of another hacker thriller, *The Net*. But, like most members of the film's audience, I found the movie pleasurable only because of the considerable winsome charms of its lead performer, Sandra Bullock. Accepting the lovely Ms. Bullock as an antisocial computer nerd was the biggest hurdle. Get past that, and the rest of this plot involving (you guessed it) corporate skullduggery seems nearly tenable.

But maybe I was so forgiving of the numerous sins of *Hackers* and *The Net* because they were infinitely more pleasant than the unrelentingly violent futuristic serial-killer movie *Virtuosity*. Like *The Net*, this one needs to rely on the magnetism of its star. And Denzel Washington certainly has charisma to spare. Unfortunately, he's allowed to display none of it here. Washington plays a former cop (and convicted killer) who is put on the trail of a hybrid VR serial killer, Sid 6.7 (Russell Crowe). Seems Sid has escaped into the real Los Angeles of 1999 after he has been conveniently programmed with the knowledge and cunning of every known multiple murderer.

The film is an ugly, bloody mess from director Brett Leonard. Now, Mr. Leonard alienated story author Stephen King with his other VR movie, *The Lawnmower Man*. And author Dean Koontz was none too pleased with what Leonard (and his writers) did to his novel *Hideaway*, which became another 1995 feature about a serial killer from another dimension. Clearly, Leonard has developed a definite movie specialty. It just doesn't seem like a very fruitful one, for adapted authors . . . or for his audience.

Mr. Leonard wasn't the only filmmaker to commemorate the coming millennium with an L.A. serial killer who laces his carnage with VR head games, however. Kathryn Bigelow's *Strange Days* also follows a multiple murderer through the City of Angels in the final days of the last year of the century. On the plus side, Bigelow is an undeniably stylish director. And she can tell a story with more noirish finesse than a sledgehammer like Brett Leonard can. On technique alone, *Strange Days* is well worth watching. And it didn't hurt it to have the power of James Cameron's name going for it. (Cameron is credited as a producer, as well as for the story and as co-writer of the screenplay of *Strange Days*.)

But big names and spiffy camera work aren't the only measures of a film's watchability. Nor are they the best. And the film's story, about a former cop and current pusher of VR "clips," Lenny (Ralph Fiennes, badly miscast), drawn into a murder plot that somehow involves his lost love (Juliette Lewis), is just the same-old same-old. I kept wishing that the movie had been about Lenny's friend Mace (Angela Bassett), a limo driver and bodyguard—and one of those strong women we've come to expect in a Cameron film. But it's not. And, finally, *Strange Days* seems like a waste of energy from several very talented people.

But if *Strange Days* disappoints, *Johnny Mnemonic* is enough to make a grown man weep. On paper, it seemed like one of those dream projects: William Gibson adapting his own classic short story for the screen; painter, sculptor, musician, and performance artist Robert Longo bringing a fresh vision to film direction; and Keanu Reeves starring as the title data courier, following up on his breakthrough triumph in *Speed*. But, alas, this was one dream team that turned out a nightmarish product.

Perhaps Longo had more money than he knew what to do with, and less experience than he needed. As for poor Keanu, someone forgot to tell him that he was an augmented human and not a robot. (His wooden line delivery is alone enough to deaden this film for the viewer.) Yet this ill-fated project met with a happy ending of sorts. When *Johnny Mnemonic* was adapted (yet again) for the pc, it became quite a popular interactive CD-ROM game. A computer is, perhaps, a more appropriate home for this particular cyberthriller.

If Hollywood had no idea what to do with high-tech suspense, it's nice to know that someone else was ready and able to lead the way. I refer to a prime example of Japanese anime, *Ghost in the Shell*. This Japan-U.K. production was released in 1995, but most of its American showings and its video release came in 1996. It was directed by Mamoru Oshii, from a manga (comic book/novel) by Masamune Shirow. And it's simply splendid, both as a story and as an example of feature animation.

The narrative's hero is one Major Kusanagi, a female cyborg who works as a special operative for Section 9 of the Security Police. Almost all of Kusanagi's humanity has been replaced and enhanced with impressive results in every skill from firearm use to surveillance hacking. She can do it all with cool to spare.

Kusanagi and her team are currently investigating a cybernetic entity called the Puppetmaster. Begun as a secret government project, the Puppetmaster has taken on a life and identity of its own, and is even capable of taking possession of the minds and actions of human beings.

Those unfamiliar with manga and anime may find the complexities of the plot (few of which are explained) more than a little daunting. Even so, the animation is impressive, and the philosophic issues the film raises, related to the concept of "ghost" (intelligence, identity, and the elusive quality called soul), are so compelling that *Ghost in the Shell* should be viewed as one of the best sf films of the year.

Not exactly Japanese, but, rather, a Western rip-off of Japanese sentai shows, *The Mighty Morphin Power Rangers* became one of the most popular television programs ever produced for kids. In the series, an assortment of multicultural youths in color-coordinated jumpsuits and helmets do battle with a variety of monsters threatening the peace of Angel Grove, California. *Mighty Morphin Power Rangers: The Movie* is more of the same, with a new bad guy, Ivan Ooze (Paul Freeman), thrown in for good measure. Unfortunately for the producers, the Rangers' popularity had already peaked when the movie appeared. (And, more to the point, parents and other elders were so sick of this kick-happy crew by the time the movie came out that many of them refused to sit through this woeful excuse for a film.)

Another martial-arts tie-in fantasy did better. And perhaps better than it deserved. But *Mortal Kombat,* based on one of the most popular—and bloodthirsty—video games that ever chopped its way into America's homes and arcades, was actually a better film than expected. Although obviously pitched to a young male audience, the good-kick-boxers-save-the-world plot had enough humor and special-effects wizardry that even some adults were willing to sit through it.

A youth-pitched fantasy film can be much more than a bearable experience for adults, however. Some are an absolute joy for viewers of all ages. Moreover, judging from the film output of 1995, the family fantasy film has become the most varied and vibrant genre of speculative cinema.

Not all of them were "instant classics" (the oxymoron Disney likes to apply to its movies). In fact, some—like *Magic in the Water* (a Pacific Northwest sea serpent fable), *A Kid in King Arthur's Court* (a junior league Mark Twain rip-off), and *Tall Tale: The Unbelievable Adventures of Pecos Bill* (in which legendary heroes help a lad save the family farm)—deserved the immediate obscurity into which they fell. Still, even the least notable of these children's films contained a few moments of wonder and infinitely more humanity than most of the sf/fantasy tales pitched to older audiences.

Even in the kiddie categories, it's name-recognition projects that most often get green-lighted. And FX rules. So it's no surprise that the most successful of these family fantasies (besides *Toy Story*) was yet another cartoon crossover loaded with dazzling visuals. *Casper* starred Bill Pullman and Christina Ricci as a ghost therapist and his adolescent daughter who come to an old mansion in Maine to exorcise it. Four ghosts inhabit the manse: three cantankerous elders and the "friendliest ghost" of TV lore, a young lad of a ghost named Casper.

Ricci makes a spunky, likable heroine. And the story line is passable. But it's the forty minutes of apparitional computer animation ILM added to the action that really stars in this film. And it's those swooping translucent ghosts in a live-action world that really packed them into theaters.

In a similar way, *Jumanji*, based on the wonderful storybook by Chris Van Allsburg, is a film in which the human actors (even the formidable Robin Williams) play second bananas to a jungle's worth of marauding CGI critters. Some critics worried that the film, about the fearsome realm unleashed by a board game, would be too frightening for children. (And, yes, it does consist of back-to-back episodes of scary moments.) But, as in *Jurassic Park*, *Jumanji*'s terrors are those a child isn't likely to meet up with in real life, and so s/he feels safe exploring them on the screen.

The people story of *Jumanji* could have been much stronger. But few viewers noticed—they were too caught up in the elephant stampede through Main Street.

The moral of *Jumanji* is that we must all confront our fears. A similarly virtuous precept, about accepting our responsibilities and caring about the feelings of others, may be gained through watching the more gentle fantasy *The Indian in the Cupboard*. Based on the well-loved children's novel by Lynne Reid Banks, Frank Oz's film—written by *E.T.*'s Melissa Mathison—is really a serious story about serious issues. That's probably one of the reasons it didn't hit it big.

Young Omri (Hal Scardino) receives a small cast-off cabinet for his ninth birthday. Shortly thereafter, he discovers that this cupboard has the power to transform toys into living beings. When a small plastic Indian becomes a man spirited away from his eighteenth-century tribe, Omri has to face many challenges that would stump even the wisest adult. *The Indian in the Cupboard* is, perhaps, a little too sincere. And Scardino is less of an actor than this particular story requires. But I'd say it deserved to do better than it did.

It's unfortunate, really, that Hollywood's spending sprees make it necessary for even a "small" children's movie to make a killing to be viewed a success. *Indian* was considered a dud at $32 million because of its high costs ($45 million). But independent filmmaker John Sayles is used to shooting a movie on a chicken-feed budget. So when his 1995 Irish fable, *The Secret of Roan Inish*, finished the year with over $6 million in earnings, it was considered an art-house hit.

And well it should have been. This film is a gem. It follows young Fiona (Jeni Courtney), a solemn child sent to live with her grandparents in coastal Ireland. There she begins to hear bits of the family lore relating to Selkies (seal-to-human changelings) and decides to investigate the disappearance of her baby brother on the family's ancestral island several years earlier.

The real magic of *The Secret of Roan Inish* is in its very naturalism. Sayles is incapable of cute, but honesty is his forte. He and cinematographer Haskell Wexler spend a lot of time photographing seals. And they manage to invest these sea creatures with intelligence and sentience without once stooping to Andre-like antics. In a similar way, Sayles doesn't resort to high-tech morphing in order to show a seal transforming itself into a woman. But, by gum, you'll believe it when you see it happen.

It will be hard for some viewers, too conditioned to whizbang, to appreciate the quiet mystery of *The Secret of Roan Inish*. But those who can surrender themselves to this enchanting tale will likely rank it as one of the finest films of the year.

Ranking a film called *The City of Lost Children* is a little more of a challenge. It concerns kiddies but is far too frightening for most of them to watch. Jean-Pierre Jeunet and Marc Caro, the two auteurs of the cult cannibalism flick *Delicatessen*, are responsible for this unique cinematic excursion. The narrative—if you can call it that—concerns a mad scientist named Krank (Daniel Emilfork) who has children kidnapped (by his Cyclopsian drones) so he can steal their dreams. Other characters include a voracious toddler, a dim-witted muscle man (Ron Perlman), a gamine orphan, a talking brain-in-a-tank, several cloned idiots, a prim midget, and two monstrous Siamese-twin sisters.

The bizarre alternative world of *The City of Lost Children* is chock-full of dark, dazzling visuals and freakish characters. And the film is, in its own way, exquisite. But you will likely wonder what any of it means as the credits roll. What can I say, it's sure to become another "cult classic"!

Extravagant obscurity isn't a problem for *Three Wishes*. If anything, this comedy-drama, bringing magic realism to Middle America in the 1950s, is a little too straight for its own good. It would have been a different—and, I suspect, much better—film if the lead character hadn't been played by Patrick Swayze. (When I picture a beatnik drifter with a Zen sensibility and a talent for various manly arts like baseball, Swayze is not the actor who comes to mind.) And *more* magic would have helped. *Three Wishes* plays most of the way through like a simple domestic drama. This account of how a mysterious stranger changes the lives of a widow and her two sons should have shown its fantastical hand earlier and more often. Or not at all.

And here's a delightful little adult fantasy hardly anyone saw: *Window to Paris*. The title tells the story of this foreign farce. A teacher takes a room in a crowded, run-down apartment house in Saint Petersburg, only to find that an old wardrobe in it opens—presto chango—onto a rooftop in Paris. The film's fantasy conceit is just an excuse for a social comedy contrasting the Parisian and the post-Communist Russian cultures, of course. And the humor is none too subtle, but genuinely amusing. One thing is apparent: the party animals of old Saint Petersburg could teach the sophisticated French a little something about joie de vivre.

Perhaps a little humor—the bitter kind, to be sure—could have helped another social-contrast fantasy, *White Man's Burden*. That, or an even harder edge was needed. As is, this turgid and uninsightful alternative history (in which blacks are the owning-class bosses of disadvantaged whites) is a waste of time. Worse, it squanders the talents of comeback-kid John Travolta and his distinguished costar, Harry Belafonte.

One of the screen controversies of the year involved a modestly budgeted fantasy film called *Powder*. But the public debate about the movie had little to do with the movie itself. Rather, it concerned the media revelation that its writer-director, Victor Salva, was a convicted child molester. Knowing something of the filmmaker's history makes it hard not to see the story as a thinly veiled allegory about his own life.

A boy (struck by lightning in his mother's womb) is born a hairless albino with a brilliant mind and certain paranormal powers. When he is forced into society as a teen, he is labeled a freak and an outcast. And although Powder (Sean Patrick Flanery) is a young man of great gifts and sensitivity, he is hounded until he chooses a Christ-like, mystical ascension out of this world that refuses to appreciate him.

As a fable about teen alienation, *Powder* definitely has its strengths. And the first two-thirds of the film definitely held my interest. But eventually it degrades into an exercise in persecution and self-pity, and that's when it lost me. *And* it gave me the creeps. For if this story represents the poor-me rationalizations of a pedophile, it brings new meaning to the term "horror film."

And while I'm on the subject of monsters with a talent for self-justification, I should mention a few of the vampire films of the year. On the arty end of the vein chain, there were two black-and-white movies that were too drab to find an audience. Michael Almereyda's *Nadja,* about the Dracula and Van Helsing clans continuing their struggles in New York, had a bit of style, at least. Abel Ferrara's *The Addiction* is some kind of deadly (or is that undeadly?) philosophical treatise masquerading as a movie. Even the brilliant Lili Taylor in the lead couldn't save that one.

But fresh ideas are hard to come by with ye olde bloodsucker stories. Even setting the right tone is as treacherous as a room filled with mirrors and crosses. Too serious doesn't work. And comedy is just as tricky. So it's no wonder that today's vampire films seem to be at a loss for the right approach.

The high-profile flop *Vampire in Brooklyn* is a perfect example of this particular problem. This Eddie Murphy vehicle (that he and his brother, Charles Murphy, and stepbrother, Vernon Lynch, Jr., helped to create) flip-flops between gross gags and an approximation of horror drama. Miserable to watch, the film failed utterly at giving Murphy a much-needed comeback. A film this bad doesn't do anything for director Wes Craven's résumé, either.

At least you can say that Mel Brooks knows what mood he's trying to set with his films. But that makes it even sadder when he can't quite pull it off. *Dracula: Dead and Loving It* is the standard Brooksian spoof. And it's actually more faithful to the original Stoker novel than most of the dramatic versions of the tale. The film's one big plus: Leslie Nielsen in the title role. Regrettably, Nielsen isn't enough to save this project, which will likely send you back to the video shelves for George Hamilton.

Mr. Brooks can comfort himself with the knowledge that his *Dracula* satire has more going for it than another spoof of a fictional horror classic: *Dr. Jekyll and Ms. Hyde.* Transsexual transmogrification is the gag of this one-joke movie, with Tim Daly and Sean Young sharing the split-personality role. I quickly tired of the lingerie and oops-I'm-growing-boobs witticisms. And I was even less thrilled with the underlying message of the movie, that the scariest monster in this world is a career woman with the drive to get ahead.

It wasn't a great year for horror drama, either. But box-office bonanzas are no longer the goal of the horror producers. After the slasher heyday of a decade ago, the horror film has comfortably slid into a lower-budget, quick-return, release-to-video strategy more in keeping with its B-movie roots. But the field is also showing the tired, knockoff characteristics of those roots, as well.

Many of the year's releases were either sequels (*Candyman 2: Farewell to the Flesh, Halloween VI: The Curse of Michael Myers*), remakes (*Village of the Damned*), or TV tie-ins (*Tales of the Crypt Presents Demon Knight*). Most of the others borrowed heavily from the past, as well. They just did it in ways that were less clearly acknowledged.

Care for an African-American riff on *The Twilight Zone?* Well, if you missed 1994's Hudlin brothers' cable experiment called *Cosmic Slop*, another hot young African-American filmmaker, Rusty Cundieff, offered his own *Zone*-ish anthology theatrically in 1995. *Tales from the Hood*, with Clarence Williams III as the maniacal mortician/host, is a slightly uneven grouping of horror stories. The flashiest fables—like one in which a white-supremacist politician (Corbin Bernsen) is hunted down by small dolls containing the spirits of slaughtered slaves—deal directly with racism. But my personal favorite was a simpler tale about how a small boy defends himself against the monster that terrorizes him in the night.

Tales from the Hood is an enjoyable mix, deserving a sequel—or a TV spin-off.

For those who prefer their horror movies to be brazen bloodfests, director Tobe Hooper seldom disappoints. *The Mangler,* based on yet another Stephen King story, is a cheerfully gory yarn about a carnivorous laundry machine.

Clive Barker fans (and those who miss Scott Bakula in *Quantum Leap*) rushed out to see *Lord of Illusions.* But they're the only ones who did. Folks who were smart enough to stay away missed a sluggish story about a demonic cult leader who comes back from the "dead" to avenge himself. The story, contrasting dark-side magic with the illusionist's art, had a lot of promise—not delivered upon. And the noirish private-eye hero (Bakula) is never adequately developed.

The Prophecy, a film by Gregory Widen, wielded its subject matter much more effectively. Openly theological, it concerns a war between God's angels and those allied with the renegade Gabriel (Christopher Walken). People—notably a cop (Elias Koteas), a Native American schoolgirl (Moriah Snyder), and her protective teacher (Virginia Madsen)—are caught in the middle. And even Lucifer (Viggo Mortensen) gets into the act.

My own favorite horror film of the year was the one that was most clearly science fiction. *Species,* which owes more than a little to the *Alien* franchise (the monster was even designed by H. R. Giger), is the story of an experiment with alien DNA gone seriously awry. But who could really quarrel with the resulting "monster," who usually looks like supermodel Natasha Henstridge? She's out to breed—and pity the fool who gets in her way. Chasing after her is an elite team (including Ben Kingsley and Marg Helgenberger), but the usually beauteous, sometimes horrific Sil is a hard gal to catch up with. It's *She's Gotta Have It* with a *really* bad attitude. If you can get into the dumb fun of it, *Species* is a solid entertainment.

But a critter doesn't have to come from a far-off planet to play protagonist in a great fantasy movie. In fact, the best fantasy film—perhaps the best *film*—of 1995 starred an earthbound barnyard animal. If you had told me in 1994 that a fable about a wee pig would win best-picture honors from the National Society of Film Critics and would come away with several Oscar noms, including best director and best picture, I would have said that you'd been pitching hay a little too long.

But *Babe,* co-written and coproduced by none other than *Mad Max*'s George Miller, is an absolute miracle of a movie. And it was a miracle ten years in the making. Miller and co-writer/director Chris Noonan had to wait for the FX technology to become affordable. But the wait was definitely worth it. Combining live animal actors (some five hundred in all) with computer animation and animatronics, first-time helmer Noonan seamlessly spins a yarn about a motherless pig who wants to be a sheepdog. And, in so doing, teaches viewers young and old a little something about prejudice.

In a year when the big-budget action SF movie, epitomized by a bloated floater called *Waterworld,* seemed to reach its nadir, *Babe* showed that fantasy film need not be creatively, spiritually, or even financially bankrupt.

I'd like to think that the critical and financial success of *Babe* has set an example that the rest of the movie industry will rush to follow. "When pigs fly," you sneer? Well, actually, this was the year one did. After *Babe,* anything is possible.

The Narcissus Plague

LISA GOLDSTEIN

Lisa Goldstein won an American Book Award for her first novel, *The Red Magician*. Since then, she has been a finalist for the Nebula, Hugo, and World Fantasy Awards. Her highly respected short fiction was recently collected in *Travellers in Magic*, and her latest novel is *Walking the Labyrinth*. Her other novels are *The Dream Years*, *A Mask for the General*, *Tourists*, *Strange Devices of the Sun and Moon*, and *Summer King, Winter Fool*. She lives in Oakland, California.

"The Narcissus Plague" offers a wry look at one of our society's particular afflictions. Of this Nebula finalist, Lisa Goldstein writes:

"There was a week when everyone I met talked about nothing but themselves. What is this, I wondered—some sort of plague?"

The man in the tollbooth had the Narcissus Plague. "We moved when I was nine," he said earnestly. I held my dollar out to him, watched it sway in the breeze. "My dog never did get used to the new house. One day he got out and chased the mailman up a tree. No one was home, and the neighbors had to call the police. . . ."

Finally he took my money and I sped away. A minute later, I looked in my rearview mirror and saw that the car after me was still trapped at the booth. A narrow escape, I thought. I checked my oxygen mask and surgical gloves and hurried toward the newspaper office where I work.

I parked in the lot and rode the elevator up to my floor. "Hi, Amy, how are you?" my editor, Thomas, asked. This is the only way we greet each other now. It's meant to assure other people that we can still take an interest in them, that we don't have the plague.

"Fine, how are you?" I said. He followed me down the hall toward my cubicle.

"Hi, guys," my co-worker Gary said, heading toward his desk. "I stayed up all last night working on that article you wanted, Thomas."

We turned and watched him go. If it had been anyone else in the office we would have worried about the plague, but Gary has talked about nothing but himself for as long as any of us can remember.

"Listen—I've got an assignment for you," Thomas said. "Someone at one of the labs says she's come up with a cure."

"A cure? You're kidding me," I said.

"I'm not, but it's possible she is. That's what I want you to find out. Her name's Dr. Leila Clark."

He gave me the doctor's address and phone number, and I hurried to my desk to call. To my annoyance an answering machine came on. "Hello, you've reached the office of Dr. Leila Clark. We can't answer your call right now, but if you leave your name and number I'll get back to you just as soon as I go visit my boyfriend. He said he was going to break up with that other woman, but I bet he hasn't done it. He's been saying he'll break up with her since last winter, when I caught them at our favorite restaurant together—"

I hung up. The chances for a cure did not look good.

The lab turned out to be on the other side of the park from the newspaper's offices. The sun had risen above the clouds; it was turning into a warm, beautiful day. I decided to walk.

The fountain in the center of the park was stagnant, green algae lapping at the rim. Its filtering mechanism had clogged; it was making strange mechanical whimpering noises as it tried to get the water to circulate. The person responsible for fixing it probably had the plague, I thought. It only took about a week for the virus to render you unfit for anything but talking about yourself. Things were breaking down all over the city.

The Narcissus Plague had not always been this virulent. Ten or twenty years ago people talked about the Me Generation, the Greed Decade, as if those things were normal, just human nature. But about six months ago the virus mutated, became far stronger. Shortly after that a team of doctors isolated the virus they think is responsible for the plague.

My boyfriend Mark was one of the first victims of the more virulent strain. At the time I had no idea what was happening to him; all I knew was that he had changed from the concerned, caring man he had once been. "What makes you think I'd be interested in your old girlfriends?" I'd asked him angrily, over and over again, and, "Why don't you ever ask me how my day went? Why do we always have to talk about you?" Now he lives with his mother, sitting in his old room and talking eagerly to anyone who comes by. I try to visit him about once a week.

I came to the end of the park, found the laboratory offices, and went inside. The receptionist area was deserted, but I heard laughter and cheering from somewhere within. I went past the receptionist's desk and down a hallway, following the sounds. A group of men and women were gathered in one of the offices. Glasses and bottles of champagne lay strewn across the desk; they had probably gone back to their offices and quickly lifted their oxygen masks for a celebratory drink.

A woman turned toward me. She was young, with blond hair braided down her back and a white lab coat with "Leila Clark" stitched on the pocket. "Hello, Dr. Clark, how are you?" I said. "I'm Amy Nunes. The paper sent me—"

"How are you?" the woman said. "I'm Debra Lowry." Her voice sounded a little slurred, but even so I thought that I'd heard it before. She looked down at her lab coat and laughed a little too loudly. "Oh, sorry—we've been celebrating. This is Dr. Clark."

Another woman detached herself from the group. She looked more like someone who'd made a major medical discovery, a woman in her mid-forties, with long black hair streaked with gray and tied back in a ponytail. "Hello, how are you?" she said. "I sent word to all the papers, but you're the only one who seems to have shown up. I suppose everyone else must be out with the plague." She stretched out a gloved hand, realized she was still holding a champagne glass, and set the glass down.

"I tried calling—" I said. I shook her hand, glove touching glove.

"Things have been a little hectic here," she said. She took a folder from a stack on the desk and gave it to me. "Here—this handout will give you the details."

I opened the folder; it had the kind of scientific detail so beloved by our science section. I took out my tape recorder and turned it on. "You say this is a cure for the plague?"

"Yes."

"But how can you be sure it works?"

"Everyone I've treated so far has recovered." Dr. Clark played with the champagne glass on her desk. "You see, I was almost certain I'd discovered a cure, but I needed subjects to test it on. Of course we couldn't experiment with animals—they don't seem to get the plague, or if they do, it takes a form we can't understand, since they don't communicate by using language. So I asked everyone working here if they would sign a release form." She waved her hand, nearly knocking over the glass. "They all agreed that if they got the plague, I could administer the drug. Our receptionist Debra was one of the people who manifested symptoms."

Debra nodded. "So she gave me a pill—"

"You're the one who did the answering machine message!" I said, recognizing her voice.

"Oh my God!" Debra said, and ran down the hallway. "You see, you don't remember what happened to you when you've been ill," Dr. Clark said. "After you recover, it seems a blur to you, as if it happened to someone else."

"How soon will your drug come on the market?" I asked.

"Not as soon as I'd like, unfortunately. Because of the crisis, the Food and Drug Administration is moving as quickly as possible, but even at their quickest they're not very fast. And a good many of them are out with the plague. Have you ever tried dealing with a bureaucrat with the plague?"

I nodded sympathetically.

"At the soonest, we'll get FDA approval in six months, maybe a year." She took a bottle of pills off her desk. "Here they are."

The pills—red and yellow capsules—caught the light and shone like jewels. "How long does the cure take?"

"A week. The pills should be taken twice a day. But the results are immediate, within a few minutes of taking the first pill."

"And are there side effects?"

"None that we know of."

I cleared my throat. "My—uh, my boyfriend Mark—"

Dr. Clark shook her head. "I'm sorry—I can't prescribe anything to anyone who hasn't signed a release form. I don't want to jeopardize our standing with the FDA."

She set the bottle back on its shelf. Just fourteen of them, and Mark would be the person he had been before. If I could distract her somehow . . . But there were at least a dozen people crowded into the doctor's office. There was no way I could get the pills.

I got some background information from Dr. Clark—where she was born, where she went to school—and made my way back to the office.

Thomas stopped me before I got to my cubicle. "Amy," he said. There was an edge of excitement in his voice I had never heard before.

Because of the plague I never knew what to expect from the paper. Some days the printers run whole sections of autobiography, some days they catch it in time and leave huge parts of the paper blank. "What is it?" I asked.

"Gary got the plague," he said. "You've got to come see this."

"Gary? How can you tell?"

"Come *on,*" he said.

Gary seems to have always had the plague—that is, Gary has never paid attention to anyone else in his life. Unlike the victims of the plague, though, he's always been very sneaky about it, managing to turn the conversation toward himself with all the subtlety and dexterity of a master chess player. Intrigued, I followed Thomas down the hall.

Gary was in his cubicle. So were a number of other people, all of them sitting around his desk and watching him. "I like to be noticed," Gary was saying. "I love it when people pay attention to me. That's what I live for. I have to have someone listening to me and watching me at every minute. . . ."

Almost everyone was trying not to laugh. "One day, I remember, we were sitting around and talking about the president," Gary was saying. "So I started talking about the president too, and then the president's brother, and then my own brother, and finally I got to my favorite topic, myself. Another time I thought that Thomas was getting too much attention, so I went down two floors and had him paged from a pay phone. Then I went back to work—it was much easier to talk about myself after he'd gone."

One of the more enterprising reporters on the paper had turned on his tape recorder. If Dr. Clark had indeed found a cure for the virus Gary was going to have a very hard time living this one down.

"How long are you going to let him go on like that?" I whispered to Thomas.

"Oh, I don't know," he said. He felt to make sure his mask and gloves were in place. "It's almost lunchtime—probably we'll send him home then."

I left Gary's cubicle and went back to my desk. Before I could start on the story about Dr. Clark my friend Barbara knocked on my partition and sat in the room's other chair. "Hi, how are you?" she said.

"Fine. How was Washington?"

"You won't believe it," she said. "The pilot on the flight back got the plague. There we all were, looking out the window or reading our in-flight magazines, and the next minute this guy comes over the intercom to tell us that his fingers are nearly all the same length. On and on—you wouldn't believe how much mileage this guy could get from his hands. Every so often you'd hear a scuffle in the cockpit, where the co-pilot was trying to gain control of the intercom, but the pilot held on grimly all the way home." She sighed. "For three and a half hours. Talk about a captive audience."

"What happened when you landed?"

"Oh, he landed fine. He wasn't that far gone. There was a stretcher waiting for him at the landing gate—I guess he'd bored the traffic controllers too."

"Listen," I said. "I just interviewed a doctor who says she found a cure for the plague."

"Really? Do you think she's on the level?"

"God, I hope so," I said.

I visited Mark after work. I'm not sure why I still see him—I guess I do it out of respect for the person he once was, for the memories I have of our times together.

Mark's mother let me in. Her eyes looked tired over her oxygen mask. "He's in his room," she said, pointing with a gloved hand.

I thanked her and went down the hallway to Mark's old room. He was staring out the window with his back to me, and I stood there a while and watched him. He was tall and thin, with straight brown hair that shone a deep red in the light. For a moment I desired him as much as I ever had before he became ill. Maybe this time, I thought, he would turn and smile at me, kiss me, lead me toward the bed.

Suddenly I realized that he was not looking out the window at all. He was admiring his reflection in the glass. "Hello, Mark," I said. "How are you?"

He turned. He seemed eager to see me. He always seems eager to see me—victims of the plague need other people to talk to. "When I was a kid, we used to turn the sprinklers on on hot days," he said. "All the kids in the neighborhood would run through them. And then the ice cream truck would come, and we'd all go and get ice cream."

He went on in the same even, contemplative tone. He never noticed that my attention wandered, that I looked out the window as often as I looked at him.

When he was well he had never talked so much. He would think before he spoke, weigh each of his words carefully. I had never met anyone before who so clearly meant what he said. Six months ago he had asked me, with no wasted words, if I thought we should move in together.

He'd gotten the plague instead. And here I was, trying to find the man I loved somewhere within this garrulous stranger. I sighed and checked my watch. I try to spend at least an hour with him.

Finally the long hour ended. I stood up to leave. He looked sad to see me go, but he did not stop his flow of reminiscences. I knew from previous weeks that he was incapable of asking me to stay. In a very real sense I was not a separate person to him. I was Audience.

I said goodbye to Mark's mother and drove home. Once there, I took off my mask and gloves and microwaved a day-old pot roast. When the beep sounded, I took it over to the couch and ate, staring bleakly at my television set. I did not want to turn on the TV; these days, with the plague so rampant, you never know what you might see.

I should call someone, I thought. I should call my friend Barbara. But I'd heard too many stories about people calling old friends who turned out to have the plague.

Still, I looked at the phone with longing. The very first words spoken over a telephone had been words of need, of desire, I thought. "Watson, come here—I need you," Alexander Graham Bell had said. How many times since then had people tried desperately to connect over the phone? Because we do need other people; we need them terribly. What would happen to us if the whole world got the plague?

I opened my handbag and took out the folder Dr. Clark had given me. I had already written and turned in my article, but I wanted reassurance. Could it be that she had actually discovered a cure?

I made my way through her technical explanations. I understood very little of it, but her conclusion was nothing if not clear. "Over a three-month period," she had written, "we have treated seventy-nine people with the plague virus, all of them successfully."

I closed the folder. Six months to a year seemed far too long to wait for Mark's cure. Tomorrow I would return to Dr. Clark's office and steal her pills.

Thomas was in a jubilant mood the next day; we'd scooped all the other papers with the news of a possible cure. He made no objection to a follow-up article on Leila Clark. I walked back across the park to the laboratory.

I passed the ragged speaker who sometimes stood by the fountain, exhorting people to come to Jesus. "Yesterday someone gave me a slice of pizza!" he was yelling. "I had just enough money to get a Coke to go with it! Coke and pizza, my friends! Coke and pizza!" He paced back and forth in front of the fountain, his arms punching the air. I gave him a wide berth.

Debra Lowry was sitting at the receptionist's desk. "Hello, how are you?" she said. "You're the reporter who was here yesterday, aren't you?"

"Yes, I'm Amy Nunes," I said. "I'd like to ask Dr. Clark some more questions. Is she in?"

Debra looked at her calendar. "She's at Channel 7 right now, doing an interview. She'll be back in about fifteen minutes, but only to meet with the staff and pick up her messages. She's got another interview after that."

"Shall I wait in her office?" I moved back toward the hallway.

"I'm sorry—no one's allowed in Dr. Clark's office."

So much for that idea. I sat in a leather-and-steel chair and picked up a *Cosmopolitan* from the glass coffee table. "Men Are Too Much Trouble: How I Learned to Love Myself," the cover said.

The phone rang constantly, all people who wanted to hear more about the cure. I looked at my watch. Fifteen minutes passed, then thirty. Dr. Clark had obviously been detained at Channel 7.

I thought of Mark. I couldn't sit still while the cure, his cure, was only a few steps away. I stood and walked toward the hallway.

"Ms. Nunes," Debra Lowry said, calling after me. "Ms. Nunes!"

I turned. Debra had come around her desk and was hurrying toward me.

Very deliberately, I took off my mask and gloves. "Last summer I went to the Grand Canyon," I said. "It was huge—I've never seen anything so big. I have pictures right here."

Debra backed away. She may have been cured of the plague, but obviously the old fear still lingered. "After I saw the Grand Canyon I went to Yellowstone," I said, moving toward her.

She looked back toward the front door, toward safety. "And then Mount Rushmore," I said. She turned and fled.

I ran down the hallway and into Dr. Clark's office. The bottle of pills was still on her desk. I grabbed it, shoved it into my coat pocket, and hurried out the door. The receptionist area was deserted.

On my way to the elevator I passed a group of people holding microphones and lights and cameras. Leila Clark stood in the center of them. She seemed to be enjoying the limelight; I hoped she'd remembered to sign a release form.

I drove to Mark's house. His mother let me in, surprised and pleased to see me so soon after my last visit. I took a glass from her kitchen, filled it with water. "What—" she asked.

I said nothing, but hurried down the hallway. Mark turned from the window. "Here," I said, giving him the pill before he could say anything. "Swallow this."

He looked into the glass, studying something—his own reflection?—that I couldn't see. "Swallow the pill," I said again, and this time he did.

"I always dreaded going to school after summer vacation," he said. "I hated having to put on shoes after going barefoot all summer. They never seemed to fit right somehow. . . ."

How long would it take? Would it even work at all? Seventy-nine successes—would Mark be the first failure?

Mark continued to talk. I heard about his friends at school, the ones he liked, the ones he hated, his first crush. I heard about his teachers.

"I never liked getting used to a new teacher," Mark said. "Some of them were nice, but some of them were horrible, like Mrs. Plauscher. I I You." He looked at me, found my eyes. "Oh, you!" he said. "Where have you *been?*"

Last Summer at Mars Hill

ELIZABETH HAND

Elizabeth Hand was honored with the James Tiptree Jr. Memorial Award and the Mythopoeic Society Fantasy Award for her recent novel *Waking the Moon;* she has also completed a new novel, *Glimmering*. Her other novels are *Winterlong, Aestival Tide,* and *Icarus Descending,* all of which were finalists for the Philip K. Dick Award.

Hand lives with her two children on the coast of Maine, where her Nebula Award–winning "Last Summer at Mars Hill" is set. About this novella, which also won the World Fantasy Award, she writes:

"For me, writing has always resembled childbirth in that afterward, regarding the product with delight (or dismay), I am blessedly without memory of the agonizing process which brought it to life. With 'Last Summer at Mars Hill,' I recall mostly that it was inspired by a Fred Frith song called 'The Welcome,' which was the original title for the story, and that it was summer when I wrote it.

"Several miles up the coast from where I live there is a real Spiritualist community, founded over a century ago and still active in the summers, when assorted clairvoyants, psychics, and readers of ectoplasm assemble from all over the country. I pass Temple Heights all the time, though I never visited until after 'Mars Hill' was completed. When I did, I found it much as I had imagined it. I drank some herb tea, received an inaccurate reading from a psychic who played the bagpipes (happily, not while he scryed my fate), and looked out across Penobscot Bay to where the windjammer fleet sailed in the August sun.

"Paul Bowles wrote, 'I had based my sense of being in the world partly on an unreasoned conviction that certain areas of the earth's surface contained more magic than others.' To me, Maine has always been one of those places. I hardly feel I can take credit for whatever magic seeped out of the earth and into my story, but I am exceedingly grateful, and touched, that readers share in it."

Even before they left home, Moony knew her mother wouldn't return from Mars Hill that year. Jason had called her from his father's house in San Francisco—

"I had a dream about you last night," he'd said, his voice cracking the way it did when he was excited. "We were at Mars Hill, and my father was there, and my mother, too—I knew it was a dream, like can you imagine my *mother* at Mars Hill?—and you had on this sort of long black dress and you were sitting alone by the pier. And you said, 'This is it, Jason. We'll never see this again.' I felt like crying, I tried to hug you but my father pulled me back. And then I woke up."

She didn't say anything. Finally Jason prodded her. "Weird, huh, Moony? I mean, don't you think it's weird?"

She shrugged and rolled her eyes, then sighed loudly so that he'd be able to tell she was upset. "Thanks, Jason. Like that's supposed to cheer me up?"

A long silence, then Jason's breathless voice again. "Shit, Moony, I'm sorry. I didn't—"

She laughed, a little nervously, and said, "Forget it. So when you flying out to Maine?"

Nobody but Jason called her Moony, not at home at least, not in Kamensic Village. There she was Maggie Rheining, which was the name that appeared under her junior picture in the high school yearbook.

But the name that had been neatly typed on the birth certificate in San Francisco sixteen years ago, the name Jason and everyone at Mars Hill knew her by, was Shadowmoon Starlight Rising. Maggie would have shaved her head before she'd admit her real name to anyone at school. At Mars Hill it wasn't so weird: there was Adele Grose, known professionally as Madame Olaf; Shasta Daisy O'Hare and Rvis Capricorn; Martin Dionysos, who was Jason's father; and Ariel Rising, née Amanda Mae Rheining, who was Moony's mother. For most of the year Moony and Ariel lived in Kamensic Village, the affluent New York exurb where her mother ran Earthly Delights Catering and Moony attended high school, and everything was pretty much normal. It was only in June that they headed north to Maine, to the tiny spiritualist community where they had summered for as long as Moony could remember. And even though she could have stayed in

Kamensic with Ariel's friends the Loomises, at the last minute (and due in large part to Jason's urging, and threats if she abandoned him there) she decided to go with her mother to Mars Hill. Later, whenever she thought how close she'd come to not going, it made her feel sick: as though she'd missed a flight and later found out the plane had crashed.

Because much as she loved it, Moony had always been a little ashamed of Mars Hill. It was such a dinky place, plopped in the middle of nowhere on the rocky Maine coast—tiny shingle-style Carpenter Gothic cottages, all tumbled into disrepair, their elaborate trim rotting and strung with spiderwebs; poppies and lupines and tiger lilies sprawling bravely atop clumps of chickweed and dandelions of truly monstrous size; even the sign by the pier so faded you almost couldn't read the earnest lettering:

MARS HILL
SPIRITUALIST COMMUNITY
FOUNDED 1883

"Why doesn't your father take somebody's violet aura and repaint the damn sign with it?" she'd exploded once to Jason.

Jason looked surprised. "I kind of like it like that," he said, shaking the hair from his face and tossing a sea urchin at the silvered board. "It looks like it was put up by our Founding Mothers." But for years Moony almost couldn't stand to even look at the sign, it embarrassed her so much.

It was Jason who helped her get over that. They'd met when they were both twelve. It was the summer that Ariel started the workshop in Creative Psychokinesis, the first summer that Jason and his father had stayed at Mars Hill.

"Hey," Jason had said, too loudly, when they found themselves left alone while the adults swapped wine coolers and introductions at the summer's first barbecue. They were the only kids in sight. There were no other families and few conventionally married couples at Mars Hill. The community had been the cause of more than one custody battle that had ended with wistful children sent to spend the summer with a more respectable parent in Boston or Manhattan or Bar Harbor. "That lady there with my father—"

He stuck his thumb out to indicate Ariel, her long black hair frizzed and bound with leather thongs, an old multicolored skirt flapping around her legs. She was talking to a slender man with close-cropped blond hair and goatee, wearing a sky-blue caftan and shabby Birkenstock sandals. "That your mom?"

"Yeah." Moony shrugged and glanced at the man in the caftan. He and Ariel both turned to look at their children. The man grinned and raised his wine glass. Ariel did a little pirouette and blew a kiss at Moony.

"Looks like she did too much of the brown acid at Woodstock," Jason announced, and flopped onto the grass. Moony glared down at him.

"She wasn't *at* Woodstock, asshole," she said, and had started to walk away when the boy called after her.

"Hey—It's a joke! My name's Jason—" He pointed at the man with Ariel. "That's my father. Martin Dionysos. But like that's not his real name, okay? His real name is Schuster but he changed it, but *I'm* Jason Schuster. He's a painter. We don't know anyone here. I mean, does it ever get above forty degrees?"

He scrambled to his feet and looked at her beseechingly. Smaller even than Moony herself, so slender he should have looked younger than her, except that his sharp face beneath floppy white-blond hair was always twisted into some ironic pronouncement, his blue eyes always flickering somewhere between derision and pleading.

"No," Moony said slowly. The part about Jason not changing his name got to her. She stared pointedly at his thin arms prickled with gooseflesh, the fashionable surfer-logo T-shirt that hung nearly to his knees. "You're gonna freeze your skinny ass off here in Maine, Jason Schuster." And she grinned.

He was from San Francisco. His father was a well-known artist and a member of the Raging Faery Queens, a gay pagan group that lived in the Bay Area and staged elaborately beautiful solstice gatherings and AIDS benefits. At Mars Hill, Martin Dionysos gave workshops on strengthening your aura and on clear nights led the community's men in chanting at the moon as it rose above Penobscot Bay. Jason was so diffident about his father and his father's work that Moony was surprised, the single time she visited him on the West Coast, to find her friend's room plastered with flyers advertising Faery gatherings and newspaper photos of Martin and Jason at various ACT-UP events. In the fall Jason would be staying in Maine, while she returned to high school. Ultimately it was the thought that she might not see him again that made Moony decide to spend this last summer at Mars Hill.

"That's what you're wearing to First Night?"

Moony started at her mother's voice, turned to see Ariel in the middle of the summer cottage's tiny living room. Wine rocked back and forth in her mother's glass, gold shot with tiny sunbursts from the crystals hung from every window. "What about your new dress?"

Moony shrugged. She couldn't tell her mother about Jason's dream, about the black dress he'd seen her wearing. Ariel set great store by dreams, especially these last few months. What she'd make of one in which Moony appeared in a black dress and Ariel didn't appear at all, Moony didn't want to know.

"Too hot," Moony said. She paused in front of the window and adjusted one of three silver crosses dangling from her right ear. "Plus I don't want to upstage you."

Ariel smiled. "Smart kid," she said, and took another sip of her wine.

Ariel wore what she wore to every First Night: an ankle-length patchwork skirt so worn and frayed it could only be taken out once a year, on this ceremonial occasion. Squares of velvet and threadbare satin were emblazoned with suns and moons and astrological symbols, each one with a date neatly embroidered in crimson thread.

Sedona, Aug 15 1972. Mystery Hill, NH, 5/80. The Winter Garden 1969. Jajouka, Tangiers, Marrakech 1968.

Along the bottom, where many of the original squares had disintegrated into fine webs of denim and chambray, she had begun piecing a new section: squares that each held a pair of dates, a name, an embroidered flower. These were for friends who had died. Some of them were people lost two decades earlier, to the War, or drugs or misadventure; names that Moony knew only from stories told year after year at Mars Hill or in the kitchen at home.

But most of the names were those of people Moony herself had known. Friends of Ariel's who had gathered during the divorce, and again, later, when Moony's father died, and during the myriad affairs and breakups that followed. Men and women who had started out as Ariel's customers and ended as family. Uncle Bob and Uncle Raymond and Uncle Nigel. Laurie Salas. Tommy McElroy and Sean Jacobson. Chas Bowen and Martina Glass. And, on the very bottom edge of the skirt, a square still peacock-bright with its blood-colored rose, crimson letters spelling out John's name and a date the previous spring.

As a child Moony had loved that skirt. She loved to watch her mother sashay into the tiny gazebo at Mars Hill on First Night and see all the others laugh and run to her, their fingers plucking at the patchwork folds as though to read something there, tomorrow's weather perhaps, or the names of suitors yet unmet.

But now Moony hated the skirt. It was morbid, even Jason agreed with that.

"They've already got a fucking quilt," he said, bitterly. "We don't need your mom wearing a goddamn *skirt*."

Moony nodded, miserable, and tried not to think of what they were most afraid of: Martin's name there beside John's, and a little rosebud done in flower-knots. Martin's name, or Ariel's.

There was a key to the skirt, Moony thought as she watched her mother sip her wine; a way to decode all the arcane symbols Ariel had stitched there over the last few months. It lay in a heavy manila envelope somewhere in Ariel's room, an envelope that Ariel had started carrying with her in February, and which grew heavier and heavier as the weeks passed. Moony knew there was something horrible in that envelope, something to do with the countless appointments Ariel had had since February, with the whispered phone calls and macrobiotic diets and the resurgence of her mother's belief in *devas* and earth spirits and plain old-fashioned ghosts.

But Moony said nothing of this, only smiled and fidgeted with her earrings. "Go ahead," she told Ariel, who had settled at the edge of a wicker hassock and peered up at her daughter through her wineglass. "I just got to get some stuff."

Ariel waited in silence, then drained her glass and set it on the floor. "Okay. Jason and Martin are here. I saw them on the hill—"

"Yeah, I know, I talked to them, they went to Camden for lunch, they can't wait to see you." Moony paced to the door to her room, trying not to look impatient. Already her heart was pounding.

"Okay," Ariel said again. She sounded breathless and a little drunk. She had ringed her aquamarine eyes with kohl, to hide how tired she was. Over the last few months she'd grown so thin that her cheekbones had emerged again, after years of hiding in her round peasant's face. Her voice was hoarse as she asked, "So you'll be there soon?"

Moony nodded. She curled a long tendril of hair, dark as her mother's but finer, and brushed her cheek with it. "I'm just gonna pull my hair back. Jason'll give me shit if I don't."

Ariel laughed. Jason thought that they were all a bunch of hippies. "Okay." She crossed the room unsteadily, touching the backs of chairs, a windowsill, the edge of a buoy hanging from the wall. When the screen door banged shut behind her Moony sighed with relief.

For a few minutes she waited, to make sure her mother hadn't forgotten something, like maybe a joint or another glass of wine. She could see out the window to where people were starting downhill toward the gazebo. If you didn't look too closely, they might have been any group of summer people gathering for a party in the long northern afternoon.

But after a minute or two their oddities started to show. You saw them for what they really were: men and women just getting used to a peculiar middle age. They all had hair a little too long or too short, a little too gray or garishly colored. The women, like Ariel, wrapped in clothes like banners from a triumphant campaign now forgotten. Velvet tunics threaded with silver, miniskirts crossing pale bare blue-veined thighs, Pucci blouses back in vogue again. The men more subdued, in chinos some of them, or old jeans that were a little too bright and neatly pressed. She could see Martin beneath the lilacs by the gazebo, in baggy psychedelic shorts and T-shirt, his gray-blond hair longer than it had been and pulled back into a wispy ponytail. Beside him Jason leaned against a tree, self-consciously casual, smoking a cigarette as he watched the First Night promenade. At sight of Ariel he raised one hand in a lazy wave.

And now the last two stragglers reached the bottom of the hill. Mrs. Grose carrying her familiar, an arthritic wheezing pug named Milton: Ancient Mrs. Grose, who smelled of Sen-sen and whiskey, and prided herself on being one of the spiritualists exposed as a fraud by

Houdini. And Gary Bonetti, who (the story went) five years ago had seen a vision of his own death in the City, a knife wielded by a crack-crazed kid in Washington Heights. Since then, he had stayed on at Mars Hill with Mrs. Grose, the community's only other year-round resident.

Moony ducked back from the window as her mother turned to stare up at the cottage. She waited until Ariel looked away again, as Martin and Jason beckoned her toward the gazebo.

"Okay," Moony whispered. She took a step across the room and stopped. An overwhelming smell of cigarette smoke suddenly filled the air, though there was no smoke to be seen. She coughed, waving her hand in front of her face.

"Damn it, Jason," she hissed beneath her breath. The smell was gone as abruptly as it had appeared. "I'll be *right there*—"

She slipped through the narrow hallway with its old silver-touched mirrors and faded Maxfield Parrish prints, and went into Ariel's room. It still had its beginning-of-summer smell, mothballs and the salt sweetness of rugosa roses blooming at the beach's edge. The old chenille bedspread was rumpled where Ariel had lain upon it, exhausted by the flight from La Guardia to Boston, from Boston via puddle-jumper to the tiny airport at Green Turtle Reach. Moony pressed her hand upon the spread and closed her eyes. She tried to focus as Jason had taught her, tried to dredge up the image of her mother stretched upon the bed. And suddenly there it was, a faint sharp stab of pain in her left breast, like a stitch in her side from running. She opened her eyes quickly, fighting the dizziness and panicky feeling. Then she went to the bureau.

At home she had never been able to find the envelope. It was always hidden away, just as the mail was always carefully sorted, the messages on the answering machine erased before she could get to them. But now it was as if Ariel had finally given up on hiding. The envelope was in the middle drawer, a worn cotton camisole draped halfheartedly across it. Moony took it carefully from the drawer and went to the bed, sat and slowly fanned the papers out.

They were hospital bills. Hospital bills and Blue Cross forms, cash register receipts for vitamins from the Waverly Drugstore with Ariel's crabbed script across the top. The bills were for tests only, tests and consultations. Nothing for treatments; no receipts for medication other than vitamins. At the bottom of the envelope, rolled into a blue cylinder and tightened with a rubber band, she found the test results. Stray words floated in the air in front of her as Moony drew in a long shuddering breath.

Mammography results. Sectional biopsy. Fourth stage malignancy. Metastasized.

Cancer. Her mother had breast cancer.

"Shit," she said. Her hands after she replaced the papers were shaking. From outside echoed summer music, and she could hear voices—her mother's, Diana's, Gary Bonetti's deep bass—shouting above the tinny sound of a cassette player—

"Wouldn't it be nice if we could wake up
In the kind of world where we belong?"

Y ou bitch," Moony whispered. She stood at the front window and stared down the hill at the gazebo, her hands clamped beneath her armpits to keep them still. Her face was streaked with tears. "When were you going to *tell* me, when were you going to fucking *tell me?*"

At the foot of Mars Hill, alone by a patch of daylilies stood Jason, staring back up at the cottage. A cigarette burned between his fingers, its scent miraculously filling the little room. Even from here Moony could tell that somehow and of course, he already knew.

Everyone had a hangover the next morning, not excluding Moony and Jason. In spite of that, the two met in the community chapel. Jason brought a thermos of coffee, bright red and yellow dinosaurs stenciled on its sides, and blew ashes from the bench so she could sit down.

"You shouldn't smoke in here." Moony coughed and slumped beside him. Jason shrugged and stubbed out his cigarette, fished in his pocket and held out his open palm.

"Here. Ibuprofen and valerian capsules. And there's bourbon in the coffee."

Moony snorted but took the pills, shooting back a mouthful of tepid coffee and grimacing.

"Hair of the iguana," Jason said. "So really, Moony, you didn't know?"

"How the hell would I know?" Moony said wearily. "I mean, I knew it was *something*—"

She glanced sideways at her friend. His slender legs were crossed at the ankles and he was barefoot. Already dozens of mosquito bites pied his arms and legs. He was staring at the little altar in the center of the room. He looked paler than usual, more tired, but that was probably just the hangover.

From outside, the chapel looked like all the other buildings at Mars Hill, faded gray shingles and white trim. Inside there was one large open room, with benches arranged in a circle around the walls, facing in to the plain altar. The altar was heaped with wilting daylilies and lilacs, an empty bottle of chardonnay and a crumpled pack of Kents—Jason's brand—and a black velvet hair ribbon that Moony recognized as her mother's. Beneath the ribbon was an old snapshot, curled at the edges. Moony knew the pose from years back. It showed her and Jason and Ariel and Martin, standing at the edge of the pier with their faces raised skyward, smiling and waving at Diana behind her camera. Moony made a face when she saw it and took another swallow of coffee.

"I thought maybe she had AIDS," Moony said at last. "I knew she went to the Walker Clinic once, I heard her on the phone to Diana about it."

Jason nodded, his mouth set in a tight smile. "So you should be happy she doesn't. Hip hip hooray." Two years before, Jason's father had tested HIV-positive. Martin's lover, John, had died that spring.

Moony turned so that he couldn't see her face. "She has breast cancer. It's metastasized. She won't see a doctor. This morning she let me feel it . . ."

Like a gnarled tree branch shoved beneath her mother's flesh, huge and hard and lumpy. Ariel thought she'd cry or faint or something but all Moony could do was wonder how she had never felt it before. Had she never noticed, or had it just been that long since she'd hugged her mother?

She started crying, and Jason drew closer to her.

"Hey," he whispered, his thin arm edging around her shoulders. "It's okay, Moony, don't cry, it's all right—"

How can you say that? she felt like screaming, sobs constricting her throat so she couldn't speak. When she did talk the words came out in anguished grunts.

"They're dying—how can they—*Jason*—"

"Shh—" he murmured. "Don't cry, Moony, don't cry . . ."

Beside her, Jason sighed and fought the urge for another cigarette. He wished he'd thought about this earlier, come up with something to say that would make Moony feel better. Something like, *Hey! Get used to it! Everybody dies!* He tried to smile, but he felt only sorrow and a headache prodding at the corners of his eyes. Moony's head felt heavy on his shoulder. He shifted on the bench, stroking her hair and whispering until she grew quiet. Then they sat in silence.

He stared across the room, to the altar and the wall beyond, where a stained glass window would have been in another kind of chapel. Here, a single great picture window looked out onto the bay. In the distance he could see the Starry Islands glittering in the sunlight, and beyond them the emerald bulk of Blue Hill and Cadillac Mountain rising above the indigo water.

And, if he squinted, he could Them. The Others, like tears or blots of light floating across his retina. The Golden Ones. The Greeters. The Light Children.

"Hey!" he whispered. Moony sniffed and burrowed closer into his shoulder, but he wasn't talking to her. He was welcoming Them.

They were the real reason people had settled here, over a century ago. They were the reason Jason and Moony and their parents and all the others came here now; although not everyone could see Them. Moony never had, nor Ariel's friend Diana; although Diana believed in Them, and Moony did not. You never spoke of Them, and if you did, it was always parenthetically and with a capital T—"Rvis and I were looking at the moon last night (They were there) and we thought we saw a whale." Or, "Martin came over at midnight (he saw Them on the way) and we played Scrabble . . ."

A few years earlier a movement was afoot to change the way of referring to Them. In a single slender volume that was a history of the Mars Hill spiritualist community, They were referred to as the Light

Children, but no one ever really called Them that. Everyone just called them Them. It seemed the most polite thing to do, really, since no one knew what They called Themselves.

"And we'd hate to offend Them," as Ariel said.

That was always a fear at Mars Hill. That, despite the gentle nature of the community's adherents, They inadvertently would be offended one day (a too-noisy volleyball game on the rocky beach; a beer-fueled Solstice celebration irrupting into the dawn), and leave.

But They never did. Year after year the Light Children remained. They were a magical commonplace, like the loons that nested on a nearby pond and made the night an offertory with their cries, or the rainbows that inexplicably appeared over the Bay almost daily, even when there was no rain in sight. It was the same with Them. Jason would be walking down to call his father in from sailing, or knocking at Moony's window to awaken her for a three A.M. stroll, and suddenly there They'd be. A trick of the light, like a sun dog or the aurora borealis: golden patches swimming through the cool air. They appeared as suddenly as a cormorant's head slicing up through the water, lingering sometimes for ten minutes or so. Then They would be gone.

Jason saw Them a lot. The chapel was one of the places They seemed to like, and so he hung out there whenever he could. Sometimes he could sense Them moments before They appeared. A shivering in the air would make the tips of his fingers go numb, and once there had been a wonderful smell, like warm buttered bread. But usually there was no warning. If he closed his eyes while looking at Them, Their image still appeared on the cloudy scrim of his inner eye, like gilded tears. But that was all. No voices, no scent of rose petals, no rapping at the door. You felt better after seeing Them, the way you felt better after seeing a rainbow or an eagle above the Bay. But there was nothing really magical about Them, except the fact that They existed at all. They never spoke, or did anything special, at least nothing you could sense. They were just *there;* but Their presence meant everything at Mars Hill.

They were there now: flickering above the altar, sending blots of gold dancing across the limp flowers and faded photographs. He wanted to point Them out to Moony, but he'd tried before and she'd gotten mad at him.

"You think I'm some kind of idiot like my mother?" she'd stormed, sweeping that day's offering of irises from the altar onto the floor. "Give me a break, Jason!"

Okay, I gave you a break, he thought now. *Now I'll give you another.*

Look, Moony, there They are! he thought; then said, "Moony. Look—"

He pointed, shrugging his shoulder so she'd have to move. But already They were gone.

"What?" Moony murmured. He shook his head, sighing.

"That picture," he said, and fumbled at his pocket for his cigarettes. "That stupid old picture that Diana took. Can you believe it's still here?"

Moony lifted her head and rubbed her eyes, red and swollen. "Oh, I can believe anything," she said bitterly, and filled her mug with more coffee.

In Martin Dionysos's kitchen, Ariel drank a cup of nettle tea and watched avidly as her friend ate a bowl of mung bean sprouts and nutritional yeast. *Just like in* Annie Hall, she thought. *Amazing.*

"So now she knows and you're surprised she's pissed at you." Martin raised another forkful of sprouts to his mouth, angling delicately to keep any from falling to the floor. He raised one blond eyebrow as he chewed, looking like some hardscrabble New Englander's idea of Satan, California surfer boy gone to seed. Long gray-blond hair that was thinner than it had been a year ago, skin that wasn't so much tanned as an even pale bronze, with that little goatee and those piercing blue eyes, the same color as the Bay stretching outside the window behind him. Oh yes: and a gold hoop earring and a heart tattoo that enclosed the name *JOHN* and a T-shirt with the pink triangle and SILENCE=DEATH printed in stern block letters. Satan on vacation.

"I'm not *surprised,*" Ariel said, a little crossly. "I'm just, mmm, disappointed. That she got so upset."

Martin's other eyebrow arched. *"Disappointed?* As in, 'Moony, darling, I have breast cancer (which I have kept a secret from you for seven months) and I am very *disappointed* that you are not self-actualized enough to deal with this without falling to pieces'?"

"She didn't fall to pieces." Ariel's crossness went over the line into full-blown annoyance. She frowned and jabbed a spoon into her tea. "I *wish* she'd fall to pieces, she's always so—" She waved the hand holding the spoon, sending green droplets raining onto Martin's knee. "—*so something.*"

"Self-assured?"

"I guess. Self-assured and smug, you know? Why is it teenagers are always so fucking smug?"

"Because they share a great secret," Martin said mildly, and took another bite of sprouts.

"Oh yeah? What's that?"

"Their parents are all assholes."

Ariel snorted with laughter, leaned forward to get her teacup out of the danger zone and onto the table. "Oh, Martin," she said. Suddenly her eyes were filled with tears. "Damn it all to *hell* . . ."

Martin put his bowl on the table and stepped over to take her in his arms. He didn't say anything, and for a moment Ariel flashed back to the previous spring, the same tableau only in reverse, with her holding Martin while he sobbed uncontrollably in the kitchen of his San Francisco townhouse. It was two days after John's funeral, and she was on her way to the airport. She knew then about the breast cancer but she hadn't told Martin yet; didn't want to dim any of the dark luster of his grief.

Now it was her grief, but in a strange way she knew it was his, too. There was this awful thing that they held in common, a great unbroken chain of grief that wound from one coast to the other. She hadn't wanted to share it with Moony, hadn't wanted her to feel its weight and breadth. But it was too late, now. Moony knew and besides, what did it matter? She was dying, Martin was dying, and there wasn't a fucking thing anyone could do about it.

"Hey," he said at last. His hand stroked her mass of dark hair, got itself tangled near her shoulder, snagging one of the long silver-and-quartz-crystal earrings she had put on that morning, for luck. "Ouch."

Ariel snorted again, laughing in spite of, or maybe because of, it all. Martin extricated his hand, held up two fingers with a long curling strand of hair caught between them: a question mark, a wise serpent waiting to strike. She had seen him after the cremation take the lock of John's hair that he had saved and hold it so, until suddenly it burst into flames, and then watched as the fizz of ash flared out in a dark penumbra around Martin's fingers. No such thing happened now, no Faery Pagan pyrotechnics. She wasn't dead yet, there was no sharp cold wind of grief to fan Martin's peculiar gift. He let the twirl of hair fall away and looked at her and said, "You know, I talked to Adele."

Adele was Mrs. Grose, she of the pug dog and suspiciously advanced years. Ariel retrieved her cup and her equanimity, sipping at the nettle tea as Martin went on, "She said she thought we had a good chance. You especially. She said for you it might happen. They might come." He finished and leaned back in his chair, spearing the last forkful of sprouts.

Ariel said, "Oh yes?" Hardly daring to think of it; no, don't think of it at all.

Martin shrugged, twisted to look over his shoulder at the endless sweep of Penobscot Bay. His eyes were bright, so bright she wondered if he were fighting tears or perhaps something else, something only Martin would allow himself to feel here and now. Joy, perhaps. Hope.

"Maybe," he said. At his words her heart beat a little faster in her breast, buried beneath the mass that was doing its best to crowd it out. "That's all. Maybe. It might. Happen."

And his hand snaked across the table to hers and held it, clutched it like it was a link in that chain that ran between them, until her fingers went cold and numb.

On Wednesday evenings the people at Mars Hill gave readings for the public. Tarot, palms, auras, dreams—five dollars a pop, nothing guaranteed. The chapel was cleaned, the altar swept of offerings and covered with a frayed red-and-white checked tablecloth from Diana's kitchen and a few candles in empty Chianti bottles.

"It's not very atmospheric," Gary Bonetti said, as someone always did. Mrs. Grose nodded from her bench and fiddled with her rosary beads.

"Au contraire," protested Martin. "It's *very* atmospheric, if you're in the mood for spaghetti carbonara at Luigi's."

"May I recommend the primavera?" said Jason. In honor of the occasion he had put on white duck pants and white shirt and red bow tie. He waved at Moony, who stood at the door taking five-dollar bills from nervous, giggly tourists and the more solemn-faced locals, who made this pilgrimage every summer. Some regulars came week after week, year after year. Sad Brenda, hoping for the tarot card that would bring news from her drowned child. Mr. Spruce, a ruddy-faced lobsterman who always tipped Mrs. Grose ten dollars. The Hamptonites Jason had dubbed Mr. and Mrs. Pissant, who were anxious about their auras. To-night the lobsterman was there, with an ancient woman who could only be his mother, and the Pissants, and two teenage couples, long blond hair and sunburned, reeking of marijuana and summer money.

The teenagers went to Martin, lured perhaps by his tie-dyed caf-tan, neatly pressed and swirling down to his Birkenstock-clad feet.

"Boat trash," hissed Jason, arching a nearly invisible white-blond eyebrow as they passed. "I saw them in Camden, getting off a yacht the size of the fire station. God, they make me sick."

Moony tightened her smile. Catch *her* admitting to envy of people like that. She swiveled on her chair, looking outside to see if there were any newcomers making their way to the chapel through the cool summer night. "I think this is gonna be it," she said. She glanced wistfully at the few crumpled bills nesting in an old oatmeal tin. "Maybe we should, like, advertise or something. It's been so slow this summer."

Jason only grunted, adjusting his bow tie and glaring at the rich kids, now deep in conference with his father. The Pissants had fallen to Diana, who with her chignon of blond hair and gold-buttoned little black dress could have been one of their neighbors. That left the lobsterman and his aged mother.

They stood in the middle of the big room, looking not exactly uneasy or lost, but as though they were waiting for someone to usher them to their proper seats. And as though she read their minds (but wasn't that her job?), Mrs. Grose swept up suddenly from her corner of the chapel, a warm South Wind composed of yards of very old rayon fabric, Jean Naté After Bath, and arms large and round and powdered as wheaten loaves.

"Mr. *Spruce*," she cried, extravagantly trilling her *rrr*'s and opening those arms like a stage gypsy. "You have come—"

"Why, yes," the lobsterman answered, embarrassed but also grateful. "I, uh—I brought my mother, Mrs. Grose. She says she remembers you."

"I do," said Mrs. Spruce. Moony twisted to watch, curious. She had always wondered about Mrs. Grose. She claimed to be a true clairvoyant. She *had* predicted things—nothing very useful, though. What the weather would be like the weekend of Moony's Junior Prom (rainy), but not whether she would be asked to go, or by whom. The day Jason would receive a letter from Harvard (Tuesday, the fifth of April), but not whether he'd be accepted there (he was not). It aggravated Moony, like so much at Mars Hill. What was the use of being a psychic if you could never come up with anything really useful?

But then there was the story about Harry Houdini. Mrs. Grose loved to tell it, how when she was still living in Chicago this short guy came one day and she gave him a message from his mother and he tried to make her out to be a fraud. It was a stupid story, except for one thing. If it really had happened, it would make Mrs. Grose about ninety or a hundred years old. And she didn't look a day over sixty.

Now Mrs. Grose was cooing over a woman who really *did* look to be about ninety. Mrs. Spruce peered up at her through rheumy eyes, shaking her head and saying in a whispery voice, "I can't believe it's you. I was just a girl, but you don't look any different at all . . . "

"Oh, flattery, flattery!" Mrs. Grose laughed and rubbed her nose with a Kleenex. "What can we tell you tonight, Mrs. Spruce?"

Moony turned away. It was too weird. She watched Martin entertaining the four golden children, then felt Jason coming up behind her: the way some people claim they can tell a cat is in the room, by some subtle disturbance of air and dust. A cat is there. Jason is there.

"They're *all* going to Harvard. I can't *believe* it," he said, mere disgust curdled into utter loathing. "And that one, the blond on the end—"

"They're all blond, Jason," said Moony. *"You're* blond."

"I am an *albino*," Jason said with dignity. "Check him out, the Nazi Youth with the Pearl Jam T-shirt. He's a legacy, absolutely. SAT scores of 1060, tops. I *know*." He closed his eyes and wiggled his fingers and made a *whoo-whoo* noise, beckoning spirits to come closer. Moony laughed and covered her mouth. From where he sat Martin raised an eyebrow, requesting silence. Moony and Jason turned and walked outside.

"How old do you think she is?" Moony asked, after they had gone a safe distance from the chapel.

"Who?"

"Mrs. Grose."

"Adele?" Jason frowned into the twilit distance, thinking of the murky shores and shoals of old age. "Jeez, I dunno. Sixty? Fifty?"

Moony shook her head. "She's got to be older than that. I mean, that story about Houdini, you know?"

"Huh! Houdini. The closest she ever got to Houdini is seeing some Siegfried and Roy show out in Las Vegas."

"I don't think she's ever left here. At least not since I can remember."

Jason nodded absently, then squatted in the untidy drive, squinting as he stared out into the darkness occluding the Bay. Fireflies formed mobile constellations within the birch trees. As a kid he had always loved fireflies, until he had seen Them. Now he thought of the Light Children as a sort of evolutionary step, somewhere between lightning bugs and angels.

Though you hardly ever see Them at night, he thought. *Now why is that?* He rocked back on his heels, looking like some slender pale gargoyle toppled from a modernist cathedral, the cuffs of his white oxford-cloth shirt rolled up to show large bony wrists and surprisingly strong square hands, his bow tie unraveled and hanging rakishly around his neck. Of a sudden he recalled being in this same spot two years ago, grinding out a cigarette as Martin and John approached. The smoke bothered John, sent him into paroxysms of coughing so prolonged and intense that more than once they had set Jason's heart pounding, certain that This Was It, John was going to die right here, right now, and it would be all Jason's fault for smoking. Only of course it didn't happen that way.

"The longest death since Little Nell's," John used to say, laughing hoarsely. That was when he could still laugh, still talk. At the end it had been others softly talking, Martin and Jason and their friends gathered around John's bed at home, taking turns, spelling each other. After a while Jason couldn't stand to be with them. It was too much like John was already dead. The body in the bed so wasted, bones cleaving to skin so thin and mottled it was like damp newsprint.

By the end, Jason refused to accompany Martin to the therapist they were supposed to see. He refused to go with him to the meetings where men and women talked about dying, about watching loved ones go so horribly slowly. Jason just couldn't take it. Grief he had always thought of as an emotion, a mood, something that possessed you but that you eventually escaped. Now he knew it was different. Grief was a country, a place you entered hesitantly, or were thrown into without warning. But once you were there, amidst the roiling formless blackness and stench of despair, you could not leave. Even if you wanted to: you could only walk and walk and walk, traveling on through the black reaches with the sound of screaming in your ears, and hope that someday you might glimpse far off another country, another place where you might someday rest.

Jason had followed John a long ways into that black land. And now his own father would be going there. Maybe not for good, not yet, but Jason knew. An HIV-positive diagnosis might mean that Death was a long ways off; but Jason knew his father had already started walking.

". . . you think they don't leave?"

Jason started. "Huh?" He looked up into Moony's wide gray eyes. "I'm sorry, what?"

"Why do you think they don't leave? Mrs. Grose and Gary. You know, the ones who stay here all year." Moony's voice was exasperated. He wondered how many times she'd asked him the same thing.

"I dunno. I mean, they *have* to leave sometimes. How do they get groceries and stuff?" He sighed and scrambled to his feet. "There's only two of them, maybe they pay someone to bring stuff in. I know Gary goes to the Beach Store sometimes. It's not like they're under house arrest. Why?"

Moony shrugged. In the twilight she looked spooky, more like a witch than her mother or Diana or any of those other wannabes. Long dark hair and those enormous pale gray eyes, face like the face of the cat who'd been turned into a woman in a fairy tale his father had read him once. Jason grinned, thinking of Moony jumping on a mouse. No way. But hey, even if she did, it would take more than *that* to turn him off.

"You thinking of staying here?" he asked slyly. He slipped an arm around her shoulders. "'Cause, like, I could keep you company or something. I hear Maine gets cold in the winter."

"No." Moony shrugged off his arm and started walking toward the water: no longer exasperated, more like she was distracted. "My mother is."

"Your *mother?*"

He followed her until she stopped at the edge of a gravel beach. The evening sky was clear. On the opposite shore, a few lights glimmered in Dark Harbor, reflections of the first stars overhead. From somewhere up along the coast, Bayside or Nagaseek or one of the other summer colonies, the sounds of laughter and skirling music echoed very faintly over the water, like a song heard on some distant station very late at night. But it wasn't late, not yet even nine o'clock. In summers past, that had been early for Moony and Jason, who would often stay up with the adults talking and poring over cards and runes until the night grew cold and spent.

But tonight for some reason the night already felt old. Jason shivered and kicked at the pebbly beach. The last pale light of sunset cast an antique glow upon stones and touched the edge of the water with gold. As he watched, the light withdrew, a gauzy veil drawn back teasingly until the shore shimmered with afterglow, like blue glass.

"I heard her talking with Diana," Moony said. Her voice was unsettlingly loud and clear in the still air. "She was saying she might stay on, after I go off to school. I mean, she was talking like she wasn't going back at all, I mean not back to Kamensic. Like she might just stay here and never leave again." Her voice cracked on the words *never leave again* and she shuddered, hugging herself.

"Hey," said Jason. He walked over and put his arms around her, her dark hair a perfumed net that drew him in until he felt dizzy and had to draw back, gasping a little, the smell of her nearly overwhelming that of rugosa roses and the sea. "Hey, it's okay, Moony, really it's okay."

Moony's voice sounded explosive, as though she had been holding her breath. "I just can't believe she's giving *up* like this. I mean, no doctors, nothing. She's just going to stay here and die."

"She might not die," said Jason, his own voice a little desperate. "I mean, look at Adele. A century and counting. The best is yet to come."

Moony laughed brokenly. She leaned forward so that her hair once again spilled over him, her wet cheek resting on his shoulder. "Oh Jason. If it weren't for you I'd go crazy, you know that? I'd just go fucking nuts."

Nuts, thought Jason. His arms tightened around her, the cool air and faraway music nearly drowning him as he stroked her head and breathed her in. *Crazy, oh yes.* And they stood there until the moon showed over Dark Harbor, and all that far-off music turned to silvery light above the Bay.

Two days later Ariel and Moony went to see the doctor in Bangor. Moony drove, an hour's trip inland, up along the old road that ran beside the Penobscot River, through failed stonebound farms and past trailer encampments like sad rusted toys, until finally they reached the sprawl around the city, the kingdom of car lots and franchises and shopping plazas.

The hospital was an old brick building with a shiny new white wing grafted on. Ariel and Moony walked through a gleaming steel-and-glass door set in the expanse of glittering concrete. But they ended up in a tired office on the far end of the old wing, where the squeak of rubber wheels on worn linoleum played counterpoint to a loudly echoing, ominous *drip-drip* that never ceased the whole time they were there.

"Ms. Rising. Please, come in."

Ariel squeezed her daughter's hand, then followed the doctor into her office. It was a small bright room, a hearty wreath of living ivy trained around its single grimy window in defiance of the lack of sunlight and, perhaps, the black weight of despair that Ariel felt everywhere, chairs, desk, floor, walls.

"I received your records from New York," the doctor said. She was a slight fine-boned young woman with sleek straight hair and a silk dress more expensive than what you usually saw in Maine. The little metal name-tag on her breast might have been an odd bit of heirloom jewelry. "You realize that even as of three weeks ago, the cancer had spread to the point where our treatment options are now quite limited."

Ariel nodded, her arms crossed protectively across her chest. She felt strange, light-headed. She hadn't been able to eat much the last day or two, that morning had swallowed a mouthful of coffee and a stale muffin to satisfy Moony but that was all. "I know," she said heavily. "I don't know why I'm here."

"Frankly, I don't know either," the doctor replied. "If you had optioned for some kind of intervention, oh, even two months ago; but now . . ."

Ariel tilted her head, surprised at how sharp the other woman's tone was. The doctor went on, "It's a great burden to put on your daughter—" She looked in the direction of the office door, then glanced down at the charts in her hand. "Other children?"

Ariel shook her head. "No."

The doctor paused, gently slapping the sheaf of charts and records against her open palm. Finally she said, "Well. Let's examine you, then."

An hour later Ariel slipped back into the waiting room. Moony looked up from a magazine. Her gray eyes were bleary and her tired expression hastily congealed into the mask of affronted resentment with which she faced Ariel these days.

"So?" she asked as they retraced their steps back through cinder-block corridors to the hospital exit. "What'd she say?"

Ariel stared straight ahead, through the glass doors to where the summer afternoon waited to pounce on them. Exhaustion had seeped into her like heat; like the drugs the doctor had offered and Ariel had refused, the contents of crystal vials that could buy a few more weeks, maybe even months if she was lucky, enough time to make a graceful farewell to the world. But Ariel didn't want weeks or months, and she sure as hell didn't want graceful goodbyes. She wanted years, decades. A cantankerous or dreamy old age, aggravating the shit out of her grandchildren with her talk about her own sunflower youth. Failing that, she wanted screaming and gnashing of teeth, her friends tearing their hair out over her death, and Moony . . .

And Moony. Ariel stopped in front of a window, one hand out to press against the smooth cool glass. Grief and horror hit her like a stone, struck her between the eyes so that she gasped and drew her hands to her face.

"Mom!" Moony cried, shocked. "Mom, what *is* it, are you all right?—"

Ariel nodded, tears burning down her cheeks. "I'm fine," she said, and gave a twisted smile. "Really, I'm—"

"What did she *say*?" demanded Moony. "The doctor, what did she tell you, *what is it?*"

Ariel wiped her eyes, a black line of mascara smeared across her finger. "Nothing. Really, Moony, nothing's changed. It's just—it's just hard. Being this sick. It's hard, that's all."

She could see in her daughter's face confusion, despair, but also relief. Ariel hadn't said *death,* she hadn't said *dying,* she hadn't since that first day said *cancer.* She'd left those words with the doctor, along with the scrips for morphine and Fiorinal, all that could be offered to her now. "Come on," she said, and walked through the sliding doors. "I'm supposed to have lunch with Mrs. Grose and Diana, and it's already late."

Moony stared at her in disbelief: was her mother being stoic or just crazy? But Ariel didn't say anything else, and after a moment her daughter followed her to the car.

In Mars Hill's little chapel Jason sat and smoked. On the altar in front of him were several weeks' accumulated offerings from the denizens of Mars Hill. An old-fashioned envelope with a glassine window, through which he could glimpse the face of a twenty-dollar bill—that was from Mrs. Grose, who always gave the money she'd earned from readings (and then retrieved it at the end of the summer). A small square of brilliantly woven cloth from Diana, whose looms punctuated the soft morning with their steady racketing. A set of blueprints from Rvis Capricorn. Shasta Daisy's battered *Ephemera.* The copy of Paul Bowles' autobiography that Jason's father had been reading on the flight out from the West Coast. In other words, the usual flotsam of love and whimsy that washed up here every summer. From where Jason sat, he could see his own benefaction, a heap of small white roses, already limp but still giving out their heady sweet scent, and a handful of blackberries he'd picked from the thicket down by the pier. Not much of an offering, but you never knew.

From beneath his roses peeked the single gift that puzzled him, a lacy silk camisole patterned with pale pink-and-yellow blossoms. An odd choice of offering, Jason thought. Because for all the unattached adults sipping chardonnay and Bellinis of a summer evening, the atmosphere at Mars Hill was more like that of summer camp. A chaste sort of giddiness ruled here, compounded of equal parts of joy and longing, that always made Jason think of the garlanded jackass and wistful fairies in *A Midsummer Night's Dream.* His father and Ariel and all the rest stumbling around in the dark, hoping for a glimpse of Them, and settling for fireflies and the lights from Dark Harbor. Mars Hill held surprisingly little in the way of unapologetic lust—except for himself and Moony, of course. And Jason knew that camisole didn't belong to Moony.

At the thought of Moony he sighed and tapped his ashes onto the dusty floor. It was a beautiful morning, gin-clear and with a stiff warm breeze from the west. Perfect sailing weather. He should be out with his father on the *Wendameen.* Instead he'd stayed behind, to write and think. Earlier he'd tried to get through to Moony somewhere in Bangor, but Jason couldn't send his thoughts any farther than from one end of Mars Hill to the other. For some reason, smoking cigarettes seemed to help. He had killed half a pack already this morning, but gotten nothing more than a headache and a raw throat. Now he had given up. It never seemed to work with anyone except Moony, anyhow, and then only if she was nearby.

He had wanted to give her some comfort. He wanted her to know how much he loved her, how she meant more to him than anyone or anything in the world, except perhaps his father. Was it allowed, to feel this much for a person when your father was HIV-positive? Jason frowned and stubbed out his cigarette in a lobster-shaped ashtray, already overflowing with the morning's telepathic aids. He picked up his notebook and Rapidograph pen and, still frowning, stared at the letter he'd begun last night.

Dearest Moony,
(he crossed out *est,* it sounded too fussy)
I just want you to know that I understand how you feel. When John died it was the most horrible thing in the world, even worse than the divorce because I was just a kid then. I just want you to know how much I love you, you mean more than anyone or anything in the world, and

And what? Did he really know how she felt? His mother wasn't dying, his mother was in the Napa Valley running her vineyard, and while it was true enough that John's death had been the most horrible thing he'd ever lived through, could that be the same as having your mother die? He thought maybe it could. And then of course there was the whole thing with his father. Was that worse? His father wasn't sick, of course, at least he didn't have any symptoms yet; but was it worse for someone you loved to have the AIDS virus, to watch and wait for months or years, rather than have it happen quickly like with Ariel? Last night he'd sat in the living room while his father and Gary Bonetti were on the porch talking about her.

"I give her only a couple of weeks," Martin had said, with that dry strained calm voice he'd developed over the last few years of watching his friends die. "The thing is, if she'd gone for treatment right away she could be fine now. She could be *fine.*" The last word came out in an uncharacteristic burst of vehemence, and Jason grew cold to hear it. Because of course even with treatment his father probably wouldn't be all right, not now, not ever. He'd never be fine again. Ariel had thrown all that away.

"She should talk to Adele," Gary said softly. Jason heard the clink of ice as he poured himself another daiquiri. "When I had those visions five years ago, that's when I saw Adele. You should too, Martin. You really should."

"I don't know as Adele can help me," Martin said, somewhat coolly. "She's just a guest here, like you or any of the rest of us. And *you* know that you can't make Them . . ."

His voice trailed off. Jason sat bold upright on the sofa, suddenly feeling his father there, like a cold finger stabbing at his brain.

"Jason?" Martin called, his voice tinged with annoyance. "If you want to listen, come in *here,* please."

Jason had sworn under his breath and stormed out through the back door. It was impossible, sometimes, living with his father. Better to have a psychic wannabe like Ariel for a parent, and not have to worry about being spied on all the time.

Now, from outside the chapel came frenzied barking. Jason started, his thoughts broken. He glanced through the open door to see Gary and his black Labrador retriever heading down to the water. Gary was grinning, arms raised as he waved at someone out of sight. And suddenly Jason had an image of his father in the *Wendameen*, the fast little sloop skirting the shore as Martin stood at the mast waving back, his long hair tangled by the wind. The vision left Jason nearly breathless. He laughed, shaking his head, and at once decided to follow Gary to the landing and meet his father there. He picked up his pen and notebook and turned to go. Then stopped, his neck prickling. Very slowly he turned, until he stood facing the altar once more.

They were there. A shimmering haze above the fading roses, like Zeus's golden rain falling upon imprisoned Danaë. Jason's breath caught in his throat as he watched Them—They were so beautiful, so *strange*. Flickering in the chapel's dusty air, like so many scintillant coins. He could sense rather than hear a faint chiming as They darted quick as hummingbirds from his roses to Mrs. Grose's envelope, alighting for a moment upon Diana's weaving and Rvis's prize tomatoes before settling upon two things: his father's book and the unknown camisole.

And then with a sharp chill Jason knew whose it was. Ariel's, of course—who else would own something so unabashedly romantic but also slightly tacky? Maybe it was meant to be a bad joke, or perhaps it was a real offering, heartfelt, heartbreaking. He stared at Them, a glittering carpet tossed over those two pathetic objects, and had to shield his eyes with his hand. It was too bright, They seemed to be growing more and more brilliant as he watched. Like a swarm of butterflies he had once seen, mourning cloaks resting in a snow-covered field one warm March afternoon, their wings slowly fanning the air as though they had been stunned by the thought of spring. But what could ever surprise *Them*, the Light Children, the summer's secret?

Then as he watched They began to fade. The glowing golden edge of the swarm grew dim and disappeared. One by one all the other gilded coins blinked into nothing, until the altar stood as it had minutes before, a dusty collection of things, odd and somewhat ridiculous. Jason's head pounded and he felt faint; then realized he'd been holding his breath. He let it out, shuddering, put his pen and notebook on the floor, and walked to the altar.

Everything was as it had been, roses, cloth, paper, tomatoes; excepting only his father's offering, and Ariel's. Hesitantly he reached to touch the book Martin had left, then recoiled.

The cover of the book had been damaged. When he leaned over to stare at it more closely, he saw that myriad tiny holes had been burned in the paper, in what at first seemed to be a random pattern. But when he picked it up—gingerly, as though it might yet release an electrical jolt or some other hidden energy—he saw that the tiny perforations formed an image, blurred but unmistakable. The shadow of a hand, four fingers splayed across the cover as though gripping it.

Jason went cold. He couldn't have explained how, but he knew that it was a likeness of his father's hand that he saw there, eerie and chilling as those monstrous shadows left by victims of the bombings at Hiroshima and Nagasaki. With a frightened gasp he tossed the book back onto the altar. For a moment he stood beside the wooden table, half-poised to flee; but finally reached over and tentatively pushed aside his roses to fully reveal the camisole.

It was just like the book. Thousands of tiny burn-holes made a ruined lace of the pastel silk, most of them clustered around one side of the bodice. He picked it up, catching a faint fragrance, lavender and marijuana, and held it out by its pink satin straps. He raised it, turning toward the light streaming through the chapel's picture window, and saw that the pinholes formed a pattern, elegant as the tracery of veins and capillaries on a leaf. A shadowy bull's-eye—breast, aureole, nipple drawn onto the silken cloth.

With a small cry Jason dropped the camisole. Without looking back he ran from the chapel. Such was his hurry that he forgot his pen and notebook and the half-written letter to Moony, piled carefully on the dusty floor. And so he did not see the shining constellation that momentarily appeared above the pages, a curious cloud that hovered there like a child's dream of weather before flowering into a golden rain.

———

Moony sat hunched on the front stoop, waiting for her mother to leave. Ariel had been in her room for almost half an hour, her luncheon date with Diana and Mrs. Grose notwithstanding. When finally she emerged, Moony could hear the soft uneven tread of her flip-flops, padding from bedroom to bedroom to kitchen. There was the sigh of the refrigerator opening and closing, the muted pop of a cork being pulled from a bottle, the long grateful gurgle of wine being poured into a glass. Then Ariel herself in the doorway behind her. Without looking Moony could tell that she'd put on The Skirt. She could smell it, the musty scents of patchouli and cannabis resin and the honeysuckle smell of the expensive detergent Ariel used to wash it by hand, as though it were some precious winding sheet.

"I'm going to Adele's for lunch."

Moony nodded silently.

"I'll be back in a few hours."

More silence.

"You know where to find me if anyone comes by." Ariel nudged her daughter gently with her toe. "Okay?"

Moony sighed. "Yeah, okay."

She watched her mother walk out the door, sun bouncing off her hair in glossy waves. When Ariel was out of sight she hurried down the hall.

In her mother's room, piles of clothes and papers covered the worn Double Wedding Ring quilt, as though tossed helter-skelter from her bureau.

"Jeez, what a mess," said Moony. She slowly crossed to the bed. It was covered with scarves and tangled skeins of pantyhose; drifts of old catering receipts, bills, canceled checks. A few paperbacks with yellowed pages that had been summer reading in years past. A back issue of *Gourmet* magazine and the *Maine Progressive*. A Broadway ticket stub from *Prelude to a Kiss*. Grimacing, Moony prodded the edge of last year's calendar from the Beach Store & Pizza to Go.

What had her mother been looking for?

Then, as if by magic, Moony saw it. Its marbled cover suddenly glimpsed beneath a dusty strata of tarot cards and Advil coupons, like some rare bit of fossil, lemur vertebrae, or primate jaw hidden within papery shale. She drew it out carefully, tilting it so the light slid across the title.

MARS HILL: ITS HISTORY AND LORE

by

Abigail Merithew Cox,

A Lover of Its Mysteries

With careful fingers Moony rifled the pages. Dried rose petals fell out, releasing the sad smell of summers past, and then a longer plume of liatris dropped to the floor, fresh enough to have left a faint purplish stain upon the page. Moony drew the book up curiously, marking the page where the liatris had fallen, and read,

> Perhaps strangest of all the Mysteries of our Colony at Mars Hill is the presence of those Enchanted Visitors who make their appearance now and then, to the eternal Delight of those of us fortunate enough to receive the benison of their presence. I say Delight, though many of us who have conjured with them say that the Experience resembles Rapture more than mere Delight, and even that Surpassing Ecstasy of which the Ancients wrote and which is at the heart of all our Mysteries; though we are not alone in enjoying the favor of our Visitors. It is said by my Aunt, Sister Rosemary Merithew, that the Passamaquoddie Indians who lived here long before the civilizing influence of the White Man, also entertained these Ethereal Creatures, which are in appearance like to those fairy lights called Foxfire or Will O' The Wisp, and which may indeed be the inspiration for such spectral rumors. The Passamaquoddie named them Akiniki, which in their language means The Greeters; and this I think is a most appropriate title for our Joyous Guests, who bring only Good News from the Other Side, and who feast upon our mortality as a man sups upon rare meats. . . .

Moony stared at the page in horror and disgust. *Feasting* upon mortality? She recalled her mother and Jason talking about the things they called the Light Children, Jason's disappointment that They had never appeared to Moony. As though there was something wrong with her, as though she wasn't worthy of seeing Them. But she had never felt that way. She had always suspected that Jason and her mother and the rest were mistaken about the Light Children. When she was younger, she had even accused her mother of lying about seeing Them. But the other people at Mars Hill spoke of Them, and Jason, at least, would never lie to Moony. So she had decided there must be something slightly delusional about the whole thing. Like a mass hypnosis, or maybe some kind of mass drug flashback, which seemed more likely considering the histories of some of her mother's friends.

Still, that left Mrs. Grose, who never even took an aspirin. Who, as far as Moony knew, had never been sick in her life, and who certainly seemed immune to most of the commonplace ailments of what must be, despite appearances, an advanced age. Mrs. Grose claimed to speak with the Light Children, to have a sort of understanding of Them that Ariel and the others lacked. And Moony had always held Mrs. Grose in awe. Maybe because her own grandparents were all dead, maybe just because of that story about Houdini—it was too fucking weird, no one could have made it up.

And so maybe no one had made up the Light Children, either. Moony tapped the book's cover, frowning. Why couldn't she see Them? Was it because she didn't believe? The thought annoyed her. As though she were a kid who'd found out about Santa Claus, and was being punished for learning the truth. She stared at the book's cover, the gold lettering flecked with dust, the peppering of black and green where salt air and mildew had eaten away at the cloth. The edge of one page crumbled as she opened it once more.

> Many of my brothers and sisters can attest to the virtues of Our Visitors, particularly Their care for the dying and afflicted. . . .

"Fucking *bullshit*," yelled Moony. She threw the book across the room, hard, so that it slammed into the wall beside her mother's bureau. With a soft *crack* the spine broke. She watched stonily as yellow pages and dried blossoms fluttered from between the split covers, a soft explosion of antique dreams. She left the room without picking up the mess, the door slamming shut behind her.

"I was consumptive," Mrs. Grose was saying, nodding as she looked in turn from Ariel to Diana to the pug sprawled panting on the worn chintz sofa beside them. "Tuberculosis, you know. Coming here saved me."

"You mean like, taking the waters?" asked Ariel. She shook back her hair and took another sip of her gin-and-tonic. "Like they used to do at Saratoga Springs and places like that?"

"Not like that *at all*," replied Mrs. Grose firmly. She raised one white eyebrow and frowned. "I mean, Mars Hill saved me."

Saved you for what? thought Ariel, choking back another mouthful of gin. She shuddered. She knew she shouldn't drink, these days she could feel it seeping into her, like that horrible barium they injected into you to do tests. But she couldn't stop. And what was the point, anyway?

"But you think it might help her, if she stayed here?" Diana broke in, oblivious of Mrs. Grose's imperious gaze. "And Martin, do you think it could help him too?"

"*I* don't think *anything*," said Mrs. Grose, and she reached over to envelop the wheezing pug with one large fat white hand. "It is absolutely not up to me at all. I am simply *telling* you the *facts.*"

"Of course," Ariel said, but she could tell from Diana's expression that her words had come out slurred. "Of *course*," she repeated with dignity, sitting up and smoothing the folds of her patchwork skirt.

"As long as you understand," Mrs. Grose said in a gentler tone. "We are guests here, and guests do not ask favors of their hosts."

The other two women nodded. Ariel carefully put her glass on the coffee table and stood, wiping her sweating hands on her skirt. "I better go now," she said. Her head pounded and she felt nauseated, for all that she'd barely nibbled at the ham sandwiches and macaroni salad Mrs. Grose had set out for lunch. "Home. I think I'd better go home."

"I'll go with you," said Diana. She stood and cast a quick look at their hostess. "I wanted to borrow that book . . ."

Mrs. Grose saw them to the door, holding open the screen and swatting threateningly at mosquitoes as they walked outside. "Remember what I told you," she called as they started down the narrow road, Diana with one arm around Ariel's shoulder. "Meditation and nettle tea. And patience."

"Patience," Ariel murmured; but nobody heard.

The weeks passed. The weather was unusually clear and warm, Mars Hill bereft of the cloak of mist and fog that usually covered it in August. Martin Dionysos took the *Wendameen* out nearly every afternoon, savoring the time alone, the hours spent fighting wind and waves—antagonists he felt he could win against.

"It's the most perfect summer we've ever had," Gary Bonetti said often to his friend. *Too* often, Martin thought bitterly. Recently, Martin was having what Jason called Millennial Thoughts, seeing ominous portents in everything from the tarot cards he dealt out to stricken tourists on Wednesday nights to the pattern of kelp and maidenhair left on the gravel beach after one of the summer's few storms. He had taken to avoiding Ariel, a move that filled him with self-loathing, for all that he told himself that he still needed time to grieve for John before giving himself over to another death. But it wasn't that, of course. Or at least it wasn't *only* that. It was fear, *The* Fear. It was listening to his own heart pounding as he lay alone in bed at night, counting the beats, wondering at what point it all began to break down, at what point It would come to take him.

So he kept to himself. He begged off going on the colony's weekly outing to the little Mexican restaurant up the road. He even stopped attending the weekly readings in the chapel. Instead, he spent his evenings alone, writing to friends back in the Bay Area. After drinking coffee with Jason every morning he'd turn away.

"I'm going to work now," he'd announce, and Jason would nod and leave to find Moony, grateful, his father thought, for the opportunity to escape.

Millennial Thoughts.

Martin Dionysos had given over a corner of his cottage's living room to a studio. There was a tiny drafting table, his portable computer, an easel, stacks of books; the week's forwarded offerings of *Out!* and *The Advocate* and *Q* and *The Bay Weekly*, and, heaped on an ancient stained Windsor chair, the usual pungent mess of oils and herbal decoctions that he used in his work. Golden morning light streamed through the wide mullioned windows, smelling of salt and the diesel fumes from Diana's ancient Volvo. On the easel a large unprimed canvas rested, somewhat unevenly due to the cant of a floor slanted enough that you could drop a marble in the kitchen and watch it roll slowly but inexorably to settle in the left-hand corner of the living room. Gary Bonetti claimed that it wasn't that all of the cottages on Mars Hill were built by incompetent architects. It was the magnetic pull of the ocean just meters away; it was the imperious reins of the East, of the Moon, of the magic charters of the Otherworld, that made it impossible to find any two corners that were plumb. Martin and the others laughed at Gary's pronouncement, but John had believed it.

John. Martin sighed, stirred desultorily at a coffee can filled with linseed oil and turpentine, then rested the can on the windowsill. For a long time he had been so caught up with the sad and harrowing and noble and disgusting details of John's dying that he had been able to forestall thinking about his own diagnosis. He had been grateful, in an awful way, that there had been something so horrible, so unavoidably and demandingly *real*, to keep him from succumbing to his own despair.

But all that was gone now. John was gone. Before John's death, Martin had always had a sort of unspoken, formless belief in an afterlife. The long shadow cast by a 1950s Catholic boyhood, he guessed. But when John died, that small hidden solace had died too. There was nothing there. No vision of a beloved waiting for him on the other side. Not even a body moldering within a polished mahogany casket. Only ashes, ashes; and his own death waiting like a small patient vicious animal in the shadows.

"Shit," he said. He gritted his teeth. This was how it happened to Ariel. She gave in to despair, or dreams, or maybe she just pretended it would go away. She'd be lucky now to last out the summer. At the thought a new wave of grief washed over him, and he groaned.

"Oh, shit, shit, shit," he whispered. With watering eyes he reached for the can full of primer on the sill. As he did so, he felt a faint prickling go through his fingers, a sensation of warmth that was almost painful. He swore under his breath and frowned. A tiny stab of fear lanced through him. Inexplicable and sudden pain, wasn't that the first sign of some sort of degeneration? As his fingers tightened around the coffee can, he looked up. The breath froze in his throat and he cried aloud, snatching his hand back as though he'd been stung.

They were there. Dozens of Them, a horde of flickering golden spots so dense They obliterated the wall behind Them. Martin had seen Them before, but never so close, never so many. He gasped and staggered back, until he struck the edge of the easel and sent the canvas clattering to the floor. They took no notice, instead followed him like a swarm of silent hornets. And as though They were hornets, Martin shouted and turned to run.

Only he could not. He was blinded, his face seared by a terrible heat. They were everywhere, enveloping him in a shimmering cocoon of light and warmth, Their fierce radiance burning his flesh, his eyes, his throat, as though he breathed liquid flame. He shrieked, batting at the air, and then babbling fell back against the wall. As They swarmed over him he felt Them, not as you feel the sun but as you feel a drug or love or anguish, filling him until he moaned and sank to the floor. He could feel his skin burning and erupting, his bones turning to ash inside him. His insides knotted, cramping until he thought he would faint. He doubled over, retching, but only a thin stream of spittle ran down his chin. An explosive burst of pain raced through him. He opened his mouth to scream, the sound so thin it might have been an insect whining. Then there was nothing but light, nothing but flame; and Martin's body unmoving on the floor.

Moony waited until late afternoon, but Jason never came. Hours earlier, Moony had glanced out the window of her cottage and seen Gary Bonetti running up the hill to Martin's house, followed minutes later by the panting figure of Mrs. Grose. Jason she didn't see at all. He must have never left his cottage that morning, or else left and returned by the back door.

Something had happened to Martin. She knew that as soon as she saw Gary's stricken face. Moony thought of calling Jason, but did not. She did nothing, only paced and stared out the window at Jason's house, hoping vainly to see someone else enter or leave. No one did.

Ariel had been sleeping all day. Moony avoided even walking past her mother's bedroom, lest her own terror wake her. She was afraid to leave the cottage, afraid to find out the truth. Cold dread stalked her all afternoon as she waited for something—an ambulance, a phone call, *anything*—but nothing happened. Nobody called, nobody came. Although once, her nostrils filled with the acrid smell of cigarette smoke, and she felt Jason there. Not Jason himself, but an overwhelming sense of terror that she knew came from him, a fear so intense that she drew her breath in sharply, her hand shooting out to steady herself against the door. Then the smell of smoke was gone.

"Jason?" she whispered, but she knew he was no longer thinking of her. She stood with her hand pressed against the worn silvery frame of the screen door. She kept expecting Jason to appear, to explain things. But there was nothing. For the first time all summer, Jason seemed to have forgotten her. Everyone seemed to have forgotten her.

That had been hours ago. Now it was nearly sunset. Moony lay on her towel on the gravel beach, swiping at a mosquito and staring up at the cloudless sky, blue skimmed to silver as the sun melted away behind Mars Hill. What a crazy place this was. Someone gets sick, and instead of dialing 911 you send for an obese old fortune-teller. The thought made her stomach churn; because of course that's what her mother had done. Put her faith in fairy dust and crystals instead of physicians and chemo. Abruptly Moony sat up, hugging her knees.

"Damn," she said miserably.

She'd put off going home, half-hoping, half-dreading that someone would find her and tell her what the hell was going on. Now it was obvious that she'd have to find out for herself. She threw her towel into her bag, tugged on a hooded pullover, and began to trudge back up the hill.

On the porches of the other cottages she could see people stirring. Whatever had happened, obviously none of *them* had heard yet. The new lesbian couple from Burlington sat facing each other in matching wicker armchairs, eyes closed and hands extended. A few houses on, Shasta Daisy sat on the stoop of her tiny Queen Anne Victorian, sipping a wine cooler, curled sheets of graph paper littering the table in front of her.

"Where's your mom?" Shasta called.

Moony shrugged and wiped a line of sweat from her cheek. "Resting, I guess."

"Come have a drink." Shasta raised her bottle. "I'll do your chart."

Moony shook her head. "Later. I got to get dinner."

"Don't forget there's a moon circle tonight," said Shasta. "Nine thirty at the gazebo."

"Right." Moony nodded, smiling glumly as she passed. What a bunch of kooks. At least her mother would be sleeping and not wasting her time conjuring up someone's aura between wine coolers.

But when she got home, no one was there. She called her mother's name as the screen door banged shut behind her, waited for a reply but there was none. For an instant a terrifying surge raced through her: something else had happened, her mother lay dead in the bedroom . . .

But the bedroom was empty, as were the living room and bathroom and anyplace else where Ariel might have chosen to die. The heady scent of basil filled the cottage, with a fainter hint of marijuana. When Moony finally went into the kitchen, she found the sink full of sand and half-rinsed basil leaves. Propped up on the drainboard was a damp piece of paper towel with a message spelled out in runny Magic Marker.

Moony: Went to Chapel
Moon circle at 9:30
Love love love Mom

"Right," Moony said, disgusted. She crumpled the note and threw it on the floor. "Way to go, Mom."

Marijuana, moon circle, astrological charts. Fucking *idiots*. Of a sudden she was filled with rage, at her mother and Jason and Martin and all the rest. Why weren't there any *doctors* here? Or lawyers, or secretaries, or anyone with half a brain, enough at least to take some responsibility for the fact that there were sick people here, people who were *dying* for Christ's sake and what was anyone doing about it? What was *she* doing about it?

"I've had it," she said aloud. "I have *had* it." She spun around and headed for the front door, her long hair an angry black blur around her grim face. "Amanda Rheining, you are going to the hospital. *Now.*"

She strode down the hill, ignoring Shasta's questioning cries. The gravel bit into her bare feet as she rounded the turn leading to the chapel. From here she could glimpse the back door of Jason and Martin's cottage. As Moony hurried past a stand of birches, she glimpsed Diana standing by the door, one hand resting on its crooked wooden frame. She was gazing out at the Bay with a rapt expression that might have been joy or exhausted grief, her hair gilded with the dying light.

For a moment Moony stopped, biting her lip. Diana at least might understand. She could ask Diana to come and help her force Ariel to go to the hospital. It would be like the intervention they'd done with Diana's ex-husband. But that would mean going to Martin's cottage, and confronting whatever it was that waited inside. Besides, Moony knew that no one at Mars Hill would ever force Ariel to do something she didn't want to do; even live. No. It was up to her to save her mother: herself, Maggie Rheining. Abruptly she turned away.

Westering light fell through the leaves of the ancient oak that shadowed the weathered gray chapel. The lupines and tiger lilies had faded with the dying summer. Now violet plumes of liatris sprang up around the chapel door beside unruly masses of sweet-smelling phlox and glowing clouds of asters. Of course no one ever weeded or thinned out the garden. The flowers choked the path leading to the door, so that Moony had to beat away a net of bees and lacewings and pale pink moths like rose petals, all of them rising from the riot of blossoms and then falling in a softly moving skein about the girl's shoulders as she walked. Moony cursed and slashed at the air, heedless of a luna moth's drunken somersault above her head, the glimmering wave of fireflies that followed her through the twilight.

At the chapel doorway Moony stopped. Her heart was beating hard, and she spat and brushed a liatris frond from her mouth. From inside she could hear a low voice; her mother's voice. She was reciting the verse that, over the years, had become a sort of blessing for her, a little mantra she chanted and whispered summer after summer, always in hopes of summoning Them—

> "With this field-dew consecrate
> Every fairy take his gait
> And each several chamber bless,
> through this palace, with sweet peace;
> Ever shall in safety rest,
> and the owner of it blest."

At the sound, Moony felt her heart clench inside her. She moved until her face pressed against the ancient gray screen sagging within its door frame. The screen smelled heavily of dust; she pinched her nose to keep from sneezing. She gazed through the fine moth-pocked web as though through a silken scrim or the Bay's accustomed fog.

Her mother was inside. She stood before the wooden altar, pathetic with its faded burden of wilting flowers and empty bottles and Jason's cigarette butts scattered across the floor. From the window facing the Bay, lilac-colored light flowed into the room, mingling with the shafts of dusty gold falling from the casements set high within the opposing wall. Where the light struck the floor a small bright pool had formed. Ariel was dancing slowly in and out of this, her thin arms raised, the long heavy sweep of her patchwork skirt sliding back and forth to reveal her slender legs and bare feet, shod with a velvety coat of dust. Moony could hear her reciting, Shakespeare's fairies' song again, and a line from Julian of Norwich that Diana had taught her:

"All will be well, and all will be well, and all manner of things will be well."

And suddenly the useless purity of Ariel's belief overwhelmed Moony. A stoned forty-three-year-old woman with breast cancer and a few weeks left to live, dancing inside a ruined chapel and singing to herself. Tears filled Moony's eyes, fell and left a dirty streak against the screen. She drew a deep breath, fighting the wave of grief and despair, and pushed against the screen to enter. When she raised her head again, Ariel had stopped.

At first Moony thought her mother had seen her. But no. Ariel was staring straight ahead at the altar, her head cocked to one side as though listening. So intent was she that Moony stiffened as well, inexplicably frightened. She glanced over her shoulder, but of course there was no one there. But it was too late to keep her heart from pounding. She closed her eyes, took a deep breath, and turned, stepping over the sill toward Ariel.

"Mom," Moony called softly. "Mom, I'm—"

Moony froze. In the center of the chapel her mother stood, arms writhing as she held them above her head, long hair whipping across her face. She was on fire. Flickers of gold and crimson ran along her arms and chest, lapped at her throat and face, and set runnels of light flaming across her clothes. Moony could hear her shrieking, could see her tearing at her breast as she tried to rip away the burning fabric.

With a howl Moony stumbled across the room—not thinking, hardly even seeing her as she lunged to grab Ariel and pull her down.

"*Mom!*"

But before she could reach Ariel she tripped, smashed onto the uneven floor. Groaning she rolled over and tried to get back up. An arm's-length away, her mother flailed, her voice given over now to a high shrill keening, her flapping arms still raised above her head. And for the first time Moony realized that there was no real heat, no flames. No smoke filled the little room. The light that streamed through the picture window was clear and bright as dawn.

Her mother was not on fire. She was with Them.

They were everywhere, like bees swarming across a bank of flowers. Radiant beads of gold and argent covered Ariel until Moony no longer saw her mother, but only the blazing silhouette of a woman, a numinous figure that sent a prismatic aurora rippling across the ceiling. Moony fell back, horrified, awe-struck. The figure continued its bizarre dance, hands lifting and falling as though reaching for something that was being pulled just out of reach. She could hear her mother's voice, muted now to a soft repetitive cry—*uh, uh!*—and a very faint clear tone, like the sustained note of a glass harmonica.

"Jesus," Moony whispered; then yelled, "*Jesus!* Stop it, *stop*—"

But They didn't stop; only moved faster and faster across Ariel's body until her mother was nothing but a blur, a chrysalis encased in glittering pollen, a burning ghost. Moony's breath scraped against her throat. Her hands clawed at her knees, the floor, her own breasts, as her mother kept on with that soft moaning and the sound of the Light Children filled the chapel the way wine fills a glass.

And then gradually it all began to subside. Gradually the glowing sheath fell from her mother, not fading so much as *thinning*, the way Moony had once read the entrance to a woman's womb will thin as its burden wakes to be born. The chiming noise died away. There was only a faint high echo in Moony's ears. Violet light spilled from the high windows, a darker if weaker wine. Ariel sprawled on the dusty floor, her arms curled up against her chest like the dried hollow limbs of an insect, scarab or patient mantis. Her mouth was slack, and the folds of tired skin around her eyes. She looked inutterably exhausted, but also somehow at peace. With a cold stab like a spike driven into her breast, Moony knew that this was how Ariel would look in death; knew that this was how she looked, now; knew that she was dead.

But she wasn't. As Moony watched, her mother's mouth twitched. Then Ariel sneezed, squeezing her eyes tightly. Finally she opened them to gaze at the ceiling. Moony stared at her, uncomprehending. She began to cry, sobbing so loudly that she didn't hear what her mother was saying, didn't hear Ariel's hoarse voice whispering the same words over and over and over again—

"Thank you, thank you, thank you!—"

But Moony wasn't listening. And only in her mother's own mind did Ariel herself ever again hear Their voices. Like an unending stream of golden coins being poured into a well, the eternal and incomprehensible echo of Their reply—

"You are welcome."

There must have been a lot of noise. Because before Moony could pull herself together and go to her mother, Diana was there, her face white but her eyes set and in control, as though she were an ambulance driver inured to all kinds of terrible things. She took Ariel in her arms and got her to her feet. Ariel's head flopped to one side, and for a moment Moony thought she'd slide to the floor again. But then she seemed to rally. She blinked, smiled fuzzily at her daughter and Diana. After a few minutes, she let Diana walk her to the door. She shook her head gently but persistently when her daughter tried to help.

"You can follow us, darling," Diana called back apologetically as they headed down the path to Martin's cottage. But Moony made no move to follow. She only watched in disbelief—*I can follow you? Of course I can, asshole!*—and then relief, as the two women lurched safely through the house's crooked door.

Let someone *else* take care of her for a while, Moony thought bitterly. She shoved her hands into her pockets. Her terror had turned to anger. Now, perversely, she needed to yell at someone. She thought briefly of following her mother; then of finding Jason. But really, she knew all along where she had to go.

Mrs. Grose seemed surprised to see her *(Ha!* thought Moony triumphantly; what kind of psychic would be *surprised?).*

But maybe there was something about her after all. Because she had just made a big pot of chamomile tea, heavily spiked with brandy, and set out a large white plate patterned with alarmingly lifelike butterflies and bees, the insects seeming to hover intently beside several slabs of cinnamon-fragrant zucchini bread.

"They just keep *mul*tiplying." Mrs. Grose sighed so dramatically that Moony thought she must be referring to the bees, and peered at them again to make sure they weren't real. "Patricia—you know, that nice lady with the lady friend?—she says, *pick* the flowers, so I pick them but I still have too many squashes. Remind me to give you some for your mother."

At mention of her mother, Moony's anger melted away. She started to cry again.

"My darling, what is it?" cried Mrs. Grose. She moved so quickly to embrace Moony that a soft-smelling pink cloud of face powder wafted from her cheeks onto the girl's. "Tell us, darling, tell us—"

Moony sobbed luxuriously for several minutes, letting Mrs. Grose stroke her hair and feed her healthy sips of tepid brandy-laced tea. Mrs. Grose's pug wheezed anxiously at his mistress's feet and struggled to climb into Moony's lap. Eventually he succeeded. By then, Moony had calmed down enough to tell the aged woman what had happened, her rambling narrative punctuated by hiccuping sobs and small gasps of laughter when the dog lapped excitedly at her teacup.

"Ah, *so*," said Mrs. Grose, when she first understood that Moony was talking about the Light Children. She pressed her plump hands together and raised her tortoiseshell eyes to the ceiling. "They are having a busy day."

Moony frowned, wiping her cheeks. As though They were like the people who collected the trash or turned the water supply off at the end of the summer. But then Moony went on talking, her voice growing less tremulous as the brandy kicked in. When she finished, she sat in somewhat abashed silence and stared at the teacup she held in her damp hand. Its border of roses and cabbage butterflies took on a flushed glow from Mrs. Grose's paisley-draped Tiffany lamps. Moony looked uneasily at the door. Having confessed her story, she suddenly wanted to flee, to check on her mother; to forget the whole thing. But she couldn't just take off. She cleared her throat, and the pug growled sympathetically.

"*Well*," Mrs. Grose said at last. "I see I will be having lots of *company* this winter."

Moony stared at her uncomprehending. "I mean, your mother and Martin will be staying on," Mrs. Grose explained, and sipped her tea. Her cheeks like the patterned porcelain had a febrile glow, and her eyes were so bright that Moony wondered if she was very drunk. "So at last! there will be enough of us here to really talk about it, to *learn*—"

"Learn what?" demanded Moony. Confusion and brandy made her peevish. She put her cup down and gently shoved the pug from her lap. "I mean, what happened? *What is going on?*"

"Why, it's Them, of course," Mrs. Grose said grandly, then ducked her head, as though afraid she might be overheard and deemed insolent. "We are so *fortunate—you* are so fortunate, my dear, and your darling mother! And Martin, of course—this is a wonderful time for us, a blessed, blessed time!" At Moony's glare of disbelief she went on, "You understand, my darling—They have come, They have *greeted* your mother and Martin, it is a very exciting thing, very rare—only a very few of us—"

Mrs. Grose preened a little before going on. "—and it is always so wonderful, so miraculous, when another joins us—and now suddenly we have *two!*"

Moony stared at her, her hands opening and closing in her lap. "But what *happened?*" she cried desperately. "What *are* They?"

Mrs. Grose shrugged and coughed delicately. "What are They," she repeated. "Well, Moony, that is a very good question." She heaved back onto the couch and sighed. "What are They? I do not know."

At Moony's rebellious glare she added hastily, "Well, many things, of course, we have thought They were many things, and They might be any of these or all of them or—well, none, I suppose. Fairies, or little angels of Jesus, or tree spirits—that is what a dear friend of mine believed. And some sailors thought They were will-o'-the-wisps, and let's see, Miriam Hopewell, whom you don't remember but was *another* very dear friend of mine, God rest her soul, Miriam thought They came from flying saucers."

At this Moony's belligerence crumpled into defeat. She recalled the things she had seen on her mother—*devouring* her it seemed, setting her aflame—and gave a small involuntary gasp.

"But why?" she wailed. "I mean, *why?* Why should They care? What can They possibly get from us?"

Mrs. Grose enfolded Moony's hand in hers. She ran her fingers along Moony's palm 'as though preparing for a reading, and said, "Maybe They get something They don't have. Maybe we *give* Them something."

"But what?" Moony's voice rose, almost a shriek. *"What?"*

"Something They don't have," Mrs. Grose repeated softly. "Something everybody else has, but They don't—

"Our deaths."

Moony yanked her hand away. "Our *deaths?* My mother like, sold her *soul*, to—to—"

"You don't understand, darling." Mrs. Grose looked at her with mild, whiskey-colored eyes. "They don't want us to *die*. They want our *deaths*. That's why we're still at Mars Hill, me and Gary and your mother and Martin. As long as we stay here, They will keep them for us—our sicknesses, our destinies. It's something They don't have." Mrs. Grose sighed, shaking her head. "I guess They just get lonely, or bored of being immortal. Or whatever it is They are."

That's right! Moony wanted to scream. *What the hell* are *They?* But she only said, "So as long as you stay here you don't die? But that doesn't make any sense—I mean, John died, *he* was here—"

Mrs. Grose shrugged. "He left. And They didn't come to him, They never greeted him . . .

"Maybe he didn't know—or maybe he didn't want to stay. Maybe he didn't want to live. Not everybody does, you know. *I* don't want to live forever—" She sighed melodramatically, her bosom heaving. "But I just can't seem to tear myself away."

She leaned over to hug Moony. "But don't worry now, darling. Your mother is going to be *okay*. And so is Martin. And so are you, and all of us. We're safe—"

Moony shuddered. "But I can't stay here! I have to go back to school, I have a *life*—"

"Of course you do, darling! We all do! *Your* life is out there—" Mrs. Grose gestured out the window, wiggling her fingers toward where the cold blue waters of the Bay lapped at the gravel. "And *ours* is *here*." She smiled, bent her head to kiss Moony so that the girl caught a heavy breath of chamomile and brandy. "Now you better go, before your mother starts to worry."

Like I was a goddamn kid, Moony thought; but she felt too exhausted to argue. She stood, bumping against the pug. It gave a muffled bark, then looked up at her and drooled apologetically. Moony leaned down to pat it and took a step toward the door. Abruptly she turned back.

"Okay," she said. "Okay. Like, I'm going. I understand, you don't know about these—about all this—I mean I know you've told me everything you can. But I just want to ask you one thing—"

Mrs. Grose placed her teacup on the edge of the coffee table and waved her fingers, smiling absently. "Of course, of course, darling. Ask away."

"How old are you?"

Mrs. Grose's penciled eyebrows lifted above mild surprised eyes. "How old am I? One doesn't *ask* a lady such things, darling. But—"

She smiled slyly, leaning back and folding her hands upon her soft bulging stomach. "If I'd been a man and had the vote, it would have gone to Mr. Lincoln."

Moony nodded, just once, her breath stuck in her throat. Then she fled the cottage.

In Bangor, the doctor confirmed that the cancer was in remission.

"It's incredible." She shook her head, staring at Ariel's test results before tossing them ceremonially into a wastebasket. "I would say the phrase 'a living miracle' is not inappropriate here. Or voodoo, or whatever it is you do there at Mars Hill."

She waved dismissively at the open window, then bent to retrieve the tests. "You're welcome to get another opinion. I would advise it, as a matter of fact."

"Of course," Ariel said. But of course she wouldn't, then or ever. She already knew what the doctors would tell her.

There was some more paperwork, a few awkward efforts by the doctor to get Ariel to confess to some secret healing cure, some herbal remedy or therapy practiced by the kooks at the spiritualist community. But finally they were done. There was nothing left to discuss, and only a Blue Cross number to be given to the receptionist. When the doctor stood to walk with Ariel to the door, her eyes were too bright, her voice earnest and a little shaky as she said, "And look: whatever you were doing, Ms. Rising—howling at the moon, whatever—you just keep on doing it. Okay?"

"Okay." Ariel smiled, and left.

"You really can't leave, now," Mrs. Grose told Martin and Ariel that night. They were all sitting around a bonfire on the rocky beach, Diana and Gary singing "Sloop John B" in off-key harmony, Rvis and Shasta Daisy and the others disemboweling leftover lobster bodies with the remorseless patience of raccoons. Mrs. Grose spread out the fingers of her right hand and twisted a heavy filigreed ring on her pinkie, her lips pursed as she regarded Ariel. "*You* shouldn't have gone to Bangor, that was *very foolish*," she said, frowning. "In a few months, maybe you can go with Gary to the Beach Store. *Maybe*. But no farther than that."

Moony looked sideways at her mother, but Ariel only shook her head. Her eyes were luminous, the same color as the evening sky above the Bay.

"Who would want to leave?" Ariel said softly. Her hand crept across the pebbles to touch Martin's. As Moony watched them she felt again that sharp pain in her heart, like a needle jabbing her. She would never know exactly what had happened to her mother, or to Martin. Jason would tell her nothing. Nor would Ariel or anyone else. But there they were, Ariel and Martin sitting cross-legged on the gravel strand, while all around them the others ate and drank and sang as though nothing had happened at all; or as though whatever *had* occurred had been decided on long ago. Without looking at each other, Martin and her mother smiled, Martin somewhat wryly. Mrs. Grose nodded.

"That's right," the old woman said. When she tossed a stone into the bonfire an eddy of sparks flared up. Moony jumped, startled, and looked up into the sky. For an instant she held her breath, thinking, *At last!*—it was Them and all would be explained. The Fairy King would offer his benediction to the united and loving couples; the dour Puritan would be avenged; the Fool would sing his sad sweet song and everyone would wipe away happy tears.

But no. The sparks blew off into ashes, filling the air with a faint smell of incense. When she turned back to the bonfire, Jason was holding out a flaming marshmallow on a stick, laughing, and the others had segued into a drunken rendition of "Leaving on a Jet Plane."

"Take it, Moony," he urged her, the charred mess slipping from the stick. "Eat it quick, for luck."

She leaned over until it slid onto her tongue, a glowing coal of sweetness and earth and fire; and ate it quick, for luck.

Long after midnight they returned to their separate bungalows. Jason lingered with Moony by the dying bonfire, stroking her hair and staring at the lights of Dark Harbor. There was the crunch of gravel behind them. He turned to see his father, standing silhouetted in the soft glow of the embers.

"Jason," he called softly. "Would you mind coming back with me? I—there's something we need to talk about."

Jason gazed down at Moony. Her eyes were heavy with sleep, and he lowered his head to kiss her, her mouth still redolent of burnt sugar. "Yeah, okay," he said, and stood. "You be okay, Moony?"

Moony nodded, yawning. "Sure." As he walked away, Jason looked back and saw her stretched out upon the gravel beach, arms outspread as she stared up at the three-quarter moon riding close to the edge of Mars Hill.

"So what's going on?" he asked his father when they reached the cottage. Martin stood at the dining room table, his back to Jason. He picked up a small stack of envelopes and tapped them against the table, then turned to his son.

"I'm going back," he said. "Home. I got a letter from Brandon today"—Brandon was his agent—"there's going to be a show at the Frick Gallery, and a symposium. They want me to speak."

Jason stared at him, uncomprehending. His long pale hair fell into his face, and he pushed it impatiently from his eyes. "But—you can't," he said at last. "You'll die. You can't leave here. That's what Adele said. You'll *die*."

Martin remained silent, before replacing the envelopes and shaking his head. "We don't know that. Even before, we—*I*—didn't know that. Nobody knows that, ever."

Jason stared at him in disbelief. His face grew flushed as he said, "But you can't! You're sick—shit, Dad, look at John, you can't just—"

His father pursed his lips, tugged at his ponytail. "No, Jason, I *can*." Suddenly he looked surprised, a little sheepish even, and said more softly, "I mean, I *will*. There's too much for me to give up, Jason. Maybe it sounds stupid, but I think it's important that I go back. Not right away. I think I'll stay on for a few weeks, maybe until the end of October. You know, see autumn in New England and all. But after that—well, there's work for me to do at home, and—"

Jason's voice cracked as he shook his head furiously. "Dad. No. You'll—you'll die."

Martin shrugged. "I might. I mean, I guess I will, sometime. But—well, everybody dies." His mouth twisted into a smile as he stared at the floor. "Except Mrs. Grose."

Jason continued to shake his head. "But—you *saw* Them—They came, They must've done *something*—"

Martin looked up, his eyes feverishly bright. "They did. That's why I'm leaving. Look, Jason, I can't explain, all right? But what if you had to stay here, instead of going on to Bowdoin? What if Moony left, and everyone else—would you stay at Mars Hill? *Forever?*"

Jason was silent. Finally, "I think you should stay," he said, a little desperately. "Otherwise whatever They did was wasted."

Martin shook his head. His hand closed around a tube of viridian on the table and he raised it, held it in front of him like a weapon. His eyes glittered as he said, "Oh no, Jason. Not wasted. Nothing is wasted, not ever." And tilting his head he smiled, held out his arm until his son came to him, and Martin embraced him, held him there until Jason's sobs quieted, and the moon began to slide behind Mars Hill.

Jason drove Moony to the airport on Friday. Most of his things already had been shipped from San Francisco to Bowdoin College, but Moony had to return to Kamensic Village and the Loomises; to gather her clothes and books for school and make all the awkward explanations and arrangements on her own. Friends and relations in New York had been told that Ariel was undergoing some kind of experimental therapy, an excuse they bought as easily as they'd bought most of Ariel's other strange ideas. Now Moony didn't want to talk to anyone else on the phone. She didn't want to talk to anyone at all, except for Jason.

"It's kind of on the way to Brunswick," he explained when Diana protested his driving Moony. "Besides, Diana, if you took her she'd end up crying the whole way. This way I can keep her intact at least until the airport."

Diana gave in, finally. No one suggested that Ariel drive.

"Look down when the plane flies over Mars Hill," Ariel said, hugging her daughter by the car. "We'll be looking for you."

Moony nodded, her mouth tight, and kissed her mother. "You be okay," she whispered, the words lost in Ariel's tangled hair.

"I'll be okay," Ariel said, smiling.

Behind them Jason and Martin embraced. "If you're still here I'll be up Columbus weekend," said Jason. "Maybe sooner if I run out of money."

Martin shook his head. "If you run out of money you better go see your mother."

It was only twenty minutes to the airport. "Don't wait," Moony said to Jason, as the same woman who had taken her ticket loaded her bags onto the little Beechcraft. "I mean it. If you do I'll cry and I'll kill you."

Jason nodded. "Righto. We don't want any bad publicity. *'Noted Queer Activist's Son Slain by Girlfriend at Local Airport. Wind Shear Is Blamed.'*"

Moony hugged him, drew away to study his face. "I'll call you in the morning."

He shook his head. "Tonight. When you get home. So I'll know you got in safely. 'Cause it's dangerous out there." He made an awful face, then leaned over to kiss her. "Ciao, Moony."

"Ciao, Jason."

She could feel him watching her as she clambered into the little plane, but she didn't look back. Instead she smiled tentatively at the few other passengers—a businessman with a tie loose around his neck, two middle-aged women with L. L. Bean shopping bags—and settled into a seat by the window.

During takeoff she leaned over to see if she could spot Jason. For an instant she had a flash of his car, like a crimson leaf blowing south through the darkening green of pines and maples. Then it was gone.

Trailers of mist whipped across the little window. Moony shivered, drew her sweatshirt tight around her chest. She felt that beneath her everything she had ever known was shrinking, disappearing, swallowed by golden light; but somehow it was okay. As the Beechcraft banked over Penobscot Bay she pressed her face close against the glass, waiting for the gap in the clouds that would give her a last glimpse of the gray and white cottages tumbling down Mars Hill, the wind-riven pier where her mother and Martin and all the rest stood staring up into the early autumn sky, tiny as fairy people in a child's book. For an instant it seemed that something hung over them, a golden cloud like a September haze. But then the blinding sun made her glance away. When she looked down again the golden haze was gone. But the others were still there, waving and calling out soundlessly until the plane finally turned south and bore her away, away from summer and its silent visitors—her mother's cancer, Martin's virus, the Light Children and Their hoard of stolen sufferings—away, away, away from them all, and back to the welcoming world.

Appendixes

About the Nebula Awards

Throughout every calendar year, the members of the Science-fiction and Fantasy Writers of America read and recommend novels and stories for the annual Nebula Awards. The editor of the "Nebula Awards Report" collects the recommendations and publishes them in the *SFWA Forum*. Near the end of the year, the NAR editor tallies the endorsements, draws up the preliminary ballot, and sends it to all active SFWA members. Under the current rules, each novel and story enjoys a one-year eligibility period from its date of publication. If the work fails to make the preliminary ballot during that interval, it is dropped from further Nebula consideration.

The NAR editor processes the results of the preliminary ballot and then compiles a final ballot listing the five most popular novels, novellas, novelettes, and short stories. For purposes of the Nebula Award, a novel is 40,000 words or more; a novella is 17,500 to 39,999 words; a novelette is 7,500 to 17,499 words; and a short story is 7,499 words or fewer. At the present time, SFWA impanels both a novel jury and a short-fiction jury to oversee the voting process and, in cases where a presumably worthy title was neglected by the membership at large, to supplement the five nominees with a sixth choice. Thus, the appearance of extra finalists in any category bespeaks two distinct processes: jury discretion and ties.

Founded in 1965 by Damon Knight, the Science Fiction Writers of America began with a charter membership of seventy-eight authors. Today it boasts about a thousand members and an augmented name. Early in his tenure, Lloyd Biggle Jr., SFWA's first secretary-treasurer, proposed that the organization periodically select and publish the year's best stories. This notion quickly evolved into the elaborate balloting process, an annual awards banquet, and a series of Nebula anthologies. Judith Ann Lawrence designed the trophy from a sketch by

Kate Wilhelm. It is a block of Lucite containing a rock crystal and a spiral nebula made of metallic glitter. The prize is handmade, and no two are exactly alike.

The Grand Master Nebula Award goes to a living author for a lifetime of achievement. In accordance with SFWA's bylaws, the president nominates a candidate, normally after consulting with previous presidents and the board of directors. This nomination then goes before the officers; if a majority approves, the candidate becomes a Grand Master. Past recipients include Robert A. Heinlein (1974), Jack Williamson (1975), Clifford D. Simak (1976), L. Sprague de Camp (1978), Fritz Leiber (1980), Andre Norton (1983), Arthur C. Clarke (1985), Isaac Asimov (1986), Alfred Bester (1987), Ray Bradbury (1988), Lester del Rey (1990), Frederik Pohl (1992), and Damon Knight (1994).

The thirty-first annual Nebula Awards banquet was held on the *Queen Mary* in Long Beach, California, on April 27, 1996, where Nebula Awards were given in the categories of novel, novella, novelette, short story, and lifetime achievement (Grand Master). As part of a program to honor older writers who are no longer writing and publishing, Wilson Tucker was honored as SFWA's second Author Emeritus; Emil Petaja, honored last year, was the first.

Selected Titles from the 1995 Preliminary Nebula Ballot

NOVEL

The Shattered Sphere by Roger MacBride Allen (Tor)
Primary Inversion by Catherine Asaro (Tor)
When Heaven Fell by William Barton (Warner)
Memory and Dream by Charles deLint (Tor)
Demon Blade by Mark Garland and Charles McGraw (Baen)
Queen City Jazz by Kathleen Ann Goonan (Tor)
Bride of the Rat God by Barbara Hambly (Del Rey)
Frostwing by Richard Knaak (Warner)
Siduri's Net by P. K. McAllister (ROC)
Aggressor Six by Wil McCarthy (ROC)
The Engines of God by Jack McDevitt (Ace)

The Bohr Maker by Linda Nagata (Bantam)
Starmind by Spider and Jeanne Robinson (*Analog*, August–
November 1994)
Once a Hero by Mike Stackpole (Bantam)
The Jericho Iteration by Allen Steele (Ace)
Resurrection Man by Sean Stewart (Ace)
Remake by Connie Willis (Bantam)

NOVELLA

"Fish Tank" by Gregory Bennett (*Analog*, June 1995)
"Up the Rainbow" by Susan Casper (*Asimov's Science Fiction*,
December 1994)
"Unto the Valley of Day-Glo" by Nicholas A. DeChario (*Tales from
the Great Turtle*, Tor, 1994)
"Tide of Stars" by Julia Ecklar (*Analog*, January 1995)
"In Forests Afloat upon the Sea" by Daniel Hatch (*Analog*, January
1995)

NOVELETTE

"The Twilight of the Guards, or the Plowshare Conundrum" by Arlan
Andrews (*Analog*, December 1994)
"The Lovers" by Eleanor Arnason (*Asimov's Science Fiction*, July
1994)
"Another Story" by Ursula K. Le Guin (*Tomorrow SF #10*, August
1994)
"Fermat's Lost Theorem" by Jerry Oltion (*Analog*, Mid-December
1994)
"Fearless" by Dave Smeds (*Warriors of Blood and Dreams*,
AvoNova, 1995)

SHORT STORY

"Curse of the Cyberhead's Wife" by Bruce Boston (*Science Fiction
Age*, September 1994)
"The Transcendentalists" by David Cleary (*Science Fiction Age*,
November 1994)
"A Cat Horror Story" by Gardner Dozois (*The Magazine of Fantasy
& Science Fiction*, November 1994)

"Wells of Wisdom" by Brad Linaweaver (*Galaxy*, June 1994)
"Dilating the Paradox" by Paula May (*Analog*, Mid-December 1994)
"Moriarty by Modem" by Jack Nimersheim (*Sherlock Holmes in Orbit*, DAW, 1995)
"Swift Thoughts" by George Zebrowski (*Amazing Stories: The Anthology*, Tor, 1995)

Past Nebula Award Winners

1 9 6 5

Best Novel: *Dune* by Frank Herbert
Best Novella: "The Saliva Tree" by Brian W. Aldiss
   "He Who Shapes" by Roger Zelazny (tie)
Best Novelette: "The Doors of His Face, the Lamps of His Mouth" by Roger Zelazny
Best Short Story: "'Repent, Harlequin!' Said the Ticktockman" by Harlan Ellison

1 9 6 6

Best Novel: *Flowers for Algernon* by Daniel Keyes
   Babel-17 by Samuel R. Delany (tie)
Best Novella: "The Last Castle" by Jack Vance
Best Novelette: "Call Him Lord" by Gordon R. Dickson
Best Short Story: "The Secret Place" by Richard McKenna

1 9 6 7

Best Novel: *The Einstein Intersection* by Samuel R. Delany
Best Novella: "Behold the Man" by Michael Moorcock
Best Novelette: "Gonna Roll the Bones" by Fritz Leiber
Best Short Story: "Aye, and Gomorrah" by Samuel R. Delany

1 9 6 8

Best Novel: *Rite of Passage* by Alexei Panshin
Best Novella: "Dragonrider" by Anne McCaffrey
Best Novelette: "Mother to the World" by Richard Wilson
Best Short Story: "The Planners" by Kate Wilhelm

1 9 6 9

Best Novel: *The Left Hand of Darkness* by Ursula K. Le Guin
Best Novella: "A Boy and His Dog" by Harlan Ellison
Best Novelette: "Time Considered as a Helix of Semi-Precious
    Stones" by Samuel R. Delany
Best Short Story: "Passengers" by Robert Silverberg

1 9 7 0

Best Novel: *Ringworld* by Larry Niven
Best Novella: "Ill Met in Lankhmar" by Fritz Leiber
Best Novelette: "Slow Sculpture" by Theodore Sturgeon
Best Short Story: no award

1 9 7 1

Best Novel: *A Time of Changes* by Robert Silverberg
Best Novella: "The Missing Man" by Katherine MacLean
Best Novelette: "The Queen of Air and Darkness" by Poul Anderson
Best Short Story: "Good News from the Vatican" by Robert
    Silverberg

1 9 7 2

Best Novel: *The Gods Themselves* by Isaac Asimov
Best Novella: "A Meeting with Medusa" by Arthur C. Clarke
Best Novelette: "Goat Song" by Poul Anderson
Best Short Story: "When It Changed" by Joanna Russ

1 9 7 3

Best Novel: *Rendezvous with Rama* by Arthur C. Clarke
Best Novella: "The Death of Doctor Island" by Gene Wolfe
Best Novelette: "Of Mist, and Grass, and Sand" by Vonda N.
    McIntyre
Best Short Story: "Love Is the Plan, the Plan Is Death" by James
    Tiptree Jr.
Best Dramatic Presentation: *Soylent Green*
    Stanley R. Greenberg for screenplay (based on the novel *Make
    Room! Make Room!*)
    Harry Harrison for *Make Room! Make Room!*

1974

Best Novel: *The Dispossessed* by Ursula K. Le Guin
Best Novella: "Born with the Dead" by Robert Silverberg
Best Novelette: "If the Stars Are Gods" by Gordon Eklund and
    Gregory Benford
Best Short Story: "The Day Before the Revolution" by Ursula K.
    Le Guin
Best Dramatic Presentation: *Sleeper* by Woody Allen
Grand Master: Robert A. Heinlein

1975

Best Novel: *The Forever War* by Joe Haldeman
Best Novella: "Home Is the Hangman" by Roger Zelazny
Best Novelette: "San Diego Lightfoot Sue" by Tom Reamy
Best Short Story: "Catch That Zeppelin!" by Fritz Leiber
Best Dramatic Writing: Mel Brooks and Gene Wilder for *Young
    Frankenstein*
Grand Master: Jack Williamson

1976

Best Novel: *Man Plus* by Frederik Pohl
Best Novella: "Houston, Houston, Do You Read?" by James
    Tiptree Jr.
Best Novelette: "The Bicentennial Man" by Isaac Asimov
Best Short Story: "A Crowd of Shadows" by Charles L. Grant
Grand Master: Clifford D. Simak

1977

Best Novel: *Gateway* by Frederik Pohl
Best Novella: "Stardance" by Spider and Jeanne Robinson
Best Novelette: "The Screwfly Solution" by Raccoona Sheldon
Best Short Story: "Jeffty Is Five" by Harlan Ellison
Special Award: *Star Wars*

1978

Best Novel: *Dreamsnake* by Vonda N. McIntyre
Best Novella: "The Persistence of Vision" by John Varley

Best Novelette: "A Glow of Candles, a Unicorn's Eye" by Charles L.
   Grant
Best Short Story: "Stone" by Edward Bryant
Grand Master: L. Sprague de Camp

1 9 7 9

Best Novel: *The Fountains of Paradise* by Arthur C. Clarke
Best Novella: "Enemy Mine" by Barry Longyear
Best Novelette: "Sandkings" by George R. R. Martin
Best Short Story: "giANTS" by Edward Bryant

1 9 8 0

Best Novel: *Timescape* by Gregory Benford
Best Novella: "The Unicorn Tapestry" by Suzy McKee Charnas
Best Novelette: "The Ugly Chickens" by Howard Waldrop
Best Short Story: "Grotto of the Dancing Deer" by Clifford D. Simak
Grand Master: Fritz Leiber

1 9 8 1

Best Novel: *The Claw of the Conciliator* by Gene Wolfe
Best Novella: "The Saturn Game" by Poul Anderson
Best Novelette: "The Quickening" by Michael Bishop
Best Short Story: "The Bone Flute" by Lisa Tuttle°

1 9 8 2

Best Novel: *No Enemy But Time* by Michael Bishop
Best Novella: "Another Orphan" by John Kessel
Best Novelette: "Fire Watch" by Connie Willis
Best Short Story: "A Letter from the Clearys" by Connie Willis

1 9 8 3

Best Novel: *Startide Rising* by David Brin
Best Novella: "Hardfought" by Greg Bear
Best Novelette: "Blood Music" by Greg Bear

°This Nebula Award was declined by the author.

Best Short Story: "The Peacemaker" by Gardner Dozois
Grand Master: Andre Norton

1 9 8 4

Best Novel: *Neuromancer* by William Gibson
Best Novella: "PRESS ENTER ■" by John Varley
Best Novelette: "Bloodchild" by Octavia E. Butler
Best Short Story: "Morning Child" by Gardner Dozois

1 9 8 5

Best Novel: *Ender's Game* by Orson Scott Card
Best Novella: "Sailing to Byzantium" by Robert Silverberg
Best Novelette: "Portraits of His Children" by George R. R. Martin
Best Short Story: "Out of All Them Bright Stars" by Nancy Kress
Grand Master: Arthur C. Clarke

1 9 8 6

Best Novel: *Speaker for the Dead* by Orson Scott Card
Best Novella: "R & R" by Lucius Shepard
Best Novelette: "The Girl Who Fell into the Sky" by Kate Wilhelm
Best Short Story: "Tangents" by Greg Bear
Grand Master: Isaac Asimov

1 9 8 7

Best Novel: *The Falling Woman* by Pat Murphy
Best Novella: "The Blind Geometer" by Kim Stanley Robinson
Best Novelette: "Rachel in Love" by Pat Murphy
Best Short Story: "Forever Yours, Anna" by Kate Wilhelm
Grand Master: Alfred Bester

1 9 8 8

Best Novel: *Falling Free* by Lois McMaster Bujold
Best Novella: "The Last of the Winnebagos" by Connie Willis
Best Novelette: "Schrödinger's Kitten" by George Alec Effinger
Best Short Story: "Bible Stories for Adults, No. 17: The Deluge" by
    James Morrow
Grand Master: Ray Bradbury

1 9 8 9

Best Novel: *The Healer's War* by Elizabeth Ann Scarborough
Best Novella: "The Mountains of Mourning" by Lois McMaster Bujold
Best Novelette: "At the Rialto" by Connie Willis
Best Short Story: "Ripples in the Dirac Sea" by Geoffrey Landis

1 9 9 0

Best Novel: *Tehanu: The Last Book of Earthsea* by Ursula K. Le Guin
Best Novella: "The Hemingway Hoax" by Joe Haldeman
Best Novelette: "Tower of Babylon" by Ted Chiang
Best Short Story: "Bears Discover Fire" by Terry Bisson
Grand Master: Lester del Rey

1 9 9 1

Best Novel: *Stations of the Tide* by Michael Swanwick
Best Novella: "Beggars in Spain" by Nancy Kress
Best Novelette: "Guide Dog" by Mike Conner
Best Short Story: "Ma Qui" by Alan Brennert

1 9 9 2

Best Novel: *Doomsday Book* by Connie Willis
Best Novella: "City of Truth" by James Morrow
Best Novelette: "Danny Goes to Mars" by Pamela Sargent
Best Short Story: "Even the Queen" by Connie Willis
Grand Master: Frederik Pohl

1 9 9 3

Best Novel: *Red Mars* by Kim Stanley Robinson
Best Novella: "The Night We Buried Road Dog" by Jack Cady
Best Novelette: "Georgia on My Mind" by Charles Sheffield
Best Short Story: "Graves" by Joe Haldeman

1 9 9 4

Best Novel: *Moving Mars* by Greg Bear
Best Novella: "Seven Views of Olduvai Gorge" by Mike Resnick

Best Novelette: "The Martian Child" by David Gerrold
Best Short Story: "A Defense of the Social Contracts" by Martha
   Soukup
Grand Master: Damon Knight

Those who are interested in category-related awards should also consult *A History of the Hugo, Nebula, and International Fantasy Awards* by Donald Franson and Howard DeVore (Misfit Press, 1987). Periodically updated, the book is available from Howard DeVore, 4705 Weddel, Dearborn, Michigan 48125.

About the Science-fiction and Fantasy Writers of America

The Science-fiction and Fantasy Writers of America, Incorporated, includes among its members most of the active writers of science fiction and fantasy. According to the bylaws of the organization, its purpose "shall be to promote the furtherance of the writing of science fiction, fantasy, and related genres as a profession." SFWA informs writers on professional matters, protects their interests, and helps them in dealings with agents, editors, anthologists, and producers of nonprint media. It also strives to encourage public interest in and appreciation of science fiction and fantasy.

Anyone may become an active member of SFWA after the acceptance of and payment for one professionally published novel, one professionally produced dramatic script, or three professionally published pieces of short fiction. Only science fiction, fantasy, and other prose fiction of a related genre, in English, shall be considered as qualifying for active membership. Beginning writers who do not yet qualify for active membership may join as associate members; other classes of membership include illustrator members (artists), affiliate members (editors, agents, reviewers, and anthologists), estate members (representatives of the estates of active members who have died), and institutional members (high schools, colleges, universities, libraries, broadcasters, film producers, futurist groups, and individuals associated with such an institution).

Anyone who is not a member of SFWA may subscribe to *The Bulletin of the Science Fiction and Fantasy Writers of America*. The magazine is published quarterly, and contains articles by well-known writers on all aspects of their profession. Subscriptions are $15 a year or $27 for two years. For information on how to subscribe to the *Bulletin*, or for more information about SFWA, write to:

SFWA, Inc.
532 La Guardia Place
Box 632
New York, NY 10012-1428

Readers are also invited to visit the SFWA site on the World Wide Web at the following address:

http://www.sfwa.org/sfwa

CPSIA information can be obtained at www.ICGtesting.com
Printed in the USA
LVOW06s1458031013

355309LV00002B/220/A

9 780156 001144